D0395122

HEMLOCK BAY

Catherine Coulter

RANDOM HOUSE
LARGE PRINT

All rights reserved under International and Pan-American Copyright Conventions. Published in the United States of America by Random House Large Print in association with G. P. Putnam's Sons, a member of Penguin Putnam Inc., New York and simultaneously in Canada by Random House of Canada Limited, Toronto. Distributed by Random House, Inc., New York.

The Library of Congress has established a cataloging-in-publication record for this title.

0-375-43115-2

Please visit our website at:
www.randomlargeprint.com

FIRST LARGE PRINT EDITION

This Large Print Edition published in accord with the standards of the N.A.V.H.

I wish to thank the following people at FBI Headquarters and at Quantico for their generosity and enthusiasm.

William Hayden Matens, Special Agent, retired.
Tom B. Locke, DAD, Inspection Division
David R. Knowlton, Assistant Director, Inspection Division
Wade Jackson, Unit Chief, Firearms Training Unit
Gary J. Hutchison, Agent Instructor
Alan Marshall, Special Agent, Indoor Range
Jeffrey Higginbotham, Assistant Director, Training Division
Douglas W. Deedrick, Unit Chief, Information and Evidence Management Unit
Lester "wingtips" Davis, Officer, National Academy Association.
Ruben Garcia, Jr., Assistant Director, Criminal Investigative Division
Kenneth McCabe, Section Chief, Laboratory Division
Michael J. Perry, Agent Instructor
Sheri A. Farrar, Deputy Assistant Director, Administrative Services Division
Royce Curtin, Special Agent, Hostage Rescue Team
Stephen R. Band, Unit Chief, Behavior Sciences Unit

I wish to thank my husband, Dr. Anton Pogany, yet again, for his excellent instincts and his eagle eye that never misses a thing—he remains the Editor from Hell.

ONE

Near the Plum River, Maryland

It was a chilly day in late October. A stiff wind whipped the last colorful leaves off the trees. The sun was shining down hard and bright on the dilapidated red barn that hadn't been painted in forty years. Streaks of washed-out red were all that was left of the last paint job. There was no charm left, at all.

FBI Special Agent Dillon Savich eased around the side of the barn, his SIG Sauer in his right hand. It had taken discipline and practice, but he'd learned to move so quietly that he could sneak up on a mouse. Three agents, one of them his wife, were some twenty feet behind him, covering him, ready to fan out in any direction necessary, all of them wearing Kevlar vests. A dozen more agents were slowly working their way up the other side of the barn, their orders to wait for a signal from Savich. Sheriff Dade of Jedbrough County and three deputies were stationed in the thick stand of maple trees just thirty feet behind them. One of the deputies, a sharpshooter, had his sights trained on the barn.

So far the operation was going smoothly, which, Savich supposed, surprised everyone, although no one spoke of it. He just hoped it would continue the way it had been planned, but chances were things would get screwed up. He'd deal with it; there was no choice.

The barn was bigger than Savich liked—there was a big hayloft, and too many shadowy corners for this sort of operation. Too many nooks and crannies for an ambush, just plain too many places from which to fire a storm of bullets.

A perfect place for Tommy and Timmy Tuttle, dubbed "the Warlocks" by the media, to hole up. They'd hopscotched across the country, but had dropped out of sight here, in Maryland, with their two latest young teenage boys taken right out of the gym where they'd been playing basketball after school, in Stewartville, some forty miles away. Savich had believed that Maryland was their destination, no sound reason really, but in his gut he just felt it. The profilers hadn't said much about that, just that

Maryland was, after all, on the Atlantic coast, so they really couldn't go much farther east.

Then MAX, Savich's laptop, had dived into land registry files in Maryland and found that Marilyn Warluski, a first cousin to the Tuttle brothers, and who, MAX had also discovered, had had a baby at the age of seventeen fathered by Tommy Tuttle, just happened to own a narrow strip of land near a good-sized maple forest that wasn't far from the serpentine Plum River. And on that sliver of property was a barn, a big ancient barn that had been abandoned for years. Savich had nearly clicked his heels together in excitement.

And now, four hours later, here they were. There'd been no sign of a car, but Savich wasn't worried. The old Honda was probably stashed in the barn. He quieted his breathing and listened. The birds had gone still. The silence was heavy, oppressive, as if even the animals were expecting something to happen and knew instinctively that it wouldn't be good.

Savich was afraid the Tuttle brothers were long gone. All they would find, despite the silence, would be their victims: teenage boys—Donny and Rob Arthur—dead, horribly mutilated, their bodies circumscribed by a large, black circle.

Savich didn't want to smell any more blood.

He didn't want to see any more death. Not today. Not ever.

He looked down at his Mickey Mouse watch. It was time to see if the bad guys were in the barn. It was time to go into harm's way. It was time to get the show on the road.

MAX had found a crude interior plan of the barn, drawn some fifty years before, documented in a computerized county record as having been physically saved and filed. Kept where? was the question. They'd finally turned up the drawing in an old file cabinet in the basement of the county planning building. But the drawing was clear enough. There was a small, narrow entry, down low, here on the west side. He found it behind a straggly naked bush. It was cracked open, wide enough for him to squeeze through.

He looked back, waved his SIG Sauer at the three agents peering around the corner of the barn, a signal to hold their positions, and went in on his belly. He pushed the narrow door open an inch at a time. Filth everywhere, some rat carcasses strewn around. He nudged his way in on his elbows, feeling bones crunch beneath him, his SIG Sauer steady in his hand.

There was a strange half-light in the barn. Dust motes filled the narrow spears of light coming through the upper windows, only shards of glass sticking up in some of the frames. He lay there quietly a moment, his eyes adjusting. He saw bales of hay so old they looked petrified, stacked haphazardly, rusted machinery—mainly odd parts—and two ancient wooden troughs.

Then he noticed it. In the far corner was another door not more than twenty feet to the right of the front double barn doors. A tack room, he thought, and it hadn't been shown on the drawing. Then he made out the outline of the Honda, tucked in the shadows at the far end of the barn. The two brothers were in the tack room, no doubt about it. And Donny and Rob Arthur? Please, God, let them still be alive.

He had to know exactly who was where before he called in the other agents. It was still, very still. He got to his feet and ran hunched over toward the tack room door, his gun fanning continuously, his breathing low and steady, his steps silent. He pressed his ear against the rotted wooden door of the tack room.

He heard a male voice, clear and strong, and angry, suddenly louder.

"Listen, you Little Bloods, it's time for you to get in the middle of the circle. The Ghouls want you; they told me to hurry it up. They want to carve you up with their axes and knives—they really like to do that—but this time they want to tuck you away in their carryalls and fly away with you. Hey, maybe you'll end up in Tahiti. Who knows? They haven't wanted to do this before. But it doesn't make any difference to us. Here come the Ghouls!" And he laughed, a young man's laugh, not all that deep, and it sounded quite happily mad. It made Savich's blood run icy.

Then another man's voice, this one deeper. "Yep, almost ready for the Ghouls. We don't want to disappoint them now, do we? Move it, Little Bloods."

He heard them coming toward the door, heard the scuffling of feet, heard the boys' crying, probably beyond reason now, heard curses and prods from the Tuttle brothers. It was then that he saw the huge, crude circle painted with thick, black paint on a cleared-out part of the rotting wooden barn floor.

Zero hour. No time, simply no time now to bring the others in.

Savich barely made it down behind a rotted hay bale before one of them opened the tack room door and shoved a slight, pale boy in front of him. The boy's filthy pants were nearly falling off his butt. It was Donny Arthur. He'd been beaten, probably starved as well. He was terrified. Then a second terrified youth was shoved out of the small tack room next to him.

Rob Arthur, only fourteen years old. Savich had never seen such fear on two such young faces in his life.

If Savich ordered the Tuttles to stop now, they could use the boys for shields. No, better to wait. What was all that crazy talk about ghouls? He watched the two men shove the boys forward until they actually kicked them into the center of the circle.

"Don't either of you move or I'll take my knife and shove it right through your arm into the floor, pin you good. Tammy here will do the other with her knife. You got that, Little Bloods?"

Tammy? Her knife? No, it was two brothers—Tommy and Timmy Tuttle, more than enough alliteration, even for the media. No, he couldn't have heard right. He was looking at two young men, both in black, long and lean, big, chunky black boots laced up the front to the knees like combat boots. They carried knives and guns.

The boys were huddled together on their knees, crying, clutching each other. Blood caked their faces, but they could move, and that meant no bones were broken.

"Where are the Ghouls?" Tammy Tuttle shouted, and Savich realized in that instant that he hadn't misheard; it wasn't the Tuttle brothers, it was one brother and one sister.

What was all this about the ghouls coming to murder the boys?

"Ghouls," Tammy yelled, her head thrown back, her voice reverberating throughout the ancient barn, "where are you? We've got your two treats for you, just what you like—two really sweet boys! Little Bloods, both of them. Bring your knives and axes! Come here, Ghouls."

It was a chant, growing louder as she repeated herself once, twice, then three times. Each time, her voice was louder, more vicious, the words ridiculous, really, except for the underlying terror they carried.

Tammy Tuttle kicked one of the boys, hard, when he tried to crawl out of the circle. Savich knew he had to act soon. Where were these ghouls?

He heard something, something that was different from the mad human voices, like a high whine, sort of a hissing sound that didn't belong here, maybe didn't belong anywhere. He felt gooseflesh rise on his arms. He felt a shock of cold. He was on the point of leaping out when, to his utter astonishment, the huge front barn doors whooshed inward, blinding light flooded in, and in the middle of that light were dust devils that looked like small tornadoes. The white light faded away, and the dust devils looked more like two whirling, white cones, distinct from each other, spinning and twisting, riding up then dipping down, blending together, then separating—no, no, they were just dust devils, still white because they hadn't sucked up the dirt yet from the barn floor. But what was that sound he heard? Something strange, something he couldn't identify. Laughter? No, that was crazy, but that was what registered in his brain.

The boys saw the dust devils, whirling and spinning far above them, and started screaming. Rob jumped up, grabbed his older brother, and managed to jerk him out of the circle.

Tammy Tuttle, who'd been looking up, turned suddenly, raised her knife, and yelled, "Get back down, Little Bloods! Don't you dare anger the Ghouls. Get back in the circle, now! GET BACK DOWN!"

The boys scrabbled farther away from the circle. Tommy Tuttle was on them in an instant, jerking them back. Tammy Tuttle drew the knife back, aiming toward Donny Arthur, as Savich leaped up from behind the bale of hay and fired. The bullet ripped into her arm at her shoulder. She screamed and fell onto her side, the knife flying out of her hand.

Tommy Tuttle whipped about, no knife in his hand now but a gun, and that gun was aimed not at Savich but at the boys. The boys were screaming as Savich shot Tommy through the center of his forehead.

Tammy Tuttle was moaning on the floor, holding her arm. The boys stood, clutched together, silent now, and all three of them looked up toward those whirling, white cones that danced up and down in the clear light coming through the barn doors. No, not dust devils, two separate things.

One of the boys whispered, "What are they?"

"I don't know, Rob," Savich said and pulled the boys toward him, protecting them as best he could. "Just some sort of weird tornado, that's all."

Tammy was yelling curses at Savich as she tried to pull herself up. She fell back. There was a shriek, loud and hollow. One of the cones seemed to leap forward, directly at them. Savich didn't think, just shot it, clean through. It was like shooting through fog. The cone danced upward, then twisted back toward the other cone. They hovered an instant, spinning madly, and in the next instant, they were gone. Simply gone.

Savich grabbed both boys against him again. "It's all right now, Donny, Rob. You're both all right. I'm very proud of you, and your parents will be, too. Yes, it's okay to be afraid; I know

I'm scared out of my mind, too. Just stay nice and safe against me. That's it. You're safe now."

The boys were pressed so tightly against him that Savich could feel their hearts pounding as they sobbed, deep, ragged sobs, and he knew there was blessed relief in their sobs, that they finally believed they were going to survive. They clutched at him and he held them as tightly as he could, whispering, "It will be all right. You're going to be home in no time at all. It's okay, Rob, Donny."

He kept them both shielded from Tammy Tuttle, who was no longer moaning. He made no move to see what shape she was in.

"The Ghouls," one of the boys kept saying over and over, his young voice cracking. "They told us all about what the Ghouls did to all the other boys—ate them up whole or if they were already full, then they just tore them up, chewed on their bones—"

"I know, I know," Savich said, but he had no idea what his eyes had seen, not really. Whirling dust devils, that was all. There were no hidden axes or knives. Unless they somehow morphed into something more substantial? No, that was crazy. He felt something catch inside him. It was a sense of what was real, what had to be real. It demanded he reject what he'd seen, bury it under a hundred tons of earth, make the

Ghouls gone forever, make it so they had never existed. It must have been some kind of natural phenomenon, easily explained, or some kind of an illusion, a waking nightmare, a mad invention of a pair of psychopaths' minds. But whatever they were that the Tuttles had called the Ghouls, he'd seen them, even shot at one of them, and they were embedded in his brain.

Maybe they had been dust devils, playing tricks on his eyes. Maybe.

As he stood holding the two thin bodies to him, talking to them, he was aware that agents, followed by the sheriff and his deputies, were inside the barn now, that one of them was bending over Tammy Tuttle. Soon there were agents everywhere, searching the barn, corner to corner, searching every inch of the tack room.

Everyone was high, excited. They'd gotten the boys back safely. They'd taken down two psychopaths.

Tammy Tuttle was conscious again, screaming, no way to keep the boys from hearing her, though he tried. They held her down on the floor. She was yelling and cursing at Savich as she cradled her arm, yelling that the Ghouls would get him, she would lead them to him, that he was dead meat, and so were those Little Bloods. Savich felt the boys nearly dissolve against him, their terror palpable.

Then one of the agents slammed his fist into her jaw. He looked up, grinning. "Took her out of her pain. Didn't like to see such a fine, up-standing young lady in such misery."

"Thank you," Savich said. "Rob, Donny, she's not going to hurt anyone ever again. I swear it to you." Sherlock came to him, and she looked angry enough to spit nails. She didn't say anything, just put her arms around the two boys.

The paramedics came through with stretch-ers. Big Bob, the lead, who had a twenty-two-inch neck, looked at the two agents comforting the boys and just held up his hand. He said to the three men behind him, "Let's just wait here a moment. I think these boys are getting the medicine they need right now. See to that woman. The guy is gone."

Three hours later, the old barn was finally empty again, all evidence, mainly food refuse, pizza boxes, some chains and shackles, a good four dozen candy bar wrappers, carted away. Both Tuttles had been removed, Tammy still alive. The boys were taken immediately to their parents, who were waiting at the sheriff's office in Stewartville, Maryland. From there they'd go on to the local hospital to be checked out. The FBI wouldn't need to speak to them again for at least a couple of days, giving them time to calm down before being questioned.

All the agents drove back to FBI headquarters, to the Criminal Apprehension Unit on the fifth floor, to write up their reports.

Everyone was bouncing off the walls. They'd won. High fives, slaps on the back. No screwups, no false leads. They hadn't been too late to save the boys. "Just look at all the testosterone flying around," Sherlock said as she walked into the office. Then she laughed. No one could talk about anything but how Savich had brought them down.

Savich called all the agents who had participated in the raid together.

"When the barn doors swung in, did anyone see anything?"

No one had seen a thing.

"Did anyone see anything strange coming out of the barn, anything at all?"

There wasn't a word spoken around the big conference table. Then Sherlock said, "We didn't see anything, Dillon. The barn doors flew inward; there was some thick dust in the air, but that was it." She looked around at the other agents. No one had seen any more than that. "We didn't see anything coming out of the barn either."

"The Tuttles called them Ghouls," Savich said slowly. "They looked so real I actually shot at one of them. It was then that they seemed to dissipate, to disappear. I'm being as objective as I can. Understand, I didn't want to see anything out of the ordinary. But I did see something. I want to believe that it was some sort of dust devil that broke into two parts, but I don't know, I just don't know. If anyone can come up with an explanation, I'd like to hear it."

There were more questions, more endless speculation, until everyone sat silent. Savich said to Jimmy Maitland, "The boys saw them. They're telling everyone about them. You can bet that Rob and Donny won't call them natural phenomena or dust devils."

Jimmy Maitland said, "No one will believe them. Now, we've got to keep this Ghoul business under wraps. The FBI has enough problems without announcing that we've seen two supernatural cones, for God's sake, in a rampaging partnership with two psychopaths."

Later, Savich realized while he was typing his report to Jimmy Maitland that he'd spelled "Ghouls" with a capital G. They weren't just general entities to the Tuttles; they were specific.

Sherlock followed Savich into the men's room some thirty minutes later. Ollie Hamish, Savich's second in command, was at the sink washing his hands when they came in.

"Oh, hi, guys. Congratulations again, Savich.

Great work. I just wish I could have been with you."

"I'm glad to see a man washing his hands," Sherlock said, and poked him in the arm. "In a few minutes I'm going to be washing my hands, too. After I've beaten some sense into my husband here, the jerk. Go away, Ollie, I know you'll want to protect him from me, and I don't want to have to hurt both of you."

"Ah, Sherlock, he's a hero. Why do you want to hurt the hero? He saved those little boys from the Warlocks and the Ghouls."

Savich said, "After what I told you about them, do you spell 'Ghouls' with a capital G in your head?"

"Yeah, sure, you said there were two of them. It's one of those strange things that will stay with you. You sure you weren't smoking something, Savich? Inhaling too much stale hay?"

"I wish I could say yes to that."

"Out, Ollie."

Once they were alone, she didn't take a strip off him, just stepped against him and wrapped her arms around his back. "I can't say that I've never been more frightened in my life, since you and I have managed to get into some bad situations." She kissed his neck and squeezed him even tighter. "But today, at that damned barn, you were a hot dog, and I was scared spitless, as were your friends."

"There was no time," he said against her curly hair. "No time to bring you in. Jesus, I scared myself, but I had no choice. And then those howling wind things were there. I honestly can't say which scared me more—Tammy Tuttle or whatever it was she called the Ghouls."

She pulled back a bit. "I really don't understand any of that. You described it all so clearly I could almost see them whirling through those barn doors. But Ghouls?"

"That's what the Tuttles called them. It was like they were acolytes to these things. I'd really like to say it was some sort of hallucination, that I was the only one who freaked out, but the boys saw them, too. I know it sounds off the wall, Sherlock, particularly since none of you guys saw a thing."

Because he needed to speak of it more, she just held him while he again described what had burst through the barn doors. Then he said, "I don't think there's anything more to do about this, but it was scary, Sherlock, really."

Jimmy Maitland walked into the men's room.

"Hey, where's a man to piddle?"

"Oh, sir, I just wanted to check Dillon out, make sure he was okay."

"And is he?"

"Oh, yes."

"Ollie caught me in the hall on my way to the unit, Savich, said you were getting the bejesus whaled out of you in the men's room. We've got a media frenzy cranking up." Jimmy Maitland gave them a big grin. "Guess what? No one's going to pound on us this time—only good news, thank the Lord. Great news. Since you were the one in the middle of it, Savich, we want you front and center. Of course, Louis Freeh will be there and do all the talking. They just want you to stand there and look like a hero."

"No mention of what we saw?"

"No, not a word about the Ghouls, not even speculation about whirling dust. The last thing we need is to have the media go after us because we claim we were attacked by some weird balls of dust called into the barn by a couple of psychopaths. As for the boys, it doesn't matter what they say. If the media asks us about it, we'll just shake our heads, look distressed and sympathetic. It will be a twenty-four-hour wonder, then it'll be over. And the FBI will be heroes. That sure feels good."

Savich said as he rubbed his hands up and down his wife's back, "But there was something very strange in there, sir, something that made the hair stand up on my head."

"Get a grip, Savich. We've got the Tuttle brothers, or rather we've got one brother dead and one sister whose arm was just amputated at the shoulder. The last thing we need is a dose of the supernatural."

"You could maybe call me Mulder?"

"Yeah, right. Hey, I just realized that Sherlock here has red hair, just like Scully."

Savich and Sherlock rolled their eyes and followed their boss from the men's room.

The boys claimed they'd seen the Ghouls, could speak of nothing else but how Agent Savich had put a bullet right in the middle of one and made them whirl out of the barn. But the boys were so tattered and pathetic, very nearly incoherent, that indeed, they weren't believed, even by their parents.

One reporter asked Savich if he'd seen any ghouls and Savich just said, "Excuse me, what did you say?"

Jimmy Maitland was right. That was the end of it.

Savich and Sherlock played with Sean for so long that evening that he finally fell asleep in the middle of his favorite finger game, Hide the Camel, a graham cracker smashed in his hand. That night at two o'clock in the morning, the phone rang. Savich picked it up, listened, and said, "We'll be there as soon as we can."

He slowly hung up the phone and looked over at his wife, who'd managed to prop herself up on her elbow.

"It's my sister, Lily. She's in the hospital. It doesn't look good."

TWO

Hemlock Bay, California

Bright sunlight poured through narrow windows. Her bedroom windows were wider, weren't they? Surely they were cleaner than this. No, wait, she wasn't in her bedroom. A vague sort of panic jumped her, then fell away. She didn't feel much of anything now, just a bit of confusion that surely wasn't all that important, just a slight ache in her left arm at the IV line.

IV line?

That meant she was in a hospital. She was breathing; she could feel the oxygen tickling her nose, the tubes irritating her. But it was reassuring. She was alive. But why shouldn't she be alive? Why was she surprised?

Her brain felt numb and empty, and even the emptiness was hazy. Maybe she was dying and that's why they'd left her alone. Where was Tennyson? Oh, yes, he'd gone to Chicago two days before, some sort of medical thing. She'd been glad to see him go, relieved, just plain solidly relieved that she wouldn't have to hear his calm, soothing voice that drove her nuts.

A white-coated man with a bald head, a stethoscope around his neck, came into the room. He leaned down right into her face. "Mrs. Frasier, can you hear me?"

"Oh, yes. I can even see the hairs in your nose."

He straightened, laughed. "Oh, that's too close then. Now that my nose hairs aren't in the way, how do you feel? Any pain?"

"No, I can barely feel my brain. I feel vague and stupid."

"That's because of the morphine. You could be shot in the belly, get enough morphine, and you wouldn't even be pissed at your mother-in-law. I'm your surgeon, Dr. Ted Larch. Since I had to remove your spleen—and that's major abdominal surgery—we'll keep you on a nice, steady dose of morphine until this evening. We'll begin to lighten up on it after that. Then we'll get you up to see how you're doing, get your innards working again."

"What else is wrong with me?"

"Let me give you the short version. First, let

me promise you that you'll be all right. As for having no spleen, nothing bad should happen in the long run because of that. An adult doesn't really need his spleen. However, you will have all the discomfort of surgery—pain for several days. You'll have to be careful about when and what you eat, and as I said, we'll have to get your system working again.

"You have a concussion, two bruised ribs, some cuts and abrasions, but you'll live. Nothing that should cause any scarring. You're doing splendidly, given what happened."

"What did happen?"

Dr. Larch was silent for a moment, his head tilted a bit to one side. Sun was pouring in through the window and gave his bald head a bright shine. He said slowly, studying her face, "You don't remember?"

She thought and thought until he lightly touched his fingers to her forearm. "No, don't try to force it. You'll just give yourself a headache. What is the last thing you do remember, Mrs. Frasier?"

Again she thought, and finally she said slowly, "I remember leaving my house in Hemlock Bay. That's where I live, on Crocodile Bayou Avenue. I remember I was going to drive to Ferndale to deliver some medical slides to a Dr. Baker. I remember I didn't like driving on 211 when it was nearly dark. That road is scary and those redwoods tower over you and surround you and you start feeling like you're being buried alive." She stopped, and he saw frustration building and interrupted her.

"No, that's all right. An interesting metaphor with those redwoods. Now, everything will probably all come back to you in time. You were in an accident, Mrs. Frasier. Your Explorer hit a redwood dead on. Now, I'm going to call in another doctor."

"What is his specialty?"

"He's a psychiatrist."

"Why do I need . . ." Now she frowned. "I don't understand. A psychiatrist? Why?"

"Well, it seems that you possibly could have driven into that redwood on purpose. No, don't panic, don't worry about a thing. Just rest and build up your strength. I'll see you later, Mrs. Frasier. If you begin to feel any pain in the next couple of hours, just hit your button and a nurse will pump some more morphine into your IV."

"I thought the patient could administer the morphine when needed."

He was stumped for a moment, she saw it clearly. He said, "I'm sorry, but we can't give you that."

"Why?" Her voice was very soft.

"Because there is a question of attempted suicide. We can't take the chance that you'd pump yourself full of morphine and we couldn't bring you back."

She looked away from him, toward the window, where the sun was shining in so brightly.

"All I remember is last evening. What day is it? What time of day?"

"It's late Thursday morning. You've been going in and out for a while now. Your accident was last evening."

"So much missing time."

"It will be all right, Mrs. Frasier."

"I wonder about that," she said, nothing more, and closed her eyes.

● Dr. Russell Rossetti stopped for a moment just inside the doorway and looked at the young woman who lay so still on the narrow hospital bed. She looked like a princess who'd kissed the wrong frog and been beaten up, major league. Her blond hair was mixed with flecks of blood and tangled around bandages. She was thin, too thin, and he wondered what she was thinking right now, right this minute.

Dr. Ted Larch, the surgeon who'd removed her spleen, had told him she didn't remember a thing about the accident. He'd also said he didn't think she'd tried to kill herself. She was just too "there," he'd said. The meathead.

Ted was a romantic, something weird for a surgeon to be. Of course she'd tried to kill herself. Again. No question. It was classic.

"Mrs. Frasier."

Lily slowly turned her head at the sound of a rather high voice she imagined could whine when he didn't get his way, a voice that was right now trying to sound soothing, all sorts of inviting, but not succeeding.

She said nothing, just looked at the overweight man—on the tall side, very well dressed in a dark, gray suit, with lots of curly black hair, a double chin, and fat, very white fingers—who walked into the room. He came to stand too close to the bed.

"Who are you?"

"I'm Dr. Rossetti. Dr. Larch told you I would be coming to see you?"

"You're the psychiatrist?"

"Yes."

"He told me, but I don't want to see you. There is no reason."

Denial, he thought, just splendid. He was bored with the stream of depressed patients who simply started crying and became quickly incoherent and self-pitying, their hands held out for pills to numb them. Although Tennyson had told him that Lily wasn't like that, he hadn't been convinced.

He said, all calm and smooth, "Evidently you do need me. You drove your car into a redwood."

Had she? No, it just didn't seem right. She said, "The road to Ferndale is very dangerous. Have you ever driven it at dusk, when it's nearly dark?"

"Yes."

"You didn't find you had to be very careful?"

"Of course. However, I never wrapped my car around a redwood. The Forestry Service is looking at the tree now, to see how badly it's hurt."

"Well, if I'm missing some bark, I'm sure it is, too. I would like you to leave now, Dr. Rossetti."

Instead of leaving, he pulled a chair close to the bed and sat down. He crossed his legs. He weaved his plump, white fingers together. She hated his hands, soft, puffy hands, but she couldn't stop looking at them.

"If you'll give me just a minute, Mrs. Frasier. Do you mind if I call you Lily?"

"Yes, I mind. I don't know you. Go away."

He leaned toward her and tried to take her hand, but she pulled it away and stuck it beneath her covers.

"You really should cooperate with me, Lily—"

"My name is Mrs. Frasier."

He frowned. Usually women—any and all women—liked to be called by their first name. It made them feel that he was more of a confidant, someone they could trust. It also made them more vulnerable, more open to him.

He said, "You tried to kill yourself the first time after the death of your child seven months ago."

"She didn't just die. A speeding car hit her and knocked her twenty feet into a ditch. Someone murdered her."

"And you blamed yourself."

"Are you a parent?"

"Yes."

"Wouldn't you blame yourself if your child died and you weren't with her?"

"No, not if I wasn't driving the car that hit her."

"Would your wife blame herself?"

Elaine's face passed before his mind's eye, and he frowned. "Probably not. All she would do is cry. She is a very weak woman, very dependent. But that isn't the point, Mrs. Frasier." It wasn't. He would be free of Elaine very soon now, thank God.

"What is the point?"

"You did blame yourself, blamed yourself so much you stuffed a bottle of sleeping pills down your throat. If your housekeeper hadn't found you in time, you would have died."

"That's what I was told," she said, and she swore in that moment that she could taste the same taste in her mouth now as she had then when she'd awakened in the hospital that first time when she'd been so bewildered, so weak she couldn't even raise her hand.

"You don't remember taking the pills?"

"No, not really."

"And now you don't remember driving your car into a redwood. Your speed, it was estimated by the sheriff, was about sixty miles per hour, maybe faster. You were very lucky, Mrs. Frasier. A guy just happened to come around a bend to see you drive into the tree, and called an ambulance."

"Do you happen to know his name? I would like to thank him."

"That isn't what's important here, Mrs. Frasier."

"What is important here? Oh, yes, do you happen to have a first name?"

"My name is Russell. Dr. Russell Rossetti."

"Nice alliteration, Russell."

"It would be better if you called me Dr. Rossetti," he said. She saw those plump, white fingers twisting, and she knew he was angry. He thought she was out of line. She was, but she just didn't care. She was tired, so very tired, and she just wanted to close her eyes and let the morphine mask the pain for a while longer.

"Go away, Dr. Rossetti."

He didn't move for some time.

Lily turned her head away and sought oblivion. She didn't even hear when he finally left the room. She did, however, hear the door close.

When Dr. Larch walked in five minutes later, his very high forehead flushed, she managed to cock an eye open and say, "Dr. Rossetti is a patronizing ass. He has fat hands. Please, I don't want to see him again."

"He doesn't think you're in very good shape."

"On the contrary, I'm in splendid shape, something I can't say about him. He needs to go to the gym very badly."

Dr. Larch laughed, couldn't help himself. "He also said your defensiveness and your rudeness to him were sure signs that you're highly overwrought and in desperate need of help."

"Yeah, right. I'm so overwrought—what with all this painkiller—that I'm ready to nap."

"Ah, your husband is here to see you."

She didn't want to see Tennyson. His voice, so resonant, so confident—it was too much like

Dr. Rossetti's voice, as if they'd taken the same Voice Lessons 101 course in shrink school. If she never saw another one of them again, she could leave this earth a happy woman.

She looked past Dr. Larch to see her husband of eleven months standing in the doorway, looking rather pale, his thick eyebrows drawn together, his arms crossed over his chest. Such a nice-looking man he was, all big and solid, his hair light and wavy, lots of hair, not bald like Dr. Larch. He wore aviator glasses, which looked really cool, and now she watched him push them back up, an endearing habit—at least that's what she'd thought when she'd first met him.

"Lily?"

"Yes," she said and wished he'd stay in the doorway. Dr. Larch straightened and turned to him. "Dr. Frasier, as I told you, your wife will be fine, once she recovers from the surgery. However, she does need to rest. I suggest that you visit for only a few minutes."

"I am very tired, Tennyson," she said and hated the small shudder in her voice. "Perhaps we could speak later?"

"Oh, no," he said. And then he waited, saying nothing more until Dr. Larch left the room, fingering his stethoscope. He looked nervous. Lily wondered why. Tennyson closed the door, paused yet again, studying her, then, finally, he walked to stand beside her bed. He gently eased her hand out from under the covers, something she wished he wouldn't do, rubbed his fingers over her palm for several moments before saying in a sad, soft voice, "Why did you do it, Lily? Why?"

He made it sound like it was all over for her. No, she was being ridiculous. She said, "I don't know that I did anything, Tennyson. You see, I have no memory at all of the accident."

He waved away her words. He had strong hands, confident hands. "I know and I'm sorry about that. Look, Lily, maybe it was an accident, maybe somehow you lost control and drove the Explorer into the redwood. One of the nurses told me that the Forest Service has someone on the spot to see how badly the tree is injured."

"Dr. Rossetti already told me. Poor tree."

"It isn't funny, Lily. Now, you're going to be here for at least another two or three days, until they're sure your body is functioning well again. I would like you to speak with Dr. Rossetti. He's a new man with quite an excellent reputation."

"I've already seen him. I don't wish to see him again, Tennyson."

His voice changed now, became even softer, more gentle, and she knew she would normally have wanted to cry, to fold into herself, to have him reassure her, tell her the bogeyman wouldn't come back, but not now. It was probably the morphine making her feel slightly euphoric, slightly disconnected. But she also felt rather strong, perhaps even on the arrogant side, and that, of course, was an illusion to beat all illusions.

"Since you don't remember anything, Lily, you've got to admit that it wouldn't hurt to cover all the bases. I really want you to see him."

"I don't like him, Tennyson. How can I speak to someone I don't like?"

"You will see him, Lily, or I'm afraid we'll have to consider an institution."

"Oh? *We* will consider an institution? What sort of institution?" Why wasn't she afraid of that word that brought a wealth of dreadful images with it? But she wasn't afraid. She was looking at him positively bright-eyed. She loved morphine. She was tiring; she could feel the vagueness trying to close her down, eating away at the focus in her brain, but for this moment, maybe even the next, too, she could deal with anything.

He squeezed her hand. "I'm a doctor, Lily, a psychiatrist, as is Dr. Rossetti. You know it isn't ethical for me to treat you myself."

"You prescribed the Elavil."

"That's different. That's a very common drug for depression. No, I couldn't speak with you like Dr. Rossetti can. But you must know that I want what is best for you. I love you and I've prayed you were getting better. One day at a time, I kept telling myself. And there were some days when I knew you were healing, but I was wrong. Yes, you really must see Dr. Rossetti or I'm afraid I will have no choice but to admit you for evaluation."

"Forgive me for pointing this out, Tennyson, but I don't believe that you can do that. I'm here—I can see, I can talk, I can reason—I do have a say in what happens to me."

"That remains to be seen. Lily, just speak to Dr. Rossetti. Talk to him about your pain, your confusion, your guilt, the fact that you're beginning to accept what your ambition wrought."

Ambition? She had such great ambition that her daughter was killed because of it?

She suddenly wanted to be perfectly clear about this. She said, "What do you mean exactly, Tennyson?"

"You know—Beth's death."

That hit her right between the eyes. Instant guilt, overwhelming her. No, wait, she wasn't going to let that happen. She wouldn't let it happen, not now. Beneath the morphine, beneath all of it, she was still there, hanging on, wanting to be whole, wanting to draw her cartoon strips of No Wrinkles Remus shafting another colleague, wanting . . . Was that the great ambition that had killed her daughter? "I can't deal with this right now, Tennyson. Please go away. I'll be better in the morning."

No, she'd feel like hell when they lessened her pain dosage, she thought, but she wouldn't worry about that now. Now she would sleep; she'd get better, both her brain and her body. She turned her head away from him on the pillow. She had no more words. She knew if she tried to speak more, she wouldn't make sense. She was falling, falling ever so gently into the whale's soft belly, and it would be warm, comforting. Move over, Jonah. She wouldn't have nightmares, not with the morphine lulling her.

She stared at the IV in her arm, upward to the plastic bag filled with fluid above her. Her vision blurred into the lazy flow of liquid that didn't seem to go anywhere, just flowed and flowed. She closed her eyes even as he said, "I will see you later this evening, Lily. Rest well." He leaned down and kissed her cheek. How she used to love his hands on her, his kissing her, but not now. She simply hadn't felt anything for such a very long time.

When she was alone again, she thought, *What am I going to do?* But then she knew, of course. She forced back the haziness, the numbing effect of the morphine. She picked up the phone and dialed her brother's number in Washington, D.C. She heard a series of clicks and then the sound of a person breathing, but nothing happened. She dialed a nine, then the number again. She tried yet again, but didn't get through. Then, suddenly, the line went dead.

She realized vaguely as she let herself be drawn into the ether that there was fear licking at her, from the deepest part of her, fear that she couldn't quite grasp, and it wasn't fear that she'd be institutionalized against her will.

THREE

Lily awoke to feel the touch of fingers on her eyebrows, stroking as light as a butterfly's wing. She heard a man's voice, a voice she'd loved all her life, deep and low, wonderfully sweet, and she opened to it eagerly.

"Lily, I want you to open your eyes now and look at me and smile. Can you do that, sweetheart? Open your eyes."

And she opened her eyes and looked up at her brother. She smiled. "My big Fed brother. I've worshiped you from the time you showed me how to kick Billy Clapper in the crotch so he wouldn't try to feel me up again. Do you remember that?"

"Yes, I remember. You were twelve and this little jerk, who was all of fourteen at the time, had put his hand up your skirt."

"I really hurt him bad, Dillon. He never tried anything again."

He was smiling, such a beautiful smile, white teeth. "I remember."

"I should have kept kicking guys in the crotch. Then none of this would have happened. I'm so glad you're here."

"I'm here, Lily, so is Sherlock. We left Sean with Mom, who was grinning and singing the 'Hallelujah Chorus' as we drove out of the driveway. We told her you'd been in an accident and that you were okay, that we just wanted to see you. You can call and reassure her later. As for the rest of the family, let Mom do the telling."

"I don't want her to worry. It's true, Dillon, I'll be okay. I miss Sean. It's been so long. I really like all the photos you e-mail me."

"Yes, but it's not the same as being in the room with him, having him gum your fingers, rub his crackers into your sweater, and drool on your neck."

Sherlock said, "You touch any surface in the house and come away with graham cracker crumbs."

Lily smiled, and it was real because she could see that precious little boy dropping wet graham cracker crumbs everywhere, and it pleased her to her very soul. "Mom must be so happy to have her hands on him."

Savich said, "Yes. She always spoils him so

rotten that when he comes home, he's a real
pain for a good two days."

"He's the cutest little button, Dillon. I miss
him."

A tear leaked out of her eye.

Savich wiped the tear away. "I know, so do
Sherlock and I and we've only been apart from
him for less than a day. How do you feel, Lily?"

"It's dark again."

"Yes. Nearly seven o'clock Thursday
evening. Now, sweetheart, talk to me. How do
you feel?"

"Like they've already lightened the morphine."

"Yeah, Dr. Larch said he was just beginning
to ease up on it now. You're gonna feel rotten
for a while, a day or two, but then it'll be less
and less pain each day."

"When did you get here?"

"Sherlock and I just got into town. The pud-
dle jumper from San Francisco to Arcata-
Eureka was late." He saw her eyes go vague and
added, "Sherlock bought Sean a Golden Gate
oven mitt at the San Francisco airport."

"I'll show it to you later, Lily," Sherlock said.
She was standing on the other side of Lily's bed,
smiling down at her, so scared for this lovely
young woman who was her sister-in-law. She'd
have bitten her fingernails if she hadn't stopped

some three years before. "It was between an oven mitt with Alcatraz on it and the Golden Gate. Since Sean gums everything, Dillon thought gumming the Golden Gate was healthier than gumming a Federal prison."

Lily laughed. She didn't know where it had come from, but she even laughed again. Pain seared through her side and her ribs, and she gasped.

"No more humor," Sherlock said and lightly kissed her cheek. "We're here and everything's going to be all right now, I promise."

"Who called you?"

"Your father-in-law, about two in the morning, last night."

"I wonder why he called," she said slowly, thinking about the pain that was now coming through and how she would deal with it.

"You wouldn't expect him to?"

"I see now," Lily said, her eyes suddenly narrow and fierce. "He was afraid Mrs. Scruggins would call you and then you would wonder why the family hadn't called. I think he's afraid of you, Dillon. He's always asking me how you're doing and where you are. When you were here before, I think you scared him really good."

"Why would I scare him?"

"Because you're big and you're smart and you're a special agent with the FBI."

Sherlock laughed. "Lots of people don't relax around FBI agents. But Mr. Elcott Frasier? I took one look at him and thought he probably chewed nails for breakfast."

"He could, you know. Everyone thinks that, particularly his son, my husband."

"Maybe he called because he knew we'd want to come here to see you," Savich said. "Maybe he isn't all that much of an iron fist."

"Yes, he is. Tennyson was here earlier." She sighed, tightened a bit from a jab of pain in her bruised ribs, the pulling in her side. "Thank goodness he finally left."

Savich looked over at Sherlock. "What happened, Lily? Talk to us."

"Everyone thinks I tried to kill myself again."

"Fine, let them. It doesn't matter. Talk, Lily."

"I don't know, Dillon, I swear I don't. I remember that I had to drive that gnarly road to Ferndale, you know, 211? And that's all. Everything else is just lost."

Sherlock said, "All right, then. Everyone thinks you tried to kill yourself because of the pills you took right after Beth's death?"

"Yes, I guess so."

"But why?"

"I suppose I haven't been exactly honest with you guys, but I just didn't want you to worry. Fact is, I have been depressed. I'll feel lots better and then it's back down again. It's gotten progressively worse the past couple of weeks. Why? I don't know, but it has. And then last night happened."

Savich pulled up a chair and sat down. He took her hand again. "You know, Lily, even when you were a little girl, you'd hit a problem, and I swear you'd worry and work and chew on that problem, never giving up until you had it solved. Dad used to say that if he was slow telling you something you really wanted to know, he could just see you gnawing on his trouser leg until you ripped it right off or he talked, whichever came first."

"I miss Dad."

"I do, too. Now, I still don't understand that first time you wanted to die. That wasn't the Lily I knew. But Beth's death—that would knock any parent on his or her butt. But now seven months have passed. You're smart, you're talented, you're not one to be in denial. This depression—that doesn't make a lot of sense to me. What's been happening, Lily?"

She sobered, frowning now. "Nothing's been happening, just more of the same. Like I said, over the past months sometimes I'd feel better, feel like I could conquer the world again, but then it would go away and I'd want to stay in bed all day.

"For whatever reason, yesterday it got really bad. Tennyson called me from Chicago and told me to take two of the antidepressant pills. I did. I'll tell you something, the pills sure don't seem to help. And then, when I was driving on that road to Ferndale—well, maybe something did happen. Maybe I did drive into that redwood. I just don't remember."

"It's okay. Now, how does your brain feel right now?" Sherlock asked, scooting in a little closer to Lily on the hospital bed.

"Not quite as vague as before. I guess since there's less morphine swimming around up in there, I'm coming back."

"Are you feeling depressed?"

"No. I'm mainly just mad because of that idiot shrink they sent by. A dreadful man, trying to be so comforting, so understanding, when really he was a condescending jerk."

"You smart-mouthed him, babe?"

"Maybe. A little bit."

"I'm glad," Sherlock said. "Not enough back-mouthing from you lately, Lily."

"Oh, dear."

"Oh, dear what?"

But Lily didn't say anything, just kept looking toward the door.

Savich and Sherlock both turned to see their brother-in-law, Tennyson Frasier, come into the room.

Savich thought, Lily doesn't want to see her husband?

What was going on here? Seven months ago, Lily had come back to Maryland to stay with their mother for several weeks after Beth's funeral. While she'd been there, Savich had done everything he could, turned over every rock he could find, called in every favor, to discover who had struck Beth and driven off. No luck. Not a clue. But then Lily had wanted to go back to Hemlock Bay, to be with her husband, who loved her and needed her, and yes, she was all right now.

A big mistake to let her come back here, Savich thought, and knew he wouldn't leave her here this time. Not again.

Savich straightened as Tennyson came striding toward him, his hand outstretched. As he pumped Savich's hand, he said, "Boy, am I ever glad to see you guys. Dad told me he called you, in the middle of the night." Then he stopped. He looked at Lily.

Sherlock never moved from her perch on

Lily's bed. She said, "Good to see you, Tennyson." Such a handsome man he was, big and in pretty good shape, and at the moment he looked terrified for his wife. Why didn't Lily want to see him?

"Lily, are you all right?" Tennyson walked to her bed, his hand out.

Lily slipped her hand beneath the covers as she said, "I'm fine, Tennyson. Do you know that I tried to call Dillon and Sherlock earlier? And my line went dead. Is it still dead now?"

Sherlock picked up the phone. There was a dial tone. "It's fine now."

"Isn't that strange?"

"Maybe," Tennyson said, leaning down to caress Lily's pale face, kiss her lightly, "with all that morphine in you, you didn't do it right."

"There was a dial tone, then a person's breathing, some clicking sounds, and then nothing."

"Hmmm. I'll check on that, but it's working now, so no harm done." He turned back to Savich. "You and Sherlock got here very quickly."

"She's my sister," Savich said, looking at his brother-in-law closely. "What would you expect?" He'd always liked Tennyson, believed he'd been a solid man, one who was trustworthy, unlike Lily's first husband, Jack Crane. He'd

believed Tennyson had been as distraught as
Lily when Beth was killed. He had worked with
Savich trying to find out who the driver was
who'd killed Beth. As for the sheriff, he'd been
next to useless. What was wrong? Why didn't
Lily want to see him?

Tennyson merely nodded, then kissed Lily
again. He said, his voice as soft as a swatch of
Bengali silk, "I can't wait to get you out of this
place, get you home. You'll be safe with me,
Lily, always."

But she hadn't been safe, Sherlock thought.
That was the bottom line. She'd run her Explorer into a redwood. Hardly safe. What was
wrong with this picture?

"What about that psychiatrist, Tennyson?"

"Dr. Rossetti? I would really like you to see
him, Lily. He can help you."

"You said you would institutionalize me if I
didn't see him."

Savich nearly went *en pointe*.

Sherlock laughed. "Institutionalize Lily?
Come on, Tennyson."

"No, no, all of you misunderstood. Listen,
Lily very probably drove into that redwood last
night. This is the second time she's tried to end
her life. You were both here after the first time.
You saw how she was. Her mother saw as well.
Well, she's been on medication, but obviously it

hasn't helped. I want her to speak to a very excellent psychiatrist, a man I respect very much."

"I don't like him, Tennyson. I don't want to see him again."

Tennyson sighed deeply. "All right, Lily. If you don't like Dr. Rossetti, then I'll find another man who could possibly help you."

"I would prefer a woman."

"Whatever. I don't know of any female psychiatrists who do anything other than family counseling."

Savich said, "I'll have some names for you by tomorrow, Lily. No problem. But we're a bit off the subject here. I want to know the name of the antidepressants Lily's been taking and I want to know why they seem to have the opposite effect on her."

Tennyson said patiently, "It's a very popular drug, Dillon. Elavil. You can ask any doctor."

"I'm sure it is. I suppose there are a certain number of people who simply don't respond appropriately?"

"Unfortunately, yes. I was considering whether or not we should try another drug— Prozac, for example."

Savich said, "Why don't you just wait on all the drugs until Lily has seen a new psychiatrist. What happened to Dr. McGill? Weren't you with him for a while, Lily?"

"He died, Dillon, not two weeks after I began seeing him. He was such a sweet man, but he was old and his heart was rotten. He had a heart attack."

Tennyson shrugged. "It happens. Hey, I saw you on TV, Savich, there with all the FBI brass. You got the Warlocks."

"Turns out there was only one warlock, the other was a witch."

"Yes, a brother and a sister. How did everyone miss that?"

"Good question." Savich saw that Lily was listening closely now. She loved hearing about their cases, so he kept talking about it. "Turns out one of them wasn't really a guy, just dressed like one—Timmy was really a she. She even lowered her voice, cropped off her hair, the whole deal. The profilers never saw it and neither did any of my unit. Instead of Tammy, to the world she was Timmy."

"Did the brother and sister sleep together?" Tennyson said.

"Not that we know of."

Lily said, "It was MAX who managed to track down that barn?"

"That's right. Once we knew the Tuttles were back in Maryland, I knew in my gut that this was their final destination, that they'd come home, even though they'd been born and raised in Utah. They kidnapped the boys in Maryland. So where were they? MAX always checks out any and every relative when we know who the suspect is. He dug deep enough to find Marilyn Warluski, a cousin who owned this property. And on the property was this old abandoned barn."

Thank God no one had mentioned anything about the Ghouls.

Lily said, "How many boys did the two of them kill, Sherlock?"

"A dozen, maybe more. All across the country. We'll probably never know unless Tammy decides to tell us, and that's not likely. Her arm was amputated thanks to Dillon's shot. She's not a happy camper. Thank God it's over and the last two boys are all right."

Tennyson asked, "You shot her? Did you kill the brother too?"

"The brother's dead, yes. It was a team effort," Savich said, and nothing more.

"Those poor little boys," Lily said. "Their parents must have been torn apart when they were taken."

"They were, but as I said, everything turned out okay for them."

Nurse Carla Brunswick said from the doorway, "We don't have to worry about crooks while you guys are in town. Now, I get to order the FBI out. Time for Mrs. Frasier's sleeping pills. Say good night—even you, Dr. Frasier. Dr. Larch's orders."

● It wasn't until they were in the hospital parking lot that Tennyson said, "I apologize for not realizing sooner that you'd only just arrived. You will stay with me, won't you?"

"Yes," Savich said. "Thank you, Tennyson. We want to be close."

An hour later, after Savich had called his mother and told her not to worry and had spoken to his son, he climbed into the king-size bed beneath the sloped-ceiling guest room, kissed his wife, tucked her against his side, and said, "Why do you really think Mr. Elcott Frasier called us?"

"The obvious: he was worried about his daughter-in-law and wanted us to know right away. Very thoughtful. He thought it through and didn't just call your mom and scare the daylights out of her."

"All right, just maybe you're right. After that heavy dose of craziness with the Tuttles, I guess my mind went automatically to the worst possible motive."

Sherlock kissed his neck, then settled back in, her leg over his belly. "I've heard so much psychobabble about Lily. She tries to kill herself because it's the only thing to do if she wants to gain peace. She has to drive her Explorer into a redwood to expiate her guilt. It just doesn't sound right. It doesn't sound like Lily. Yes, yes, I remember the first time. But that was then."

"And this is now."

"Yes. Seven months. Lily isn't neurotic, Dillon. I've always thought she was strong, stable. And now I feel guilty because we didn't make an effort to see her over the last months."

"You had a baby, Sherlock, not a week after Beth's funeral."

"And Lily was there for me."

"She wasn't there with you—not like I was. My God, Sherlock, that was the longest day of my life." He squeezed her so hard, she squeaked.

"Yeah, yeah," she said.

"You never curse, but toward the end there you called me more names than I'd ever been called, even by linebackers during football games in college."

She laughed, kissed his shoulder again, and said, "Look, I know Lily's been through a very hard time. She's been understandably depressed. But we've talked to her a lot since Beth died. I just don't believe she was in a frame of mind to try to kill herself again."

"I don't know," he said. He frowned and turned off the lamp on the bedside table. He pulled Sherlock against him again and held her tight. "It really shakes me up, Sherlock, this happening to Lily. It's so hard to know what to do."

She held him harder than she had in her life. And she was thinking how fragile Lily had been seven months before, so hurt and so very broken, and then she'd taken those pills and nearly died. Savich and their mother had flown out to California for the second time, not more than a week after Beth's funeral, to see Lily lying in that narrow hospital bed, a tube in her nose, an IV line in her arm. But Lily had survived. And she'd been so sorry, so very sorry that she'd frightened everyone. And she'd come back with them to Washington, D.C., to rest and get her bearings. But after three weeks, she'd decided to go back to her husband in Hemlock Bay.

And seven months later, she'd driven her Explorer into a redwood.

She squeezed more tightly against him. "I just don't know how I'd handle it if anything happened to Sean. I couldn't bear that, Dillon. I just couldn't. No wonder Lily didn't."

After a long time, he said, "No, I couldn't bear it either, but you know what? You and I would survive it together. Somehow we would.

But I think your instincts on this were right. You said something doesn't feel right. What did you mean?"

She nuzzled her nose into his shoulder, hummed a bit, a sure sign she was thinking hard, and said, "Well, just last week, Lily sent us a *No Wrinkles Remus* strip she'd just finished, her first one since Beth was killed, and she sounded excited. So what happened over the past four days to make her want to try to kill herself again?"

FOUR

Hemlock Bay, California

"I stole the bottle of pills," Savich said, as he walked into the kitchen.

Sherlock grinned at her husband, gave him a thumbs-up, and said, "How do we check them out?"

"I called Clark Hoyt in the Eureka field office. I'll messenger them up to him today. He'll get back to me tomorrow. Then we'll know, one way or the other."

"Ah, Dillon, I've got a confession to make." She took a sip of her tea, grinned down at the few tea leaves on the bottom of the cup. "The pills you took, well, they're cold medicine. You see, I'd already stolen the pills and replaced them with Sudafed I found in the medicine cabinet."

Sometimes she just bowled him over. He

toasted her with his tea. "I'm impressed, Sherlock. When did you switch them?"

"About five A.M. this morning, before anyone was stirring. Oh, yes, Mrs. Scruggins, the housekeeper, should be here soon. We can see what she's got to say about all this."

Mrs. Scruggins responded to Sherlock's questions by sighing a lot. She was a tall woman, nearly as tall as Savich, and she looked strong, very strong, even those long fingers of hers including her thumbs, that each sported a ring. She had muscles. Sherlock didn't think she'd want to tangle with Mrs. Scruggins. She had to be at least sixty years old. It was amazing. There were pictures of her grandchildren lining the window ledge in the kitchen and she looked like she could take any number of muggers out at one time.

Savich sat back and watched Sherlock work her magic. "An awful thing," Sherlock said, shaking her head, obviously distressed. "We just can't understand it. But I'll bet you do, Mrs. Scruggins, here with poor Lily so much of the time. I'll bet you saw things real clearly."

And Mrs. Scruggins said then, her beringed fingers curving gracefully around her coffee cup, "I'd think she was getting better, you know?"

Both Savich and Sherlock nodded.

"Then she'd just fall into a funk again and curl

up in the fetal position and spend the day in bed. She wouldn't eat, just lie there, barely even blinking. I guess she'd be thinking about little Beth, you know?"

"Yes, we know," Sherlock said, sighed, and moved closer to the edge of her chair, inviting more thoughts, more confidences.

"Every few weeks I'd swear she was getting better, but it wouldn't last long. Just last week I thought she was really improving, nearly back to normal. She was in her office and she was laughing. I actually heard her. It was a laugh. She was drawing that cartoon strip of hers, and she was laughing."

"Then what happened?"

"Well, Mrs. Savich, I can't rightly say. Before I left, Dr. Frasier had come home early and I heard them talking. Then she just fell back again, the very next day. It was really fast. Laughing one minute, then, not ten hours later, she was so depressed, so quiet. She just walked around the house that day, not really seeing anything, at least that's what I think. Then she'd disappear and I knew later that she'd been crying. It's enough to break your heart, you know?"

"Yes, we know," Sherlock said. "These pills, Mrs. Scruggins, the Elavil, do you refill the prescription for her?"

"Yes, usually. Sometimes Dr. Frasier just brings them home for her. They don't seem to do much good, do they?"

"No," said Savich. "Maybe it's best that she be off them for a while."

"Amen to that. Poor little mite, such a hard time she's had." Mrs. Scruggins gave another deep sigh, nearly pulling apart the buttons over her large bosom. "I myself missed little Beth so much I just wanted sometimes to lie down and cry and cry and never you mind anything else. And I wasn't her mama, not like Mrs. Frasier."

"What about Dr. Frasier?" Savich asked.

"What do you mean?"

"Was he devastated by Beth's death?"

"Ah, he's a man, Mr. Savich. Sure, he looked glum for a week or so. But you know, men just don't take things like that so much to heart, leastwise my own papa didn't when my little sister died. Maybe Dr. Frasier keeps it all inside, but I don't think so. Don't forget, he wasn't Beth's real father. He didn't know little Beth that long, maybe six months in all."

Sherlock said, "But he's been so very worried about Lily, hasn't he?"

Mrs. Scruggins nodded, and the small diamond studs in her ears glittered in the morning sunlight pouring through the window. Diamonds and muscles and rings, Sherlock thought, and wondered. Mrs. Scruggins said, "Poor man, always fretting about her, trying to make her smile, bringing her presents and flowers, but nothing really worked, leastwise in the long term. And now this." Mrs. Scruggins shook her head. She wore her gray hair in a thick chignon. She had lots of hair and there were a lot of bobby pins worked into the roll.

It occurred to Sherlock to wonder if Mrs. Scruggins really cared for Lily, or if it was all an act. Could it be that she was really Lily's companion, or maybe even her guard?

Now where had that thought come from? Hadn't Mrs. Scruggins saved Lily's life that first time Lily had taken the bottle of pills right after Beth's funeral? She was getting paranoid here; she had to watch it.

"I have a little boy, Mrs. Scruggins," Savich said. "I've only had him a bit more than seven months, and you can believe that I would be devastated if anything were to happen to him."

"Well, that's good. Some men are different, aren't they? But my daddy, hard-nosed old bastard he was. Didn't shed a tear when my little sister got hit by that tractor. Ah, well, I'm afraid I have things to do now. When is Mrs. Frasier coming home?"

"Perhaps as soon as tomorrow," Sherlock said. "She's had major surgery and won't be feeling very well for several days."

"I'll take care of her," Mrs. Scruggins said and popped her knuckles.

Sherlock shuddered, shot Savich a look, and thanked the older woman for all her help. She shook Mrs. Scruggins's hand, feeling all those rings grind into her fingers.

Just before they left the kitchen, Mrs. Scruggins said, "I'm real glad you're staying here. Being alone just isn't good for Mrs. Frasier."

Savich felt a deep shaft of guilt. He remembered he hadn't said very much when Lily had insisted on returning here after recuperating with their mother. She'd seemed just fine, wanted to be with her husband again, and he'd thought, *I would want to be with Sherlock, too,* and he'd seen her off at Reagan Airport with the rest of the family. Tennyson Frasier seemed to adore her, and Lily, it seemed then to Savich, had adored him as well.

During the months she was home, she hadn't ever called to complain, to ask for help. Her e-mails were invariably upbeat. And whenever he and Sherlock had called, she'd always sounded cheerful.

And now, all these months later, this happened. He should have done something then, shouldn't have just kissed her and waved her onto the flight to take her three thousand miles away from her family. To take her back to where Beth had been killed.

He looked down to see Sherlock squeezing his hand. There was immense love in her eyes and she said only, "We will fix things, Dillon. This time we'll fix things."

He nodded and said, "I really want to see Lily's in-laws again, don't you, Sherlock? I have this feeling that perhaps we really don't know them at all."

"Agreed. We can check them out after we've seen Lily."

At the Hemlock County Hospital, everything was quiet. When they reached Lily's room, they heard the sound of voices and paused at the door for a moment.

It was Tennyson.

And Elcott Frasier, his father.

Elcott Frasier was saying, his voice all mournful, "Lily, we're so relieved that you survived that crash. It was really dicey there for a while, but you managed to pull through. I can't tell you how worried Charlotte has been, crying, wringing her hands, talking about her little Lily dying and how dreadful it would be, particularly such a short time after little Beth died. The Explorer, though, it's totaled."

That, Savich thought, was the strangest declaration of caring he'd ever heard.

"It's very nice of all of you to be concerned," Lily said, and Savich heard the pain in her voice, and something else. Was it fear? Dislike? He didn't know. She said, "I'm very sorry that I wrecked the Explorer."

"I don't want you to worry about it, Lily," Tennyson said and took her hand. It was limp, Savich saw, she wasn't returning any pressure.

"I'll buy you another one. A gift from me to you, my beautiful little daughter-in-law," Elcott said.

"I don't want another Explorer," she said.

"No, of course not," continued Elcott. "Another Explorer would remind you of the accident, wouldn't it? We don't want that. We want you to get well. Oh yes, we'll do anything to get you well again, Lily. Just this morning, Charlotte was telling me how everyone in Hemlock Bay was talking about it, calling her, commiserating. She's very upset by it all."

Savich, quite simply, wanted to throw Elcott Frasier out the window. He knew Frasier was tough as nails, that he was a powerful man, but Savich was surprised that he hadn't been a bit more subtle, not this in-your-face bludgeoning. Why? Why this gratuitous cruelty?

Savich walked into the room like a man bent

on violence until he saw his sister's white face, the pain that glazed her eyes, and he calmed immediately. He ignored the men, walked right to the bed, and leaned down, pressed his forehead lightly against hers.

"You hurt, kiddo?"

"Just a bit," she whispered, as if she were afraid to speak up. "Well, actually a whole lot. It's not too awful if I don't breathe too deeply or laugh or cry."

"More than a bit, I'd say," Savich said. "I'm going to find Dr. Larch and get you some more medication." He nodded to Sherlock and was out the door.

Sherlock smiled brightly at both her brother-in-law and Elcott Frasier. He looked the same as he had the first time she'd met him, eleven months before—tall, a bit of a paunch, a full head of thick, white hair, wavy, quite attractive. His eyes were his son's—light blue, reflective, slightly slanted. She wondered what his vices were, wondered if he really loved Lily and wanted her well. But why wouldn't he? Lily had been his son's wife for eleven months now. She was sweet, loving, very talented, and she'd lost her only child and fallen into a deep well of grief and depression.

She knew Elcott was sixty, but he looked no older than mid-fifties. He'd been a handsome

man when he was younger, perhaps as handsome as his only son.

There was a daughter as well. Tansy was her
name and she was, what? Twenty-eight?
Thirty? Older than Lily, Sherlock thought.
Tansy—an odd name, nearly as whimsical as
Tennyson. She lived in Seattle, owned one of
the ubiquitous coffeehouses near Pioneer
Square. Sherlock had gotten the impression
from Lily that Tansy didn't come back to Hemlock Bay all that often.

Elcott Frasier walked to Sherlock and
grabbed her hand, shook it hard. "Mrs. Savich,
what a pleasure." He looked ever so pleased to
see her. She wondered how pleased he was to
see Dillon, since she knew, right to her toes,
that Mr. Elcott Frasier had little respect for
women. It was in his eyes, in his very stance—
condescending, patronizing.

"Mr. Frasier," she said and gave him her
patented, guileless sunny smile. "I wish we
could meet again under less trying circumstances." Go ahead, she thought, believe I'm an
idiot, worth less than nothing in brainpower.

"Your poor husband is very upset by all this,"
Mr. Frasier said. "Given all that's happened, I
can't say I blame him."

Sherlock said, "Certainly he's upset. It's good
to see you again, Tennyson." She went directly

to sit on the side of Lily's bed. She lightly stroked her pale hair that was getting oily now. Thick, lank strands framed her face. Sherlock saw the pain in her eyes, how stiffly she was holding her body. She wanted to cry. "Dillon will be back in just a moment, Lily. You shouldn't have to suffer like this."

"It is about time for a bit more pain medication," a nurse said as she came through the door, Savich at her heels. No one said a word as she injected the painkiller into Lily's IV. She leaned over, checked Lily's pulse, smoothed the thin blanket to her shoulders, then straightened. "The pain will lessen almost immediately. Call if you have too much more discomfort, Mrs. Frasier."

Lily closed her eyes. After a few minutes, she said quietly, "Thank you, Dillon. It was pretty bad, but not now. Thank you." Then, without another word, she was asleep.

"Good," said Savich and motioned for them all to leave. "Let's go to the waiting room. Last time I looked, it was empty."

"My wife and I are grateful to you for being here," Elcott Frasier said. "Tennyson needs all the support he can get. The past seven months have been very hard on him."

"That's just what I was thinking," Savich said. "Lily hitting that redwood gave us just the excuse we needed to come here and support Tennyson."

"My father didn't mean it the way it sounded, Dillon," Tennyson said. "It's just been diffi-cult—for all of us." He looked down at his watch. "I'm afraid I have patients to see. I will be back to check on Lily in about four hours."

He left them with Elcott Frasier, who asked a passing nurse to fetch him a cup of coffee. She did without hesitation because, Sherlock knew, she wasn't stupid. She recognized the Big Man on the hospital board of directors when she saw him. Sherlock wanted to punch his lights out.

Savich leaned down, kissed Sherlock on the mouth, and said low, "No, don't belt him. Now, I've got all sorts of warning whistles going off in my head. I'm going to look at that car. Grill our brother-in-law's father, okay?"

"No problem," Sherlock said.

When Dillon found Sherlock two hours later, she was in the hospital cafeteria eating a Caesar salad and speaking to Dr. Theodore Larch.

"So do you think she was so depressed that she decided to end it? Again?"

"I'm a surgeon, Mrs. Savich, not a psychia-trist. I can't speculate."

"Yeah, but you see lots of people in distress, Dr. Larch. What do you think of Lily Frasier's state of mind?"

"I think the surgical pain is masking a lot of her symptoms right now—that is, if she has any symptoms. I haven't seen any myself. But what do I know?"

"What do you think of Dr. Rossetti?"

Dr. Larch wouldn't quite meet her eyes. "He's, ah, rather new here. I don't know him all that well. Dr. Frasier, however, knows him very well. They went to medical school together, I understand. Columbia Presbyterian Medical School, in New York City."

"I didn't know that," Sherlock said and tucked it away. She wanted to meet this Dr. Rossetti, the pompous man Lily didn't like and whom Tennyson appeared to be pushing very hard on his wife.

She smiled at Dr. Larch, took a bite of her salad, which was surprisingly good, and said, "Well, you know, Dr. Larch, if Lily didn't try to kill herself, then that means that just perhaps someone is up to no good. What do you think?"

Dr. Ted Larch nearly swallowed the ice cube he was rolling around in his mouth.

"I can't imagine, no, surely not—that's crazy. If she didn't do it on purpose, then it's more likely that something just went wrong with the car, an accident, nothing more than a tragic accident."

"Yes, you're probably right. Since I'm a cop, I always leap to the sinister first. Occupational hazard. Hey, I know. She just lost control of the car—maybe a raccoon ran in front of the Explorer and she tried not to hit it—and ended up smacking the redwood."

"That sounds more likely than someone trying to kill her, Mrs. Savich."

"Yes, the raccoon theory is always preferable, isn't it?"

Sherlock saw Dillon out of the corner of her eye. She rose, patted Dr. Larch on his shoulder, and said, "Take good care of Lily, Doctor." At least now, she thought, walking quickly toward Dillon, Dr. Larch would keep a very close eye on Lily because he wouldn't forget what she'd said. He would want to dismiss it as nonsense, but he wouldn't be able to, not entirely.

Savich nodded across the cafeteria to Dr. Larch, then smiled down at his wife. Her light blue eyes seemed brighter than when he'd left her, and he knew why. She was up to something. And she was very pleased with herself.

"What about the car?"

"Nothing at all. It's been compacted."

"That was awfully fast, wasn't it?"

"Yeah, sort of like cremating a body before the autopsy could be done."

"Exactly. Dr. Larch thinks Lily is just fine,

mentally, thank you very much. Actually, I think he has a crush on her. It's Dr. Rossetti he doesn't like, but who knows why? Did you know that Dr. Rossetti and Tennyson went to medical school together? Columbia Presbyterian?"

"No. That's interesting. Okay, Sherlock. I know that look. You either want me to haul you to the nearest hot tub and have my way with you, or you've done something. No hot tub? Too bad. All right, then. What have you done?"

"I planted a small bug just inside the slat on Lily's hospital bed. I already heard some interesting stuff. Come along and I'll play it back for you. Hmmm. About that hot tub, Dillon . . ."

They went to Lily's room, saw that she was still asleep and no one else was there, and Sherlock shut the door. She walked to the window, fiddled with the tiny receiver and recorder, turned on rewind, then play.

"Dammit, she needs more pain medication."

Savich said, "Who's that?"

"Dr. Larch."

"I cut it back, just like you ordered, but it was too much. Listen, there's no need to make her suffer like this."

"She doesn't react well to pain meds, I've told you that several times. It makes her even crazier than she

already is. Keep the pain meds way down. I don't want her hurt anymore."

Sherlock pressed the stop button and said, "That was Tennyson Frasier. What do you think it means?"

Sherlock slipped the tiny recorder back into her jacket pocket.

"It could be perfectly innocent," Savich said. "On the other hand, the Explorer has been compacted. The guy at the junked car yard told me that Dr. Frasier told him to haul the Explorer in and compact it immediately. Will this thing click on whenever someone's speaking?"

"Yes, it's voice-activated. It turns off when there's more than six seconds of silence. I got it from Dickie in Personnel. He's a gadget freak, owed me one after I busted his sister's boyfriend—you know, the macho drug dealer who was slapping her around."

"Sherlock, have I ever told you that you never cease to amaze and thrill me?"

"Not recently. Well, not since last night, and I don't think you had the same sort of intent then."

He laughed, pulled her against him and kissed her. Her curly hair tickled his cheek. "Let's call Mom and talk to Sean."

FIVE

Eureka, California

Clark Hoyt, SAC of the new Eureka FBI field office, which had opened less than a year before, handed Savich the bottle of pills. "Sorry, Agent Savich. What we've got here is a really common antidepressant, name of Elavil."

"Not good," Savich said and looked out the window toward the small park just to the left of downtown. The trees were bright with fall colors. If he turned his head a bit to the right, he'd see the Old Town section on the waterfront. A beautiful town, Humboldt's county seat, Eureka was filled with countless fine Victorian homes and buildings.

"Something I can help you with, Agent Savich? Sounds like something's happening you don't like."

Savich shook his head. "I wish there was

something, but the pills are exactly what they should be. I guess it would have been really easy if they were something different. I told you that the Explorer my sister totaled has been compacted. I was really holding out big hopes for those pills. Oh yeah, call me Savich."

"Okay, Hoyt here. Now, the Explorer—that was done awfully fast."

"Yes, maybe too fast, but then again, my life's work is to be suspicious. Maybe it was just very straightforward. As of right now, it's all a dead end. However, I think it's time I did a bit of digging on my brother-in-law, Dr. Tennyson Frasier."

Clark Hoyt, who had heard of some of the exploits of Sherlock, Savich, and MAX, Savich's transvestite laptop, said, "Don't tell me that you didn't do a background search on this guy before he married your sister? Seems to me a brother would have checked out the fillings in his teeth."

"Well, yeah, sure I did. But not a really deep one. Just that he didn't have a record, hadn't ever been in rehab for drugs or alcohol, stuff like that."

"And that he wasn't a bigamist?"

"No, I didn't check on that. Lily told me he'd been right up front about the fact that he'd been married before and that his wife had died. You know something, Hoyt? I wonder now what the first wife died of. I wonder how long they were married before she died." His eyes brightened.

"Savich, you don't really think he's trying to kill his wife? The pills were just what they were supposed to be."

"They were indeed, and I'm not sure. But you know, information is just about the most important thing any cop can have." Savich rubbed his hands together. "MAX is going to love this."

"You know that the Frasiers are a really big deal down in Hemlock Bay and the environs. Daddy Frasier has dealings all over the state, I understand."

"Yeah. Before, I didn't see the need to check into Papa's finances and dealings, but now it's time to be thorough."

"Is your sister going to be all right?"

"Yes, she'll be just fine."

"I've got the names of some excellent psychiatrists in the area—all women, just like you wanted. I hope one of them will be able to help your sister."

"Yeah, me too. But you know—no matter there's no proof of any funny stuff, that it really does look like she just drove the Explorer into that redwood on purpose—I simply can't believe that Lily tried to kill herself. No matter what anyone says, I find myself coming back again and again to the fact that it just doesn't fit."

"People change, Savich. Even people we love dearly. Sometimes we can't see the change because we're just too close."

Savich took another look at that lovely park and said, "When Lily was thirteen, she was running a gambling operation in the neighborhood. She would take bets on anything from the point spread in college football games to who could shoot the most three-point baskets in any pro game. Drove my parents nuts. Since my dad was an FBI agent, the local cops didn't do anything, just snickered a lot. I think they all admired her moxie, but they gave my dad lots of grief about it, called her a chip off the old block.

"When she hit eighteen, she suddenly realized that she liked to draw and she was very good at it. She's an artist, you know, very talented."

"No, I hadn't heard."

"Actually, her talent comes from our grandmother, Sarah Elliott."

"Sarah Elliott? Good grief, *the* Sarah Elliott, the artist whose paintings are in all the museums?"

"Yep. Lily's talents lie in a different direction—she's an excellent cartoonist, lots of humor and irony. Have you ever heard of the cartoon strip *No Wrinkles Remus?*"

Agent Hoyt shook his head.

"That's all right. It's political satire and shenanigans, I guess you could say. She hasn't done much for the past seven months, since the death of her daughter. But she will, and once she gets herself back together again, I'm sure she's going to be syndicated in lots of papers across the country."

"She's that good?"

"I think so. Now, given her talent, her background, can you really believe that she would try to kill herself seven months after her daughter was killed?"

"A girl who was the neighborhood bookie, then a cartoon strip artist?" Hoyt sighed. "I'd like to say no, I can't imagine it, Savich, but who knows? Aren't artists supposed to be high-strung? Temperamental? You said she still can't remember a thing about the accident?"

"Not yet."

"What are you going to do?"

"After MAX checks everything out, we'll see. No matter what, I'm taking Lily back to Washington with my wife and me. I think it's been proved that Hemlock Bay isn't healthy for her."

"Everything could be perfectly innocent," Clark Hoyt said. "She could have simply lost control of the car."

"Yeah, but you know something? I saw my brother-in-law differently this time. I saw him through Lily's eyes, maybe. It's not a pretty sight. I want to strangle him. Actually, I wanted to throw his daddy through the hospital window."

Clark Hoyt laughed. "Let me know if there's anything I can do."

"I will, thank you, Hoyt. Count on it. Thanks for the names of the shrinks."

Hemlock Bay, California

● On the following Sunday afternoon, four days after her surgery, Lily was pronounced well enough to leave the hospital. She suffered only mild discomfort, because Dr. Larch had stopped by her room, looking determined, and given her some pills to keep the worst of the pain at bay. She still walked bent over like an old person, but her eyes were clear, her mood upbeat.

Sherlock had wanted to ask Dr. Larch about lowering Lily's meds temporarily on Dr. Frasier's orders, but Savich said, "Nope, let's just hold off on that for a while."

"Nothing else good on the tape," Sherlock said in some disgust as she removed the small bug from beneath Lily's hospital bed while Lily was in the small bathroom bathing. "Not even doctors or nurses gossiping."

Ten minutes later Savich said to his sister as he pushed her wheelchair toward the elevator, "I told Tennyson that Sherlock and I are taking you to see your new shrink. He wasn't happy about that, said he didn't know anything about this woman. She could be a rank charlatan and he'd lose all sorts of money, maybe even get you more depressed. I just let him talk on, then gave him my patented smile."

"That smile," Sherlock said, "translates into 'You mess with me, buddy, and even your toenails are gonna hurt.'"

"In any case, at the end of all his ranting, there was nothing he could do about it. He tried to get me to convince you to see Dr. Rossetti. I do wonder why he thinks the guy is so great."

"He's not," Lily said. "He's horrible." She actually shuddered. "He came back again this morning. The nurse had just washed my hair for me, so I looked human and felt well enough to take him on."

"What happened?" Sherlock asked. She was carrying Lily's small overnight bag. Savich pushed her wheelchair onto the elevator, punched the button. No one else was on board.

Lily shuddered yet again. "I think he'd talked to Tennyson some more. He tried to change his tactics. He actually attempted to be ingratiating, at least at first. When he slithered into my room—yes, that's it exactly, he slithered— Nurse Carla Brunswick had just finished blow-drying my hair."

Nurse Brunswick turned toward him and said, "Doctor."

"Leave us alone for a bit, Nurse. Thank you."

Lily said, "I don't want Nurse Brunswick to leave, Dr. Rossetti. I want you to leave."

"Please, Mrs. Frasier, just a moment of your time. I fear we got off on the wrong foot when I was here before. You were just out of surgery; it was simply too soon for you to want to hear about anything. Please, just a few minutes of your time."

Nurse Brunswick smiled at Lily, patted her hand, then left the hospital room.

"I see that I have little choice here, Russell. What do you want?"

If he was angered at her use of his first name, he didn't let on. He kept smiling, walked to her bed, and stood there, towering over her. She looked at his hands; his plump hands sported a ring this time—a huge diamond on his pinkie. She wished she could throw him out of her room.

"I just wanted to speak to you, Mrs. Frasier— Lily. See if perhaps we could deal better with each other, perhaps you could come to trust me, to let me help you."

"No."

"Are you in pain, Lily?"

"Yes, Russell, I am."

"Would you like me to give you a mild anti-depressant?"

"My pain is from my ribs and my missing spleen."

"Yes, well, that pain will likely suppress the other, deeper pain for a while longer."

"I hope so."

"Mrs. Frasier—Lily—won't you come to my office, perhaps next Monday? That will give you another week to recuperate."

"No, Russell. Ah, here's Dr. Larch. Hello. Do come in. Dr. Rossetti was just leaving."

Savich looked ready to spit by the time Lily finished, but she just laughed. "No need to go pound him, Dillon. He left, didn't say another word, just walked out. Dr. Larch didn't move until he was gone."

"What I don't understand," Sherlock said thoughtfully, "is why both Tennyson and Dr. Rossetti want you as his patient so very much. Isn't that strange? You give Rossetti grief and he still wants you?"

"Yes," Savich said slowly, "it is strange. We'll have to see what MAX has to say about Russell Rossetti. He was ready to give you some anti-depressants, right there, on the spot?"

"It seems so."

After Lily was in the car, a pillow over her stomach and ribs, the seat belt as loose as possible over the pillow, Savich said, "I have a psychiatrist for you, Lily. No, not someone to shrink you and give you more medication, but a woman who is very good at hypnosis. What do you think?"

"Hypnosis? Oh, goodness, she'll help me remember what happened?"

"I hope so. It's a start anyway. Maybe it will jump-start your memory. Since it's Sunday, she's coming into her office especially for you."

"Dillon, I think I just gained a whole ton of energy."

Sherlock heard her say under her breath, "I'll know, finally, if I'm really crazy."

"Yes, you'll know, and that's the best thing to happen," Sherlock said and patted her shoulder. "Then we're off right now to Eureka."

● Dr. Marlena Chu was a petite Chinese-American woman who looked barely old enough to buy liquor. Lily was tall, nearly five feet eight in her ballet flats, which were what she was wearing today, and she wondered how she could trust someone so small she could easily tuck her beneath her armpit.

Dr. Chu met them in her outer office, since there was no one else there on Sunday. "Your brother has told me what has happened," she said. "This must be very difficult for you, Mrs. Frasier." She took Lily's hands in her own small ones and added, "You need to sit down. I can see that you're still very weak. Would you like a glass of water?"

Her hands felt warm, Lily thought; she didn't want to let them go. And her voice was incredibly soothing. She suddenly felt much calmer, and surely that was odd, but true nonetheless. Also, the nagging pain in her ribs seemed to fade. She smiled at Dr. Chu, hanging on to her hands like a lifeline.

"No, I'm just fine. Well, maybe a bit tired."

"All right, then. Come into my office and sit down. I have a very comfortable chair and a nice high, footstool so you won't feel like you're pulling anything. Yes, here we are."

Her inner office was perfectly square with soft blue furnishings and lots of clean, oak parquet floor. Again, Lily felt a wave of peace and calm wash through her.

"Do let me help you sit down, Mrs. Frasier."

"Please, call me Lily."

"Thank you. I'd like that." As soon as Lily was seated, Dr. Chu brought her chair alongside and took Lily's left hand in hers again. Dr. Chu watched Lily's eyelids flutter as warmth and calm flowed through her, and was pleased. She watched Mr. Savich ease the footstool beneath his sister's narrow feet and saw it immediately lessened the pull on her stitches. She studied her patient. Even though she was pale, her eyes were bright. Lovely eyes, a soft light blue that went very nicely with her blond hair. She was a lovely young woman, but that didn't really matter. What was important was that she was in trouble. What was more important was that she was soaking up the strength Dr. Chu was giving her. "Lily is such a romantic name. It sounds like soft music; it's the sort of name to make one dream of fanciful things."

Lily smiled. "It's my grandmother's name.

Coincidence, maybe, but she grew the most beautiful lilies."

"It's interesting how some things work out, isn't it?"

"Yes, interesting, but sometimes it's also terrifying."

"True, but there is nothing here to harm you, Lily." She patted Lily's hand again. Dr. Chu knew that Lily Frasier was an artist, and that meant she was creative, probably very bright. Such folk usually went under very easily. She said in her soft voice, "You understand that I'm going to try to help you remember what happened last Wednesday evening. Do you want this?"

"Yes, I want to know very badly what really happened. Just tell me what to do. I've never been hypnotized before."

"It's nothing, really. I just want you to relax." She lightly squeezed Lily's hand.

Lily felt more warmth flow through her, all the way to her bones, felt herself becomimg utterly calm. Those small hands of Dr. Chu's, how could they make her feel like this?

Savich pulled a chair next to Lily's and took her other hand. A strong hand, she thought, strong fingers. His hand didn't make hers feel warm, but it did make her feel safe. He said nothing at all, was just there beside her, there for her. Sherlock sat on a sofa behind Lily, quiet as could be.

Dr. Chu said, "You will perhaps believe this a bit odd, Lily, but I don't swing a watch in front of your eyes or let you lie on the sofa and chant this and that over and over. No, we'll just sit here and chat. I understand you draw a cartoon strip. *No Wrinkles Remus?* Such an interesting title. What does it mean?"

Lily actually smiled. She felt the familiar pain of Beth's death ease away. "Remus is a United States senator from the state of West Dementia, located in the Midwest. He's very bright, utterly ruthless, completely amoral, has overweening ambition, and loves to pull fast ones on his opponents. He's also known as 'Ept Remus,' as opposed to inept, because he's so fast to come up with a new angle to get what he wants. He's a spin master. He never gives up, just ignores what people say because he knows that soon enough they'll forget, ignores what the truth is, and continues until he gets what he wants. What he wants now is the presidency, and he's shafted a friend of his to get it."

Dr. Chu raised a thin, perfectly arched black brow and smiled. "An interesting character study, and not all that unfamiliar."

Lily actually chuckled. "I finished another strip just last week. His friend Governor Braveheart isn't taking being shafted well. He's fighting back. Although he's tough as hell, he's got one big problem—he's honest. It's good. At least I hope it is."

"Did you take it to your editor at the paper?"

Lily paused a moment and closed her eyes. "No, I didn't."

"Why not?"

"Because I started feeling bad again."

"What do you mean by 'feeling bad'?"

"Like nothing really mattered. Beth was dead and I was alive, and nothing was worth anything, including me and anything I did."

"You went from feeling great and creative, from smiles and laughter to utter depression?"

"Yes."

"In just a day?"

"Yes. Maybe less. I don't remember."

"On the day your husband left for Chicago, how did you feel, Lily?"

"I don't remember feeling much of anything. I was . . . just there."

"I see. Your husband called you the next day—Wednesday—and he wanted you to take some medical slides to a doctor in Ferndale?"

"That's right."

"And the only road is 211."

"Yes. I hate that road, always have. It's dangerous. And it was dusk. Driving at that time of day always makes me antsy. I'm always very careful."

"It makes me nervous as well. Now, you took two more antidepressant pills, right?"

"That's right. Then I slept. I had terrible nightmares."

"Tell me what you remember about the nightmares."

Dr. Chu wasn't holding her hand now, but still Lily felt a touch of warmth go through her, felt like it was deep inside her now, so deep it was warming her very soul. "I saw Beth struck by that car, over and over, struck and hurled screaming and screaming, at least twenty feet, crying out my name, over and over. When I awoke, I could still see Beth. I remember just lying there and crying and then I felt lethargic, my brain dull."

"You felt leached of hope?"

"Yes, that's it exactly. I felt like nothing was worth anything, particularly me. I wasn't worth anything. Everything was black, just black. Nothing mattered anymore."

"All right, Lily, now you're driving away from your house. You're in your red Explorer. What do you think of your car?"

"Tennyson yells every time I call it a car. I haven't done that for months now. It's an Explorer and nothing else is like it and it isn't a car, so you call it by its name and that's it."

"You don't like the Explorer much, do you?"

"My in-laws gave it to me for my birthday. That was in August. I turned twenty-seven."

Dr. Chu didn't appear to be probing or delving; she was merely speaking with a friend, nothing more, nothing less. She was also lightly stroking Lily's left hand. Then she turned to Savich and nodded.

"Lily."

"Yes, Dillon."

"How do you feel, sweetheart?"

"So warm, Dillon, so very warm. And there's no nagging pain anywhere. It's wonderful. I want to marry Dr. Chu. She's got magic in her hands."

He smiled at that and said, "I'm glad you feel good. Are you driving on 211 yet?"

"Yes, I just made a right onto the road. I don't mind the beginning of it, but you get into the redwoods and it's so dark and the trees press in on you. I've always thought that some maniac carved that road."

"I agree with you. What are you thinking, Lily?"

"I'm thinking that when it's dark, it will be just like a shroud is thrown over all those thick redwoods. Just like Beth was in a shroud and I'm so depressed that I want to end it, Dillon, just end it and get it over with. It's relentless, this greedy pain. I'm thinking it's settled into my soul and it won't leave me, ever. I just can't stand it any longer."

"This pain," Dr. Chu said in her soft voice, holding Lily's hand now, squeezing occasionally, "tell me more about this pain."

"I know the pain wants to be one with me. I want to give over to it. I know that if I become the pain and the pain becomes me, then I'll be able to expiate my guilt."

"You came to the conclusion that you had to kill yourself because it was the only way you could make reparation? To redress the balance?"

"Yes. A life for a life. My life—worth nothing much—for her small, precious life."

Then Lily frowned.

Dr. Chu lightly ran her palm over Lily's forearm, then back to clasp her limp hand. "What are you thinking now, Lily?"

"I just realized that something isn't right. I didn't kill Beth. No, I'd been at the newspaper, giving my cartoon to Boots O'Malley, seeing what he thought, you know?"

"I know. And he laughed, right?"

"Yes. I heard the sheriff say later that Beth's body had been thrown at least twenty feet."

Lily stopped. She squeezed Dr. Chu's hand so tightly her knuckles whitened.

"Just stay calm, Lily. Everything is just fine. I'm here. Your brother and Mrs. Savich are here. Forget what the sheriff said. Now, you suddenly recognized that you didn't kill Beth."

"That's right," Lily whispered, her eyelids fluttering. "I realize that something is wrong. I suddenly remember taking those sleeping pills that Tennyson put on the bedside table. I took so many of them, felt them stick in my throat and I swallowed and swallowed to get them down, and I sat with that bottle and chanted, more, more, more, and then the bottle was nearly empty and I thought suddenly, *Wait, I don't want to die,* but then it was too late, and I felt so sorry for the loss of Beth and the loss of me."

"I don't understand, Lily," Savich said in that darkly smooth voice of his. "You told me about the pills you took just after Beth's funeral. Why are you thinking about that now, while you're driving?"

"Because I realize that I can't really remember actually taking those pills. Now isn't that odd?"

"It's very odd. Tell us more."

"Well, I realize I didn't want to die then, and I don't want to die now. But why is the guilt eating at me like this? What's inside my brain that's making me want to simply drive the Explorer right into the thick trees that line this horrible road?"

"And did you find an answer, Lily?"

"Yes, I did." She stopped, just stopped and sighed deeply. She was asleep. Her head fell lightly to the side.

"It's all right, Mr. Savich. Let's just let her rest awhile, then I'll wake her and we can carry on. She'll be back with us when she wakes up. We'll see if she needs to go under again.

"You know, Mr. Savich, I'm getting more and more curious about that first time when she took all those sleeping pills. Just maybe we should go into that as well."

"Oh, yes," Sherlock said from behind them.

However, they didn't have to wake Lily up. Not more than another minute passed when suddenly Lily opened her eyes, blinked, and said, "I remember everything." She smiled at Dr. Chu, then said to her brother, "I didn't try to kill myself, Dillon, I didn't."

Dr. Chu took both of her hands now and leaned very close. "Tell us exactly what happened, Lily."

"I came back to myself. I felt clear and alert and appalled at what I'd been considering. Then the road twisted, started one of those steep descents. I realized I was going too fast and I pressed down on the brake."

"What happened?" Savich said, leaning toward her.

"Nothing happened."

Sherlock whispered "I knew it, I just knew it."

Savich said, "Did you pump the brakes the way Dad taught you way back when?"

"Yes, I pumped gently, again and again. Still there was nothing. I was terrified. I yanked up the emergency brake. I know it only works on the rear tires, but I figured it would have to slow me down."

"Don't tell me," Savich said. "The emergency brake didn't work either."

She just shook her head, swallowed convulsively. "No, it didn't. I was veering from the center toward the deep ravine on my left. I pulled back, but not too far because the redwoods were directly to my right, thick, impenetrable. I was going too fast, and the downhill grade was becoming even steeper. That stretch twists and wheels back on itself a whole lot before it flattens out at the outskirts of Ferndale."

Sherlock said from behind her, "Did you slam the shift into park?"

"Oh, yes. There was an awful grinding noise, like the transmission was tearing itself up. The

Explorer shuddered, screamed, and all the wheels locked up. I went into a skid. I tried to let the side of the Explorer scrape against the redwoods, to slow me down, but then the road twisted again. I knew I was going to die."

Savich pulled her very gently into his arms, settling her on his lap. Dr. Chu never released her left hand. Lily lay against him, her head on his shoulder. She felt Sherlock's fingers lightly stroking her hair. She drew a deep breath and said, "I remember so clearly slamming head-on into that poor redwood, thinking in that split second that the redwood had survived at least a hundred years of violent Pacific storms but it wouldn't survive me.

"I remember hearing the blaring of the horn, so loud, like it was right inside my head. And then there just wasn't anything."

She pulled back and smiled, a beautiful smile, clean and filled with self-awareness and hope. "Now, this is a very strange thing, Dillon. The brakes didn't work. Did someone try to kill me?"

Since Dr. Chu was still holding her hand, Lily wasn't frightened. Actually, she felt good all the way to her toes. Her smile didn't fade a bit with those awful words.

"Yeah," Savich said, looking directly into her eyes. "Probably so. Isn't that a kick?"

"Now," Dr. Chu said, "let's just go back and see how it happened that you ended up in the hospital with all those sleeping pills in your stomach."

Lily felt peaceful and excited at the same time. "Yes, let's go back."

SIX

Hemlock Bay, California

"All right, MAX, whatcha got?"

Sherlock walked over, looked down at the laptop screen. "Oh, dear, he's not doing anything. You don't think he's becoming MAX-INE again so soon, do you, Dillon? He's in a mood?"

"Nah, MAX is still a he, and he's just concentrating. He's going to turn up something for us."

"You hope."

"MAX just shuddered a bit. That means he's digging deep. Is Lily asleep?"

"Yes, I just checked on her. She didn't want a pain pill. Said she didn't need it. Isn't that amazing?"

"Lily told me that a doctor who could make her feel good without hurting her was sure an improvement over a husband who can't. She said she still feels better for having met her."

"Since Dr. Chu didn't hold our hands, we'll have to work out our stress at the gym. Too bad." Then Sherlock laughed. "Remember when she asked Dr. Chu to marry her? That was good, Dillon. She wants out of this mess.

"Now, according to Mrs. Scruggins, Tennyson will be home in about two hours. She told me she's making a vegetarian dinner just for you—her special zucchini lasagna, and an apple-onion dish that she assured me would make you hum and help you keep your, er, physique perfect. I think she'd like to see you on a calendar, Dillon. What do you think?"

Savich just laughed, then smacked MAX very lightly on his hard drive with the palm of his hand.

"Not going to commit yourself, are you? Okay, she's got a big crush on you, Dillon. I think it struck when she saw you in your T-shirt this morning, your pants zipped up but not fastened. There was lust in her eyes when she said your name. She had her hands clasped on her bosom. That's a sure sign of palpitations. She wants you."

Savich cocked a dark eyebrow at his wife. "Don't go there, Sherlock, it scares me too much."

She thought about how she felt whenever she saw him in a T-shirt—or less—and didn't doubt Mrs. Scruggins's fast-beating heart one bit. She lightly touched her fingertips to the back of his neck and began to knead.

MAX beeped.

"He's jealous."

"No, that was a burp. Well, maybe he's telling me he's distracted, what with you draped all over me."

Sherlock leaned down to kiss the back of his neck, then just grinned at him as she did some stretching. "It really is time for the gym. Do you think there's one here in Hemlock Bay?"

"We'll find one. Tomorrow morning, if Lily's still feeling fine, we'll go get the kinks out and lower our stress levels."

She stretched a bit more, rubbing the back of her neck. "You think Tennyson was giving her pills to make her depressed, don't you? You think he changed the pills back, just to be on the safe side since her big brother Fed was here."

"Sounds good to me. After Dr. Chu couldn't get anything conclusive about Lily's so-called attempt to commit suicide right after Beth's funeral, I'm thinking that maybe she never tried to kill herself at all."

"It was strange how Lily sort of remembered,

but she didn't really. If she didn't do it, then it had to be Tennyson, and that was the bastard's first try. They'd been married all of four months, Dillon. That's incredibly cold-blooded. It makes me really mad. Let's prove it so we can pound him."

"We'll try, Sherlock. Here we go. Good work, MAX."

Both of them read the small print on the screen, as Savich slowly scrolled. A couple of minutes later, Savich raised his head and looked up into Sherlock's blue eyes.

"Not really all that much of a surprise, is it? So, our Tennyson was married once before, just like he told Lily. Only thing is, he didn't bother to mention that his first wife committed suicide only thirteen months after they'd tied the knot."

Savich hit his palm against his forehead. "I'm an idiot, Sherlock. I shouldn't have given him the benefit of the doubt, shouldn't have respected his privacy. Some brother I am after that bastard first husband of hers. After Jack Crane, I should have opened every closet in his house, checked his bank statements for the past twenty years. You know something else? All I had to do was flat-out ask Tennyson just how his first wife died."

"He probably would have lied."

"It wouldn't have mattered. You know I can

tell when someone's lying. Also, I could have done then what I'm doing now. My holding back, my respecting Lily's decision, could have cost Lily her life. I want you to flay me, Sherlock."

Sherlock was twining one curly strand of hair round and round her finger, a sure sign she was upset. He immediately took her hand between his two large ones. She said, "I'd just as soon flay myself, Dillon. Do you think Lily would still have married him if she'd known that the first wife killed herself?"

"We can ask her. You can bet she'll be asking herself the same question, over and over. But the thing is that this is now, and her eyes are wide open. Eleven months ago she believed she loved him, thought she'd found a really wonderful father for Beth. If Tennyson had told her, she'd probably have felt sorry for him—poor man—losing his wife like that. She probably would have married him anyway. If I'd told her, it probably would have pissed her off, she'd have resented me, and she would have married him."

"Okay, so no flaying. You know, Dillon, sometimes we women do think with our hearts, not like you men, who think with your . . . well, that's better left unsaid, isn't it?"

He grinned up at her. "Yep, probably so."

"All of it was an illusion. Look, the first wife—her name was Lynda—was rich, Dillon, had a nice, fat trust fund from her grandfather. Oh, my, she was only twenty-five."

"Ah, just read this, Sherlock." Savich stroked his fingers over his jaw and added, disgust thick in his voice, "That immoral bastard. It usually comes down to money, doesn't it? Daddy got himself into a mess and so his son tries to bail him out. Or maybe it was both of them in the mess up to their necks. That sounds more likely."

"Yes," Sherlock said. "It's so mundane, really, just a couple of greedy men trying to get what they want."

Savich nodded as he read to the end of MAX's information. He sat back a moment, then said, "It seems very likely to me that Tennyson killed his first wife as well as trying to kill Lily. Was Daddy in on it with him? Very likely. Doesn't matter. I don't want to take any more chances. I want Lily out of here. I want you to take her to that very nice bed-and-breakfast we stayed at once in Eureka. What was it?"

"The Mermaid's Tail, just off Calistoga Street. It's late fall. Tourist season is over so they'll have room. What will you do?"

"I'm going to have a nice vegetarian dinner with Tennyson. I love lasagna. I'm going to see if I can get him to admit to anything useful. I really want to nail him. I'll join you and Lily later."

He rose and pulled her tightly against him. "Take MAX with you. Keep after him to find out all he can about Daddy Frasier's efforts to get that public road built to the lovely resort spot on the coast he's so hot to build. Without the state legislature passing it, the project would be doomed. He's having trouble. Maybe they ran out of bribery money."

"Don't forget the condos he's planning, too— Golden Sunset."

"Yes, lots of potential profit from those as well. Elcott Frasier has lots and lots of bucks already invested. I wonder if they ran into more roadblocks. Maybe that's why they wanted Lily out of the way. They were in deep financial trouble again. Now, let's get you guys packed up and out of this house."

But Lily didn't cooperate. She was awake, she still didn't hurt very much at all, and she was very clearheaded. She smacked her palm to the side of her head and announced, delight and wonder in her voice, "Would you look at me— I'm not depressed. In fact I can't imagine being depressed. Nope, everything inside there is rattling around clockwise, just as it should be."

They were in the hallway outside her bedroom. Lily was dressed in loose jeans and a baggy sweater, hair pulled back in a ponytail, no makeup, hands on hips, reminding Savich of his once sixteen-year-old sister who stood tall and defiant in front of their parents, who were dressing her down but good for her latest bookie scheme. "No, Dillon, I won't just turn tail and leave. I want to read everything MAX has come up with so far. I want to speak to Tennyson, confront him with all this. It's my right to find out if my husband of eleven months married me only to kill me off. Oh, dear. There's a big problem here. Why would he do it? I don't have any money."

"Unfortunately, sweetheart," Savich said, his voice very gentle, "you are very rich. All us kids tend to forget what Grandmother left us."

"Oh, my Sarah Elliott paintings. You're right, I forget about them, since they're always on loan to a museum."

"Yes, but they're legally yours, all eight paintings, willed to you. I just e-mailed Simon Russo in New York. You remember him, don't you? You met him way back when he and I were in college."

"I remember. That was way back in the dark ages before I started screwing up big time."

"No, you were screwing up then, too," Savich said, lightly punching her arm. "Remember that point spread you had on the Army-Navy game? And Dad found out that you'd gotten twenty dollars off Mr. Hodges next door?"

"I hid out in your room, under your bed, until he calmed down."

They laughed. It sounded especially good to Sherlock, who beamed at both of them. Lily depressed? It was hard, looking at her now, to believe that she'd ever been depressed.

Lily said, "Yes, I remember Simon Russo. He was a real pain in the butt and you said yeah, that was true enough, but it didn't matter because he was such a good wide receiver."

"That's Simon. He's neck-deep in the art world, you know. He got back to me right away, said eight Sarah Elliotts are worth in the neighborhood of eight to ten million dollars."

Lily stared at him blank-faced. She was shaking her head. "That's unbelievable. No, you're pulling my leg, aren't you? Please tell me you're kidding, Dillon."

"Nope. The paintings have done nothing but gain in value since Grandmother died seven years ago. Each of the four grandchildren got eight paintings. Each painting is worth about one million dollars right now, more or less, according to Simon."

"That's an enormous responsibility, Dillon."

He nodded. "Like you, I think the rest of us have felt like we're the guardians; it's our responsibility to see that the paintings are kept safe throughout our lifetimes and exhibited so that the public can enjoy them. I remember yours were on loan to the Chicago Art Institute. Are they still there?"

Lily said slowly, rubbing her palms on the legs of her jeans, "No. When Tennyson and I married he thought they should be here, in a regional museum, close to where we lived. So I moved them to the Eureka Art Museum."

Savich said without missing a beat, "Does Tennyson know anyone who works in the museum?"

Lily said very quietly, "Elcott Frasier is on the board of the museum."

"Bingo," Sherlock said.

● When Tennyson Frasier walked through the front door of his house that evening, he saw his wife standing at the foot of the stairs, looking toward him. She watched his eyes fill with love and concern. But it didn't take him long to realize that something was up. He sensed it, like an animal senses danger lying in wait ahead. His step slowed. But when he reached Lily, he said gently, as he took her hands, "Lily, my dear, you are very pale. You must still be in pain. After all, the surgery wasn't long ago at all. Please, sweetheart, let me take you up to bed. You need to rest."

"Actually, I feel fine, Tennyson. You needn't worry. Mrs. Scruggins has made us a superb dinner. Are you hungry?"

"If you're sure you want to eat downstairs, then yes, I'm hungry." He sent a wary look to his brother and sister-in-law, who had just walked into the entrance hall from the living room. "Hello, Sherlock, Savich."

Savich just nodded.

"Hope you had a good day, Tennyson," Sherlock said and gave him a sunny smile. She hoped he couldn't tell just yet that she wanted to strangle him with his own tie.

"No, I didn't actually," Tennyson said. He took a step back from Lily and stuck his hands in his pockets. He didn't take his eyes off his wife. "Old Mr. Daily's medication isn't working anymore. He talked about sticking his rifle in his mouth. He reminded me of you, Lily, that awful hopelessness when the mind can't cope. It was a dreadful day. I didn't even have time to come visit you before you left the hospital. I'm sorry."

"Well, these unpleasant sorts of things occasionally happen, don't they?" Sherlock patted his arm and just smiled at the disgusted look he gave her.

Savich winked at her as they walked to the dining room.

Tennyson tenderly seated Lily in her chair in the long dining room. Lily loved this room. When she'd moved in, she had painted it a light yellow and dumped all the heavy furniture. It was very modern now, with a glossy Italian Art Deco table, chairs, and sideboard. On the walls were five Art Deco posters, filled with color and high-living stylized characters. Tennyson was no sooner seated than Mrs. Scruggins began to serve. Normally, she simply left the food in the oven and went home, but not this evening.

Tennyson said, "Good evening, Mrs. Scruggins. It's very nice of you to stay."

"My pleasure, Dr. Frasier," she said.

Sherlock, who was watching her pile food onto Lily's plate, knew that Mrs. Scruggins wasn't about to leave unless she was booted out. "I couldn't very well leave when Mrs. Frasier was coming home, now could I?"

Savich nearly smiled. Mrs. Scruggins wanted to hear everything. She knew the air was hot, even if she didn't know the reason, and would become hotter.

Lily took a small bite of a homemade dinner roll that tasted divine. She said to her husband,

"Oh yes, Tennyson, you'll be pleased, I hope, to hear that I didn't try to kill myself by running the Explorer into the redwood. Actually, neither the brakes nor the emergency brake worked. Since I was on that very gnarly part of 211, I didn't stand a chance. Doesn't that relieve your mind?"

Tennyson was silent, frowning a bit over a forkful of lasagna, beautifully flavored, that was nearly to his mouth. He swallowed, then said slowly, his head cocked to the side, "You remembered, Lily?"

"Yes, I remembered."

"Ah, then you mean that you changed your mind? But it was too late because then the brakes failed?"

"That's it exactly. I realized that I didn't want to kill myself, but then it didn't matter, since someone had evidently disabled the brakes."

"Someone? Come on, Lily, that's absurd."

Savich said easily, "Unfortunately, the Explorer was compacted the very next day after the accident, so we can't check it out to see if it is or isn't absurd."

"Perhaps, Lily," Tennyson said very gently, "just perhaps you're wanting to remember something different, something that could alleviate the pain of the past seven months."

"I don't think so, Tennyson. You see, I remembered while I was under hypnosis. And then when I came out of it, I remembered the rest of it, all by myself. All of it."

A thick eyebrow went straight up. Savich had never before seen an eyebrow do a vertical lift like that. Tennyson turned to Savich and spoke, his voice low and controlled, but it was obvious to everyone that he was very angry. "You're telling me you took Lily to see a hypnotist? One of those charlatans who plant garbage in their patients' minds?"

"Oh, no," Sherlock said, taking Lily's clenched fist beneath the table. "This doctor didn't plant anything, Tennyson. She simply helped Lily to remember what happened that evening. Both Dillon and I were there the whole time, and he and I are very familiar with hypnotists as part of our work. It was all on the up-and-up. Now, don't you think it's strange that the brakes didn't work? Don't you think it's at least possible that someone disabled them from what Lily said?"

"No, what I think is that Lily disremembers. I'm not sure if she's doing it on purpose or if she's simply confused and wants desperately for it to be this way. Don't you see? She made up the brakes failing so she wouldn't have to face up to what she did. I don't think the brakes failed. I certainly don't think anyone cut the lines. That's beyond what is reasonable, and her saying that, claiming that that's what happened, well, it really worries me. I don't want Lily to even consider such a thing; it could make her lose ground again.

"Listen, I'm a psychiatrist—a real one—one who doesn't use hocus-pocus on people to achieve some sort of preordained result. I am not pleased about this, Savich. I am Lily's husband. I am responsible for her."

Sherlock pointed her fork at him and said, her voice colder than a psychopath's heart, "You haven't been doing such a good job of it, have you?"

SEVEN

Tennyson looked as if he wanted to throw his plate at Sherlock's head. His breathing was hard and fast.

Sherlock continued after a moment of chewing thoughtfully on a green bean. "I've also wondered at the timing. You remember, don't you, Tennyson? You called to ask Lily to deliver those medical slides to Ferndale, knowing it would be dusk to dark when she was on 211. Then the brakes failed. That sounds remarkably fortuitous, doesn't it?"

"Damn you, you both went behind my back, did something you knew I wouldn't approve of! Lily is fine now. She no longer needs you here. I repeat, I am her husband. I will take care of her. As for your ridiculous veiled accusations, I won't lower myself to answer them."

"I think you should consider lowering yourself," Sherlock said, and in that moment, Tennyson looked fit to kill.

Savich waited a moment for him to regain some calm, then said, "All right, no lowering right now. Let's just move along. Let's suppose, Tennyson, that Lily does remember everything exactly as it happened. That raises a couple of good questions. Why did the brakes fail? Perhaps it was simply a mechanical problem? But then the emergency brake failed, too. It's rather a difficult stretch to make if there's also a second mechanical problem, don't you think? And that means that someone had to have disabled the systems. Who, Tennyson? Who would want Lily dead? Realize, too, that if she had died, why then, everyone would have declared it a clear case of suicide. Who would want that, Tennyson?"

Tennyson rose slowly to his feet. Sherlock could see the pulse pounding in his neck. He was furious, and he was also something more. Frightened? Desperate? She just couldn't tell, which disappointed her. He was very good, very controlled.

Tennyson said, the words nearly catching in his throat, "You are a cop. You see bad things. You deal with bad people, evil people. What happened wasn't caused by someone out to kill

Lily—other than Lily. She's been very ill. Everyone knows that. Lily knows that; she even accepts it. The most logical explanation is that she simply doesn't remember what happened because she can't bring herself to admit that she really tried to commit suicide again. That's all there is to it. I won't stand for your accusations any longer. This is my home. I want you both to leave. I want you both out of our lives."

Savich said, "All right, Tennyson, Sherlock and I will be delighted to leave. Actually, we'll leave right after dinner. Mrs. Scruggins made it just for me, and I don't want to miss any of it. Oh, yes, did I tell you that we know all about Lynda—you remember, don't you? She was your first wife who killed herself only thirteen months after marrying you?"

They hadn't told Lily about Lynda Middleton Frasier. She froze where she sat, her mouth open, utter disbelief scored on her face, any final hope leached out with those words. When her husband had spoken so calmly, so reasonably, she had wondered if it was possible that her mind had altered what really happened, that her mind was so squirrelly that she simply couldn't trust any thought, any reaction. But not any longer. Now she knew she hadn't disremembered anything. Oh, God, had he killed his first wife? It was horrible, unbelievable. Lily was shaking from the inside out—she couldn't help it.

She said slowly, holding her knife in a death grip, her knuckles white from the strain, "I remember that you told me you'd been married for a very short time, Tennyson, a long time ago."

"A long time ago?" Sherlock said, an eyebrow arched. "Sounds like maybe it was a decade or more, doesn't it? Like he ran away with a girl when he was eighteen? Actually, Lily, Tennyson's first wife, Lynda, killed herself two years ago—just eight months before you came to Hemlock Bay and met him." She looked over at Tennyson and said, her voice utterly emotionless, "However, you didn't say a word about your wife having killed herself. Why is that, Tennyson?"

"It was a tragic event in my life," Tennyson said calmly, in control again, as he picked up his wineglass and sipped at the Napa Valley Chardonnay. It was very dry, very woody, just as he preferred. "It is still painful. Why would I wish to speak of it? Not that it was a secret. Lily could have heard it from anyone in town, from my own family even."

Sherlock leaned forward, her food forgotten. The gauntlet was thrown. This was fascinating.

She smiled at Tennyson Frasier. "Still, doesn't it seem like it would be on the relevant side, Tennyson, for her to know, particularly after Lily tried to kill herself seven months ago? Wouldn't you begin to think, Oops, could there be something wrong, just maybe, with me? Two wives trying to do away with themselves after they've been married to me only a short time? What are the odds on that, do you think, Tennyson? Two dead wives, one live husband?"

"No, that's all ridiculous. None of it was at all relevant. Lily isn't anything like Lynda. Lily was simply bowled over by her child's death, by her role in her child's death."

"I didn't have a role in Beth's death," Lily said. "I realize that now."

"Do you really believe that, Lily? Just think about it, all right? Now, as for Lynda, she had a brain tumor. She was dying."

This was a corker, Savich thought. "A brain tumor?"

"Yes, Savich, she was diagnosed with a brain tumor. It wasn't operable. She knew she was going to die. She didn't want the inevitable pain, the further loss of self, the deterioration of her physical abilities. Her confusion was growing by the day because of the tumor. She hated it. She wanted to be the one to decide her own end, and so she did. She gave herself an injection of potassium chloride. It works very quickly. As for the tumor, I saw to it that it was kept quiet. I saw no reason to tell anyone." He paused for a moment, looked at Savich, then at Sherlock. "There are, of course, records. Check if you want to, I don't care. I'm not lying."

"Hmmm," Sherlock said. "So you think it's better for a woman to be known as a suicide for no good reason at all?" Sherlock sat back in her chair now, arms crossed over her breasts.

"It was my call and that's what I decided to do at the time."

"Thirteen months," Savich said. "Married the first time only thirteen months. If Lily had managed to die in that accident, then she would have beaten Lynda to the grave by two months. Or, if she had died in her first attempt, right after Beth's death, then she would have really broken the record."

Tennyson Frasier said slowly, looking directly at his wife, "I don't find that amusing, Savich. You have judged me on supposition, on a simple coincidence, no evidence that would stand up anywhere, and surely a cop shouldn't do that. Lily didn't die, thank God, either time. If she had died in that accident, I doubt I would have survived. I love her very much. I want her well."

He was good, Savich thought, very good indeed. Very fluent, very reasoned and logical, and the appeal to gut emotion was surefire. Tennyson was certainly right about one thing— they didn't have any proof. He was right about another thing—Savich had already judged him guilty. Guilty as sin. They had to have proof. MAX had to dig deeper. There would be something; there always was.

Sherlock chewed on a homemade roll that was now cold, swallowed, then said in the mildest voice imaginable, "Where did Lynda get the potassium chloride?"

"From her doctor, the one who diagnosed her in the first place. He was infatuated with her, which is why, I believe, he assisted her. I knew nothing about any of it until she was dead and he told me what had happened, what he had helped her do. I didn't file charges because I'd known she'd wanted to end her life herself, on her own terms. Dr. Cord died only a short while later. It was horrible, all of it."

Lily said, "I heard about Dr. Cord's death from a woman in Casey's Food Market. She said he shot himself while cleaning his rifle, such a terrible accident. She didn't mention anything about your wife."

"The townspeople didn't want to see me hurt any more, I suppose, particularly since I had a new wife, so I guess they just kept quiet." He turned to his wife and said, his voice pleading, his hand stretched out toward her, "Lily, when you came to town, just over a year and a half ago, I couldn't believe that someone else could come into my life who would make me complete, who would love me and make me happy, but you did. And you brought precious little Beth with you. I loved her from the first moment I saw her, just as I did you. I miss her, Lily, every day I miss her.

"What you've been going through—maybe now it's over. Maybe what happened with the Explorer, maybe that snapped you back. Believe me, dearest, I just want you to get well. I want that more than anything. I want to take you to Maui and lie with you on the beach and know that your biggest worry will be how to keep from getting sunburned. Don't listen to your brother. Please, Lily, don't believe there was anything sinister about Lynda's death. Your brother is a cop. Cops think everyone has ulterior motives, but I don't. I love you. I want you to be happy, with me."

Savich, who'd been finishing off his lasagna during this impassioned speech, looked only mildly interested, as if he were attending a play. He laid down his fork and said, "Tennyson, how long has your dad been on the board of the Eureka Art Museum?"

"What? Oh, I don't know, for years, I suppose. I've never really paid any attention. What the hell does that have to do with anything?"

"You see," Savich continued, "at first we couldn't figure out why you would want to marry Lily if your motive was to kill her. For what? Then we realized you knew about our grandmother's paintings. Lily owns eight Sarah Elliotts, worth a lot of money, as you very well know."

For the first time, Savich felt a mild surge of alarm. Tennyson was a man nearing the edge. He was furious, his face red, his jaw working. He readied himself for an attack, just in case.

But what Tennyson did was bang his knife handle on the table, once, twice, then a really hard third time. "You bastard! I did not marry Lily to get her grandmother's goddamned paintings! That's absurd. Get out of my house!"

Lily slowly rose to her feet.

"No, Lily, not you. Please, sit down. Listen to me, you must. My father and I are familiar with the excellent work of the folk at the Eureka Art Museum. They have a splendid reputation. When you told me your grandmother was Sarah Elliott—"

"But you already knew, Tennyson. You knew before you met me that first time. And then you acted so surprised when I told you. You acted so pleased that I had inherited some of her incredible talent. You wanted so much to have her paintings here, in Northern California. You wanted them here so you could be close to them, so you could control them. So that when I was dead, you wouldn't have any difficulty getting your hands on them. Or maybe your father wanted the paintings close? Which, Tennyson?"

"Lily, be quiet, that's not true, none of it. The paintings are great art. Why should the Chicago Art Institute have them when you live here now? Also, administration of the paintings is much easier when they're exhibited locally."

"What administration?"

Tennyson shrugged. "There are phone calls coming in all the time, questions about loaning the paintings out, about selling them to collectors, the schedule for ongoing minor restoration, about our approval on the replacement of a frame. Endless questions about tax papers. Lots of things."

"There was very little of what you just described before I married you, Tennyson. There was only one contract with the museum to sign every year, nothing else. Why haven't you said anything about any administration to me? You make it sound like an immense amount of work."

Was that sarcasm? Savich wondered, rather hoping that it was.

"You weren't well, Lily. I wasn't about to burden you with any of that."

Suddenly, the strangest thing happened. Lily saw her husband as a grayish shadow, hovering without substance, his mouth moving but nothing really coming out. Not a man, just a shadow, and shadows couldn't hurt you. Lily smiled as she said, "As Dillon said, I'm very rich, Tennyson."

Savich saw that his brother-in-law was trying desperately to keep himself calm, to keep himself logical in his arguments, not to get defensive, not to let Lily see what he really was. It was fascinating. Could a man be that good a liar, that convincing an actor? Savich wished he knew.

Tennyson said, "It's always been my understanding that you simply hold the paintings in a sort of trust. That they aren't yours, that you're merely their guardian until you die and one of your children takes over."

"But you've been in charge of their administration all these months," Lily said. "How could you not know that they were mine, completely mine, no trust involved?"

"I did believe that, I tell you. No one ever said anything different, not even the curator,

Mr. Monk. You've met him, Lily, up front, so pleased to have the paintings here."

Savich sipped at the hot tea Mrs. Scruggins had poured into his cup. "None of us hold the paintings in trust," he said. "They're ours, outright." He knew Mrs. Scruggins was listening to everything, forming opinions. He didn't mind it a bit. Just maybe she'd have something more to say to him or to Sherlock when this little dinner meeting was over. "If Lily wants to, she can sell one or two or all of the paintings. They're worth about one million dollars each. Maybe more."

Tennyson looked stunned. "I . . . I never realized," he said, and now he sounded a bit frantic.

"Difficult not to," Lily said. "You're not a stupid man, Tennyson. Surely Mr. Monk told you what they're worth. When you found out I was Sarah Elliott's granddaughter, it would have been nothing at all for you to find out that she willed them to me. You saw me as the way to get to those paintings. You must have rubbed your hands together. I left everything in my will to Beth, at your urging, Tennyson, if you'll remember, and I named you the executor."

"As it happened," Savich said, "Beth did predecease Lily. Who inherits?"

"Tennyson. My husband." She continued

after a moment, so bitter she was nearly choking on it. "How easy I made everything for you. What happened? Big money troubles? You needed me out of the way, fast?"

Tennyson was nearly over the edge now. "No, no, listen to me. I suppose I just saw the paintings as your grandmother's, nothing more than that. Valuable things that needed some oversight, particularly after you became so ill. All right, I was willing to do that work. Please, Lily, believe me. When you told me that she was your grandmother, I was very surprised and pleased for you. Then I just dismissed it. Lily, I didn't marry you for your grandmother's paintings. I swear to you I didn't. I married you because I love you, I loved Beth. That's it. My father—no, I don't believe there could possibly be anything there. You've got to believe me."

"Tennyson," Lily said, her voice low, soothing, "do you know that I've never been depressed in my life until I married you?"

"Dammit, before Beth's death, you had no reason to be depressed."

"Well, maybe I did. Didn't I tell you a bit about my first husband?"

"Yes, he was horrible, but you survived him. But, Lily, it was completely different when your daughter was killed by a hit-and-run driver. It's only natural that you'd be overcome with grief, that you would experience profound depression."

"Even after seven months?"

"The mind is a strange instrument, unpredictable. It doesn't always behave the way we would like it to. I've prayed and prayed for your full recovery. I agree it's been taking you a long time to recover but, Lily, you'll get well now, I know it."

"Yes," she said very slowly and pushed back her chair. "Yes, I know I'll get well now." She felt her stitches pull, a tug that made her want to bend over, but she didn't. "Yes, Tennyson," she said, "I fully intend to get well now. Completely well."

She pressed her palms flat on the table. "I will also love Beth for the rest of my life, and I will know sadness at her loss and grief until I die, but I will come to grips with it. I will bear it. I will pray that it will slowly ease into the past, that I won't fall into that black depression again. I will face life now and I will gain my bearings. Yes, Tennyson, I will get well now because, you see, I'm leaving you. Tonight."

He rose so quickly his chair slammed down to the floor. "No, dammit, you can't leave me . . . Lily, no! It's your brother. I wish my father hadn't called him; I wish Savich hadn't come here to ruin everything. He's filled your mind with lies. He's made you turn on me. There's no proof of anything at all, just ask him. No, none of it's true. Please, Lily, don't leave me."

"Tennyson," Lily said very quietly now, looking directly at him, "what sort of pills have you been feeding me these last seven months?"

He howled, literally howled, a desperate, frightened sound of rage and hopelessness. He was panting hard when he said, "I tried to make you well. I tried, God knows, and now you've decided to believe this jerk of a brother and his wife and you're leaving me. Dammit, I've been giving you Elavil!"

Lily nodded. "Actually, even though there doesn't seem to be any solid proof to haul you to the sheriff. The sheriff is something of a joke anyway, isn't he? When I remember how he tried so hard to apprehend Beth's killer."

"I know he did the best he could. If you'd been with Beth, maybe you would have made a better witness, but you—"

She ignored his words and said, "If we find proof, then even Sheriff Bozo will have to lock you away, Tennyson—no matter what you or Daddy say, no matter how much money you've put in his pocket, no matter how many votes you got for him—until we manage to get some competent law enforcement in Hemlock Bay. The truth of the matter is, I would leave you even if you didn't kill your first wife, if you hadn't, in truth, tried to kill me, because, Tennyson, you've lied to me; from the very beginning you lied to me. You used Beth's death to make me feel the most profound guilt. You milked it, manipulated me—you're still doing it—and you very likely drugged me to make me depressed, to make me feel even more at fault. I wasn't at fault, Tennyson. Someone killed Beth. I didn't. I realize that now. Were you planning on killing me even as you slid the ring on my finger?"

He was holding his head in his hands, shaking his head back and forth, not looking at anyone now.

"I found myself wondering today, Tennyson—did you kill Beth, too?"

His head came up, fast. "Kill Beth? Oh, my God! No!"

"She was my heir. If I died, then the paintings would be hers. No, surely even you couldn't be that evil. Your father could, maybe your mother could, but not you, I don't think. But then again, I've never been good at picking men. Look at my pathetic track record—two tries and just look what happened. Yes, I'm obviously rotten at it. Hey, maybe it's my bookie genes getting in the way of good sense. No, you couldn't have killed or had Beth killed. Maybe we'll find something on your daddy. We'll see.

"Good-bye, Tennyson. I can't begin to tell you what I think of you."

Both Savich and Sherlock remained silent, looking at the man and woman facing each other across the length of the dining table. Tennyson was as white as a bleached shroud, the pulse in his neck pounding wildly. His fingers clutched the edge of the table. He looked like a man beyond himself, beyond all that he knew or understood.

As for Lily, she looked calm, wonderfully calm. She didn't look to be in any particular discomfort. She said, "Dillon and Sherlock will pack all my things while you're at your office tomorrow, Tennyson. Tonight, the three of us are going to stay in Eureka." She turned, felt the mild pulling in her side again, and added, "Please don't destroy my drawing and art supplies, Tennyson, or else I'll have to ask my brother or sister-in-law to break your face. They want to very badly as it is."

She nodded to him, then turned. "Dillon, I'll be ready to leave in ten minutes."

Head up, back straight, as if she didn't have stitches in her side, she left the dining room. Lily saw Mrs. Scruggins standing just inside the kitchen door. Mrs. Scruggins smiled at her as she walked briskly past, saying over her shoulder, "It was an excellent dinner, Mrs. Scruggins. My brother really liked it. Thank you for saving my life seven months ago. I will miss you and your kindness."

EIGHT

**Eureka, California
The Mermaid's Tail**

Lily swallowed a pain pill and looked at herself in the mirror. She'd looked better, no doubt about that. She sighed as she thought back over the months and wondered yet again what had happened to her. Had she looked different when she'd first arrived in Hemlock Bay? She'd been so full of hope, both she and Beth finally free of Jack Crane, on their own, happy. She remembered how they'd walked hand in hand down Main Street, stopping at Scooters Bakery to buy a chocolate croissant for Beth and a raisin scone for herself. She hadn't realized then that she would soon marry another man she'd believe with all her heart loved both her and Beth, and this one would gouge eleven months out of her life.

Fool.

She'd married yet another man who would have rejoiced at her death, who was prepared to bury her with tears running down his face, a stirring eulogy coming out of his mouth, and joy in his heart.

Two husbands down—never, never again would she ever look at a man who appeared even mildly interested in her. Fact was, she was really bad when it came to choosing men. And the question that had begun to gnaw at her surfaced again. Was Tennyson responsible for Beth's death?

Lily didn't think so—she'd been honest the night before about that—but it had happened so quickly and no one had seen anything at all useful. Could Tennyson have been driving that car? And then the awful depression had smashed her, had made her want to lie in a coffin and pull down the lid.

Beth was gone. Forever. Lily pictured her little girl's face—a replica of her father's, but finer, softer—so beautiful, that precious little face she saw now only in her mind. She'd just turned six the week before she died. Beth hadn't been evil to the bone like her father. She'd been all that was innocent and loving, always telling her mother any- and everything until . . . Lily raised her head and looked at herself again in the mirror. Until what? She thought back to the week before Beth was killed. She had been different, sort of furtive, wary—maybe even scared.

Scared? Beth? No, that didn't make any sense. But still, Beth had been different just before she died.

No, not died. Beth had been killed. By a hit-and-run driver. The pain settled heavily in Lily's heart as she wondered if she would ever know the truth.

She shook her head, drank more water from the tap. Her brother and Sherlock had just left, after she'd assured them at least a half dozen times that she still felt calm, didn't hurt at all. She was fine, go, go, pack up her things in Hemlock Bay. She hoped that Tennyson hadn't trashed her drawing supplies.

She drew a deep, clean breath. Yes, she wanted her drawing supplies today, as soon as possible. She wanted to hold her #2 red sable brush again, but it would be foolish to buy another one just to use today. No, she'd just buy a small sampler set of pens and pen points, inexpensive ones because it didn't really matter. Maybe she'd get a Speedball cartooning set, just like the one her folks had given her when she'd wanted to try cartooning so many years before. Those pens would still feel familiar in her hand. And a bottle of India ink, some standard-size, twenty-pound typing paper, durable paper that would last, no matter how many times it was shoved into envelopes or worked on by her and the editors. Yes, just some nice bond paper, not more than a hundred sheets. Usually, since she did political cartoons, she used strips of paper cut from larger sheets of special artist paper, thicker than a postcard—bristol board, it was called, well suited for brushwork. And one bottle of Liquid Paper. She could just see herself— not more than an hour from now—drawing those sharp, pale lines that would become the man of the hour, Senator No Wrinkles Remus, the soon-to-be president of the U.S., from that fine state of West Dementia, where the good senator has managed to divide his state into halves, to conduct the ultimate experiment with gun control. One half of the state has complete gun control, as strict as in England; the other half of West Dementia has no gun control at all. He gives an impassioned speech to the state legislature, with the blessing of the governor, whom he's blackmailed for taking money from a contractor who is also his nephew: "One year, that's all we ask," Remus says, waving his arms to embrace all of them. "Just one year and we'll know once and for all what the answer is."

And what happens in the west of West Dementia is that criminals auction off areas to one another since civilians aren't allowed to own any device that shoots a bullet out of a barrel. Criminals break-and-enter at their leisure, whenever the spirit moves them. Houses, banks, gas stations, 7-Elevens, nothing is safe.

In east West Dementia, every sort of gun abounds, from sleek pistols that fire one round a minute to behemoths that kick out eight hundred zillion rounds a second. There are simply no limits at all. Because of the endless supply, guns are really cheap. What happens surprises everyone: robbery stats go down nearly seventy percent after a good dozen would-be robbers are killed breaking in—to homes, banks, filling stations, 7-Elevens.

On the other side of it, killing abounds. Everything that moves, and doesn't move, gets shot—deer, rabbits, cars, people. Some people even take to target-shooting in the rivers. Many trout, it is said, die from gunshot wounds.

There are rumors of payoffs from both the National Rifle Association and the Mafia to No Wrinkles Remus, but like his name, no matter what he does—or people believe he does—that face of his remains smooth and absolutely trustworthy.

She was grinning like a madwoman. She rubbed her hands together. She wanted to draw *No Wrinkles Remus*—now, right this minute, as soon as she could get a pen between her fingers. She didn't need a drawing table, the small circular Victorian table in her room would be perfect. The sun was coming in at exactly the right angle.

She just didn't want to wait. Lily grabbed her purse, her leather jacket, and headed out of the bed-and-breakfast. Mrs. Blade, standing behind the small counter downstairs, waved her on. Lily didn't know Eureka well, but she knew to go to Wallace Street. A whole bunch of artists lived over in the waterfront section of town, and a couple of them ran art supply stores.

The day was cloudy, nearly cold enough to see your breath, a chilly breeze swirling about in the fallen autumn leaves that strengthened the salty ocean taste when you breathed in. She managed to snag a taxi across the street that was letting off an old man in front of an apartment building.

The driver was Ukrainian, had lived in Eureka for six years, and his high-schooler son liked to doodle, even on toilet paper, he said, which made you wonder what sort of poisoning you could get using that toilet paper. He knew just where to go.

It was Sol Arthur's art supply shop. She was in and out in thirty minutes, smiling from ear to ear as she shifted the wrapped packages in her arms. She had maybe eleven dollars left in her purse—goodness, eleven whole dollars left in the world. She wondered what had happened to her credit cards. She would ask Dillon to deal with it.

She stood on the curb looking up and down the street. No way would a taxi magically appear now even though she was ready to part with another four dollars from her stash. No, no taxi. Such good lightning luck didn't strike twice. A bus, she thought, watching one slowly huff toward her. The bed-and-breakfast wasn't all that far from here, and the bus was heading in the right direction. She jaywalked, but not before she was sure that no cars were coming from either direction. There weren't a whole lot of people on the street.

No Wrinkles Remus is looking particularly handsome and wicked, right there, full-blown in her mind again. He looks annoyed when a colleague hits on a staffer Remus himself fancies, his absolute joy when he discovers that the wife of a senator cheated on her husband with one of his former senior aides.

She was singing when the bus—twenty years old if not older, belching smoke—lumbered toward her. She saw the driver, an old coot, grinning at her. He had on headphones and was chair-dancing to the music. Maybe she was the only passenger he'd seen in a while.

She climbed on board, banging her packages about as she found change in her wallet. When she turned to find a seat, she saw that the bus was empty.

"Not many folk out today?"

He grinned at her and pulled off his headphones. She repeated her question. He said, "Nah, all of 'em down at the cemetery for the big burying."

"Whose big burying?"

"Ferdy Malloy, the minister at the Baptist Church. Kicked it, just last Friday."

She'd been lying in the hospital last Friday, not feeling so hot.

"Natural causes, I hope?"

"You can think that if you want, but everyone knows that his missus probably booted him to the other side. Tough old broad is Mabel, tougher than Ferdy, and mean. No one dared to ask for an autopsy, and so they're planting Ferdy in the ground right about now."

"Well," Lily said, then couldn't think of another thing. "Oh, yes, I'm at The Mermaid's Tail. Do you go near there?"

"Ain't nobody on board to tell me not to. I'll

take you right to the front door. Watch that
third step, though, board's rotted."

"Thank you, I'll be careful."

The driver put his headphones back on and
began bouncing up and down in the seat. He
stopped two blocks down, just in front of
Rover's Drive-In with the best hamburgers
west of the Sillow River, sandwiched next to a
storefront that advertised three justices of the
peace, who were also notaries, on duty 24/7.

Lily closed her eyes. The bus started up again.
No Wrinkles Remus was in her mind again,
playing another angle.

"Hey."

She looked up to see a young man swinging
into the seat next to her. He simply lifted off the
packages, set them on the seat opposite, and sat
down.

For a moment, Lily was simply too surprised
to think. She stared at the young man, no older
than twenty, his black hair long, greasy, and tied
back in a ratty ponytail. He had three silver
hoops marching up his left ear.

He was wearing opaque sunglasses, an Ori-
oles cap on his head, turned backward, and a
roomy black leather jacket.

"My packages," she said, cocking her head to
one side. "Why did you put them over there?"

He grinned at her, and she saw a gold tooth toward the back of his mouth.

"You're awful pretty. I wanted to sit next to you. I wanted to get real close to you."

"No, I'm not particularly pretty. I'd like you to move. Lots of seat choice, since the bus is empty."

"Nope, I'm staying right here. Maybe I'll even get a little closer. Like I said, you're real pretty."

Lily looked up at the bus driver, but he was really into his rock 'n' roll, bouncing so heavily on the seat that the bus was swerving a bit to the left, then back to the right.

Lily didn't want trouble, she really didn't. "All right," she said and smiled at him. "I'll move."

"I don't think so," he said, his voice barely a whisper now, and he grabbed her arm to hold her still.

"Let go of me, buster, now."

"I don't think so. You know, I really don't want to hurt you. It's too bad because, like I said, you're real pretty. A shame, but hey, I need money, you know?"

"You want to rob me?"

"Yeah, don't worry that I'll do anything else. I just want your wallet." But he pulled a switch-blade out of his inside jacket pocket, pressed a small button, and a very sharp blade flew out, long and thin, glittering.

She was afraid now, her heart pumping, bile rising in her throat. "Put the knife away. I'll give you all my money. I don't have much, but I'll give you all I've got."

He didn't answer because he saw that the bus was slowing for the next stop. He said, low, "Sorry, no time for the money."

He was going to kill her. The knife was coming right at her chest. She tightened, felt the stitches straining, but it didn't matter.

"You fool," she said. She drove her elbow right into his Adam's apple, then right under his chin, knocking his head back, cutting off his breath. Still he held the knife, not four inches from her chest.

Twist left, make yourself a smaller target.

She turned, then did a right forearm hammer, thumb down smashing the inside of his right forearm.

Attack the person, not the weapon.

She grabbed his wrist with her left hand and did a right back forearm hammer to his throat. He grabbed his throat, gagging and wheezing for breath, and she slammed her fist into his chest, right over his heart. She grabbed his wrist and felt the knife slide out of his fingers, heard it thunk hard on the floor of the bus and slide beneath the seat in front of them.

The guy was in big trouble, couldn't breathe, and she said, "Don't you ever come near me again, you bastard." And she smashed the flat of her palm against his ear.

He yelled, but it only came out as a gurgle since he still couldn't draw a decent breath.

The bus had stopped right in front of The Mermaid's Tail. The driver waved to her in the rearview mirror, still listening to his music, still chair-dancing. She didn't know what to do. Call the cops? Then it was taken out of her hands. The young man lurched up, knowing he was in deep trouble, scooped up his knife, waved it toward the bus driver, who was now staring back at the two of them wide-eyed, no longer dancing. He waved the knife at her once, then ran to the front of the bus, jumped to the ground, and was running fast down the street, turning quickly into an alley.

The bus driver yelled.

"It's okay," Lily said, gathering her bags together. "He was a mugger. I'm all right."

"We need to get the cops."

The last thing Lily wanted was to have to deal with the cops. The guy was gone. She felt suddenly very weak; her heart was pounding hard and loud. But her shoulders were straight. She was taller than she'd been just five minutes before. It hadn't been much more than five minutes when she'd first gotten onto that empty bus, and then the young guy had come on and sat down beside her.

It didn't matter that she felt like all her stitches were pulling, that her ribs ached and there were jabs of pain. She'd done it. She'd saved herself. She'd flattened the guy with the knife. She hadn't forgotten all the moves her brother had taught her after she'd finally told him about Jack and what he'd done.

Dillon had said, squeezing her so hard she thought her ribs would cave in, "Dammit, Lily, I'm not about to let you ever be helpless again. No more victim, ever." And he'd taught her how to fight, with two-year-old Beth shrieking and clapping as she looked on, swinging her teddy bear by its leg.

But he hadn't been able to teach her for real—how to handle the bubbling fear that pulsed through her body when that knife was just a finger-length away. But she'd dealt with the fear, the brain-numbing shutdown. She'd done it.

She walked, straight and tall, her stitches pulling just a bit now, into The Mermaid's Tail.

"Hello," she called out, smiling at Mrs. Blade, who was working a crossword puzzle behind the counter.

"You look like you won the lottery, Mrs. Frasier. Hey, do you know a five-letter word for a monster assassin?"

"Hmmm. It could be me, you know, but Lily is only four letters. Sorry, Mrs. Blade." Lily laughed and hauled her packages up the stairs.

"I've got it," Mrs. Blade called out. "The monster assassin is a 'slayer.' You know, 'Buffy the Vampire Slayer.' "

"That's six letters, Mrs. Blade."

"Well, drat."

Upstairs in her room, Lily arranged the small Victorian table at just the right angle to the bright sun. She carefully unwrapped all her supplies and arranged them. She knew she was on an adrenaline high, but it didn't matter. She felt wonderful. Then she stopped cold.

Her Sarah Elliott paintings. She had to go right now to the Eureka Art Museum and make sure the paintings, all eight of them, were still there. How could she have thought only of drawing Remus?

No, she was being ridiculous. She could simply call Mr. Monk, ask him about her paintings. But what if he wasn't trustworthy—no one else had proved the least trustworthy to date—he could lie to her.

Tennyson or his father could have stolen

them last night after they'd left the house. Mr. Monk could have helped them.

No, someone would have notified her if the paintings were gone. Or maybe they would just call Elcott Frasier or Tennyson. No, they were her paintings, but she was sick, wasn't she? Another suicide attempt. Incapable of dealing with something so stressful.

She was out the door again in three minutes.

NINE

The Eureka Art Museum took up an entire block on West Clayton Street. It was a splendid old Victorian mansion surrounded by scores of ancient, fat oak trees madly dropping their fall leaves in the chilly morning breeze. What with all the budget cuts, the leaves rested undisturbed, a thick red, yellow, and gold blanket spread all around the museum and sidewalks.

Lily paid the taxi driver five dollars including a good tip because the guy had frayed cuffs on his shirt, hoping she had enough cash left for admission. The old gentleman at the entrance told her they didn't charge anything, but any contributions would be gracefully accepted. "Not gratefully?"

"Maybe both," he said and gave her a big grin. All she had to give him in return was a grin to match and a request that he tell Mr. Monk that Mrs. Frasier was here.

She'd seen the paintings here only once, during a brief visit, before the special room was built, right after she'd married Tennyson. She'd met Mr. Monk, the curator, who had gorgeous, black eyes and looked intense and hungry, and two young staffers, both with Ph.D.s, who'd just shrugged and said there were no jobs in any of the prestigious museums, so what could you do but move to Eureka? At least, they said, big smiles on their faces, the Sarah Elliott paintings gave the place class and respectability.

It wasn't a large museum, but nonetheless, they had fashioned an entirely separate room for Sarah Elliott's eight paintings, and they'd done it well. White walls, perfect lighting, highly polished oak floor, cushion-covered benches in the center of the room to sit on and appreciate.

Lily just stood there for a very long time in the middle of the room, turning slowly to look at each painting. She'd been overwhelmed when her grandmother's executor had sent them to her where she was waiting for them in the office of the director of the Chicago Art Institute. Finally, she'd actually touched each one, held each one in her hands. Every one of them was special to her, each a painting she'd mentioned to her grandmother that she loved especially, and her grandmother hadn't forgotten. Her favorite, she discovered, was still *The Swan*

Song—a soft, pale wash of colors, just lightly veiling an old man lying in the middle of a very neat bed, his hands folded over his chest. He had little hair left on his head and little flesh as well, stretched so taut you could see the blood vessels beneath it. The look on his face was beatific. He was smiling and singing to a young girl, slight, ethereal, who stood beside the bed, her head cocked to one side. Lily felt gooseflesh rise on her arms. She felt tears start to her eyes.

Dear God, she loved this painting. She knew it belonged in a museum, but she also knew that it was hers—hers—and she decided in that moment that she wanted to see it every day of her life, to be reminded of the endless pulse of life with its sorrowful endings, its joyous beginnings, the joining of the two. This one would stay with her, if she could make that happen. The value of each of the paintings still overwhelmed her.

She wiped her eyes.

"Is it you, Mrs. Frasier? Oh my, we heard that you had been in an accident, that you were in serious condition in the hospital. You're all right? So soon? You look a bit pale. Would you like to sit down? May I get you a glass of water?"

She turned slowly to see Mr. Monk standing in the doorway of the small Sarah Elliott room, with its elegant painted sign over the oak door. He looked so intense, like a taut bowstring, he seemed ready to hum with it. He was dressed in a lovely charcoal gray wool suit, a white shirt, and a dark blue tie.

"Mr. Monk, it's good to see you again." She grinned at him, her tears dried now, and said, "Actually, the rumors of my condition were exaggerated. I'm just fine; you don't have to do a thing for me."

"Ah, I'm delighted to hear it. You're here. Is Dr. Frasier here as well? Is there some problem?"

Lily said, "No, Mr. Monk, there's no problem. The past months have been difficult, but everything is all right now. Oh, yes, which of these paintings is your favorite?"

"The Decision," Mr. Monk said without hesitation.

"I like that one very much as well," Lily said. "But don't you find it just the least bit depressing?"

"Depressing? Certainly not. I don't get depressed, Mrs. Frasier."

Lily said, "I remember I told my grandmother I loved that one when I'd just lost a lot of money on a point spread between the Giants and Dallas. I was sixteen at the time, and I do remember that I was despondent. She laughed and loaned me ten dollars. I've never forgotten that. Oh, yes, I paid her back the next week when a whole bunch of fools bet New Orleans would beat San Francisco by twelve."

"Are you talking about some sort of sporting events, Mrs. Frasier?"

"Well, yes. Football, actually." She smiled at him. "I am here to tell you that I will be leaving the area, Mr. Monk, moving back to Washington, D.C. I will be taking the Sarah Elliott paintings with me."

He looked at her like she was mad. He fanned his hands in front of him, as if to ward her off. "But surely, Mrs. Frasier, you're pleased with their display, how we're taking such good care of them; and the restoration work is minor and nothing to concern you—"

She lightly laid her fingers on his forearm. "No, Mr. Monk, it looks to me like you've done a splendid job. It's just that I'm moving, and the paintings go where I go."

"But Washington, D.C., doesn't need any more beautiful art! They have so many beautiful things that they're sinking in it, beautiful things that are stuck in basements, never seen. They don't need any more!"

"I'm very sorry, Mr. Monk."

Those gorgeous dark eyes of his glittered. "Very well, Mrs. Frasier, but it's obvious to me that you haven't discussed this with Dr. Frasier. I'm sorry but I cannot release any of the paintings to you. He is their administrator."

"What does that mean? You know very well the paintings are mine."

"Well, yes, but it's Dr. Frasier who's made all the decisions, who's directed every detail. Also, Mrs. Frasier, it's common knowledge here that you haven't been well—"

"Lily, what are you doing out of bed? Why are you here?"

Dillon and Sherlock stood just behind Mr. Monk, and neither of them looked very pleased.

She smiled, saying only, "I'm here to tell Mr. Monk that the paintings go where I go, and in this case, it's all the way to Washington, D.C. Unfortunately, he says that everyone knows I'm crazy and that Dr. Frasier is the one who controls everything to do with the paintings—and so Mr. Monk won't release them to me."

"Now, Mrs. Frasier, I didn't quite mean that . . ."

Savich lightly tapped him on the shoulder, and when Mr. Monk turned, in utter confusion, he said, "The paintings can't be released to my sister? Would you care to explain that to us, Mr. Monk? I'm Dillon Savich, Mrs. Frasier's brother, and this is my wife. Now, what is all this about?"

Mr. Monk looked desperate. He took a step back. "You don't understand. Mrs. Frasier isn't mentally competent, that's what I was told, and thus the paintings are all controlled by Dr. Frasier. Appropriate, naturally, since he is her husband. When we heard that she'd been in an accident, an accident that she herself caused, there were some who thought she was dying and thus Dr. Frasier would inherit the paintings and then they would never leave the museum."

"I'm not dead, Mr. Monk."

"I can see that you're not, Mrs. Frasier, but the fact is that you aren't as well as you should be to have charge of such expensive and unique paintings."

Savich said, "I assure you that Mrs. Frasier is mentally competent and is legally entitled to do whatever she wishes to with the paintings. Unless you have some court order to the contrary?"

Mr. Monk looked momentarily flummoxed, then, "A court order! Yes, that's it, a court order is what's required."

"Why?" said Savich.

"Well, a court could decide whether she's capable of making decisions of this magnitude."

Sherlock patted his shoulder. "Hmm, nice suit. I'm sorry, Mr. Monk, as this seems to be quite upsetting to you, but she is under no such obligation to you. I suppose you could try to get her declared incompetent, but you would lose, and I'm sure it would create quite a stir in the local papers."

"Oh, no, I wouldn't do that. What I mean is that I suppose then that everything is all right, but you understand, I have to call Dr. Frasier. He has been dealing with everything. I haven't spoken to Mrs. Frasier even once over all the months the paintings have been here."

Savich pulled out his wallet, showed Mr. Monk his ID, and said, "Why don't we go to your office and make that phone call?"

Of course Savich had shown Mr. Monk his FBI shield. He swallowed, looked at Lily like he wanted to shoot her, and said, "Yes, of course."

"Good," Savich said. "We can also discuss all the details of how they'll be shipped, the insurance, the crating, all those pesky little details that Dr. Frasier doesn't have to deal with anymore. By the way, Mr. Monk, I do know what I'm doing since I also own eight Sarah Elliott paintings myself."

"Would you like to go now, Mr. Savich?"

Savich nodded, then said over his shoulder as he escorted Mr. Monk from that small, perfect room, "Sherlock, you stay here with Lily, make sure she sits down and rests. Mr. Monk and I will finalize matters. Come along, sir."

"I hope the poor man doesn't cry," Lily said. "They built this special room, did a fine job of exhibiting the paintings. I think that Elcott and Charlotte Frasier donated the money to build the room. Wasn't that kind of them?"

"Yes. You know, Lily, many people have enjoyed the paintings over the past year. Now people in Washington can enjoy them for a while. You need to think about where you want the paintings housed. But we can take our time there, no rush, let people convince you they're the best.

"Oh, Lily, don't feel guilty. There are a whole lot of people there who have never seen these particular Sarah Elliott paintings."

"Truth be told, I'm just mighty relieved that they're all present and accounted for and I'm not standing here looking at blank walls because someone stole the paintings. That's why I came, Sherlock. I just realized that since Tennyson married me for the paintings, maybe they were already gone."

Sherlock patted a cushion and waited until Lily eased carefully down beside her. "We didn't want to wait either." She paused to look around. "Such beauty. And it's in your genes,

Lily, both yours and Dillon's. You're very lucky. You draw cartoons that give people great pleasure, and Dillon whittles the most exquisite pieces. He whittled Sean, newly born, in the softest rosewood. Whenever I look at that piece, touch it, I feel the most profound gratitude that Dillon is in my life.

"Now, I'm going to get all emotional and that won't help anything. Did I have a point to make? Oh yes, such different aspects of those splendid talent genes from your grandmother."

"What about your talent, Sherlock? You play the piano beautifully. You could have been a concert pianist, if it hadn't been for your sister's death. I want to listen to you play when we get back to Washington."

"Yes, I'll play for you." Sherlock added, without pause, "You know, Lily, I was very afraid that Tennyson and his father had stolen the paintings as well, and you hadn't been notified because you'd been too ill to deal with it."

"I suppose they had other plans. All of this happened very quickly."

"Yes, they did have time, but don't you see? If the paintings were suddenly gone, they would have looked so guilty Sing Sing would have just opened its doors and ushered them right on in. I suppose they were waiting to sell them off when you were dead and they legally belonged to Tennyson."

"Dead." Lily said the word again, then once more, sounding it out. "It isn't easy to believe that someone wants you dead so they can have what you own. That's really low."

"Yes, it is."

"I feel shock that Tennyson betrayed me, probably his father as well, but I don't want to wring my hands and cry about it. Nope, what I really want to do is belt Tennyson in the nose, maybe kick him hard in his ribs, too."

Sherlock hugged her, very lightly. "Good for you. Now, how do you feel, really?"

"Calm, just a bit of pain, nothing debilitating. I believed I loved him, Sherlock, believed I wanted to spend the rest of my life with him. I trusted him, and I trusted him with Beth."

"I know, Lily. I know."

Lily got ahold of herself, tried to smile. "Oh yes, I've got something amazing to tell you. Remus was dancing in my head this morning, yelling at me so loud that I went out and bought art supplies. Then, strange thing, I get on this empty city bus to go back to The Mermaid's Tail and this young guy tries to mug me."

Sherlock blinked, her mouth open.

Lily laughed. "Finally I've managed to surprise you so much you can't think of anything to say."

"I don't like this, Lily. Tell me exactly what happened."

But Mr. Monk appeared in the doorway. "I will contact our lawyers and have them prepare papers for your signature. I've detailed to Mr. Savich how the paintings will be packed and crated in preparation to be shipped to Washington. You will need to inform us of their destination so that we can make arrangements with the people at the other end. There will be two guards as well for the trip. It's quite an elaborate process, necessary to keep them completely safe. I will phone you when the papers are ready. Did you plan to leave the area soon?"

"Fairly soon, Mr. Monk." Lily rose slowly, her stitches pulling, aching more now, and took his hand. "I'm sorry, but I really can't leave them here."

"It's a pity. Dr. Frasier said on the phone that you were divorcing him and that he had no more say in anything."

"I'm relieved that he didn't try anything underhanded," Lily said.

Mr. Monk looked profoundly uncomfortable at that. "He's a fine man, and so are his esteemed father and mother."

"I understand that many people think that. Yes, we're divorcing, Mr. Monk."

"Ah, such a pity. You've been married such a short time. And you lost your little girl just a few months ago. I do hope you're making this decision with a clear head."

"You still think my mental condition is in question, Mr. Monk?"

Mr. Monk seemed to pump himself up. He swallowed and said, "Well, I think that just maybe you're acting in haste, not really thinking things through. And here you are divorcing poor Dr. Frasier, who seems to love you and wants only the best for you. Of course, Mrs. Frasier, this is a very bad thing for me and for the museum."

"Well, these things happen, don't they? And I'd have to say that Dr. Frasier loves my paintings, sir, not me. I'm staying at The Mermaid's Tail here in Eureka. Please call when I can finalize all this."

Lily's last view of Mr. Monk was of him standing in the doorway to the Sarah Elliott room, hunched in on himself, looking like he'd just lost all his money in a poker game. The museum had run just fine before Sarah Elliott's paintings had arrived, and it would do so after they went away.

When they were walking down the stone steps of the museum, Savich on one side of Lily, her arm resting heavily on his, Sherlock on the other, Savich said, not looking at her, "I was wondering if Tennyson would be obstructive when we called him up. To be honest, if it had been you, Lily—by yourself on the phone—he would have been, no doubt in my mind about that. But he couldn't this time, not with two of us federal agents and one of them your brother."

He stopped abruptly, turned, and grasped Lily's shoulders in his big hands. "I'm not pleased with you, Lily. You should have let Sherlock and me take care of all this. I'll bet you pulled your stitches and now your belly aches like you've been punched."

"Yes," Sherlock said, "Dillon's right. You look like you're ready to fall over."

Lily smiled down at her sister-in-law—small, fine-boned, all that incredible curly red hair, and the sweetest smile—who could take down a guy three times her size. And she played the piano beautifully. She'd known from the moment they'd first met at her and Dillon's wedding that Sherlock's love for Dillon was steady and absolute. Beth had been three years old at the time, so excited to see her uncle Dillon, and so proud of her new patent-leather shoes. Lily swallowed, got herself together. She said, "Do you know that you and Dillon could finish each other's sentences? Now, don't fret, either of you. I am feeling a bit on the shaky side, but I can hold on until we get back to the inn." She hugged him tight, then stepped back. "You know what, Dillon? I've decided that I'm going to check into my own credit card situation."

"What does that mean?"

Lily just smiled. He helped her into the back-seat, gently placed the pillow over her stomach, and fastened her seat belt. She lightly touched her fingertips to his cheek. "I'm glad you came to the museum. I don't think I had enough money to pay for a taxi back to the B-and-B."

Savich shook his head at her as he slipped his hand beneath the seat belt to make sure it wouldn't press too hard against her middle, got in the driver's seat, and drove off.

"Now then, Lily," Sherlock said, turning in her seat. "You can't put it off any longer. Dillon will want to hear all about this, too. I want you to tell us about the mugger who attacked you on that empty bus this morning. No more than two hours ago."

Savich nearly drove into a fire hydrant.

● They were eating lunch in a small Mexican restaurant, The Toasted Taco, on Chambers

Street, just down the block from The Mermaid's Tail, Lily having decided she was starving more than she was aching.

"Good salsa," Lily said and dipped in another tortilla chip and stuffed it in her mouth. "That's a sure sign that the food will be okay. Goodness, I don't think I've ever been so hungry in my life."

Savich said, "Talk."

She'd told them about the bus driver who had explained to her that the bus was empty because of the big burying and was having a fine time chair-dancing while he drove, headphones turned up high, and about the young man with three earrings in his left ear, the switchblade that was sharp and silver and nearly went into her heart.

Savich blew out a big breath, picked up a tortilla chip, and absently chewed on it. "I suppose it's occurred to you it may not have been a mugger."

"He talked like one, maybe, I'm not sure since I've never been mugged before. Then he ruined it by pulling this switchblade knife. One thing I'm absolutely sure of—there was death in his eyes. And you know what? I knew all the way to my stomach lining that it was the end of the line. But then I went after him, Dillon, wrecked him good—all the moves you taught me. I could hear your voice telling me things, 'Make yourself as small as possible,' stuff like that. I hammered him—my hand a tight fist and whap! Then I hammered him hard against his chest, then polished him off by slamming my palm against his ear. Unfortunately, he got himself together and jumped off the bus, got away. Hey, I smashed him, Dillon, really smashed him."

She looked so proud of herself that Dillon wanted to hug her until she squeaked, but he was still too scared. She could have been killed so very easily.

He cleared his throat. "Did you call the police?"

Lily shook her head. "To be honest, all I wanted to do was get back to the B-and-B. Then I thought of the paintings and got to the museum as fast as I could. Why don't you think it was a mugger?"

Savich was still shaking with reaction. "I'm upset about this, Lily, really upset. He most certainly wasn't a mugger. Listen, an empty bus, a guy starts with a throwaway line about taking your wallet to keep things real calm, then he brings out the knife? A mugger? No, Lily, I don't think so."

"The question is," Sherlock said, chewing on a chip that she'd liberally dipped in salsa, her right hand near her glass of iced tea, "who found him, got him up to speed and moving so fast? You told Tennyson just last night that you were leaving him. Talk about fast action—that really surprises me. Tennyson, his father, whoever else is involved in this—they're not pros, yet they got this guy after you very quickly. He must have been watching the B-and-B, then followed you to the art supply shop, got ahead of you and on the bus at the next stop. It was well planned, well executed, except, thank God, he failed."

"Yeah, they didn't know what Dillon had taught me." She actually rubbed her hands together, realized she'd gotten salsa all over herself, and laughed. "Can we have another basket of chips?" she called out to the young Mexican waitress, then, "I saved myself, Dillon, and it felt really good."

Savich understood then, of course. Her life had been out of control for so very long, but no longer. He patted her back. "I wonder if it would help to check hospitals. Did you hurt him that bad?"

"Maybe. Good idea, I didn't think of that."

"He's paid to think of things like that," Sherlock said and got out her cell phone. She looked up at them after a moment, "We've got a lot of possibilities here."

Savich said, "You know, I was going to call the cops. But now that I think about it, I don't think the local constabulary is what we need just yet. What I want is Clark Hoyt from the FBI field office right here in Eureka. If he knows the local cops, thinks they could help with this, then we can bring them into it. But for the time being, let's use our own guys."

Sherlock said, as she dialed information, "Great idea, Dillon. I'm sure glad they opened up this field office last year. The one in Portland wouldn't be able to help us with much. Clark can get all the hospitals checked in no time. Now, Lily, tell me where you hit this guy. Be as specific as you can."

"Yeah, I can do that, and then hand me a napkin so I can draw the guy for you."

TEN

Eureka, California
The Mermaid's Tail

Savich flipped open his cell phone, which was softly beeping the theme song from *The Lion King,* listened, and said, "Simon Russo? Is this the knucklehead who shot himself in the foot with my SIG Sauer?" Then he laughed and listened some more. Then he talked. Savich realized quickly enough that Simon didn't like what he had been hearing, didn't like it at all. What the hell was going on here? He listened as Simon said slowly, "Listen, Savich, just get your grandmother's paintings safely back to Washington. Do it right away, don't dither or let the museum curator put you off. Don't take any shortcuts with their safety, but move quickly. I'll be down to Washington as soon as the paintings get there. I want to see them. It's very important that I see them. Don't take any chances."

Savich frowned into his cell phone. What was this all about? "I know you like my grandmother's paintings, Simon. She gave you your favorite when you graduated from MIT, but you don't have to come down to Washington to see them right away."

"Yes," Simon said, "trust me on this, I do." And he hung up.

Sherlock was standing on the far side of the bedroom, her own cell phone dangling from her hand. "Sweetheart," he called out to her, "strangest thing. Simon is all hot under the collar to see Lily's eight Sarah Elliott paintings. He's being mysterious, won't tell me a thing, just insists he has to see the paintings as soon as they arrive in Washington."

Sherlock didn't say anything. Savich felt a sharp point of fear. Jesus, she looked shell-shocked, no, beyond that. She looked drop-dead frightened, her pupils dilated, her skin as pale as ice. He was at her side in an instant. He gathered her against him, felt that she was as cold as ice as well, and held on to her tightly. "What's wrong? Tell me what's wrong. It's Sean, isn't it? Oh God, something's happened to our boy?"

She shook her head hard, but still no words.

He pulled back, saw the shock of fear still deep in her eyes, and shook her lightly. "Please tell me, Sherlock, talk to me. What's going on? What happened?"

She swallowed, and managed finally to get the words out. "Sean's all right. I checked in at the office. I heard Ollie yell in the background that he had to speak to us. Oh, God, Dillon, Ollie said that Tammy Tuttle just up and walked out of the jail wing of Patterson-Wright Hospital."

"No," Savich said, shaking his head in utter disbelief, "you've got to be kidding me." Things like that just didn't happen. She was very dangerous, and everyone at the hospital knew it. He continued to stare down at his wife, wanting to see some flicker of doubt that wasn't there. "That can't be possible," he went on slowly. The panic of it was nearly under control, but he just didn't want to believe it, to accept it. "She was in the jail ward. She was well guarded. The woman is nuts. Everyone knows what she's done. She couldn't just walk out."

"They were going to put her in restraints tomorrow or the next day, when they thought she was well enough to be a danger to them. Then there was a screwup in the scheduling of the guards. Evidently, she was ready for something to give her a chance. When she got her break, she snagged a nurse, knocked her out cold, and took her white pantsuit. At least she didn't kill her. But she walked out."

"It hasn't been even a week since they amputated her arm. How could she have the strength to take down a nurse? They're used to violent patients; they're trained. She's got only one arm, for God's sake."

"Obviously no one thought she had the strength or the ability, and that's why when there was the scheduling foul-up. No one was really concerned. And that's why no one even discovered she was gone until a nurse went in to give her a shot and found another nurse tied up naked in the closet. They figure she got herself at least a two-hour window."

Savich shook himself. His brain was back in gear, finally. "All right. Where would she go? Do they have any leads?"

"Ollie says there are more cops looking for her than the hunt for Marlin and Erasmus Jones. Everyone knows she's really scary, that she's truly dangerous. No one wants her free again." Sherlock cleared her throat. "There's the question of those things you saw in the barn, Dillon—the Ghouls."

He squeezed her again and said against her temple, her curly hair tickling his nose, "I know what I want to do right this minute. I want to talk to Sean and listen to him gurgle. That little guy is so sane, and that's what we need right now, a big dose of normalcy." He didn't add that he just wanted to know for sure, all the way to his soul, that his little boy was all right. As for the Ghouls—if they were real, and Savich knew to his bones that they were—then it was possible there was more danger than anyone could begin to imagine. Would the FBI let all the people looking for Tammy Tuttle know that she could have accomplices? Or were they just going to ignore everything he'd told them?

They took turns gurgling with their son, who was busy gnawing a banana, not a graham cracker. Then they called Ollie back to see if there was any news yet.

"Yes," Ollie Hamish said, "but not good." Sherlock could see him leaning back in his chair, spinning it just a bit, because he was nervous and scared. "Tammy Tuttle just murdered a teenage boy a block outside of Chevy Chase, Maryland. She left a note on the body. Well, actually, she didn't leave it *on* the body, she left it attached to the body. It's addressed to you, Savich."

"Read it, Ollie."

"Here goes: 'I'll get you and I'll rip your arm

off and then I'll cut your fucking head off, you murdering bastard. Then I'll give you to the Ghouls.' "

"That's real cheery," Savich said. "Was it addressed specifically to me?"

"Yeah, which means she knows your name. How? Everyone thinks she probably heard people talking about you in the hospital. She left her fingerprints all over the paper and envelope, obviously didn't care. Oh yes, at the murder scene, there was also a black-painted circle, and the boy was inside it. She's loose, Savich. Everyone is shaken to their toes. It was a really gruesome crime scene. That poor kid, he was only thirteen years old."

"Black-painted circle," Savich said. "Tammy called to the Ghouls to come get the boys in the circle."

"I was hoping maybe you really hadn't seen anything, Savich, that maybe you'd just experienced a temporary vision distortion. Since the boy's body was a mess, maybe more of a mess than a single one-armed sick woman could have done, then maybe these things—these Ghoul characters—were somehow involved. Jimmy Maitland brought it up. And the bosses even had a big meeting about it. They've all decided that what you saw in that barn were dust devils."

Savich said finally, "Mr. Maitland has my number here if he wants to talk about it. Now, here's something to do. Bring in Marilyn Warluski."

"We already went looking. She's long gone, no one knows where."

"MAX found out that she has an ex-boyfriend in Bar Harbor, Maine, name of Tony Fallon. Check there. Just maybe she'll be with him and know something. Tammy has to go somewhere, and Marilyn loaned her and her brother that barn for their use. Did Tammy steal any money?"

"Not at the hospital, but elsewhere? We haven't heard of anything yet. Also, there have been a dozen reports of stolen vehicles. We're checking all those out as well."

"Okay. Find Marilyn and wring her out, Ollie. I think you should be the one in direct contact with her. You know more than the others."

"Okay. Let me take a deep breath here. I'm very glad you aren't listed in the phone book and your phone number's private. It's unlikely she could find you where you are, but I want you to be careful, Savich, really careful."

"You can count on that, Ollie."

"Okay. How are things going out there with Lily?"

Savich said, "She managed to hurt a guy who tried to kill her on an empty bus a couple of hours ago. Clark Hoyt in the new Eureka field office is checking all the hospitals. No word yet. Lily drew a picture of him and we just heard from a Lieutenant Dobbs at the Eureka Police Department that the guy's a local hood-for-hire, a freelancer, who would kill his own mom for the right price. Name of Morrie Jones. Everyone's looking for him. He's a kid, just turned twenty."

Savich could see Ollie shaking his head back and forth as he said, "Big troubles on both coasts. Ain't nothing easy anywhere in this world, is there?"

● Lily slept for three hours—no nightmares, thank God—and awoke to see her brother seated on a big wing chair pulled near her lovely Victorian canopied bed, a gooseneck lamp beaming light over his right shoulder, reading through a sheaf of papers.

He looked up immediately.

"You're fast. I just opened one eye and you knew I was awake."

"Sean got both Sherlock and me trained in a matter of days. He yawns or grunts, and we're ready to move."

She managed a smile, but truth be told, the day's events had caught up with her. She'd gone from being euphoric about drawing Remus again, to nearly being murdered, to getting back her paintings. At least she'd had a great Mexican lunch and it hadn't made her sick to her stomach.

But now, even after a very long sleep, she still felt wrung out. Her side ached something fierce, and her head sat heavy and dull on her shoulders. "No, Dillon, don't get up. What are you reading?"

"Articles and reports MAX found for me on weird phenomena. I'm trying to find other reported crimes with similarities to the Tuttles' rampage and the Ghouls."

"You told me just a little bit about the Tuttles and these Ghoul things, Dillon. Tell me more."

"There were two of them, two distinct white cones that sometimes came together. You can imagine how the two boys—Tammy and Timmy Tuttle called them 'Little Bloods'— were reacting. I've never seen such terror. I nearly swallowed my own tongue I was so afraid. Then Tammy Tuttle called to the Ghouls, yelled for them to bring their axes and knives, their 'treats' were ready for them. The boys wanted out of that circle and Tammy pulled her knife. She was going to nail them to the barn floor, inside that damned circle. That's when I shot her, and the bullet nearly tore her arm off. Timmy pulled his gun then, but he wasn't going to shoot me, no, he was aiming at the boys, so I had to kill him clean and quick, no choice. Then one of those white cones was coming at us, and I shot it. Did the bullet hurt it? I have no idea. I pulled the boys out of that circle and then both of the white cones just whooshed out of there. No one outside the barn saw them. So it was just the two boys, me, and Tammy, who had called them."

"My God, that's scary."

"More than you can imagine."

Lily said, "I wonder, did their victims have to be inside that circle?"

"Good question. Since I was there and saw all of it, I think they did have to have their victims inside the circle. Or maybe it was just a ritual that they themselves had developed over time, a ceremony that gave the Tuttles more of a kick out of what they were doing. However, I didn't see that the Ghouls had any knives or axes, so why did they say that?" He paused a moment, thinking back. "You know, Tammy had a knife but I didn't see any axes anywhere."

"Maybe she was just speaking dramatically."

Savich thought about the teenage boy, his body mutilated. "Maybe. I don't think so."

"What sorts of things has MAX dug up?"

He paused for a moment, then gave a slight shake of his head as he said, "You'd be surprised what's turned up over the years."

"Yeah, I bet I would, only you're not going to tell me anything, are you?"

There was a knock on the door.

Sherlock's voice. "Quick, Dillon. Open up!"

She was carrying three covered trays, stacked on top of one another. "From Mrs. Blade, downstairs," she said and handed them to Savich. "Besides doing crossword puzzles, she likes to cook. She insisted that if we couldn't come down to the dining room, she was sending this up."

Two huge plates of spaghetti with meatballs, one huge plate without the meatballs for Savich, lots of Parmesan cheese in a big bowl on the side, eight slices of garlic bread, and three large bowls of Caesar salad.

No one said a word for at least seven minutes, just groaned with pleasure and chewed. Finally, Lily sat back, patted her stomach, and sighed. "That garlic bread makes your back teeth sing the Italian anthem. Goodness, that was nearly as good as our Mexican lunch."

Sherlock wanted to laugh, but her mouth was full of spaghetti. Savich said, "Nah, Lily, give me a salty tortilla and salsa hot enough to burn the rubber off my soles any day. I wonder which one of your in-laws is going to pay us a visit this evening?"

Lily turned a bit pale. "But why would any of them want to see me again?"

Sherlock took the tray off her lap and said matter-of-factly, "Because their pigeon is bent on flying out of the nest. You survived the attack on the city bus this morning. No more attacks since Dillon have been with you. Nope, now they've got to visit you and try to convince you that Tennyson can't live without you."

"A final shot," Lily said.

"Yes, that's right," Sherlock said.

Savich just smiled. "Only thing is, they also know that their little pigeon has two big crows guarding her. We'll see exactly what tack they take. Ah, look at that dessert Sherlock was hiding from us. Chocolate mousse, one of my favorites."

Tennyson and his mother showed up an hour later, at precisely eight o'clock.

Charlotte Frasier had come to the hospital only once, stood by Lily's bed, and told her at least three times that she desperately needed to see dear Dr. Rossetti, a fine doctor, an excellent man who would help her. She was so worried about her dear Lily, everyone was. No one wanted her to try to kill herself again. To which

Lily had simply stared at her, not a single word coming to mind after that outrageous speech. This evening, she was beautifully dressed in a dark wine-colored wool suit, a pale pink silk blouse beneath. Her thick black hair, not a hint of white, was cut short and tousled in loose curls and waves around her face. It was a very young style, but it didn't look ridiculous at all. Her teeth were white and straight, her lipstick blood red. Charlotte looked good; she always had.

As for Tennyson, he paid no attention to either Savich or Sherlock, just marched directly to Lily's bed, grabbed her hand, and held on tightly.

"Come home with me, Lily. I need you."

"Hello, Tennyson. Hello, Charlotte. What more could we possibly have to say to each other? Dillon thought you would come by this evening, but I have to admit I'm very surprised." Lily finally got her hand back and asked, "Oh yes, where is your father? Isn't he well?"

Savich said easily, "Maybe they don't think they need him. They're hopeful they can talk you around by themselves."

Lily said to her husband, "You can't."

Charlotte said in her rich-as-sin Savannah-smooth voice, "Elcott wanted to come tonight, but he had a slight indigestion. Now, listen to me for a moment, Lily. My son loves you very much. Since he's a man, it's difficult for him to speak from his heart—that's a woman sort of thing to do, so I am telling you for him that he really does need you."

"Actually, Charlotte, Tennyson can speak very eloquently. However, I don't think his heart has anything to do with it. No, Charlotte, what Tennyson really needs is my Sarah Elliott paintings."

"That's not true!" Tennyson whirled about to face Savich. "You have filled her head with suspicions, doubts, with lies about me and my family and my motives. I don't have any ulterior motives! I love my wife, do you hear me? Yes, that is from my bruised and bleeding heart! I wouldn't do anything to harm her. She's precious to me. Why don't you and your wife just go back to Washington and fight criminals, you know, people who have really done bad things, not innocent people you've just taken a dislike to. That's what you're paid to do, not rip apart a loving family! Leave us the hell alone!"

"That was a very impassioned speech," Sherlock said, smiling and nodding in approval. She knew from the furious pulse pounding in Tennyson's neck that he would cheerfully murder her.

Charlotte's voice was still as silky and soft as gently flowing honey. "Now, now, my dears, all of you need to calm down. Lily dearest, you're a grown woman. My Tennyson is just as protective of his own younger sister as your brother is of you. But your brother and his wife have gone over the line. They dislike my son, for whatever reasons I'm sure I can't say. But there can simply be no proof to any of their accusations, not a shred. Mad accusations, all of them. Lily, how could you possibly believe such things of my son?"

Sherlock said, "I wouldn't call them particularly 'mad accusations,' but, yes, ma'am, you're right about proof. If we had proof, we'd haul his butt to jail."

Charlotte said, "So, then, why are you continuing to poison poor Lily's mind? You're doing her a disservice. She's really not well, you know, and you're pushing her farther down a road none of us want her to travel."

"Mother—"

"No, it's true, Tennyson. Lily is mentally ill. She needs to come home so we can take care of her."

Lily said in a loud, clear voice that brought everyone's eyes back to her, "A young guy tried to murder me this morning."

"What? Oh, God, no!" Tennyson nearly

jerked her up into his arms, but Lily managed to press herself against the headboard and hold firm. Even as she was struggling, she said, "No, Tennyson, I'm quite all right. He didn't succeed, as you can see. Actually, I beat the stuffing out of him. The cops know who he is. Do back away now before my sister-in-law bites you."

Sherlock laughed.

"That's right," Savich said. "His name is Morrie Jones. Ring a bell, Tennyson? Charlotte? No? Well, you certainly got to him quickly enough, set everything in motion with nary a wasted moment. The cops will catch him anytime now and he'll spill his guts to them, and then we'll have our proof."

Tennyson said, "It's another lie, Lily. The guy must have mistaken you for someone else; that, or more likely, the guy was just a mugger. Where did it happen?"

"That's right, you couldn't have known where he'd find me, could you? He got on a local city bus that was empty except for me and the bus driver, because of the funeral."

"Yes," Charlotte said. "Dear old Ferdy Malloy died, probably poisoned by his wife. Everybody knows it, but no one was about to insist on an autopsy, least of all the coroner."

"Yes, yes, but that's not important, Mother. Someone tried to hurt Lily."

"A sharp knife probably meant he was planning to do more than hurt me," Lily said. "Lucky for me that Dillon had taught me how to protect myself."

"Just maybe," Tennyson said now, his voice all soft and gentle, his patented shrink's voice, "just maybe there was this young guy who came on to you, maybe even asked you out. I know Dr. Rossetti believes that a young woman, vulnerable like you are, uncertain, her mind clouded, can imagine many different things to disguise her sickness—"

Lily, who'd been staring at him like he had sprouted a TV antenna from his head, said, "Why did I ever think I loved you? You're the biggest jerk."

"I'm not, I'm just trying to understand you, to make you face things. Besides, that's what Dr. Rossetti thinks."

Lily began laughing, rich, deep laughter that didn't stop for a good, long time. Finally, wiping her eyes, she said, "You're really good, Tennyson, both you and Dr. Rossetti. You combined all your shrink analysis with some pills to drive me over the edge, and no wonder I wanted to do away with myself. So I made the guy up to assuage my guilt. Do you know what, Tennyson? I think I'm just about over blaming myself."

Charlotte said, "Lily dearest, I'm glad to hear you say that, actually—"

Lily interrupted her mother-in-law. She was waving Tennyson away even as she said, her voice light, amused, "Please go now, both of you. I hope that I'm lucky enough never to see either of you again."

Sherlock said, "Oh, I hope we do see them again, Lily. In a courtroom."

Savich said suddenly, "Your first wife, Tennyson. I don't suppose Lynda's fondest wish was to be cremated?"

Tennyson was shaking so much from rage, Sherlock was sure he was going to go after her husband, a singularly stupid thing for him even to consider. She stepped quickly to him, laid her hand on his forearm and said, "Don't even think about it. You couldn't take me and I'm half your size. Even five days after surgery, I doubt you could take Lily either. So please just leave, Tennyson, and take your mother with you."

"I am appalled that you have relatives who are so very close-minded and obnoxious, Lily," Charlotte Frasier said, her words smooth out of her mouth. They left, not another word out of either mouth, but Tennyson did pause to give Lily a tormented look over his shoulder.

Sherlock said thoughtfully, "He was trying to reproduce a patented Heathcliff look there, all down-in-the-mouth and pathetic. He didn't do it well, but he tried."

Lily said, "Did you notice that lovely black turtleneck sweater Tennyson was wearing? I gave it to him for Christmas."

"You know what I think, Lily?" Savich asked, shaking his head at her. "I think the next time a guy appeals to you, red lights need to flash in your brain. Then we need to take him in for questioning."

"I was just thinking about that this morning. Maybe I'm too gullible. Okay, no more good-looking men; actually, no more men at all, Dillon, or I'll kick myself from here to Boston. Nothing but gnomes with pocket protectors for me in the future, and they'll just be friends."

That was going overboard, Sherlock was thinking, but for the time being, not a bad way for Lily to think about the opposite sex.

Lily said, "I wish I had a beer so I could drink to that."

Savich said, "No beer. Here's more iced tea."

"Thanks." Lily sipped the tea and laid her head back against the pillow. "I wonder where my father-in-law was. You think they really thought he'd be a liability?"

"Evidently so," Savich said. "What amazes me is they don't seem to realize what a liability the both of them are."

"I've never heard such a charming Southern accent," Sherlock said. She sat down on the bed beside Lily and lightly rubbed her arm. "Talk about candy coating."

"She frightened me more than Tennyson." She gave both of them a fat smile. "I held up," she said, gave a deep sigh, and said again, "I held up. He never guessed that I was so scared."

Savich felt her pain in his gut. He gathered her against him, very careful with her stitches. He kissed the top of her head. "Oh no, sweetheart, there isn't a reason for you to be afraid of him, ever again. I was proud of you. You held up great."

"Yes, you did, Lily, so no more talk about being scared. Remember, you've got your two bulldogs right here. You know something? I don't know what they thought they could gain by coming here. They didn't try to be very conciliatory. Are they stupid or was there some method to their approach?"

"I surely hope not," Lily said and closed her eyes.

Savich's cell phone rang.

ELEVEN

Washington, D.C.
Three days later

"You go to bed now, Lily. No arguments.
You look like a ghost out of *A Christmas Carol.*"

Lily managed a small smile and did as she was told. She was still weak, and the long plane trip back east had knocked her flat. She awoke an hour later to hear Dillon and Sherlock talking to Sean. They cuddled, hugged, and kissed him until finally he was so exhausted he hollered big time for about two minutes. Then he was out like the proverbial light. His nursery was right next to the guest room, where she lay quietly in the dim light. She didn't realize she was crying until a tear itched her cheek. She wiped it away.

She closed her eyes when she heard her door open slightly. No, she wasn't ready to see anyone just yet, although she loved them both dearly for caring about her so very much. She pretended to be asleep. When she heard them go downstairs, she got up and went into the baby's room. Sean was sleeping on his knees, his butt in the air, two fingers in his mouth, his precious face turned toward her. He looked just like his father, but he had his mother's dreamy blue eyes. She lightly rubbed her fingers over his back. So small, so very perfect.

She cried for the beauty of this little boy and for the loss of Beth.

Late that evening, over a good-sized helping of Dillon's lasagna, she said, "Have you checked back with your office? Did they find Marilyn Warluski?"

Savich said, "Not yet. They found the boyfriend, Tony Fallon, but he claims she hasn't contacted him. But there were a couple of folk in Bar Harbor who identified a photo of her, said they'd seen her recently. They're going back to put his feet to the coals. We'll know something soon."

"We hope," Sherlock said. Then she smiled. "You should have seen Dillon's mother when we picked up Sean—she didn't want us to take him. She said we'd promised her at least a week with him all to herself, but we'd lied; it was barely a week. She was shouting 'Foul' even as we were pulling out of her driveway."

Savich shook his head. "Now he'll be so spoiled that we'll actually have to say no to him a couple of times to get him grounded back into reality."

"I bet Mom would love to baby-sit him on a regular basis," Lily said.

"Well," Savich said, "she's got her own life. She's his treat; two or three times a week he gets big doses of Grandma. It works well that way. Our nanny, Gabriella Henderson, is the best. She's young, so she's got the energy and stamina to keep up with him. Believe me, he can wear you down very fast."

Lily was laughing, looking over at Sean, who was seated in his walker, a nifty contraption that let him scoot all over the downstairs. If he ran into something, he just changed directions.

Savich said, "Those wheels are bad for the floor, but Sherlock and I decided we'd just have them refinished when he moves on to crawling and walking."

Lily said slowly, "Isn't it strange? I never imagined you with a kid, Dillon."

Savich smiled and helped her down on his big stuffed chair. "I didn't either, but here came Sherlock, blasted right into my comfortable life, and it just seemed like the right thing. We're very lucky, Lily. Now, sweetheart, we've been traveling all day and you're jet-lagged, probably really bad what with the surgery a week ago. I want you to sleep at least ten hours before you face the world here in Washington tomorrow."

"You and Sherlock have to be jet-lagged too. Even though you travel a lot and you are FBI agents, you—"

The front doorbell rang.

Savich walked around Sean, who was speeding toward the front door. It was Simon Russo. Savich knew him as a man of immense energy and focus, a man who just didn't quit. And now Simon was looking beyond him to the living room.

"Simon, it's good to see you. What the devil are you doing here?"

Simon grinned at his friend, shook his hand, and said, "Yeah, good to see you, Savich. I came to see the paintings. Where are they? Not here, I hope. You don't have the kind of security to keep the paintings here, even overnight."

"No we don't. Come on in. No, the paintings are in the vault in the Beezler-Wexler Gallery, safe as can be."

"Good, good. I'd like you to arrange for me to see them, Savich."

"So you said. First, however, you need a cup of tea and a slice of apple pie. My mom made it."

"Oh, not your blasted tea. Coffee, please,

Savich, I'm begging you. Coffee, black. Then we can see the paintings."

"Simon, come on in and say hello to Sherlock and meet my sister, Lily."

Simon shook his head and said, "Not until tomorrow? How early?"

"Get a grip, Simon. Come along. Hey, guys, look who just flew through our front door? Simon Russo."

Lily's first impression of Simon Russo was that he was too good-looking, that he was a man who looked like a Raphaelesque angel, hair black and thick and a bit too long. Yeah, the angel Gabriel, probably, the head angel, the big kahuna. He was taller than her brother, long and lean, his eyes brighter and bluer than a winter sky over San Francisco Bay, and he looked distracted. He hadn't shaved. He was wearing blue jeans, sneakers, a white dress shirt, a yellow-and-red tie, and a tweed jacket. He looked like a gangster academic, an odd combination, but it was true. Or maybe a nerd gangster, what with a name like Simon. He also looked like he knew things, maybe dangerous things. Lily was sure all the way to her bones that she wouldn't trust him if he pledged his name in blood.

Red lights flashed in her brain. No, she wouldn't let herself even see him as a man. He

was an expert who wanted to see her Sarah Elliott paintings for some reason. He was Dillon's
friend. She wouldn't have to worry about him.
Still, she found herself drawing back into the
big chair, just in case.

"Simon!" Sherlock was across the living
room in under three seconds, her arms thrown
around him, laughing and squeezing him. She
came barely to his chin. He was hugging her,
kissing her bouncing hair. She pulled back
finally, kissed his scratchy cheek, and said,
"Goodness, you're here in a hurry. Yes, I know
it isn't us you want to see, it's those paintings.
Well, you'll just have to wait until morning."

Lily watched him hug her sister-in-law close
once again, kiss her hair once again, and say, "I
love you, Sherlock, I'd love to keep kissing you,
but Dillon can kill me in a fair fight. The only
time I ever beat him up, he was sick with the flu,
and even then it was close. He also fights dirty. I
don't want him to mess up my perfect teeth." He
lifted her over his head, then slowly lowered her.

Savich said, crossing his arms over his chest,
"You kiss her hair again and I'll have to see
about those teeth."

Simon said, "Okay, I'll stay focused on the
paintings, but, Sherlock, I want you to know
that I wanted you first." He started to kiss her
again, then sighed deeply. "Oh, what the hell."

Then he turned those dark blue eyes on Lily, and he smiled at her, far too nice a smile, and she wished she could just stand up and walk out of the room. He was dangerous.

"Why," she said, not moving out of her chair, actually pressing her back against the cushions, "are you so hot to see my paintings?"

Savich frowned at her, his head cocked to one side. She sounded mad, like she wanted to kick Simon through a window. He said easily, "Lily, sweetheart, this is Simon Russo. You've heard me talk about him over the years. Remember, we roomed together our senior year at MIT?"

"Maybe," Lily said. "But what does he want with my paintings?"

"I don't know yet. He's a big-time dealer in the art world. He's the one I called to ask how much Grandmother's paintings are worth in today's market."

"I remember you," she said to Simon. "I was sixteen when you came home with Dillon on Christmas your senior year. Why do you want to see my paintings so badly?"

Simon remembered her, only she was all grown up now, not the wily, fast-talking teenager who'd tried to con him out of a hundred bucks. He didn't remember the scheme—some bet, maybe, but he did remember that she would have gotten it out of him, too, if her father hadn't warned him away and told him to keep his money in his wallet.

Simon wasn't deaf. He heard wariness, maybe even distrust in her voice. Why would she dislike him? She didn't even know him, hadn't seen him in years. She didn't look much like that teenager, either. She still looked like a fairy princess, but this grown-up fairy princess looked ground under—alarmingly pale, shadows beneath her eyes. Her hair was pulled back in a ratty ponytail and badly needed to be washed. She also needed to gain some weight to fill out her clothes. Antipathy was pouring off her in waves, a tsunami of dislike to drown him. Why?

"Are you in pain?" he asked, taking a step toward her.

Lily blinked at him, drawing herself in even more. "What?"

"Are you in pain? I know you had surgery last week. That's got to be tough."

"No," she said, still looking as though she was ready to gut him. Then Lily realized that she had no reason at all to dislike this man. He was her brother's friend, nothing more, no reason to be wary of him. The only problem was that he was good-looking, and surely she could overlook that flaw. He was here to see her paintings.

The good Lord save her from good-looking

men who wanted her paintings. Two had been more than enough.

She tried to smile at him to get that puzzled look off his face.

Now what was this? Simon wondered, but he didn't get an answer, of course. He didn't say anything more. He turned on his heel and walked to where Sean had come to a halt in his walker and was staring up at him, a sodden graham cracker clutched in his left hand. Crumbs covered his mouth and chin and shirt.

"Hi, champ," Simon said and came down on his haunches in front of Sean's walker.

Sean waved the remains of the graham cracker at him.

"Let me pass on that." He looked over his shoulder. "He's still teething?"

Sherlock said, "Yep, for a while yet. Don't let Sean touch you, Simon, or you'll regret it. That jacket you're wearing is much too nice to have wet graham cracker crumbs and spit all over it."

Simon merely smiled and stuck out two fingers. Sean looked at those two fingers, gummed his graham cracker faster, then shoved off with his feet. The walker flew into Simon. He was so startled, he fell back on his butt.

He laughed, got back onto his knees, and lightly ran his fingers over Sean's black hair. "You're going to be a real bruiser, aren't you, champ? You're already a tough guy, mowed me right down. Thank God you've got your mama's gorgeous blue eyes or you'd scare the bejesus out of everybody, just like your daddy does." He turned on his heel to say to Lily, "Are you the changeling or is Savich?"

Savich laughed and gave Simon a hand up. "She's the changeling in our immediate family. However, she looks just like Aunt Peggy, who married a wealthy businessman and lives like a princess in Brazil."

"Okay, then," Simon said, "let's see if she tries to bite my hand off." He stuck out his hand toward Lily Frasier. "A pleasure to meet another Savich."

Good manners won out, and she gave him her hand. A soft hand, smooth and white, but there were calluses on her fingertips. He frowned as he felt them. "I remember now, you're an artist, like Savich here."

"Yes, I told you about her, Simon. She draws *No Wrinkles Remus,* a political cartoon strip that—"

"Yes, of course I remember. I've read the strip, but it's been a while now. It was in the *Chicago Tribune,* if I remember correctly."

"That's right. It ran there for about a year. Then I left town. I'm surprised you remember it."

He said, "It's very biting and cynical, but hilarious. I don't think it matters if the reader is a Democrat or a Republican, all the political shenanigans ring so true it just doesn't matter. Will the world see more of Remus?"

"Yes," Lily said. "Just as soon as I'm settled in my own place, I'm going to begin again. Now, why are you so anxious to see my paintings?"

Sean dropped the graham cracker, looked directly at his mother, and yelled.

Sherlock laughed as she lifted him out of the walker. "You ready for a bath, sweetie? Goodness, and a change, too. It's late, so let's go do it. Dillon, why don't you make Lily and Simon some coffee. I'll be back with the little prince in a while."

"Some apple pie would be nice," Simon said. "I haven't had dinner yet; it would fill in the cracks."

"You got it," Savich said, gave Lily the once-over to make sure she was okay, and went to the kitchen.

"Why do you want to see my paintings so badly?" Lily asked again.

"I'd just as soon not say until I actually see them, Mrs. Frasier."

"Very well. What do you do in the art world, Mr. Russo?"

"I'm an art broker."

"And how do you do that, exactly?"

"A client wants to buy, say, a particular paint-ing. A Picasso. I locate it, if I don't know where it is already—which I do know most of the time—see if it's for sale. If it is, I procure it for the client."

"What if it's in a museum?"

"I speak to the folk at the museum, see if there's another painting, of similar value, that they'd barter for the one my client wants. It happens that way, successfully sometimes, if the museum wants what I have to barter more than the painting they have. Naturally, I try to keep up with the wants and needs of all the major museums, the major collectors as well." He smiled. "Usually, though, a museum isn't all that eager to part with a Picasso."

"You know all about the illegal market, then."

Her voice was flat, no real accusation in it, but he knew to his toes that she was very wary of him. Why? Ah, yes, her paintings, that was it. She didn't trust him because she was afraid for her paintings. Okay, he could deal with that.

He sat down on the sofa across from her, picked up the afghan, and held it out to her.

Lily said, "Thanks, I am a bit cold. No, no, just toss it to me."

But he didn't. He spread it over her, aware that she didn't want him near her, frowned, then sat down again and said, "Of course I know about the illegal market. I know all of the main players involved, from the thieves to the most immoral dealers, to the best forgers and the collectors who, many of them, are totally obsessed if there is a piece of art they badly want. 'Obsession' is many times the operative word in the business. Is there anything you want to know about it, Mrs. Frasier?"

"You know the crooks who acquire the paintings for the collectors."

"Yes, some of them, but I'm not one of them. I'm strictly on the up-and-up. You can believe that because your brother trusts me. No one's tougher than Savich when it comes to trust."

"You've known each other for a very long time. Maybe trust just starts between kids and doesn't end, particularly if you rarely see each other."

"Whatever that means," Simon said. "Look, Mrs. Frasier, I've been in the business for nearly fifteen years. I'm sorry if you've had some bad experiences with people in the art world, but I'm honest, and I don't dance over the line. You can take that to the bank. Of course I know about the underside of the business or I wouldn't be very successful, now would I?"

"How many of my grandmother's paintings have you dealt with?"

"Over the years, probably a good dozen, maybe more. Some of my clients are museums themselves. If the painting is owned by a collector—legally, of course—and a museum wants to acquire it, then I try to buy it from the collector. Since I know what all the main collectors own and accumulate, I will try to barter with them. It cuts both ways, Mrs. Frasier."

"I'm divorcing him, Mr. Russo. Please don't call me that again."

"All right. 'Frasier' is a rather common sort of name anyway, doesn't have much interest. What would you like to be called, ma'am?"

"I think I'll go back to my maiden name. You can call me Ms. Savich. Yes, I'll be Lily Savich again."

Her brother said from the doorway, "I like it, sweetheart. Let's wipe out all reminders of Tennyson."

"Tennyson? What sort of name is that?"

Lily actually smiled. If it wasn't exactly at him, it was still in his vicinity. "His father told me that Lord or Alfred just wouldn't do, so he had to go with Tennyson. He was my father-in-law's favorite poet. Odd, but my mother-in-law hates the poet."

"Perhaps Tennyson, the poet—not your nearly ex-husband—is a bit on the 'pedantic' side."

"You've never read Tennyson in your life," Lily said.

He gave her the most charming smile and nodded. "You're right. I guess 'pedantic' isn't quite right?"

"I don't know. I haven't read him either."

"Here's coffee and apple pie," Savich said, then cocked his head, looking upward. He said, "I hear Sherlock singing to Sean. He loves a good, rousing Christmas carol in the bathtub. I think she's singing 'Hark! The Herald Angels Sing.' You guys try to get along while I join the sing-along. You can trust him, Lily."

When they were alone again, Lily heard the light slap of rain on the windows for the first time. Not a hard, drenching rain, just an introduction, maybe, to the winter rains that were coming. It had been overcast when they'd landed in Washington, and there was a stiff wind.

Simon sipped Savich's rich black coffee, sighed deeply, and sat back, closing his eyes. "Savich makes the best coffee in the known world. And he rarely drinks it."

"His body is a temple," she said. "I guess his brain is, too."

"Nah, no way. Your brother is a good man, sharp, steady, but he ain't no temple. I bet Savich would fall over in shock if he heard you say that about him."

"Probably so, but it's true nonetheless. Our dad taught all of us kids how to make the very best coffee. He said if he was ever in an old-age home, at least he'd know he could count on us for that. Our mom taught Dillon how to cook before he moved to Boston to go to MIT."

"Did she teach all of you?"

"No, just Dillon." She stopped, listening to the two voices singing upstairs. "They've moved on to 'Silent Night.' It's my favorite."

"They do the harmony well. However, what Savich does best is country and western. Have you ever heard him at the Bonhomie Club?"

She shook her head, drank a bit of coffee, and knew her stomach would rebel if she had any more.

"Maybe if you're feeling recovered enough, we could all go hear him sing at the club."

She didn't say anything.

"Why do you distrust me, Ms. Savich? Or dislike me? Whatever it is."

She looked at him for a good, long time, took a small bit of apple pie, and said finally, "You really don't want to know, Mr. Russo. And I've decided that if Dillon trusts you, why, then, I can, too."

TWELVE

Raleigh Beezler, co-owner of the Beezler–Wexler Gallery of Georgetown, New York City, and Rome, gave Lily the most sorrowful look she'd seen in a very long time, at least as hangdog as Mr. Monk's at the Eureka museum.

He kissed his fingers toward the paintings. "Ah, Mrs. Frasier, they are so incredible, so unique. No, no, don't say it. Your brother already told me that they cannot remain here. Yes, I know that and I weep. They must make their way to a museum so the great unwashed masses can stand in their wrinkled walking shorts and gawk at them. But it brings tears to my eyes, clogs my throat, you understand."

"I understand, Mr. Beezler," Lily said and patted his arm. "But I truly believe they belong in a museum."

Savich heard a familiar voice speaking to Dyrlana, the gorgeous twenty-two-year-old gallery facilitator, hired, Raleigh admitted readily, to make the gentlemen customers looser with their wallets. Savich turned and called out, "Hey, Simon, come on back here."

Lily looked through the open doorway of the vault and watched Simon Russo run the distance to the large gallery vault in under two seconds. He skidded to a stop, sucked in his breath at the display of the eight Sarah Elliott paintings, each lovingly positioned against soft black velvet on eight easels, and said, "My God," and nothing else.

He walked slowly from painting to painting, pausing to look closely at many of them, and said finally, "You remember, Savich, that your grandmother gave me *The Last Rites* for my graduation present. It was my favorite then and I believe it still is. But this one—*The Maiden Voyage*—it's incredible. This is the first time I've seen it. Would you look at the play of light on the water, the lace of shadows, like veils. Only Sarah Elliott can achieve that effect."

"For me," Lily said, "it's the people's faces. I've always loved to stare at the expressions, all of them so different from each other, so telling. You know which man owns the ship just by the look on his face. And his mother—that look of superior complacency at what he's achieved, mixed with the love she holds so deeply for her son and the ship he's built."

"Yes, but it's how Sarah Elliott uses light and shadow that puts her head and shoulders above any other modern artist."

"No, I disagree with you. It's the people, their faces, you see simply everything in their expressions. You feel like you know them, know what makes them tick." She saw he would object again and rolled right over him. "But this one has always been my favorite." She lightly touched her fingertips to the frame on *The Swan Song.* "I really hate to see it go to a museum."

"Keep it with you then," Savich said. "I've kept *The Soldier's Watch.* The insurance costs a bundle as well as the alarm system, but very few people know about it, and that's what you'll have to do. Keep it close and keep it quiet."

Simon looked up from his study of another painting. "I have *The Last Rites* hung in a friend's gallery near my house. I see it nearly every day."

"That's an excellent idea," Raleigh Beezler said and beamed at Lily, seeing hope. "Do you know, Mrs. Frasier, that there is an exquisite townhouse for sale not two blocks from my very safe, very beautiful, very hassle-free gallery that would accord you every amenity? What do you say I call the broker and you can have a look at it? I understand you're a cartoonist. There is this one room that is simply filled with light, just perfect for you."

That was well done, Lily thought. She had to admire Mr. Beezler. "And I could leave some of my paintings here, in your gallery, on permanent display?"

"An excellent idea, no?"

"I'd like to see the townhouse, sir, but the price is very important. I don't have much money. Perhaps you and I could come to a mutually satisfying financial arrangement. My painting displayed right here for a monthly stipend, a very healthy one, given that this house sits in the middle of Georgetown and I'd have to afford to live here. What do you think?"

Raleigh Beezler was practically rubbing his hands together. There was the light of the negotiator in his dark eyes.

Simon cleared his throat. He'd continued studying the rest of the paintings, and now he turned slowly to say, "I think that's a very good idea, Ms. Savich, Mr. Beezler. Unfortunately, there is a huge problem."

Lily turned to frown at him. "I can't see any

problem if Mr. Beezler is willing to pay me a sufficient amount to keep up mortgage payments, at least until I can get an ongoing paycheck for *No Wrinkles Remus,* maybe even get it syndicated . . ."

Simon just shook his head. "I'm sorry, but it's just not possible."

"What's wrong, Simon?" Because he knew Simon, knew that tone of voice, Savich automatically took Lily's hand. "All right, the floor's yours. You really wanted to see the paintings. You've seen them. I've watched you studying them. What's wrong?"

"No easy way to say this," Simon said. "Oh damn, four of them are fakes, including *The Swan Song.* Excellent fakes, but there it is."

"No," Lily said. "No. I would know if it weren't real. You're wrong, Mr. Russo, just wrong."

"I'm sorry, Ms. Savich, but I'm very sure. Like I said, the way Sarah Elliott uses light and shadows makes her unique. It's the special blend of shades that she mixed herself and the extraordinary brush strokes she used; no one's really managed to copy them exactly.

"Over the years I've become an expert on her paintings. Still, if I hadn't also heard some rumors floating around New York that one of the big collectors had gotten a hold of some Sarah Elliott paintings in the last six months, I wouldn't have come rushing down here."

Savich said, "I'm sorry, Lily, but Simon is an expert. If he says they're fake, then it's true."

"I'm sorry," Simon said. "Also, there were no Sarah Elliotts for sale that I knew of. When I heard *The Swan Song* as one of the paintings acquired, I knew something was wrong. I immediately put out feelers to get more substantial information. With any luck, I'll find out what's going on soon. Unfortunately, I haven't yet heard a thing about what happened to the fourth painting. Since I knew that you, Ms. Savich, owned them, and that they'd been moved from the Chicago Art Institute to the Eureka Art Museum eleven months ago, I didn't want to believe it—there are always wild rumors floating through the art world. I couldn't be sure until I'd actually seen them. I'm sorry, they are fakes."

"Well," Sherlock said, her face nearly as red as her hair, "shit."

Savich stared at his wife and said slowly, "You really cursed, Sherlock? You didn't even curse when you were in labor."

"I apologize for that, but I am so mad I want to chew nails. This is very bad. I'm really ready to go over the edge here. Those bastards—those officious, murdering bastards. There, I don't have to curse anymore. I'm sorry, Dillon, but this really is too much. This is so awful, Lily, but at least we have a good idea who's responsible."

Lily said, "Tennyson and his father."

Sherlock said, "And Mr. Monk, the curator of the Eureka museum. He had to be in on it. No wonder he was near tears when you told him you were taking the paintings. He knew the jig would be up sooner or later. He had to know that in Washington, D.C., experts would be viewing the paintings and one of them would spot the fakes."

"So did Tennyson," Savich said.

Lily said, "Probably my father-in-law as well. Maybe the whole family was in on this. But they couldn't have known we would find out the very day after we got here." She turned to Simon Russo. "I'm madder than Sherlock. Thank you, Mr. Russo, for being on top of this and getting to us so quickly."

Simon turned to Savich. "There is one positive thing here. At least Tennyson Frasier didn't have time to have all eight of them forged. Now that I know for certain that we've got four forgeries, I can find out the name of the forger. It won't be difficult. You see, it's likely to be one of three or four people in the world—the only ones with enough technique to capture the essence of Sarah Elliott and fool everyone except an expert who's been prepared for the possibility."

Lily said, "Would you have known they were fakes if you hadn't heard about them being sold to a collector?"

"Maybe not, but after the second or third viewing, I probably would have realized something was off. They really are very well done. When I find out who forged them, I'll pay a visit to the artist."

"Don't forget, Simon, we need proof," Savich said, "to nail Tennyson. And his family, and Mr. Monk at the Eureka museum."

Sherlock said, "No wonder that guy tried to murder you on the bus, Lily. They knew they had to move quickly and they did. It's just that you're no wuss and you creamed the guy. I wanna lock them all up, Dillon. Maybe stomp on them first."

Simon, who had been studying *The Maiden Voyage,* looked up. "What do you mean she creamed the guy? Someone attacked you? But you were just out of surgery."

"Sorry, I forgot to mention that," Savich said.

Lily said, "There was no reason to tell him. But yes, I'd been five or six days out of surgery. I was okay, thanks to a psychiatrist who . . .

well, never mind about that. But I was feeling just fine. A young guy got on an empty bus, sat beside me, and pulled out this really scary switchblade. He was lucky to get away." And Lily gave him a big smile, the first one he'd gotten from her. He smiled back.

"Very good. Your brother taught you?"

"Yes, after Jack . . . No, never mind that."

"You have a lot of never minds, Ms. Savich."

"You may have to get used to it." But she saw him file Jack's name away in that brain of his.

Simon said, "As for the fourth painting, *Effigy*, I thought it was just fine at first, but then I realized that the same forger who did the other three did that one as well. No leads yet on *Effigy*, but we'll track it down. It probably went to the same collector."

Mr. Beezler, shaken, wiped a beautiful linen handkerchief over his brow and said, "This would be a catastrophe to a museum, Mr. Savich, like a stick of dynamite stuck in the tailpipe of my Mercedes. You, Mr. Russo, you are, I gather, in a position to perhaps get the original paintings back?"

"Yes," said Simon, "I am. Keep the black velvet warm, Mr. Beezler."

Savich said, "I'll speak to the guys in the art fraud section, see what recommendations they have. The FBI doesn't do full-blown stolen art investigations at this time, so our best bet is Simon finding out who acquired the paintings."

Simon said, "First thing, I'll do some digging around, hit up my informants to get verification on who our collector is, find the artist, and squeeze him. The instant our collector hears that I'm digging—and he'd hear about it real quick—he'll react, either go to ground, hide the paintings, or maybe something else, but it won't matter."

"What do you mean 'something else'?" Lily asked.

Savich gave him a frown, and Simon said quickly, shrugging, "Nothing, really. But since I plan to stir things up, I'll be really careful who's at my back. Oh yeah, Savich, I'm relieved you didn't use the shippers that Mr. Monk wanted you to use."

Savich said, "No, I used Bryerson. I know them and trust them. There's no way Mr. Monk or Tennyson or any of the rest of them could know, at least for a while, where the paintings ended up. However, I will call Teddy Bryerson and have him let me know if he gets any calls about the paintings. Simon, do you think anyone will realize that these four paintings are fakes if they're out in the open for all to see?"

"Sooner or later someone would notice and ask questions."

Lily said to Mr. Beezler, "I can't very well let a museum hang the four fakes. What do you think about hanging all of them here for a while, Mr. Beezler, and we can see what happens?"

"Yes, I will hang them," said Raleigh, "with great pleasure."

Lily said to Simon, "Do you really think you can get the paintings back?"

Simon Russo rubbed his hands together. His eyes were fierce, and he looked as eager as a boy with his first train set. "Oh, yes."

She imagined him dressed all in black, even black camouflage paint on his face, swinging down a rope to hover above an alarmed floor.

Savich said, "Just one thing, Simon. When you find out who bought the paintings, I go with you."

Sherlock blinked at her husband. "You mean that you, an FBI special agent, unit chief, want to go steal four paintings?"

"Steal back," Savich said, giving her a kiss on her open mouth. "Bring home. Return to their rightful owner."

Lily said, "I'll be working with Mr. Russo to find the person who forged them and the name of the collector who bought them. And then we'll have proof to nail Tennyson."

"Oh no," Savich said. "I'm not letting you out of my sight, Lily."

"No way," Sherlock said. "No way am I letting you out of my sight either. Sean wants his auntie to hang out with him for a while."

Simon Russo looked at Lily Savich and slowly nodded. He knew to his bones that when this woman made up her mind, it would take more than an offering of a dozen chocolate cakes to change it. "Okay, you can work with me. But first you need to get yourself back to one-hundred-percent healthy."

"I'll be ready by Monday," Lily said. She raised her hand, palm out, to her brother before he could get out his objection. "You guys have lots to worry about—this Tammy Tuttle person. She's scary, Dillon. You've got to focus on catching her. This is nothing, in comparison, just some work to track these paintings, maybe talking to these artists. I know artists. I know what to say to them. It won't be any big deal. I can tell Mr. Russo exactly how to do it."

"Right," said Simon.

Sherlock was pulling on a hank of curly hair, something, Savich knew, she did when she was stressed or worried. She said, "She's right, Dillon, but that doesn't mean I like it." She sighed.

"And it's not just Tammy Tuttle. Oh well, I'll just spit it out. Ollie phoned just before we left the house this morning."

"He did?" Savich turned the full force of his personality on his wife, a dark brow raised. "And you didn't see fit to mention it to me?"

"It's Friday morning, Gabriella was at the dentist and running late; she's our nanny," Sherlock added to Simon. "Besides, you'd already told Ollie and Jimmy Maitland that you wouldn't be in until late morning. I was going to tell you on the way in."

"I know I don't want to hear this, but out with it, Sherlock. I can take it."

"Besides worrying about Tammy Tuttle, there's been a triple murder in a small town called Flowers, Texas. The governor called the FBI and demanded that we come in, and so we will. Both the ATF and the FBI are involved. There's this cult down there that they suspect is responsible for the murder of the local sheriff and his two deputies, who'd gone out to their compound to check things out. Their bodies were found in a ditch outside of town."

"That's nuts," Simon said.

"Yes," Sherlock said, "it is. Ah, Raleigh, would you mind visiting with Dyrlana for a moment? All this stuff is sort of under wraps."

Raleigh looked profoundly disappointed, but

he left them in the vault. At the doorway, he said, "What about your sister and Mr. Russo? They're civilians, too."

"I know, but I can control what they say," Savich said. "I really couldn't get away with busting your chops."

They heard him chuckling as he called out, "Dyrlana! Where is my gumpoc tea?"

"One problem is," Sherlock said, "that the cult has cleared out, split up into a dozen or more splinter groups and left town in every direction. Nobody knows where the leader is. They've pulled in a few of the cult members, but these folks just shake their heads and claim they don't know anything about it. The only good thing is that we have a witness, of sorts. It seems that one of the women is pregnant by the guru. Lureen was rather angry when she found him seducing another cult member, actually at least three or four other cult members. She slipped away and told the town mayor about it."

Savich said, "A witness, then. Did she identify the guru as the guy who ordered the murders?"

"Not yet. She's still thinking about it. She's afraid she'd screw up her child's karma if she identified the father as a murderer."

"Great," Savich said and sighed. "Like Ollie said, there doesn't seem to be anything in this life that's easy. Do we have some sort of name on this guy?"

"Oh, sure, that's no secret," Sherlock said. "Wilbur Wright. Lureen just wouldn't say his name out loud, but everybody knows it, since he was around town for a couple of months."

"Isn't that clever?" Savich rubbed the back of his neck, nodded to Simon, grabbed his wife's hand, and walked out of the vault. He said over his shoulder, "It's settled then. Lily, you rest and recuperate. Simon, you can stay at the house. I'd feel better if you did. Sherlock and I will call you guys later. Oh yes, don't spoil Sean. Gabriella is besotted with him already; she doesn't need any more help. Holler if you want MAX to check anything out for you, Simon."

"Will do."

"Oh, yes, there's one other thing," Sherlock said to Savich once they were out of the vault and in the gallery itself, alone and beyond the hearing of Lily or Simon. She glanced at Raleigh and Dyrlana, who were drinking gumpoc tea over by the front glass doors.

Savich knew he didn't want to hear this. He merely looked at her, nodding slowly.

"The guru. He had the hearts cut out of the sheriff and his two deputies."

"So this is why the Texas governor wants us involved. This guy has probably done something this sick before in other states. Ah, Sherlock, I just knew it couldn't be as straightforward as you presented it. So, is Behavioral Sciences also involved?"

"Yes. I didn't want Lily to have to hear that."

"You're right. All right, love, let's go track down Tammy Tuttle and Wilbur Wright."

Lily Savich and Simon Russo stood in the silent vault, neither of them saying a word. She walked to one of the paintings that was real, not forged—*Midnight Shadows*. She said, "I wonder why he tried to kill me when he did? What was the hurry? He had four more paintings to have forged. Why now?"

Savich had told Simon most of what had happened to his sister the previous evening, after she'd gone to bed, looking pale and, truth be told, wrung out. All except for the murder attempt on the city bus in Eureka. What had happened to her—what was still happening—was tragic and evil, and it all came on top of the death of her daughter.

But just perhaps they could recover the paintings. He sure wanted to. He said, "That's a good question. I don't know why they cut the brake lines. My guess is that something must have happened to worry them, something to make them move up the timetable."

"But why not just kill me off right away?

Surely it would have been easier for Tennyson to simply inherit the paintings, to own them himself. Then he wouldn't have had to go to all the trouble and risk of finding a first-class forger and then collectors who would want to buy the paintings."

"Count on Mr. Monk to help with all that. I bet you Mr. Monk doesn't have all that sterling a reputation. I'll check into that right away."

"Yes," Lily continued, her head cocked to one side, still thinking. "He could have killed me immediately, and then he would have owned the paintings. He could then have sold them legally, right up front, with no risk that someone would turn on him, betray him. Probably he would have made more money that way, you know, in auctions."

"First of all, Lily, killing you off would have brought Savich down on their heads, with all the power of the FBI at his back. Never under-estimate your brother's determination or the depths of his rage if something had happened to you. As for legal auctions for the paintings, you're wrong there. Collectors involved in ille-gal art deals pay top dollar, many times outra-geous amounts because they want something utterly unique, something no one else on the face of the earth owns. The stronger the obses-sion, the more they'll pay. Going this route was

certainly more risky, but the payoff was probably greater, even figuring in the cost of the forgery. It was trying to kill you that was the real
risk. As I said, something very threatening must
have happened. I don't know what, but we'll
probably find out. Now, you ready to go have
some lunch before you go home to bed?"

Lily thought about how tired she was, how
she could simply sit down and sleep, then she
smiled. "Can I have Mexican?"

THIRTEEN

Quantico

Savich was seated in his small office in the Jefferson dorm at the FBI academy when two agents ushered in Marilyn Warluski, who'd borne a child by her cousin Tommy Tuttle, now deceased, the child's whereabouts unknown. They'd nabbed her getting on a Greyhound bus in Bar Harbor, Maine, headed for Nova Scotia. Since she'd been designated a material witness, and Savich wanted to keep her stashed away, they'd brought her in a FBI Black Bell Jet to Quantico.

He'd never met her, but he'd seen her photo, knew she was poorly educated, and guessed that she was not very bright. He saw that she looked, oddly, even younger than in her photo, that she'd gained at least twenty pounds, and that her hair, cropped short in the photo, was longer and hung in oily hanks to her shoulders. She looked more tired than scared. No, he was wrong. What she looked was defeated, all hope quashed.

"Ms. Warluski," he said in his deep, easy voice, waving her to a chair as he said her name. The two agents left the office, closing the door behind them. Savich gently pressed a button on the inside of the middle desk drawer, and in the next room, two profilers sitting quietly could also hear them speak.

"My name is Dillon Savich. I'm with the FBI."

"I don't know nothin'," Marilyn Warluski said.

Savich smiled at her and seated himself again behind the desk.

He was silent for several moments, watched her fidget in that long silence. She said finally, her voice jumpy, high with nerves, "Just because you're good-lookin' doesn't mean I'm gonna tell you anythin', mister."

This was a kick. "Hey, my wife thinks I'm good-looking, but I'm wondering, since you said it, if you're just trying to butter me up."

"No," she said, shaking her head, "you're good-lookin' all right, and I heard one of the lady cops on the airplane say you're a hunk.

They were thinkin' that a sexy guy will make me talk, so they got you."

"Well," Savich said, "just maybe that's so." He paused a fraction of a second, then said, his voice unexpectedly hard, "Have you ever seen the Ghouls, Marilyn?"

He thought she'd keel over in her chair. So she knew about the Ghouls. She paled to a sickly white, looked ready to bolt.

"They're not here, Marilyn."

She shook her head back and forth, back and forth, whispering, "There's no way you could know about the Ghouls. No way at all. Ghouls are bad, real bad."

"Didn't Tammy tell you that I was there in the barn, that I saw them, even shot at them?"

"No, she didn't tell me . . . ah, shit. I don't know nothin', you hear me?"

"Okay, she didn't tell you that I saw them and she didn't tell you my name, which is interesting since she knows it. But she did tell you that she wanted to have at me, didn't she?"

Marilyn's lips were seamed tight. She shook her head and said "Oh, yeah, and she will. She called you that creepy FBI fucker. I don't know why she didn't tell me that you saw the Ghouls."

"Maybe she doesn't trust you."

"Oh, yeah, Tammy trusts me. She doesn't have anybody else now. She'll get you, mister, she will."

"Just so you know, Marilyn, I'm the one who shot her, the one who killed Tommy. I didn't want to, but they left me no choice. They had two kids there, and they were going to kill them. Young boys, Marilyn, and they were terrified. Tommy and Tammy had kidnapped them, beaten them, and they were going to murder them, like they've murdered many young boys all across the country. Did you know that? Did you know your cousins were murderers?"

Marilyn shrugged. Savich saw a rip beneath the right arm of her brown, cracked leather jacket. "They're my kin. I could miss Tommy— seein' as how he's dead now—but he killed our baby, cracked its poor little head right open, so I was really mad at him for a long time. Tommy was hard, real hard. He was always doin' things you didn't expect, mean things, things to make you scream. You killed him. He was one of a kind, Tommy was. Tammy's right, you're a creepy fucker."

Savich didn't respond, just nodded, waiting.

"You shouldn't have shot Tammy like you did, tearing her arm all up so they had to saw it off. You shouldn't have been there in my barn in the first place. It wasn't none of your damned business."

He smiled at her, sat forward, his palms flat on his desk. "Of course it's my business. I'm a cop, Marilyn. You know, I could have killed Tammy, not just shot her arm off. If I had killed her in the barn then she wouldn't have killed that little boy outside Chevy Chase. Either she did it or the Ghouls did it. Maybe the Ghouls did kill the boy, since there was a circle. Do the Ghouls have to have a circle, Marilyn? You don't know? Were you with her when she took that boy? Did you help her murder him?"

Marilyn shrugged her shoulders again. "Nope, I didn't even know what she was going to do, not really. She left me at this grungy motel on the highway and told me to stay put or she'd bang me up real bad. She looked real happy when she got back. There was lots of blood on her nurse's uniform; she said she'd have to find somethin' else to wear. She thought it was neat that there was blood on the uniform, said it was a-pro-pos or somethin' like that. Now, I'm not goin' to say any more. I already said too much. I want to leave now."

"You know, Marilyn, your cousin's very dangerous. She could turn on you, like this." He snapped his fingers, saw her cower in the chair, saw her shudder. He said, "How would you like to be ripped apart?"

"She wouldn't turn on me. She's known me all my life. I'm her cousin, her ma and mine were sisters, at least half-sisters. They wasn't real sure since their pa was always cattin' around."

"Why did Tammy pretend to be Timmy?"

Marilyn focused her eyes on the pile of books along the side wall of the office and didn't answer. Savich started to leave it for the moment since it obviously upset her, when she burst out, "She wanted me, you know, but she weren't no dyke and so she played with me only when she was dressed like Timmy, but never when she was Tammy."

For an instant, Savich was too startled to say a word. What a wild twist. He said finally, "Okay then, tell me what kind of shape Tammy is in right now."

That brought Marilyn up straight in her chair. "No thanks to you she's going to be okay, at least she kept telling me that. But she hurts real bad and her shoulder looks all raw and swollen. She went to a pharmacy late one night, just when they was closing, and got the guy to give her some antibiotics and pain pills. He nearly puked when he saw her shoulder."

"I didn't hear about any robbery in a pharmacy," Savich said slowly. They'd been looking, but hadn't gotten any news as yet.

"That's because Tammy whacked the guy after she got the medicine from him, tore the place up. She said that'd make the cops go after the local druggies."

"Where was this, Marilyn?"

"In northern New Jersey somewhere. I don't remember the name of that crummy little town."

Local law enforcement hadn't connected the pharmacist's murder to the Tammy Tuttle bulletin the FBI had circulated all over the eastern seaboard. Well, at least now they'd find out everything the local cops had on the murder. He said, "Where did Tammy go after you went off to Bar Harbor?"

"She said she wanted some sun so's it would heal her shoulder. She was going down to the Caribbean to get herself well. No, I don't know where; she wouldn't tell me. She said there were lots of islands down there and she'd just find the one that was best for her. Of course she didn't have enough money, so she robbed this guy and his wife in a real fancy house in Connecticut. Got three thousand and change. That's when she told me she'd be all right and I could take off."

"Naturally she's going to call you, let you know how she's doing?"

Marilyn nodded.

"Where will she call you?"

"At my boyfriend's, in Bar Harbor. But I'm not there anymore, am I? My boyfriend will tell her that the cops came around and I left."

That was true enough, Savich thought, no hope for it. He just hoped that Tammy wouldn't call until they'd found out where she was in the Caribbean.

Marilyn said, "I'll bet she really wants to kill you bad because of what you done to her. She'll come back when she's really well, and she'll take you down. Tammy's the meanest female in the world. She beat the shit out of me every time I saw her when we was growin' up. She'll get you, Dillon Savich. You're nuthin' compared to Tammy."

"What are the Ghouls, Marilyn?"

Marilyn Warluski seemed to grow smaller right in front of him. She was pressed against the back of her chair, her shoulders hunched forward. "They're bad, Mr. Savich. They're really bad."

"But what are they?"

"Tammy said she found them when she and Tommy were hiding out in some caves in the Ozarks a couple years ago. That's in Arkansas, you know. It was real dark, she told me, real dark in that stinkin' cave, smelled like bat shit, and Tommy was out takin' a leak, and she was alone and then, all of a sudden, the cave filled with weird white light and then the Ghouls came."

"They didn't hurt her?"

Marilyn shook her head.

"What else did she say?"

"Said she knew they were the Ghouls, just knew, that somehow they'd got inside her head and told her their name, then told her that they needed blood, lots of young blood, and then they laughed and told her they were counting on her, and then they just winked out. That's what Tammy said: they laughed, spoke in her head, and just 'winked out.' "

"But what are they, Marilyn? Do you have any idea?"

She was silent for the longest time, then she whispered, "Tammy told me just a couple of days ago that the Ghouls were pissed off at her because she and Tommy hadn't given them their young blood in the barn, that if Tommy was still alive, they'd eat him right up."

"Do you think that's why Tammy got that kid? So the Ghouls could have their young blood?"

She didn't say anything, just looked at him and slowly nodded. Then she started crying, hunched over, her bowed head in her hands.

"Do you know anything else, Marilyn?"

She shook her head. Savich believed her. He also understood why she was shivering. He was close to shivering himself. He had goose bumps on his arms.

Two FBI agents escorted Marilyn Warluski out of Savich's office. She would remain here at Quantico, a material witness and the FBI's guest until Savich and Justice made a decision about what to do with her.

He was standing by his desk, deep in thought, looking out the window toward Hogan's Alley, the all-American town that the FBI Academy had created and used to train their agents in confronting and catching criminals, when Jeffers, a profiler in the Behavioral Sciences, housed three floors down here at Quantico, said in his slow, Alabama drawl even before he cleared the doorway, "This is about the strangest shared delusion I've ever heard, Savich. But what are the things to them? How do they interact with Tammy Tuttle? Marilyn said Tammy told her the Ghouls got in her head and told her to do things."

"What we've got to do is predict what Tammy Tuttle will do next given this belief of hers in the Ghouls," said Jane Bitt, a senior profiler who'd lasted nearly five years without burning out.

Jane Bitt came around Jeffers and leaned against the wall, her arms crossed over her chest. "Lots of other monsters but not anything like this. Tammy Tuttle is a monster. She's got monsters inside her—monsters within a monster. The problem is that we don't have any markers, any clues to give us even a glimmer of an idea of what we're working with here. We're faced with something we've never seen before."

"That's right," said Jeffers, the two words so drawn out in his accent that Savich wanted to say them for him, that or just pull them out of his mouth. "How do we get her, Agent Savich? I sure want to hear what she has to say about the Ghouls."

Savich said, "You heard Marilyn say that Tammy went to the Caribbean, to an island 'right' for her. She couldn't have walked there, and she sure can't be hard to spot. Just a moment, let me call Jimmy Maitland. They can get on that right away." He placed the phone call, listened, and when he finally hung up, he said, "Mr. Maitland was nearly whistling. He's sure they'll get her now. What else do you guys think from listening to her?"

"Well," Jane said as she sat down, crossing her legs and leaning forward, "it seems to be some sort of induced hallucination. Marilyn seems to think they're real, and both you and the boys saw *something* unusual in that barn, isn't that right, Agent Savich?"

"Yes," Savich said.

"Maybe Tommy and Tammy have some sort of ability to alter what you see and feel, some sort of hypnotic ability."

Savich said to Jeffers, "You did a profile on Timmy Tuttle before he turned out to be Tammy."

"Savich is right, Jane," Jeffers said. "We ain't got nothing useful that fits a psychotic cross-dresser who may have hypnotic skills."

Savich laughed, said, "You know what I want to try? I want to talk Marilyn into letting us hypnotize her. Maybe if you're right about this, she can tell us a lot more when she's under."

Jeffers laughed. "Hey, maybe the Ghouls are real, maybe they're entities, aliens from outer space. What do you think, Jane?"

"I like the sound of that, Jeffers. It'd perk up our boring lives a bit, add some color to our humdrum files. White cones whirling around black circles—maybe they're from Mars, you think?"

Savich said, "Actually, I've been reading articles, studies on various phenomena involved in past crimes."

"Found anything?" Jeffers asked.

"Nothing like this," Savich said. "Not a thing like this." He added as he stood, "Joke all you want, but just don't do it in front of the media."

"Not a chance," Jane said. "I don't want to get committed." She rose, shook Savich's hand. "Marilyn told you that Tammy met up with the Ghouls in a cave. My husband is really into speleology and we usually go spelunking on our vacations. In fact, we were planning on visiting some of the caves in the Ozarks this summer. No matter how much I can laugh about this, I might want to rethink that plan."

Washington, D.C.

● Lily was leaning over her drawing table, looking at her work. No Wrinkles Remus was emerging clear and strong and outrageous from the tip of her beloved sable brush. The brush was getting a bit gnarly, but it was good for another few weeks, maybe.

First panel: Remus is sitting at his desk, a huge, impressive affair, looking smug as he says to someone who looks like Sam Donaldson, "Here's a photo of you without your wig. You're really bald, Sam. I'm going to show this photo to the world if you don't give me what I want."

Second panel: Sam Donaldson clearly isn't happy. He grabs the photo, says, "I'm not bald, Remus, and I don't wear a wig. This photo is a fake. You can't blackmail me."

Third panel: Remus is gloating. "Why don't you call Jessie Ventura? Just ask him what I did to him."

Fourth panel: Sam Donaldson, angry, defeated, says, "What do you want?"

Fifth panel: Remus says, "I want Cokie Roberts. You're going to fix it so I can have dinner with her. I want her and I'm going to have her."

Lily was grinning when she turned to see Simon Russo standing in the doorway.

He looked fit, healthy, and tanned. She felt suddenly puny and weak, still bowed over a bit. She wished he'd just go away, but she said, "Yes?"

"Sorry to bother you, but you should be in bed. I just spoke to Savich, and he said to check on you. He knew you wouldn't be following orders. You've got a strip nearly ready?"

"Yep. It's not the final version yet, but close. Remus is in fine form. He's blackmailing Sam Donaldson."

Simon wandered over to look down at the

panels. He laughed. "I've missed Remus, the amoral bastard. Glad to see him back."

"Now I've got to see if the *Washington Post* would like to take me and *Remus* in. Keep your fingers crossed that they'll agree. I won't get rich anytime soon, but it's a start."

Simon said after a moment, looking down at the *Remus* strip, "I know a cartoonist doesn't make much money until he or she is syndicated. Hey, I just happen to know Rick Bowes. He runs the desk. How about I give him a call, go to lunch, show him the strips?"

Lily didn't like it, obvious enough, so he didn't say anything more until she shook her head. "All right, then, you bring some of these strips to show him and I'll take you both to a Mexican restaurant."

"Well," she said, "maybe that would be okay."

"Will you take a nap now, Lily? You should take some of your meds, too."

Sean hollered from the nursery down the hall. They heard Gabriella telling him that if he'd just stop chewing his knuckles as well as hers, she'd get him a graham cracker and they'd go for a walk in the park. Sean let out one more yell, then burbled. Gabriella laughed. "Let's go get that cracker, champ."

Lily heard Sean cooing as Gabriella carried him down the hall. She tried to swallow the tears, but it just wasn't possible. She stood there, not making a sound, tears rolling down her cheeks.

Simon knew about tragedy, knew about the soul-deep pain that dulled over time but never went away. He didn't say a word, just very slowly pulled her against him and pressed her face to his shoulder.

When the phone rang a minute later, Lily pulled away, wouldn't look him straight in the eye, and answered it.

She handed it to him. "It's for you."

FOURTEEN

New York City

It was nearly ten o'clock Sunday night. Simon was back in New York and had just finished a hard workout at his gym. He felt both exhausted and energized, as always. He toweled off his face, wiped the sweat off the back machine, stretched, and headed for the showers. There were at least a dozen guys in the men's locker room, all in various stages of undress—cracking jokes, bragging about their dates, and complaining about injured body parts.

Simon stripped and nabbed the only free shower. It was late when he finally stepped out and grabbed up his towel. Only two guys were left, one of them blow-drying his hair, the other peeling a Band-Aid off his knee. Then, not three minutes later, they were gone. Simon had on his boxer shorts when the lights went out.

He grabbed for his pants. He remembered the circuit breaker was outside the men's locker room, right there on the left wall.

He heard something, a light whisper of sound. It was the last thing he remembered. The blow just over his right ear knocked him out cold. He fell flat to the locker room floor.

"Hey, man, wake up! Oh God, please, man, don't be dead. I'd lose my job for sure. Please, man, open your eyes!"

Simon cracked open an eye to see an acne-ridden face, a very young face that was scared to death, staring down at him. The young guy was shaking his shoulder.

"Yeah, yeah, I'm not dead. Stop shaking me." Simon raised his hand and felt the lump behind his right ear. The skin was broken, and he felt the smear of his own blood. He looked up at the kid and said, "Someone turned out the lights and hit me with something very hard."

"Oh, man," the kid said, "Mr. Duke is going to blame me for sure. I'm supposed to take care of this place, and I've only been here a week and he's going to fire me. I'm roadkill." He began wringing his hands, looking around wildly, as if expecting to see Mr. Duke, the manager, at any minute.

"The guy who hit me—I guess you didn't see him?"

"Nah, I didn't see any guy."

"All right. Don't worry, chances are he's long gone. Help me up, I've got to check my wallet." Once on his feet, Simon opened his locker door and reached for his ancient black bomber jacket that had seen its best days at MIT a dozen years before. His wallet was gone.

A robber trips the circuit breaker, then comes into the gym locker room to steal a wallet? He must have known only one guy was left, which meant that he'd had to look in, to check. A mugger in a men's locker room?

"Sorry, kid, but we should call the cops. Can't hurt. Just maybe they'll turn up something."

Simon canceled his credit cards while he waited for the cops to show up. The police, two young patrolmen, took a statement, looked around the gym and in the locker room, but—

Simon waited to call Savich until he was back at his brownstone on East Seventy-ninth Street.

Savich said, "What's happening?"

Simon said, "I had a bit of trouble just a while ago."

Savich said, "You leave my house this afternoon after you get a phone call, don't call me to tell me what's going on, and you're telling me you've already landed into trouble?"

"Yeah, that's about the size of it. Is Lily better?"

"Lily is indeed better, and she's pissed. She said tomorrow is Monday, her stitches are out in the morning, and she's coming up to New York, no matter what kind of excuses you try to pawn off on her."

"I'll have to think about that," Simon said.

"All right, tell me what happened."

After Simon had finished, Savich said, "Go to the hospital. Have a doctor check out your head."

"Nah, it's nothing, Savich, the skin's barely split. Don't worry about that. Thing is my wallet was taken, and I really don't know what to make of it all."

Savich said slowly, "You think some people know you're after my grandmother's paintings?"

"Could be. Thing is, when I got that phone call at your house, I wasn't exactly truthful with Lily. It wasn't an emergency with a client here in New York. It was from an art world weasel I do business with occasionally. I'd called him from your house earlier and he said he'd heard some things, too, and now he's put out some feelers for me on the Sarah Elliott paintings. He was expecting some solid results soon, would have something to show me, and he needed me up here in New York. I was supposed to meet him tonight, but he called earlier and said he didn't have everything together yet. So it's on for tomorrow night, at the Plaza Hotel, the Oak Room Bar, one of his favorite places. The guy's good, really knows what he's doing, so I'm hopeful."

"All right, sounds promising. Now, just in case you were wondering how good a liar you are, Lily didn't believe you for a minute. Your mugging, Simon, maybe it was just a mugging or maybe it was a warning. They didn't hurt you seriously, and they could have. I'll bet you a big one that your wallet is in a Dumpster somewhere near the gym. So take a look."

Simon could picture Savich pacing up and down that beautiful living room with its magnificent skylights.

"How's Sean?"

"Asleep."

"Is Lily asleep, too?"

"Nope. She's here, knows it's you on the phone, and wants to lay into you. I can't stop her from coming up, Simon."

Simon said, "Okay, give her my address, tell her to take a shuttle up here. I'll meet her unless there's a problem. I wish you could keep her with you longer, Savich."

"No can do."

Simon said, "I changed my mind, Savich. It may be turning dangerous, real fast. I really don't want Lily involved in this. She's a civilian.

For God's sake, she's your sister. I take it all back. Tie her to a chair; don't let her come up here."

"Do you happen to have any suggestions about what I should do, other than tying her up?"

"Put her on the phone. I want to talk to her."

"Sure. She's about to rip the phone away from me in any case. Good luck, Simon."

A moment later, Lily said, "I'm here. I don't care what you have to say. Just be quiet, go to the hospital, get a good night's sleep, and meet my plane tomorrow. I'll take the two-o'clock United shuttle to JFK. Then we can handle things. Good night, Simon."

"But Lily—"

She was gone.

Then Savich's voice came on. "Simon?"

"Yeah, Savich. Well, I'd have to say it was a nonstarter."

Savich laughed. "Lily's my sister. She's smart, and they are her paintings. Let her help with it, Simon, but keep her safe."

Simon bowed to the inevitable. "I'll try."

He took two aspirins and went back to his gym. There was a Dumpster half a block away. Lying on the top was his wallet, with only the cash gone. He looked up to see two young guys staring at him.

When one of them yelled an obscenity at him, Simon started forward. They didn't waste time and swaggered away, then turned when they figured they were far enough away from him and gave him the finger.

Simon smiled and waved.

● He was waiting for her, standing right in front of the gate, arms crossed, looking pissed.

Lily smiled, said even before she got to him, "I didn't want to carry much because of my missing spleen. I've got a bag down on carousel four."

"I've decided you're going back to Washington to draw your cartoons."

"While you find my paintings? Doesn't look like you started out very well, Mr. Russo. You don't look so hot. I think I did better on that bus than you did in your men's locker room last night. And I want to find my grandmother's paintings worse than you do."

And she walked past him to follow the signs to Baggage Claim.

Simon didn't own a car, had never felt the need to, so they took a taxi to East Seventy-ninth, between First and Second. He assisted her out of the cab, took her purse and suitcase, grunted because it had to weigh seventy pounds, and said, "This is it. I've got a nice guest room with its own bath. You should be comfortable until you wise up and go back home. How are they doing on that cult case in Texas? They got him yet? Wilbur Wright?"

"Not yet. What Dillon does is feed all the pertinent information into protocols he developed for the CAU—Criminal Apprehension Unit. Put that eyebrow back down. So you already know what he does and how he does it."

"I should have asked, has MAX got Wilbur yet?"

"MAX found out that Wilbur Wright is Canadian, that he attended McGill University, that he's a real whiz at cellular biology, and that his real name is Anthony Carpelli—ancestry, Sicily. Oh my, Simon, this is very lovely."

Lily stepped into a beautifully marbled entryway, and felt like she'd stepped back into the 1930s. The feel was all Art Deco—rich dark wood paneling, lamps in geometric shapes, a rich Tabriz carpet on the floor, furniture right out of the Poirot series on PBS.

"I bought it four years ago, after I got a really healthy commission. I knew the old guy who'd owned it for well nigh on to fifty years, and he gave me a good deal. Most of the furnishings were his. I begged and he finally sold me most of them. Neat, huh?"

"Very," she said, a vast understatement. "I want to see everything."

There was even a small library, bookshelves to the ceiling with one of those special library ladders. Wainscoting, leather furniture, rich Persian carpets on the dark walnut floor. He didn't show her his bedroom, but guided her directly to a large bedroom at the end of the hall. All of the furniture was a rich Italian Art Deco, trimmed with glossy black lacquer. Posters from the 1930s covered the walls. He put her suitcase on the bed and turned. She said, shaking her head, "You are so modern, yet here you are in this museum of a place that actually looks lived in. This is a beautiful room."

"Wait till you see the bathroom."

He didn't tell her that he was leaving until he had the key in his hand that evening at 10:30.

"I'm meeting a guy with information. No, you're not coming with me."

"All right."

He distrusted her, she could see it, and she just smiled. "Look, Simon, I'm not lying. I'm not going to sneak out after you and follow you like some sort of idiot. I'm really tired. You can go hear what your informant has to say. Just be careful. When you get back, I'll still be awake. Tell me what you find out, okay?"

He nodded and was at the Plaza Hotel by ten minutes to eleven.

LouLou was there, pacing back and forth along the park side of the Plaza, beautifully dressed, looking like a Mafia don. The uniformed Plaza doormen paid him little attention.

He nodded to Simon, motioned to the entrance to the Plaza's Oak Room Bar. It was dark and rich, filled with people and conversation. They found a small table, ordered two beers. Simon leaned back, crossing his arms over his chest. "How's it going, LouLou?"

"Can't complain. Hey, this beer on you? Drinks aren't cheap here, you know?"

"Since we're in New York, I figured the Oak Room would be our venue. Yeah, I'm paying for the beer. Now, what have you got for me?"

"I found out that Abe Turkle did the Elliotts. Talk is he had a contract to do eight of them. Do you know anything about which eight?"

"Yeah, I do, but you don't need to know any more. I would have visited Abe Turkle second. You sure it's not Billy Gross?"

"He's sick—his lungs—probably cancer. He's always smoked way too much. Anyway, he took all his money and went off to Italy. He's down living on the Amalfi Coast, nearly dead. So it's Abe who's your guy."

"And where can I find him?"

"In California, of all places."

"Eureka, by any chance?"

"Don't know. He's in a little town called Hemlock Bay, on the ocean. Don't know where it is. Whoever's paying him wants him close by where he is."

"You're good, LouLou. I don't suppose you'll tell me where you heard this?"

"You know better, Simon." He drank the rest of his beer in one long pull, wiped his mouth gently on a napkin, then said, "Abe's a mean sucker, Simon, unlike most artists. When you hook up with him, you take care, okay?"

"Yeah, I'll be real careful. Any word at all on who our likely collectors are?"

LouLou fiddled with a cigarette he couldn't light, even here in a bar, for God's sake. "Word is that it just might be Olaf Jorgenson."

This was a surprise, a big surprise, to Simon. He wouldn't have put Olaf in the mix. "The richest Swede alive, huge in shipping. But I heard that he's nearly blind, nearly dead, that his collecting days are over."

LouLou said, "Yeah, that's the word out. Why buy a painting if you're blind as a bat and can't even see it? But, hey, that's what I heard from my inside gal at the Met. She's one of the curators, has an ear that soaks up everything. She's been right before. I trust her information."

"Olaf Jorgenson," Simon said slowly, taking a pull on his Coors. "He's got to be well past eighty now. Been collecting mainly European art for the past fifty years, medieval up through the nineteenth century. After World War Two, I heard he got his hands on a couple of private collections of stolen art from France and Italy. Far as I know, he's never bought a piece of art legally in his life. The guy's certifiable about his art, has all his paintings in climate-controlled vaults, and he's the only one who's got the key. I didn't know he'd begun collecting modern painters, like Sarah Elliott. I never would have put him on my list."

LouLou shrugged. "Like you said, Simon, the guy's a nut. Maybe nuts crack different ways when they get up near the century mark. His son seems to be just as crazy, always out on his yacht, lives there most of the time. His name's Ian—the old guy married a Scotswoman and that's how he got his name. Anyway, the son now runs all the shipping business. From the damned yacht."

Simon gave a very slight shake of his head to a very pretty woman seated at the bar who'd been staring at him for the past couple of minutes. He moved closer to LouLou to show that he was in very heavy conversation and not interested. "LouLou, how sure are you that it's Olaf who bought the paintings?"

"Besides my gal at the Met, I went out of my way to get it verified. You know my little art world birdies that are always singing, Simon. I spread a little seed, and they sing louder and I heard three songs, all with the same words. One hundred percent? Nope, but it's a start. Cost me a cool thousand bucks to get them to sing to me."

"Okay, you done good, LouLou." Simon handed him an envelope that contained five thousand dollars. LouLou didn't count it, just slipped the fat envelope inside his cashmere jacket pocket. "Hey, you know what the name of Ian Jorgenson's yacht is?"

Simon shook his head.

"Night Watch."

Simon said slowly, "That's the name of a painting by Rembrandt. That particular painting is hanging in the Rijksmuseum in Amsterdam. I saw it there a couple of years ago."

LouLou cocked his head to one side, his hairpiece not moving a bit because it was expensive and well made, and gave Simon a cynical smile. "Who knows? Just maybe *Night Watch* is hanging in Ian's stateroom, right over his bed. I've often wondered how many real paintings there are left in the museums and not beautifully executed fakes."

"Actually, LouLou, I don't want to know the answer to that question."

"Since Sarah Elliott just died some seven years ago, all her materials—the paints, the brushes—still exist. You take a superb talent with an inherent bent toward her sort of technique and visualization, and what you get is so close to the real thing, most people wouldn't even care if you told them."

"I hate that."

"I do, too," LouLou said. "I need another beer."

Simon ordered them another round, ate a couple of peanuts out of the bowl on their table, and said, "Remember that forger Eric Hebborn, who wrote that book telling would-be forgers exactly how to do it—what inks, papers, pens, colors, signatures, all of it? Then he up and dies in ninety-six. The cops said it was under mysterious circumstances. I heard it was a private collector who killed Hebborn because a dealer friend had sold him an original Rubens that turned out to be a fake that Hebborn himself had done. Supposedly the dealer died shortly thereafter in a car accident."

LouLou said, "Yeah, I met old Eric back in the early eighties. Smart as a whip, that guy, and so talented it made you cry. You wondering if it was Olaf Jorgenson who popped him? Hey, Simon, there's a whole bunch of collectors who'd cut off hands to have a certain medal or stamp or train or painting. They've got to have it or life loses its meaning for them. Look, Simon, when you get down to it, they're the people who keep us in business."

"I wonder if Olaf ordered all eight paintings. I wonder what he's paying for them."

"Huge bucks, my man, huge, count on it. All eight Sarah Elliotts? Don't know. I haven't heard any other names floated around. Simon, I heard those eight paintings are owned privately by a member of the Elliott family?"

"Yes, Lily Savich owns them. And therein lies a very long, convoluted tale." Simon rose, putting a fifty-dollar bill on the table. "LouLou, thank you. You know where to find me. I think I'll be heading out to California soon to track down one of the major players—Abraham Turkle. He's English, right?"

"Half Greek. Weird guy. Very eccentric, said to eat only snails that he raises himself." LouLou shuddered. "You take care around him, Simon. Abe killed a guy who tried to rip him off with his bare hands, just a couple of years ago. So have a care. Hey, this Lily Savich hire you?"

Simon paused, cocked his head to the side.

"Not exactly, but that's about it. I want to get those four paintings back."

"I hope the others are safe."

"Much safer than the snails in Abe's garden. Take care, LouLou."

"Why are you going after Abe?"

Simon said, "I want to see if I can shake something loose. It's not just the art scam. There are other folk involved in this deal who have done very bad things, and I want to nail them. Just maybe Abe can help me do that."

"He won't help you do squat."

"We'll see. His forging days in Hemlock Bay are over. I want to catch him before he takes off to parts unknown. Who knows what I can get out of him."

"Good luck shaking the wasp nest. You know, I've always liked the name Lily," LouLou said and gave Simon a small salute. Then, when Simon left, LouLou turned his attention to that very pretty lady at the bar who'd kept looking over at them.

FIFTEEN

Quantico

Dr. Hicks said quietly, "Marilyn, tell me, how did Tammy look when she came back to the motel?"

"She had on a coat and she just ripped it apart and showed me her nurse's uniform. It was soaked with blood."

"Did she seem pleased?"

"Oh yes. She was crazy happy that she got away. She just kept laughing and rubbing her bloody hands together. She loves the feel of fresh blood on her hands."

"How did she get back to the motel? You said her hands were all bloody. Wouldn't somebody have noticed?"

"I don't know." Marilyn looked worried, shaking her head just a bit.

"No, no, that's okay. It's not important. Now, you said she was wearing a coat. Do you know where she got the coat?"

"I don't know. When she came to get me, she was wearing it. It was too big for her, but it covered her arm where she didn't have one, you know?"

"Yes, I know. Mr. Savich would like to ask you some questions now. Is that all right, Marilyn?"

"Yes. He was nice to me. He's sexy. I'm kinda sorry that Tammy's gonna kill him."

Dr. Hicks raised a thick brow at Savich, no look of shock on his face since he'd heard it all. He just shook his head as Savich eased his chair nearer to Marilyn's.

"She's well under, Savich. You know what to do."

Savich nodded, said, "Marilyn, how are you feeling about Tammy right now?"

She was silent, her forehead creased in a frown, then she shook her head and said slowly, "I think I love her; I'm supposed to since she's my cousin, but she scares me. I never know what she's going to do. I think she'd kill me, laugh while she rubbed my blood all over her hands, if she was in the mood, you know?"

"Yes, I know."

"She's going to kill you."

"Yes, she might try, you told me. How do you think she contacts the Ghouls?" Savich ignored Dr. Hicks, who didn't have a clue who or what the Ghouls were. He just shook his head and repeated the question. "Marilyn?"

"I've thought about that, Mr. Savich. I know they were there when she killed that little boy. Maybe, from what she said, she just thinks about them and they come. Or maybe they follow her around and she just says that to prove how powerful she is. Do you know what the Ghouls are?"

"No, I don't have any idea, Marilyn. You don't either, do you?"

She shook her head. She was sitting in a comfortable chair, her head leaning back against the cushion, her eyes closed. She'd been staying in a room at the Jefferson dormitory at the FBI complex, watched over by female agents. She'd washed her hair, and they'd given her a clean skirt and sweater. Even hypnotized, she looked pale and frightened, her fingers continually twitching and jerking. He wondered what would happen to her. She had no other family, no education to speak of, and there was Tammy, in the Caribbean, who'd scared her all of her life. He hoped the FBI would find her soon and Marilyn wouldn't have to be scared of her anymore.

He said, "Has Tammy been to the Caribbean before?"

"Yeah. She and Tommy visited the Bahamas a couple years ago. In the spring, I think."

"Did they take the Ghouls with them?"

Marilyn frowned and shook her head.

"You don't know if they killed anyone while they were there?"

"I asked Tommy, and he just laughed and laughed. That was right before he got me pregnant."

Savich made a note to check to see if there'd been any particularly vicious, unsolved killings during their stay.

"Has Tammy ever talked about the Caribbean, other than the Bahamas? Any islands that she'd like to visit?"

She shook her head.

"Think, Marilyn. That's right, just relax, lean your head back, and think about that. Remember back over the times you've seen her."

There was a long silence, and then Marilyn said, "She said once—it was Halloween and she was dressed like a vampire—that she wanted to go to Barbados and scare the crap out of the kids there. Then she laughed. I never liked that laugh, Mr. Savich. It was the same kind of laugh that Tommy had after the Bahamas."

"Did she ever talk about what the Ghouls did to those kids?"

"Once, when she was being Timmy, she said they just gobbled them right up."

"But the Ghouls don't just gobble them up, do they? They maybe take an arm, a leg?"

"Oh, Mr. Savich, they just do that when they're full and aren't interested in anything but a taste. But I can't be sure because both Tommy and Tammy never really told me."

Savich felt sick. Jesus, did she really mean what he thought she meant? That there were young boys who'd simply disappeared and would never be found because the Tuttles had eaten them? Were they cannibals? He unconsciously rubbed his arms at a sudden chill he felt.

He looked over at Dr. Hicks. His face was red, and he looked ready to be ill himself.

Savich lightly touched her forearm and said, "Thank you, Marilyn, you've been a big help. If you could choose, right now, what would you like to do with your life?"

She didn't hesitate for a second. "I want to be a carpenter. We lived for about five years in this one place and the neighbor was a carpenter. He built desks and tables and chairs, all sorts of stuff. He spent lots of time with me, taught me everything. 'Course I paid him just like he wanted, and he liked that a lot. In high school they told me I was a girl and girls couldn't do that, and then Tommy got me pregnant and killed the baby."

"Just one more question. Was Tammy planning to contact you from the Caribbean?" He'd asked her this before. He wanted to see if she added anything under hypnosis because now he had a plan.

"Yeah. She didn't say when, just that she would, sometime."

"How would she find you?"

"She would call my boyfriend, Tony, up in Bar Harbor. I don't think he likes me anymore. He said if the cops were after me, then he was out of there."

Savich hoped that Tony wouldn't take off too soon. He was still there, working as a mechanic at Ed's European Motors. He'd check in again with the agents in Bar Harbor, keep an eye on him, maybe some wiretaps. Now they had something solid. A call from Tammy.

"Thank you, Marilyn." Savich rose and went to stand by the door. He watched as Dr. Hicks brought her gently back. He listened as he spoke quietly to her, reassuring her, until he nodded to Savich and led her from the room, holding her shoulder.

Savich said, "It's time for lunch, Marilyn. We'll eat in the Boardroom, not the big cafeteria. It's just down the hall on this floor."

"I'd really like a pizza, Mr. Savich, with lots of pepperoni."

"You've got it. The Boardroom is known for its pizza."

Eureka, California

Simon was pissed. He'd sent Lily back to Washington. She'd been as pissed as he was now, but she'd finally given up, seen reason, and slid her butt into the taxi he'd called for her. Only she hadn't gone back to Washington. She'd simply taken the same plane he had to San Francisco, keeping out of sight in the back, then managed to make an earlier connection from San Francisco to Arcata-Eureka Airport. She'd waltzed right up to him at the damned baggage carousel and said in a chirpy voice, "I never thought I'd be traveling back to Hemlock Bay only two weeks after I finally managed to escape it."

And now they were sitting side by side in a rental car, and Simon was still pissed.

"You shouldn't have pulled that little sneaking act, Lily. Some bad stuff could happen.

We're in their neck of the woods again, and I—"

"We're in this together, Russo, don't forget it," she said. She gave him a long look, then glanced out the back window of their rental car to study the three cars behind them. None appeared to be following them. She said, "You're acting like I've cut off your ego. This isn't your show, Russo. They're my paintings. Back off."

"I promised your brother I wouldn't let you get hurt."

"Fine. Okay, keep your promise. Where are we going? I was thinking it would be to Abe Turkle. You said maybe you could get something out of him, not about the collector he was working for, but maybe about the Frasiers. Since he's here, that pretty well proves he's involved with them, doesn't it?"

"That's right."

"You said Abraham Turkle is staying in a beach house just up the coast from Hemlock Bay. Do we know who owns it? Don't tell me it's my soon-to-be-ex-husband."

Simon gave it up. He turned to her as he said, "No, it's not Tennyson Frasier. It's close, but no, the cottage is in Daddy Frasier's name."

"Why didn't you tell me that sooner? That really nails it, doesn't it? Isn't that enough proof?"

"Not yet. Just be patient. Everything will come together. Highway 211 is a very gnarly road, just like you told me. Are we going to be passing the place where you lost your brakes and plowed into that redwood?"

"Yes, just ahead." But Lily didn't look at the tree as they passed it. The events of that night were growing more faint, the terror fading a bit, but it was still too close to her.

Simon said, "Turns out that Abraham Turkle has no bank account, no visible means of support. So the Frasiers must be paying him in cash."

"I still can't get over their going to all this trouble," Lily said.

"After we verify that Mr. Olaf Jorgenson of Sweden now has three in his possession—no, we want him to have all four of the paintings, it'd keep things simple—we may be able to find out how much he's paid for them. I'm thinking in the neighborhood of two to three million per painting. Maybe higher. Depends on how obsessed he is. From what I hear, he's single-minded when he wants a certain painting."

"Three million? That's a whole lot of money. But to go to all this trouble—"

"I can tell you stories you don't want to hear about how far some collectors will go. There was one German guy who collected rare stamps. He found out that his mother had one that he'd wanted for years, only she wanted to keep it for herself. He hit her over the head with a large bag of coins, killed her. Does that give you an idea of how completely obsessed some of these folk are?"

Lily could only stare at him. "It's just hard to believe. This Olaf Jorgenson—you told me he's very old and nearly blind in the bargain."

"It is amazing that he can't control his obsession, not even for something as incidental as, say, going blind. I guess it won't stop until he's dead."

"Do you think his son Ian has the real *Night Watch* aboard his yacht?"

"I wouldn't be at all surprised."

"Are you going to tell the people at the Rijksmuseum?"

"Yeah, but trust me on this, they won't want to hear it. They'll have a couple of experts examine the painting on the sly. If the experts agree that it's a forgery, they'll try to get it back, but will they announce it? Doubtful.

"We've been checking out Mr. Monk, the curator of the Eureka Art Museum. He does have a Ph.D. from George Washington, and a pedigree as long as your arm. If something's off there, Savich hasn't found it yet. We're going deeper on that, got some feelers out to a couple

of museums where he worked. You keep looking back there. Is anyone following us?"

Lily shifted in her seat to face his profile.
"No, no one's back there. I can't help it. To me,
this is enemy territory."

"You're entitled. You had a very bad experience here. You met Mr. Monk, didn't you?"

"Oh yes."

"Tell me about him."

Lily said slowly, "When I first met Mr. Monk,
I thought he had the most intense black eyes,
quite beautiful really, 'bedroom eyes' I guess
you could call them. But he looked hungry.
Isn't that odd?"

Simon said, "He has beautiful eyes? Bedroom
eyes? You women think and say the strangest
things."

"Like men don't? If it were Mrs. Monk,
you'd probably go on about her cleavage."

"Well, yeah, maybe. And your point would
be?"

"You'd probably never even get to her face.
You men are all one-celled."

"You think? Really?"

She laughed, she just couldn't help it. He
pushed his sunglasses up his nose, and she saw
that he was grinning at her. He said with a good
deal of satisfaction, "You're feeling better.
You've got a nice laugh, Lily. I like hearing it.

Mind you, I'm still mad because you followed me out here, but I will admit that this is the first time I've seen you that you don't look like you want to curl up and take a long nap."

"Get over it, Simon. We must be nearly to Abraham Turkle's cottage. Just up ahead, Highway 211 turns left to go to Hemlock Bay. To the right there's this asphalt one-lane track that goes the mile out to the ocean. That's where the cottage is?"

"Yes, those were my directions. You've never been out to the ocean on that road?"

"I don't think so," she said.

"Okay now, listen up. Abe has a bad reputation. He's got a real mean side, so we want to be careful with him."

They came to the fork. Simon turned right, onto the narrow asphalt road. "This is it," Simon said. "There's no sign and there's no other road. Let's try it."

The ocean came into view almost immediately, when they were just atop a slight rise. Blue and calm as far as you could see, white clouds dotting the sky, a perfect day.

"Look at this view," Lily said. "I always get a catch in my throat when I see the ocean."

They reached the end of the road very quickly. Abe Turkle's cottage was a small gray clapboard, weathered, perched right at the end of a promontory towering out over the ocean. There were two hemlock trees, one on either side of the cottage, just a bit protected from the fierce ocean storms. They were so gnarly and bent, though, that you wondered why they even bothered to continue standing.

There was no road, just a dirt driveway that forked off the narrow asphalt. In front of the cottage was a black Kawasaki 650 motorcycle.

Simon switched off the ignition and turned to Lily. She held up both hands. "No, don't say it. I'm coming with you. I can't wait to meet Abe Turkle."

Simon said as he came around to open her car door, "Abe only eats snails and he grows them himself."

"I'm still coming in with you."

She carefully removed the seat belt, laid the small pillow on the backseat, and took his hand. "Stop looking like I'm going to fall over. I'm better every day. It's just that getting out of a car is still a little rough." He watched her swing her legs over and straighten, slowly.

Simon said, "I want you to follow my lead. No reason to let him know who we are just yet."

When he reached the single door, so weathered it had nearly lost all its gray paint, he listened for a moment. "I don't hear any movement inside."

He knocked.

There was no answer at first, and then a furious yell. "Who the hell is that and what the hell do you want?"

"The artist is apparently home," Simon said, cocking a dark eyebrow at Lily, and opened the door. He kept her behind him and walked into the cottage to see Abraham Turkle, a brush between his teeth, another brush in his right hand, standing behind an easel, glaring over the top toward them.

There was no furniture in the small front room, just painting supplies everywhere, at least twenty canvases stacked against the walls. The place smelled of paint and turpentine and french fries and something else—maybe fried snails. There was a kitchen separated from the living room by a bar, and a small hallway that probably led to a bedroom and a bathroom.

The man, face bearded, was indeed Abe Turkle; Simon had seen many photos of him.

"Hi," Simon said and stuck out his hand.

Abe Turkle ignored the outstretched hand. "Who the hell are you? Who is she? Why the hell is she standing behind you? She afraid of me or something?"

Lily stepped around Simon and said, extending her hand, "I like snails. I hear you do, too."

Abraham Turkle smiled, a huge smile that

showed off three gold back teeth. He had big shoulders and hands the size of boxing gloves. He didn't look at all like an artist, whatever that was, Simon thought. A painter was supposed to wear paint-encrusted black pants, long hair fastened in a thong at the back of the neck. Instead, Abraham Turkle looked like a lumberjack. He was wearing a flannel shirt and blue jeans and big boots that were laced halfway to his knees. There were, however, paint splotches all over him, including his tangled dark beard and grizzled hair.

"So," Abe said, and he put down the brushes, wiped the back of his hand over his mouth to get off the bit of turpentine, and shook Lily's hand. "The little gal here likes snails, which means she knows about me, but I don't know who the hell you are, fella."

"I'm Sully Jones, and this is my wife, Zelda. We're on our honeymoon, just meandering up the coast, and we heard in Hemlock Bay that you were an artist and that you liked snails. Zelda loves art and snails, and we thought we'd stop by and see if you had anything to sell."

Lily said, "We don't know yet if we like what you paint, Mr. Turkle, but could you show us something? I hope you're not too expensive."

Abraham Turkle said, "Yep, I'm real expensive. You guys aren't rich?"

Simon said, "I'm in used cars. I'm not really rich."

"Sorry, you won't want to buy any of my stuff."

Simon started to push it, then saw that Lily looked on the shaky side. Simon nodded to Abe Turkle and just looked at him.

"Wait here." Abe Turkle picked up a towel and wiped his hands. Then he walked past them to the far wall, where there were about ten canvases piled together. He went through them, making a rude noise here, sighing there, and then he thrust a painting into Lily's hand. "Here, it's a little thing I did just the other day. It's the Old Town in Eureka. For your honeymoon, little gal."

Lily held the small canvas up to the light and stared at it. She said finally, "Why, thank you, Mr. Turkle. It's beautiful. You're a very fine artist."

"One of the best in the world actually."

Simon frowned. "I'm sure sorry we haven't heard of you."

"You're a used-car salesman. Why would you have heard of me?"

"I was an art history major," Lily said. "I'm sorry, but I haven't heard of you either. But I can see how talented you are, sir."

"Well, just maybe I'm more famous with certain people than with the common public."

"What does that mean?" Simon asked.

Abe's big chest expanded even bigger. "It means, used-car salesman, that I reproduce great paintings for a living. Only the artists themselves would realize they hadn't painted them."

"I don't understand," Lily said.

"It ain't so hard if you think about it. I reproduce paintings for very rich people."

Simon looked astonished. "You mean you forge famous paintings?"

"Hey, I don't like that word. What do you know, fella, you're nothing but a punk who sells heaps of metal; the lady could do a lot better than you."

"No, you misunderstand me," Simon said. "To be able to paint like you do, for whatever purpose, I'm really impressed."

"Just hold it," Abe said suddenly and pulled at his ponytail. "Yeah, just wait a minute. You aren't a used-car salesman, are you? What's your deal, man? Come on, what's going on here?"

"I'm Simon Russo."

That brought Abe to a stop. "Yeah, I recognize you now. Dammit, you're that dealer guy . . . Russo, yeah, you're him. You're Simon

Russo, you son of a bitch. You'd better not be here to cause me any trouble. What the hell are you doing here?"

"Mr. Turkle, we—"

"Dammit, give me back that painting! You aren't on any honeymoon now, are you? You lied to me. As for you, Russo, I'm going to have to wring your scrawny neck."

SIXTEEN

Lily didn't think, just assumed a martial arts position that Dillon had shown her, the painting still clutched in her right hand.

She looked both ridiculous and defiant, and it stopped Abe Turkle in his tracks. He stared at her. "You want to fight me? You going to try to karate chop me with my own painting?"

She moved back and forth, flexed her arms, her fists. "I won't hurt your bloody painting. Listen, pal, I don't want to fight you, but I can probably take you. Yes, I can take you. You're big but I'll bet you're slow. So go ahead, if you want, let's just see how tough you are."

"Lily, please don't," Simon said as he prepared to simply lift her beneath her armpits and move her behind him. To Simon's surprise, Abe Turkle began shaking his head. He laughed, and then he laughed some more.

"Jesus, you're something, little lady."

Abe made to grab the painting from Lily's hand, and she said quickly, whipping it behind her back, "Please let me keep it, Mr. Turkle. It really is beautiful. I'll treasure it always."

"Oh, hell, keep the stupid thing. I don't want to fight you either. It's obvious to me that you're real tough. Hell, I might never get over being scared of you. All right, now. Let's just get it over with. What do you want, Simon Russo? And who is the little gal here?"

"I'm just here to see which Sarah Elliott you're working on now."

Abe Turkle glanced back at his easel, and his face blotched red as he said, "Listen to me, Russo, I barely heard of the broad. You want to look?"

"Okay." Simon smiled and walked toward Abe.

Abe held up a huge hand still stained with daubs of red, gold, and white paint. "You try it and I'll break your head off at your neck. Even the little lady here won't be able to hold me off."

Simon stopped. "Okay. Since there were no paintings missing from the Eureka Art Museum, you must be having trouble working from photographs they brought to you. Which one is it? Maybe *The Maiden Voyage* or *Wheat*

Field? If I were selecting the next one, it would be either of those two."

"Go to hell, boyo."

"Or maybe you had to stop with the Sarah Elliotts altogether now that they're gone from the museum? So you're doing something else now?"

"I'd break your head for you right this minute, right here, but not with my new stuff around. You want to come outside?"

"You were right about the lady," Simon said. "She isn't my wife. She's Lily Savich, Sarah Elliott's granddaughter. The eight paintings that were in the museum, including the four you've already copied, belong to her."

"Are you finishing a fifth one, Mr. Turkle? If you are, it's too bad because you won't get paid for it. The real one is back in my possession so there won't be any chance to switch it."

Simon said, "Actually, I'm surprised you're still here in residence since the paintings have flown the coop. They're hoping they'll get them back? No chance.

"To be honest, Abe, the real reason we're here is that we want to know who commissioned you. Not the collector, but the local people who are paying you and keeping you here."

"Yes," Lily said. "Please, Mr. Turkle, tell us who set this up."

Abe Turkle gave a big sigh. He looked at Lily and his fierce expression softened, just a bit. "Little gal, why don't you marry me and then I could look at those paintings for the rest of my life. I swear I'd never forge anything again."

"I'm sorry, but I'm still married to Tennyson Frasier."

"Not for long. I heard all about how you just walked out on him."

"That's right. But even so, the paintings belong in a museum, Mr. Turkle, not in a private collection somewhere, locked away, to be enjoyed by only one person."

"They're the ones with all the money. They call the shots."

Simon said, "Abe, she's divorcing Tennyson. She wants to fry that bastard's butt, not yours. You'd do yourself a favor if you helped us."

Abe said slowly, one eyebrow arched up a good inch, "You've got to be joking, boyo."

Lily stepped forward and laid her hand on Abe Turkle's massive shoulder. "We're not joking. You could be in danger. Listen, Tennyson tried to kill me, and I wondered, Why now? Do you know? Did something happen to make him realize that I was a threat to him, before you'd finished copying all the paintings? Please,

Mr. Turkle, tell us who hired you to copy my paintings. We'll help you stay safe."

"That really so? Your old man tried to kill you? I'm sorry about that, but I don't have a clue what you're talking about. Both of you need to just get out of here now."

He was standing with his legs spread, his big arms crossed over his chest. "I'm sorry you were almost killed, but it doesn't have anything to do with me."

"We know," Simon said, "that this cottage is owned by the Frasiers. You're staying here. It isn't a stretch to figure it out."

"I don't have anything to say about that. Maybe when this is over, the little gal will share some lunch with me, I'll marinate up some snails, then broil them. That's the best, you know."

Lily shook her head, then walked to the easel. Abe didn't get in her way, didn't try to block her. She stopped and sucked in her breath. On the easel was a magnificent painting nearly finished—it was Diego Velázquez's *Toilet of Venus,* oil on canvas.

"It's incredible. Please, Mr. Turkle, don't let some collector take the original. Please."

Abe shrugged. "I'm just painting that for the fun of it. I'm in between jobs right now. No, you don't want to say that it's because you took all the Sarah Elliott paintings away from the museum. Nah, don't say that. There's nothing going on here so I'm just having me some fun."

Simon came around and looked at the nearly completed painting. "The original is in the National Gallery in London. I hope your compatriots elect to leave it there, Abe."

"Like I said, this is just for fun. A guy's got to keep practicing, you know what I mean? Look, I painted this from a series of photos. If I were in it for bucks, I wouldn't have let her see it. I'd be in London, too."

Lily couldn't give up, not yet. "Won't you just tell us the truth, Mr. Turkle? Tennyson Frasier married me only to get his hands on the paintings. Then he tried to kill me. Did he tell you that, Mr. Turkle? It's possible that he murdered my child as well, I don't know for sure. Please, we won't involve you. Just tell us."

Abe Turkle looked back and forth between the two of them. He slowly shook his head.

"I wish you hadn't found me, Russo," Abe Turkle said, shaking his big head. "I really wish you hadn't." He turned then and walked out the cottage door.

"Wait!" Lily started after him.

Simon grabbed her sleeve and pulled her back. "Let him go, Lily."

They watched from the doorway as the big,

black Kawasaki scattered rocks and dirt as it picked up speed. Then he was gone.

"We screwed up," Simon said.

"I wish he'd stayed and fought me," Lily said.

Simon looked down at her, remembering the image of her in a fighting position, with that painting in her right hand. He grinned. He lightly touched his hand to her hair. "You're all blond and blue-eyed, you're skinny as a post, your pants are hanging off your butt, and knowing you for just a short time, I know you've got more guts than brains. I swear to you, when I tell Savich how his little sister was ready to take on Abe Turkle, he'll . . . No, better not tell him how I nearly got you into a fight. Well, shit."

Lily punched him in the gut. "You jerk. I didn't see you trying to do anything."

Simon grunted, rubbed his palm over his belly, and grinned down at her. "I hope you didn't pull anything loose when you hit me. Not in me, in you."

"I might have, no thanks to you."

She didn't speak to him until they were back in the car and headed down to Hemlock Bay.

"We're going to see Tennyson?"

"Nope, we've got other fish to fry."

Washington, D.C.
The Hoover Building
Fifth Floor, The Criminal
Apprehension Unit

It was one o'clock in the afternoon. Empty sandwich wrappers were strewn on the conference table, leaving the vague smell of tuna fish with an overlay of roast beef, and at least a dozen soda cans stood empty. They'd just finished their daily update meeting. Savich's second in charge, Ollie Hamish, said to the assembled agents around the CAU conference table, "I'm going to be going to Kitty Hawk, North Carolina, in the morning. Our research says that he not only took the real Wilbur's name, he's spent a lot of time in Wright's hometown. Chances are, though, that he's not going to Dayton, since everyone's looking for him there, but to Kitty Hawk. I've gotten all the data over to Behavioral Sciences, to Jane Bitt. We'll see what she's got to add, but that's it, so far.

"I'm going to our office down there, fill them all in, and get things set up for when he turns up."

Savich nodded. "Sounds good, Ollie. No more supposed sightings of the guru in Texas?"

"Oh, yeah," Ollie said, "but we're letting the

agents there deal with them. Our people here believe guru Wilbur is already heading across country, due east to North Carolina. Our offices across the South are all alerted. Maybe we can get him before he hits Kitty Hawk. It might be that Kitty Hawk will be his last stand. We don't want him to bring real havoc when he gets there. We'll see if Jane Bitt agrees."

Sherlock said, "Have we got photos?"

"The only photo we've got is old and fuzzy, unfortunately. We're looking at getting more."

Special Agent Dane Carver, newly assigned to the unit, said, "Why don't you give me the photo, Ollie, and let me work on it. Maybe we can clean it up in the lab."

"You got it."

Savich looked around the conference table. "Everyone on track now?"

There were grunts, nods, and groans.

Millie, the CAU secretary, said, "What about Tammy, Dillon? Any sightings? Any word at all yet?"

"Not a thing as yet. It's only been a day since I spoke to Marilyn Warluski at Quantico. Our people are staying with Tony, Marilyn's boyfriend, in Bar Harbor. His phone's covered. If Tammy calls, we'll hear it all. He's cooperating." Savich paused a moment, then shrugged. "It's frustrating. She's not in good shape, yet no one's seen her. Chances are very good that she did indeed murder a pharmacist in Souterville, New Jersey. The other pharmacist checked and said someone had rifled through the supplies. Vicodin, a medication to control moderate pain, and Keflex, an oral antibiotic, a good three or four days' supply, were missing. Evidently she killed the guy because he refused to give her anything.

"As you know, we alerted police on all islands to Tammy's possible presence. Now they also know to keep a close eye on doctors and pharmacies, and why."

Ollie said, sitting forward, his hands clasped, "Look, Savich, she threatened you. I read you the note. She means it. We've all been talking about it, and we think you should have some protection. We think Jimmy Maitland should assign you some guards."

Savich thought about it a minute, then looked down the table to Sherlock. He realized that she was thinking about Tammy finding out where they lived and coming to the house. She was thinking about Sean. He said to Ollie, "I think that's a great idea. I'll speak to Mr. Maitland this afternoon. Thanks, Ollie, I really hadn't thought it through."

He called a halt, scheduled a meeting with his boss, Jimmy Maitland, within the hour, and kissed Sherlock behind a door. Then he went to his office and punched in Simon's cell phone.

Simon answered on the third ring. "Yo."

"Savich here. Is Lily all right? What's going on?"

"Yes, she's fine." Simon then told him about their meeting with Abe Turkle, omitting Lily's challenge to beat the crap out of Abe. Then he told him about their much shorter meeting in Hemlock Bay with Daddy Frasier. "That old guy's really something, Savich. The guy hates Lily, you can see it in his eyes, colder than a snake's, and in his body language. I think he would have threatened her if I hadn't been there."

Savich wanted details, and so Simon told him exactly what had happened.

They'd gone to Elcott Frasier's office because they wanted to get in the old man's face, scare the bejesus out of him, let him know that everyone was on to him. Since he was the president and big cheese of the Hemlock National Bank, he had the shiny corner office on the second floor, all windows, a panoramic view of both the ocean and the town. Simon had wondered if Frasier would see them. His administrative assistant, Ms. Loralee Carmichael, at least twenty-one years old, and so beautiful it made your teeth ache to look at her, left them to kick

up their heels for only twelve minutes, acceptable, Simon decided, since they'd caught the old
man off guard and he'd probably want to get
himself and his stories together. But Simon was
worried about Lily. He'd have given anything
to put her on a plane back to Washington, D.C.,
where she'd be safe. She looked nearly flattened,
her face pale and set. If there'd been a bed
nearby, he'd have tied her down in it. She
moved slowly, but she had that lockjaw determined look, and so he kept his mouth shut.

Elcott Frasier welcomed them into his office,
patted Lily's shoulder, his hand a bit on the
heavy side, and said, "Lily, dear. May I say that
you don't look well."

"Mr. Frasier." She immediately moved away
from him. "Since you've already said it, I don't
suppose there's anything I can do about it." She
gave him a smile as cold as his own. "This is Mr.
Russo. He's a dealer of art. He's the one who
verified that four of my Sarah Elliott paintings
are forgeries."

Elcott Frasier nodded to Simon and motioned to them to be seated. "Well, this comes
as quite a surprise. You say so you're an art
dealer, Mr. Russo. I don't know many art dealers who can spot forgeries. Are you quite sure
about this?"

"I'm not exactly an art dealer, Mr. Frasier, as

in running a gallery. I'm more a dealer/broker.
I bring buyers and sellers together. Occasionally
I track down forgeries and return them to their
rightful owners. Since I own a Sarah Elliott and
know her work intimately, I was able to spot the
fakes among the eight paintings that Lily owns,
particularly since I knew which four had been
forged."

Simon paused a moment, wondering how
much to tell Frasier and if it would frighten the
man. He'd known, of course, abut the forgeries,
didn't even try to act shocked. Why not push it
all the way, since he had a pretty good idea of
how it had gone down? It would have to make
him act. He hadn't told Lily this and hoped she
wouldn't act surprised. He smiled toward her,
then added, "I originally thought that you ini-
tiated the whole deal. But then I got to thinking that you're really a very small man, with no
contacts at all. There's a collector, a Swede
named Olaf Jorgenson, who isn't a small man.
He's very powerful, actually. When he wants
something, he goes after it, no obstacle too
great. I believe that it was Jorgenson who insti-
gated the whole thing. It went this way: Olaf
wanted the Sarah Elliott paintings when they
were in the Chicago Institute, but he couldn't
pull it off and had to wait. He knew exactly
when Lily Savich left Chicago to move to

Hemlock Bay, California. He put out feelers and found you very quickly, and your son, Tennyson, who was the right age. Then you all cut a deal. Actually, I heard Olaf had only three of the paintings. I don't know where the fourth one is as of yet. Hopefully, he has it as well. It makes everything cleaner, easier." Simon snapped his fingers right in Frasier's face. "We'll get them back fast as that. So, Mr. Frasier, did I get it all right?"

Elcott Frasier didn't bat an eye. He looked faintly bored. Lily, though, who knew him well, saw the slight tic in his left eye, there only when he was stressed out or angry. He could be either or both at this moment in time. She was surprised initially at what Simon had said but realized that it had probably happened just as Simon had said. She said, "Jorgenson is indeed powerful, Elcott. He isn't a small man at all, not like you."

Simon thought their father-in-law would belt her. He was ready for it, but Frasier managed to hold himself in. He said, dismissively and as smoothly as a politician accepting a bribe for a pardon, "That's quite a scenario, Mr. Russo. I'm sorry to hear four of the paintings were forged. No matter what you say, it must have happened while they were at the Chicago Institute. All this elaborate plot by this fellow Olaf Jorgenson sounds like a bad movie. However, none of this has anything to do with me or my family. I really don't know why you came here to accuse me of it."

He turned to Lily and there was a good deal of anger in those eyes of his. "As for you, Lily, you left my son. I fear for his health. He is not doing well. All he talks about is you. He says that your brother and sister-in-law slandered him, and none of it's true. He wants to see you, although if I were him, and I've told him this countless times, I'd just as soon see the back of you for good. You weren't a good wife to him. You gave him nothing, and then you just up and left him. His mother is also very concerned. The mere idea that he would marry you to get ahold of some paintings, it's beyond absurd."

"I don't think it's absurd at all, Elcott. It could have happened the way Mr. Russo said. Or maybe it was Mr. Monk who found Mr. Jorgenson. Either way, four of my paintings are fakes and you are the one responsible.

"Now, if Tennyson isn't doing well, I recommend that he pay a visit to Dr. Rossetti, the psychiatrist he very badly wanted me to see when I was still in the hospital. One wonders what he had to do with all this." Lily paused a moment, shrugged, then continued. "But of course you would know about that. How much did you pay Morrie Jones to kill me?"

"I didn't pay him a—" She'd snagged him, caught him completely off guard. He'd burst right out with it, then cut off like a spigot, but too late. Simon was impressed.

The tic was very pronounced now, and added to it was a face turning red with outrage.

"You're quite a bitch, you know that, Lily? I can see why you brought your bodyguard with you. This painting business, I don't know what you've done, but you can't lay it on me. I'm not to blame for anything."

Simon wanted, quite simply, to stand, reach over Mr. Frasier's desk, and yank the man up by his expensive shirt collar and smash him in the jaw. It surprised him, the intense wish to do this man physical damage. But when he spoke, he was calm, utterly measured. "Trust me, Mr. Frasier, Lily isn't a bitch. As for your precious son, what he is isn't in much doubt. Would you like to tell us why Abe Turkle is staying at your cottage?" Simon sat slightly forward in his chair, the soul of polite interest.

"I don't know who that is or why he's there. The real estate agent handles rentals."

"Naturally Abe knows you, Mr. Frasier, knows everything, since he's forged the paintings for you. I do know that he's expensive. Or perhaps Olaf is handling his payments as part of the deal?"

Mr. Frasier got to his feet. The pulse was pounding in his heavy neck. He was nearly beyond control, his hands shaking. Almost there, Simon thought. Elcott Frasier pointed to the door and yelled, "I don't know any damned Olaf! Now, get out, both of you. Lily, I don't wish to see you again. It's a pity that the mugger didn't teach you a lesson."

Simon said, "We'll return for a very nice visit, along with the FBI, when we have our proof. Not much longer. Consider this a reality check. You might want to consider cutting a deal right now, with us. If you don't, just think of all those big, mean prisoners in the federal lockups; they like vulnerable old guys like you."

"Get out or I'll call the sheriff!"

Lily laughed, couldn't help it. "Sheriff Bozo?"

Elcott Frasier yelled, "His name is Scanlan, not Bozo!" Then he nearly ran to the door, jerked it open, and left them staring after him. Simon said to Lily as he helped her to her feet, "It's been quite a morning, first Abe and now your soon-to-be-ex-father-in-law, both of them leaving us in their lairs and stalking off. But everyone is shook up now, Lily. We've stirred the pot as much as we can. Now we wait to see who does what. Just maybe old man Frasier will decide to cut a deal. Now, you ready for a light lunch, maybe Mexican?"

"There isn't a Mexican restaurant in Hemlock Bay. We'll have to go to Ferndale."

Loralee Carmichael looked them over very carefully as they left the reception area. Simon wiggled his fingers in good-bye to her. There was no sign of Elcott Frasier.

He said carefully, as he walked slowly beside her to the elevator, "I want you to consider leaving the rest of this to me. Can I talk you into going back to Washington?"

"No, don't even try, Simon."

"I had to try. When bad men are afraid, Lily, they do things that aren't necessarily smart, but are, many times, deadly."

"Yes. We will be very careful."

He sighed and gave it up. "Over tacos we can discuss our next foray."

"Do you really think that Olaf Jorgenson set this whole thing up?"

"When you think about it, he's the one with all the contacts and the expertise, unless our Mr. Monk knows more about the illegal side of the business than we're aware of yet. I'm sure that Frasier will be speaking to Mr. Monk if he hasn't already. I can't wait to hear what this guy with his bedroom eyes has to say."

Simon paused a moment, then said, "That's all of it, Savich, every gnarly detail."

Simon switched his cell phone to his other ear, waiting for Savich to ask him questions, but Savich didn't say anything. Simon could practically hear him sorting through possible scenarios.

"Lily did really good, Savich. She's tired, but she's hanging in. I've tried to talk her into going back to Washington, but she won't hear of it. I swear I'll keep her safe."

"I know you will," Savich said finally. "Just to let you know, Clark Hoyt, the SAC in the Eureka FBI office, is going to provide you backup. I figured you guys would stir everything up and that could be very dangerous. I don't want you to be on your own. If you happen to see a couple of guys following you, they're there to keep you safe. If you have any concerns, just give Clark Hoyt a call. Now, you make Lily rest. How many tacos did she get down?"

"Three ground beef tacos, a basketful of chips, and an entire bowl of hot salsa. We're going to hole up now, then see Mr. Monk in the morning. By then, they'll all have spoken together, examined their options, made plans. I can't wait to see what they'll do. Give my love to Sherlock, and let Sean teethe on your thumb. Any word on Tammy Tuttle?"

"No."

"I'll call you after we've seen Mr. Monk tomorrow."

"Clark told me they've got a line on Morrie Jones. It shouldn't be long before he's in the local jail."

"Thank God for that. I'll call the cops in Eureka and find out." He paused, then added, "I'm not planning on letting Lily out of my sight."

SEVENTEEN

Eureka, California
The Mermaid's Tail

Lily was deeply asleep, dreaming, and in that dream, she was terrified. There was something wrong, but she didn't know what. Then she saw her daughter, and she knew Beth was crying, sobbing, but Lily didn't know why. Suddenly, Beth was far away, her sobs still loud, but Lily couldn't get to her. She called and called, and then Beth simply wasn't there and Lily was alone, only she wasn't really. She knew there was something wrong, but she didn't know what.

Lily jerked up in bed, drenched with sweat, and groaned with the sharp ache the abrupt movement brought to her belly. She grabbed her stomach and tried to breathe in deeply.

When she did, she smelled smoke. Yes, it was

smoke and it was in her room. That was what
was wrong, what had brought her out of the
nightmare. The smell of smoke, acrid, stronger
now than just a moment before. Then she saw
it billowing up around the curtains in the window, black and thick, the curtains just catching
fire.

Dear God, the bed-and-breakfast was on fire!
She hauled herself out of the high tester bed
with its drapey gauze hangings and hit the floor
running.

Her door was locked. Where was the key?
Not in the door, not on the dresser. She ran to
the bathroom, wet a towel, and pressed it
against her face.

She ran to the phone, dialed 911. The phone
was dead. Someone had set the fire and cut the
phone lines. Or had the fire knocked out the
lines? Didn't matter, she had to get out. Flames
now, in the bedroom, licking up around the
edges of the rug beneath that window with its
light and gauzy draperies. She raced, bowed
over, to the wall and began banging on it.
"Simon! Simon!"

She heard him then, shouting back to her.
"Lily, get the hell out of there, now!"

"My door's locked. I can't get it open!"

"I'm coming! Stay low to the floor."

But Lily couldn't just lie down and wait to be rescued. She was too scared. She ran back to the door and banged her shoulder hard against it. The collision jarred her and left her gasping. She picked up a chair and smashed it hard into the door. The chair nearly bounced off it. The door shuddered a bit but nothing happened. The damned door wasn't hollow. It was old-fashioned and solid wood. She heard Simon jerk his door open, heard him knocking on doors, yelling. Thank God he hadn't been locked in like she was.

Then he was at her door, and she quickly moved back. She heard him kick it, saw it shudder. Then he kicked it hard again and the door slammed inward. "You okay?"

"Yes. We've got to warn everyone." She began coughing, doubled over, and he didn't hesitate. He picked her up in his arms and carried her down the wide mahogany staircase.

Mrs. Blade was in the lobby, and she was helping out a very old lady who was sobbing quietly.

"It's Mrs. Nast. She's a permanent resident. I tried to call nine-one-one but the line's dead, of all things. There are people on the third floor, Mr. Russo. Please get them."

"I've already called nine-one-one on my cell

phone. They're on their way." Simon set Lily down and ran back up the stairs. He heard her hacking cough as he ran.

He didn't get to the top of the stairs alone. Beside him at the last minute were firemen, all garbed up and yelling for him to get back downstairs and out of the building.

He nodded, then saw a young woman struggling with two children, coughing, trying to pull them down the corridor. The two firemen had their hands full with other guests. Simon simply grabbed all three of them up in his arms and carried them downstairs. They were all coughing by the time they got out the front door, the kids crying and the mother holding herself together, comforting them, thanking him again and again until he just put his hand over her mouth. "It's okay. Take care of your kids."

They saved a lot of The Mermaid's Tail, thank God, and all of the ten people staying there. No serious injuries, just some smoke inhalation.

Colin Smith, the agent sent over by Clark Hoyt to maintain an overnight watch on the bed-and-breakfast, told them he'd seen two men sneaking around, followed and lost them, turned back to see the smoke billowing up, and immediately called the fire department. That was why most of The Mermaid's Tail was still standing.

Agent Smith left them, after making certain they were okay, to repeat his story to the fire chief and the arson investigator, who'd just arrived.

Simon was holding Lily close to him. She was barefoot, wearing a long white flannel night-gown that came to her ankles, and her hair was straggling around her shoulders. He'd managed to scramble into jeans and a sweater and sneak-ers before he'd left his bedroom. He blew out, but didn't see his breath. It was cold, probably just below fifty degrees, and the firemen were distributing coats and blankets to all the victims. Neighbors were coming out with more blan-kets and coffee, even some rolls to eat.

Simon said, "You okay, Lily?"

She only nodded. "We're alive. That's all that matters. The bastards. I can't believe they set the entire place on fire. So many people could have been hurt, even killed."

"Your brother realized before I did that they'd probably try something. You met Agent Colin Smith. Your brother got the SAC here in Eureka to send him to watch over us."

She sighed and just stayed where she was. She was exhausted, doubted that any part of her would move, even if she begged. "Yeah, I realized he was a guard for us. I sure wish he'd caught them before they set the fire."

"He does, too. He's really beating himself up. He was calling in his boss, Clark Hoyt, last time I saw him. Hoyt will probably be here soon. I'll bet you he's already called Savich."

"At four o'clock in the morning?"

"Good point."

"It's really cold, Simon."

He was sitting on a lawn chair that a neighbor had brought over. He pulled her onto his lap, wrapping the blankets around both of them. "Better?"

She just nodded against his shoulder and whispered, "This really sucks."

He laughed.

"You know, Simon, even Remus wouldn't go so far as to do this sort of thing. Someone so desperate, so malevolent, they don't care how many people they kill? That's really scary."

"Yes," he said slowly, "it is. I didn't expect anything like this."

"You got mugged in New York so soon after you left Washington. These people work really fast. I'm beginning to think it's Olaf Jorgenson behind all this, not the Frasiers, just like you said. How would the Frasiers have even known about you or where you were?"

"I agree. But you know, the guy didn't try to kill me, at least I don't think he did."

"Probably a warning."

"I guess. This wasn't a warning. This was for real. We're in pretty deep now, Lily. I'll bet you that Clark Hoyt isn't going to let us out of his sight for as long as we're in his neck of the woods."

"At this point I'm glad. No, Simon, don't say it. I'm not about to leave you alone now." She fell silent, and for a little while he thought she'd finally just given out. Then she said, "Simon, did I ever tell you that Jeff MacNelly was my biggest influence for Remus?"

Who was Jeff MacNelly? He shook his head slowly, fascinated.

"Oh, yes, he was. I admired him tremendously." When she realized he didn't have a clue, she added, "Jeff MacNelly was a very famous and talented cartoonist. He won three Pulitzer Prizes skewering politicos. But he never once said that they were evil. He died in June of 2000. I really miss him. It upsets me that I never told him how much he meant to me, and to Remus."

"I'm sorry to hear that, Lily." He realized then that she was teetering on the edge of shock, so he pulled another blanket around her.

It was too much even for her. Her life had flown out of control when she'd married Tennyson Frasier. He couldn't imagine what she'd gone through when her daughter had been killed and she'd managed to survive months of depression. And then all this.

Lily said, "Jeff MacNelly said that 'when it comes to humor, there's no substitute for reality and politicians.' I don't like this reality part, Simon, I really don't."

"I don't either."

Washington, D.C.
Hoover Building

Savich slowly hung up the phone, stared out his window a moment, then lowered his face to his hands.

He heard Sherlock say, "What is it, Dillon? What's happened?" Her competent hands were massaging his shoulders, her breath was warm on his temple.

He slowly raised his head to look up at her. "I should have killed her, Sherlock, should have shot her cleanly in the head, just like I did Tommy Tuttle. This is all my fault—that boy's death in Chevy Chase, and now this."

"She's killed again?"

He nodded, and she hated the despair in his eyes, the pain that radiated from him. "In Road Town, Tortola, in the British Virgin Islands."

"Tell me."

"That was Jimmy Maitland. He said the police commissioner received all our reports, alerted his local officers, waited, and then a local pharmacist was murdered, his throat cut. The place was trashed, impossible to tell what drugs were taken, but we know what was stolen— pain meds and antibiotics. They don't have any leads, but they're combing the island for a one-armed woman who's not in good shape. No sign of her yet. Not even a whiff. Tortola isn't like Saint Thomas. It's far more primitive, less populated, more places to hide, and the bottom line is there's just no way to get to and from the island except by boat."

"I'm very sorry it happened. You know she's gotten ahold of a boat. By now she's probably long gone from Tortola, to another island."

"It's hard to believe that no one's reported a boat stolen."

"It's late," Sherlock said. "E-mail all the other islands, then let it go for a while. Let's go home, play with Sean, then head over to the gym. You need a really hard workout, Dillon."

He rose slowly. "Okay, first I've got to talk to

all the local cops down there, make sure they know what's happened on Tortola, tell them again how dangerous she is." He kissed her, hugged her tightly, and said against her temple, "Go home and start playing with Sean. I'll be there in a while. Have him gum some graham crackers for me."

Quantico, Virginia
FBI Academy

Special Agent Virginia Cosgrove cocked her head to one side and said, "Marilyn, it's for you. A woman, says she's with Dillon Savich's unit at headquarters. I'll be listening on the other line, okay?"

Marilyn Warluski, who was folding the last of her new clothes into the suitcase provided by the FBI, nodded, a puzzled look on her face. She was staying in the Jefferson dorm with two women agents, just starting to get used to things. What did Mr. Savich want from her now? She took the phone from Agent Cosgrove and said, "Hello?"

"Hi, sweet chops. It's Timmy. You hot for me, baby?"

Marilyn closed her eyes tight against the

shock, against the disbelief. "Tammy," she whispered. "Is it really you?"

"No, it's Timmy. Listen up, sweetie, I need to see you. I want you to fly down here, to Antigua, tomorrow; that's when I'll be there. I'll be at the Reed Airport, waiting for you. Don't disappoint me, baby, okay?"

Marilyn looked frantically over at Virginia.

Virginia quickly wrote on a pad of paper, then handed it to Marilyn. "Okay, I can do it, but it'll be late."

"They treating you all right at that cop academy? Do you want me to come up with the Ghouls and level the place?"

"No, no, Tammy, don't do that. I'll fly down late tomorrow. Are you all right?"

"Sure. Had to get me some more medicine on Tortola. Lousy place, dry and boring, no action at all. Can't wait to get out of here. See you tomorrow evening, baby. Bye."

Marilyn slowly placed the phone in its cradle. She looked blankly at Virginia Cosgrove. "How did she know where I was? I need to call Dillon Savich. Damn, it's really late."

Assistant Director Jimmy Maitland called Dillon Savich to mobilize the necessary agents. He got it done in two hours and set himself up to coordinate the group leaving for Antigua.

Maitland called in the SWAT Team at the

Washington, D.C., field office because they were bringing this all down very possibly in an airport, and there could always be trouble. He told Savich, "Yeah, I threw them some meat and they agreed to come out and play. We got one team, six really good guys."

Vincent Arbus, point man for the team, built like a bull, bald as a Q-tip, and many times too smart for his own good, looked at Savich, then at Sherlock, who was standing at his side, and said in his rough, low voice, "Call me Vinny, guys. I have a feeling that we're going to be getting tight before this is all over.

"Now, how the hell did this crazy one-armed woman know that Marilyn Warluski was holed up in Jefferson dorm at Quantico? How the hell did she get her number?"

"Well," Savich said slowly, not looking at Sherlock, "I sort of let it be known. Actually, I set the whole thing up."

EIGHTEEN

Eureka

Mr. Monk was gone, his office left looking as if he would be returning the next day. There were no notes, no messages, no telltale appointments listed in his date book, which sat in the middle of his desk. There was no clue at all as to where he'd gone.

Nor was he at his big bay-windowed apartment on Oak Street. He hadn't cleaned out his stuff, had just, apparently, taken off without a word to anyone.

Hoyt said to Simon when he opened his hotel room door, "He's gone. I just stood in the middle of that empty living room with its fine paintings by Jason Argot on the white walls, with its own specialized lighting, and I tell you, Russo, I wanted to kick myself. I knew we should have covered his place, but I didn't. I'm an idiot. Kick me. There's got to be a clue somewhere in there about where his bolt-hole is. Or maybe not, but I haven't found a bloody thing. Really, Russo, just kick my ribs in."

"Nah," Simon said as he zipped the fly on his new jeans and threaded his new belt. He waved Hoyt into his deluxe room with its king-size bed that took up nearly three-quarters of the room. Lily was right through the adjoining door. They were staying at the Warm Creek Lodge, both with an ocean view from one window and an Old Town view from the other. "I appreciate your checking him out for us first thing, since Lily and I didn't have any clothes at all. Though I wouldn't have minded paying the jerk a visit myself. Thank God I left my wallet in my jeans pocket last night or we'd be in really deep caca. Actually, if the credit card companies hadn't sent me replacement credit cards after my wallet was stolen in New York, we'd still be in deep caca. We're all outfitted now, real spiffy. Now, what about Monk's car? Any sign of it?"

"We've got an APB out on it—a Jeep Grand Cherokee, 'ninety-eight, dark green. And we're covering the Arcata airport. We've sent out alerts as far down as SFO, though I don't think he could have gotten that far."

"Problem is, we don't know when he bolted.

Don't you think it would be better if you issued a tri-state airport alert?"

"Yeah, good idea. I'm thinking he probably got scared. I doubt he has a fake ID or a passport. If he tries to take a flight, we'll nail him."

Simon nodded. "Would you like a cup of coffee? Room service just sent some up with croissants."

Clark Hoyt looked like he would cry. He didn't say another word until he'd downed two cups of coffee and eaten a croissant, smeared with a real butter pat and sugarless apricot jam.

When Lily came in a few minutes later, Simon smiled at the sight. She looked even better than he'd imagined. She was wearing black stretch jeans, a black turtleneck sweater, and black boots. She looked like a fairy princess who was also a cat burglar on her nights off. Clark Hoyt, when he rose to greet her, said, "Quite a change from how you looked early this morning. I like all the black."

Lily thanked him, poured herself a cup of coffee, and watched him eat a second croissant. He filled Lily in on what they hadn't found so far.

Hoyt said, "I called Savich back at Disneyland East and filled him in. He made me swear on the head of my schnauzer, Gilda, that you guys didn't have a single singed hair on your heads. It was arson, all right, but no idea yet who the perps were or who hired them."

"Disneyland East?" Lily asked, an eyebrow up.

"Yep, just another loving name for FBI Headquarters. Hey, thanks for breakfast. You guys still smell like smoke. It's really tough to get it all out. I should know, I was overenthusiastic with my barbeque last summer and lost my eyebrows, although my face was so black you couldn't tell. Just lay low; keep out of sight until I get some news for you, okay?"

● It was early afternoon when Hoyt came to get them from the lodge. Mr. Monk hadn't tried to fly out of harm's way. Actually, he hadn't flown anywhere. He was quite dead, head pressed against the steering wheel, three bullets through his back. The Jeep was in a sparse stand of redwood trees, and some hikers, poking around, had found him.

Lieutenant Larry Dobbs of the Eureka Police Department knew that the situation was dicey, that it involved a whole lot more than this one body, and even that the FBI was involved. He agreed to let Clark Hoyt bring out the two civilians, after the crime scene had been gone over.

Simon and Lily stood looking at the Jeep.

"They didn't really try to hide him," she said. "On the other hand, it could have been a long time before someone accidentally came upon him. God bless hikers."

"The medical examiner estimates he's been dead about seven hours, give or take," said Clark Hoyt. "He'll know a lot more after the autopsy. Our lab guys will crawl all over that Jeep to see what's what. Ah, here comes Lieutenant Dobbs. You've met, haven't you?"

"We've spoken on the phone," Simon said and shook Dobbs's hand. Simon saw quickly enough that the lieutenant was impressed with how Clark Hoyt deferred to him.

"Do you think he was with someone?" Lily asked both men. "And that someone killed him and then moved his body to the driver's side?"

Lieutenant Dobbs said, "No. From the trajectory of the bullets, there was someone, the shooter, riding in the backseat, behind Monk. Maybe someone else riding in the passenger seat. I don't know. Maybe Monk knew they were taking him out to kill him. But if so, why did he calmly pull over? Again, I don't know. But the fact is he did pull off the road into the redwoods, and the guy in the backseat shot him."

Simon and Lily were given permission to walk over the area. They looked everywhere, but there wasn't anything to see. The hikers had made a mess of things in their initial panic. There were five cop cars and two FBI cars adding to the chaos. There weren't any tire tracks except the Jeep's, which meant that the other car must have stayed parked on the paved road.

Lieutenant Dobbs eyed Simon and Lily and said, "Agent Hoyt tells me you guys are involved in this up to your eyeballs. Let me tell you, you two have brought me more woes than I've had for the last ten years, beginning with that jerk who attacked you on the public bus, Mrs. Frasier. Oh, yeah, Officer Tucker just found Morrie Jones a couple of hours ago, holed up in a fleabag hotel down on Conduit Street."

"Keep him safe, Lieutenant," Lily said. "He was part of this, too, as was Mr. Monk. And look what happened to him."

"You got it." Lieutenant Dobbs said then, "You know, it hasn't been all bad. I've met Hoyt here, a real federal agent and all, and I haven't had to watch *Wheel of Fortune* with my wife. I haven't had a single bored minute since I got that first call from you guys. Only bad thing is this body over there. A body's never good." He sighed and waved to one of the other officers. He said over his shoulder, "Clark, try to keep these two out of more mischief, all right? Oh, yes, I'm going to be interviewing all the Frasiers, including your husband, Mr. Tennyson Frasier. Maybe it'll scare them, make them do something else stupid. I understand you've already tried, got them all riled up. Now let's see how they handle the law." He waved toward the body bag containing Mr. Monk. "This wasn't a bright thing to do."

"Don't forget Charlotte Frasier, Lieutenant," Lily said, "and don't be fooled by that syrupy accent. She's terrifying."

Hoyt said, "Then I'm going to wait until the lieutenant is through with them, wait until they're nice and comfortable at their homes in Hemlock Bay again, and then I'm going to pay them a little visit and grill them but good. Savich has sent me lots of stuff. I've been speaking to some of our representatives in Sacramento, checking real close into Elcott Frasier's financial situation. Lots of conflicting info so far, but there's been a lot of flow in and out of his accounts there. Something will shake loose; it usually does. Oh, yeah, I heard that Elcott Frasier has hired Mr. Bradley Abbott, one of the very best criminal lawyers on the West Coast, to represent him and his family." Hoyt rubbed his hands together. "This is going to be really interesting."

As they drove back to Eureka, Simon was brooding. Lily recognized the signs. He looked single-minded as he drove, looking neither right nor left, saying nothing to Lily, who was hungry and wanted to go to the bathroom.

"Stop it, Simon."

That jerked him around to stare at her. "Stop what?"

"You've got a look that says you're far away, like maybe the Delta Quadrant."

"Yeah, I was just thinking. About Abe Turkle. He's a loose end, Lily, just like Mr. Monk. So is Morrie Jones, but he's in jail, and hopefully safe there. The lieutenant is going to put a guard on him."

Lily said, "I forgot to tell you, when you and Hoyt were talking back there, Lieutenant Dobbs told me that Morrie claims he doesn't know a thing, that a couple of thugs hurt him when he was minding his own business in a bar. He claimed no broad could ever hurt him. Oh yes, Morrie's got a big-time lawyer. I wonder how much money Morrie's being paid to keep his mouth shut."

Simon said, "Can Lieutenant Dobbs find out who hired the lawyer?"

"I asked him if he knew. He said he'd sniff around. Now, Simon, you're brooding because you think Abe Turkle might be in danger." In that instant, Lily forgot she was hungry, forgot she needed to go to the bathroom. "You've just made my stomach drop to my knees. Let's go see Abe, Simon."

He grinned over at her, braked, and did a wide U-turn.

"Hey," she said, "not bad driving. Won't this piece of garbage go any faster?"

Simon laughed. "You're the best, Lily, do you know that? Hey, I see someone doing another U-turn behind us. Must be our protection."

"Good. Hope he can keep up with us."

Simon laughed.

"My dad, Buck Savich, used to tell me that if I decided to become a professional bookie, I'd be the best in the business. Except for one thing."

"What's that?"

"He'd say my eyes changed color whenever I lied, and if anyone noticed that, my days as a bookie would be over."

"Your eyes are blue right now. What color do they go to when you lie?"

"I don't know. I've never looked at myself in the mirror and lied to it."

"I'll keep that in mind, though, and let you know."

Simon turned his attention back to the road. He saw big Abe Turkle in his mind, a paintbrush between his teeth, ready to beat the crap out of him. Then Abe's smile when he looked at Lily. The man was a crook, but he was an excellent artist. Simon didn't want him to get killed.

He sped up to sixty because his gut was crawling. Bad things, bad things. But he said in a smooth, amused voice, "I met your dad when Dillon and I were in our senior year at MIT. He was something else."

"Yes," she said. "He was the best. I miss him very much. All us kids do. As for Mom, she was a mess for a long time. She met this guy, a congressman from Missouri, just last year, still claims they're only friends, but she's a lot happier, smiles a lot more, just plain gets out and does more things. She adores Sean, too. He's the only grandkid close by."

"What did your mom think of all the legends about Buck Savich? There were so many colorful ones floating about long before he died."

"She'd just shake her head, grin like a bandit, and say she didn't think the tales were exaggerations at all. Then, I swear it to you, she'd blush. I think she was talking about intimate things, and it always freaked us kids out. You just can't think of your parents in that way, you know what I mean?"

"Yeah, I do. I guess, on the other side of the

coin, our parents look at us and see little kids who will be virgins for the rest of their lives."

Lily laughed. "What about your parents? Where do they live?"

"My folks have been divorced for a very long time. My dad's a lawyer, remarried to a woman half his age. They live in Boston. No little half-brothers or half-sisters. My mom didn't re-marry, lives in Los Angeles, runs her own makeover consulting firm. If they ever had any liking for each other, it was over before I could remember it. My sisters, both older than I am, told me they'd never seen anything resembling affection either." He paused just a moment, slowed a bit for a particularly gnarly turn, then sped up again. "You know, Lily, I have a hard time seeing you as a bookie. Did you make some money for college?"

She gave him a shark's grin, all white teeth, ready to bite. "You bet. Thing was, though, Mom decided it was better that Dad not know exactly what my earnings totaled from age six-teen to eighteen, especially since I hadn't paid any taxes."

"It boggles the mind." He looked at her then, saying nothing, just looking. "Do you know that you're looking more like a fairy princess again? I like you in all that black. How's your scar doing?"

"My innards are fine; the scar itches just a bit. It's no wonder you like all black since you bought all my clothes. You want me to look like Batgirl, Simon?"

"I always did like to watch her move." He grinned at her. "Truth is, I saw the black pants and knew it would have to be black all the way." He gave her a sideways look. "I don't mean to be indelicate, but did all the underwear fit?"

"Too well," she said, "and I don't like to think about it, so stop looking at me."

"Okay." For a couple of seconds, Simon kept his eyes on the road. Then he said, chuckling, "As I said, when I saw the black, I knew it was you. But you know, I think the biggest change was your getting all that ash and soot washed out of your hair and off your face."

Every stitch she was wearing was black, even the boot socks. She said, not intending to, "Why haven't you ever married?"

"I was married, a very long time ago."

"Tell me."

He gave her another sideways look, saw that she really wanted to know, and said, "Well, I was twenty-two years old, in overwhelming lust, as was Janice, and so we got married, divorced within six months, and both of us joined the army."

"That was a long time ago. Where is Janice now?"

"She stayed in the army. She's a two-star general, stationed in Washington, D.C. I heard she's gorgeous as a general. She's married to a four-star. Hey, maybe someday she'll be chief of staff."

"I wonder why Dillon didn't tell me."

"He would have been my best man in the normal course of things, but we eloped and he was off in Europe that summer, living on a shoestring, so I knew he didn't have the money to fly home, then back to Europe again." Simon shrugged. "It was just as well. Who was your first husband? Beth's father?"

"His name was Jack Crane. He was a stockbroker for Phlidick, Dammerleigh and Pierson. He was a big wheeler-dealer at the Chicago Stock Exchange."

"Why'd you split up?"

She tried to just shrug it off, give him a throwaway smile, but it wasn't possible. She drew a deep breath and said, "I don't want to talk about that."

"Okay, for now. Here we are. Keep your eyes open, Lily, I really have a bad feeling about this." He turned right onto the narrow asphalt road that led to the cottage, looked back, and saw their protection turning in behind them.

No motorcycle.

Simon did a quick scan, didn't see a thing. "I really don't like this."

"Maybe he just went into town to get some barbeque sauce to go with his snails."

Simon didn't think so, but he didn't argue as they walked up to the cottage. The door wasn't locked. He didn't say a word, just picked Lily up under her armpits and moved her behind him. He opened the door slowly. It was gloomy inside, all the blinds pulled down. The room was completely empty—no stacked paintings against the walls, no easel, no palette, not even a drop of paint anywhere or the smell of turpentine, just empty.

"Check the kitchen, Lily. I'm going to look in the bedroom." They met back in the empty living room five minutes later.

Agent Colin Smith stood in the open doorway. "No sign of Abe Turkle?"

Simon shook his head and said, "Nope. All that's left is a box of Puffed Wheat, a bit of milk, not soured, and a couple of apples, still edible, so he hasn't been gone long."

Lily said, "He's packed up and left. All his clothes, suitcase, everything gone, even his toothpaste."

"Do you think he went to London with that painting he was finishing?"

"I hope not. It was really very good, too good."

Colin Smith asked, "You were afraid he was dead, weren't you? Murdered. Like Mr. Monk."

Simon nodded. "I had a bad feeling there for a while. Let's tell Lieutenant Dobbs about this. Agent Smith, if you'll call Clark Hoyt, fill him in. You know, Abe had lots of stuff—at least thirty paintings leaning against the walls. All he had was a motorcycle. Maybe he rented a U-Haul to carry everything away."

"Or maybe one of the Frasiers loaned him a truck."

"Maybe. Now then, Agent Smith, Lily and I are off to pay a visit to Morrie Jones. I need to speak to Lieutenant Dobbs and the DA, get their okay. I've got an offer for Morrie he can't refuse."

Lily held up a hand. "No, I don't want to know. Maybe by now they know who's paying his lawyer." Simon closed the cottage door and waved to Agent Smith.

"Don't count on it," Simon said as he set the pillow gently over Lily's stomach and fastened the seat belt.

NINETEEN

Saint John's, Antigua
Public Administration Building,
near Reed Airport

"It's so bright and hot and blue," Sherlock said, scratching her arm. Then she sighed. "You know, Sean would really like this place. We could strip him down and play in that sand, build a castle with him, even a moat. I can just see him rolling over on the castle, flattening it, laughing all the while."

For the first time in as long as she could remember, Sherlock realized Dillon wasn't listening. She could only imagine what was going through his mind, all the ifs and buts. It was his show, and naturally he was worried, impossible not to be. They were working through the American Consular Agent with the Royal Police Force at Police Headquarters located on, strangely enough, American Road. But they were still in a foreign country, dealing with locals who were both bewildered by the extreme reaction of the United States federal cops—all fifty of them—to one woman, who only had one arm and was supposedly coming to their airport. But they were cooperating, really serious now after Savich had shown the entire group photos of her victims, including the latest one on Tortola. That one really brought it home.

Tammy couldn't have gotten to Antigua before late morning, no way, even with a fast boat. Tortola was just too far away. The weather had been calm, no high winds or waves. She couldn't have gotten here ahead of them, except by plane, and they'd been checking air traffic from Tortola and nearby islands. And there was no indication at all that she knew how to fly. They'd had time to get everything set up, to get everyone in position.

Sherlock gave him a clear look. "We have time. Stop worrying. Marilyn will be here in about two hours. We'll go over everything with her, step by step."

"What if Tammy isn't alone? What if Tammy has been traveling around as Timmy this whole time? Remember, it was Timmy who called Marilyn at Quantico."

Sherlock had never before seen him so questioning of what he was doing.

When she spoke, Sherlock's voice was as calm as the incredible blue water not one hundred yards away, "One arm is one arm, despite anything else. No one on any of the islands has reported anyone jiggering about with just one arm. The odds are stacked way against her. You know all the local police in both the British Virgin Islands and the U.S. Virgin Islands are on full alert. The Antiguan authorities aren't used to mayhem like this, so you can bet they're very concerned, probably more hyper than we are, particularly after those crime-scene photos. Dillon, everyone is taking this very seriously."

"So you think I should just chill out?"

"No, that's impossible. But you're very smart, top drawer. Just stop trying to second-guess yourself. You've done everything to prepare. If we have to deal with something other than just Tammy, we will."

The local cops, of which there weren't many, had converged on the airport. They were trying to look inconspicuous and failing, but they were trying, a couple of them even joking with tourists. All of them were used to dealing with locals who occasionally smoked too much local product or drank too much rum, or an occasional tourist who tried to steal something from a duty-free store. Nothing like this. This was beyond their experience.

Savich just couldn't help himself. He checked and rechecked with Vinny Arbus on the status of the SWAT team. If Tammy Tuttle managed to grab a civilian, they were ready. Marksmen were set up, six of them, in strategic spots around the airport as well as inside. Half the marksmen were dressed like tourists, the other half, like airport personnel. They blended right in.

Would Tammy come in by plane? Would she simply walk in? No one knew. All hotels and rooming houses had been checked, rechecked. Jimmy Maitland was seated in the police commissioner's office with its overhead fan, boiling alive in his nice fall suit.

There were nearly fifty FBI personnel involved in the operation, now named Tripod. Special Agent Dane Carver had picked the name because the perp had only one arm and two legs, so Tuttle was the tripod.

A couple of hours later, Marilyn Warluski, scared to the soles of her new Nike running shoes, pressed close to Agent Virginia Cosgrove, her lifeline. Cosgrove was jittery, too, but too new an agent to be as scared as she should be. As she saw it, she was the most important agent present. It was to her that Tammy

Tuttle would come. She was an excellent shot. She would protect Marilyn Warluski. She was ready.

"She's coming, Mr. Savich," Marilyn said, her voice dull and flat when he checked in with her again at six o'clock that evening. She was standing by the Information Desk in the airport, the Caribbean Airlines counter just off to the left.

"It will be all right, Marilyn," Virginia said, her voice more excited than soothing, and patted her hand for at least the thirtieth time. "Agent Savich won't let anything happen, you'll see. We'll nail Tammy."

"I told you it was Timmy who called me. When she's Timmy, she can do anything."

"I thought she could do anything when she was Tammy, too," Savich said.

"She can. He can. If they're both here, not just Timmy, then there'll be real trouble."

Savich felt a twist of fear in his guts. He said slowly, his voice deep and calm, "Marilyn, what do you mean if they're both here? You mean both Tammy and Timmy? I don't understand."

Marilyn shrugged. "I didn't think to tell you, but I saw it happen once, back a couple of years ago. We were in that dolled-up tourist town, Oak Bluffs. You know, on Martha's Vineyard. I saw Tammy comin' out of this really pretty pink Victorian house where we were all stayin' and she just suddenly turned several times, you know, real fast, like Lynda Carter did whenever she was goin' to change into Wonder Woman. Same thing. Tammy turned into Timmy, like they were blended together somehow, and it was the scariest thing I'd ever seen until Tammy walked into that motel room all covered in that little boy's blood."

Savich knew this was nuts. Tammy couldn't change from a woman into a man. That was impossible, but evidently Marilyn believed it. He said, carefully, "It seemed to you that Tammy and Timmy somehow coalesced into one person?"

"Yeah, that's it. She whirled around several times and then there was Timmy, all horny and smart-mouthed."

"When Tammy turned into Timmy, what did he look like?"

"Like Tammy but like a guy, you know?"

Virginia Cosgrove looked thoroughly confused. She started to say something, but Savich shook his head at her. Savich wanted to ask Marilyn to describe Timmy. Marilyn was suddenly standing perfectly still. She seemed to sniff the air like an animal scenting danger. She whispered, "I can feel Timmy close, Mr. Savich. He's real close now. Oh, God, I'm scared. He's going to wring my neck like a chicken's for helping you."

"I don't understand any of this." Virginia Cosgrove whispered low, just like Marilyn had. "So Tammy is really a guy?"

"I guess we'll find out, Agent Cosgrove. Don't dwell on it. Your priority is Marilyn. Just protect Marilyn."

Marilyn leaned close and took Virginia's hand. "You won't let him take me, will you, Agent Cosgrove?"

"No, Marilyn, I won't even let him get close to you." She said to Savich, "You can count on me. I'll guard her with my life."

It was seven o'clock in the evening, just an hour later. Since it was fall, the sun had set much earlier, and it was dark now, the sky filling with stars and a half-moon. It was beautiful and warm. The cicadas and the coquis were playing a symphony if anyone was inclined to listen.

The airport looked fairly normal except it was probably a bit too crowded for this time of day, something Savich hoped Tammy Tuttle wouldn't realize. But he knew she would notice because the local cops looked jumpy, too ill at ease for her not to notice. Or for Timmy to notice. Or whichever one of them showed.

Savich drew a deep breath as he watched the crowd. He said, "Timmy is close, Sherlock, that's what Marilyn said. She said she could feel him. That was an hour ago. I think she's even more scared than I am. She also firmly believes—no doubt at all in her mind—that Tammy can change into a guy at will, into this Timmy."

Sherlock said, "If a Timmy shows up, then I'll check us both into Bellevue."

"You got that right."

There weren't that many tourists in the airport now, real tourists at least. The major flights from the States had arrived, passengers dispersed, and just a few island-to-island flights were going out in the evening. This was both good and bad. There was less cover, but also less chance that a civilian would be harmed.

When it happened, it was so quick that no one had a chance to stop it. A short, rangy man, pale as death itself, with close-cropped black hair, except for some curls on top of his head, seemed suddenly to simply appear behind Agent Virginia Cosgrove. He said against her ear, "Just move, sweetie, make any movement at all to alert all the Feds hanging around here and I'll slice your throat from ear to ear. What'll be fun is that you'll live long enough to see your blood gush out in a bright red fountain."

Virginia heard Marilyn whimper. How had he gotten behind her? Why hadn't someone alerted her? Why hadn't someone seen him? Yes, it sounded like a man, like this Timmy Tuttle Marilyn had talked about. What was going on here? She had to be calm, wait for her chance. She slowly nodded. "I won't make a move. I won't do anything."

"Good," the man said and sliced her throat. Blood gushed out. Virginia had only a brief moment to cry out, but even then it wasn't a cry, it was only a low, blurred gurgling sound.

He turned to Marilyn, smiled, and said, "Let's go, baby. I've missed my little darlin'. You ready, baby?"

Marilyn whispered, "Yes, Timmy, I'm ready."

He took her hand in his bloody one, and with his other hand, he raised the knife to her throat. At that moment, Savich, who'd been in low conversation with Vinny Arbus, saw the blood spurting out of Virginia Cosgrove's neck. He'd been looking at her just a moment before. How was it possible? Then he saw a guy dragging Marilyn with him, a knife at her throat. A dozen other agents and at least a dozen civilians saw Virginia fall, her blood splattering everywhere, and saw a pale-as-death man dragging Marilyn Warluski.

All hell broke loose. It was pandemonium,

people screaming, running, frozen in terror, or dropping to the floor and folding their arms over their heads. But what was the most potent, what everyone would remember with stark clarity, was the smell of blood. It filled the air, filled their lungs.

It was a hostage situation, but it wasn't a by-stander who was the hostage. It was Marilyn Warluski.

Savich spotted the man, finally free of screaming civilians, and he'd recognize that face anywhere. It was Tammy Tuttle's face—only it wasn't quite. No, not possible. But Savich would go to his grave swearing that it was a man with the knife held to Marilyn's throat, and he had two arms, that man, because Savich saw two hands with his own eyes. It had to be someone else, not Tammy Tuttle dressed up like a man. Someone who looked enough like Tammy to fool him. But how had that crazy-looking man gotten so close to Virginia and Marilyn so quickly, and no one had even no-ticed? Suddenly nothing made sense.

Agents grabbed tourists who were still stand-ing and pushed them to the floor, clearing the way to get to the man and his hostage.

A local police officer, a very young man with a mustache, closed with them first. He shouted at the man to stop and fired a warning shot in the air.

The man calmly turned in the officer's direction, pulled a SIG Sauer from his pocket so fast it was a blur, and shot him in the forehead. Then he turned around and it seemed he saw Savich, who was at least fifty feet from him. He yelled, "Hey, it's me, Timmy Tuttle! Hell-ooooo, everyone!"

Savich tuned him out. He had to or he couldn't function. He knew that the marksmen stationed inside the terminal had Tuttle in their sights. Soon now, very soon, it would be over.

He moved around the perimeter, slid behind the Caribbean Airlines counter with half a dozen agents behind him, and kept moving toward Timmy Tuttle.

Three shots rang out simultaneously. Loud, clear, sharp. It was the marksmen, and they wouldn't have fired without a clear shot at Timmy Tuttle.

Savich raised his head. He knew he couldn't be more than twenty feet from Timmy Tuttle. He couldn't see him. Could they have missed?

Then there were half a dozen more shots, screaming, and deep and ugly moans wrung out of people's throats from terror.

Savich felt something, something strong and

sour, and he turned quickly. He saw Sherlock some ten feet away, just off to his left, with three other agents, rising from her kneeling position, her SIG Sauer aimed toward where Timmy Tuttle and Marilyn had been just moments before. She looked as confused as he felt. It took everything in him not to shout for her to stay back, please God, just stay back, he didn't want her hurt. And what would hurt her? A man who really wasn't a man, but an image in whole cloth spun from Tammy Tuttle's crazy brain?

Savich saw a flash of cloth, smelled the scent of blood, and he simply knew it was Timmy Tuttle. He ran as fast as he could toward a conference room, the only place Timmy could have taken Marilyn. He kicked open the door.

He stopped cold, his gun steady, ready to fire. There was a big rectangular table in the center and twelve chairs, an overhead projector, a fax, and two or three telephones.

There wasn't anyone in the room. It was empty. But even in here he smelled Virginia's blood; he could swear that he smelled her blood, rich, coppery, sickening. He swallowed convulsively as he took in every inch of the room.

So Timmy hadn't come in here. Another room then. Agents on his heels, he ran across the hall to see his wife, gun held in front her, pushing open a door with SECURITY stenciled on the glass.

He was across that hall and into the room in an instant. He saw Sherlock standing in the middle of the room, the three agents fanned out behind her, all of them searching the room. But Sherlock wasn't doing anything, just standing there staring silently at the single large window that gave onto the outside.

She turned slowly to see him in the open doorway, agents at his back, staring at her, shock and panic alive in his eyes. She cocked her head to one side in silent question, then simply closed her eyes and fell over onto the floor.

"Sherlock!"

"My God, is she shot?"

"What happened?"

The other three agents converged.

Savich knew he couldn't stop, but it was the hardest thing he'd ever done in his life. He yelled, "Make sure she's all right! Conners, check everyone out! Deevers, Conlin, Marks, Abrams, you're with me!"

He heard one of the agents shout after him, "She's breathing, can't see anything wrong with her. The guy wasn't in here, Savich. We don't know where he went."

The window, he thought, Sherlock had been

staring at that window. He picked up a chair and smashed it into the huge glass window.

When they managed to climb out the window they'd cleared of glass, they knew, logically, that Timmy Tuttle and Marilyn Warluski couldn't have come this way since the glass hadn't been broken. But it didn't matter. Where else could Timmy Tuttle have gone? They covered every inch of ground, looked into all the buildings, even went onto the tarmac where one American 757 sat waiting, calling up to the pilot. But Tammy or Timmy Tuttle was gone, and Marilyn as well. As if they'd just vanished into thin air, with nothing left to prove they'd even been there except for Virginia Cosgrove's body, bloodless now, lying on her side, covered with several blankets, local technicians working over her. And the one local officer Timmy Tuttle had shot through the head.

He'd used his right hand when he'd shot that officer.

Savich had shot Tammy Tuttle through her right arm in that barn in Maryland, near the Plum River.

At the hospital, they'd amputated her right arm.

He wondered if they were all going mad.

No, no, there was an explanation.

Somehow a man had gotten into the airport,

killed Virginia Cosgrove, and grabbed Marilyn. And no one had seen him until he had Marilyn by the neck and was dragging her away.

No one much wanted to talk. Everyone who had been in the airport appeared confused and looked, strangely, hungover.

Savich and his team went back to the security room. Sherlock was still unconscious, covered with blankets, a local physician sitting on the floor beside her.

No one had much to say. Jimmy Maitland was sitting in a chair near Sherlock.

Savich picked up his wife, carried her to a chair, and sat down with her in his arms. He rocked her, never looking away from her face.

"It's as if she's asleep," the physician said, standing now beside him. "Just asleep. She should wake up soon and tell us what happened."

Jimmy Maitland said, "We've put out an island-wide alert for Timmy Tuttle, with description, and Marilyn Warluski, with description. The three agents with Sherlock didn't see a single blessed thing. Nada."

Savich nodded, touched his wife's hair. He didn't think he'd be surprised by anything ever again.

A few minutes later, Sherlock opened her eyes. She looked up and, surprisingly, smiled.

"You're holding me, Dillon. Why? What happened?"

"You don't remember?" He spoke very slowly, the words not really wanting to speak themselves, probably because he didn't want an answer.

She closed her eyes for a moment, frowned, then said, "I remember I ran into this room, three other agents behind me. No one was here." She frowned. "No, I'm not sure. There was something—a light maybe—something. I can't remember."

"When I came in, you were standing perfectly still, staring out that big window. The other agents were searching the room. But you didn't move, didn't twitch or anything, and then you just fell over."

Jimmy Maitland said, "Did you see anything of Timmy Tuttle or Marilyn?"

Sherlock said, "Timmy Tuttle—yes, that crazy-looking guy who was as pale as an apocalypse horseman—yes, I remember. He was holding Marilyn around her neck—a knife, yes, he had a knife. I was terrified when I saw Dillon go in after him into that conference room."

"You saw Timmy go into the conference room?"

"I think so. But that can't be right. Didn't he come in here?"

"We don't know. None of the agents saw him in here," Savich said. "No, Sherlock, that's okay. You just rest now. You'll probably remember more once you get yourself together. Does your head ache?"

"A bit, why?"

"You feel maybe a bit like you're hungover?"

"Well, yes, that's right."

Savich looked up at Jimmy Maitland and nodded. "Everyone I've spoken to, agents and civilians alike, everyone feels like that."

"Sherlock," Maitland said, crouching down beside her. "Why was it just you who collapsed? You must have seen something."

"I'm thinking, sir, as hard as I can."

Dillon slowly eased her up until she was sitting on his lap. She started shaking. Savich nearly lost it. He pulled her hard against him, protecting her, from what, he didn't know. He just didn't want her hurt, no more hurt, no more monsters from the unknown.

Then she said, pulling away from him just a little bit, her voice firm and steady, "Dillon, I'm all right. I promise. I've got stuff to think about. Something really weird happened, didn't it?"

"Yes."

"It's there, in the back of my brain, and I'll get it out."

TWENTY

Eureka, California

Morrie Jones stared at the young woman who had taken him down, hurt him, dammit, before he could get away from her. He just couldn't believe it. She was skinny, looked like a damned little debutante with her blond hair and blue eyes and innocent face, like the prototypical little WASP. That damned lawyer of his had even told him that she'd been recovering from surgery and she'd still stomped his ass. He really wanted to hurt her. Hell, he'd even do it for free, this time.

He said to Simon, "You claimed I didn't need my lawyer, that you just wanted to talk to me, that you had something to offer that I couldn't refuse. You from the DA's office?"

Simon said, "No, but I have her approval. I see you remember Ms. Savich."

"Nah, I heard her name was Frasier. I know that's right because that's the name of the broad I'm going to sue for attacking me."

Lily gave him a big smile. "You go ahead and sue me, boyo, and I'll just smack your face off again. What do you think?" She cracked her knuckles, a sound Morrie Jones had hated since was a kid and his old man did it whenever he was drunk.

"Stop that," Morrie said, staring at her hands. "Why'd the cops let you two in here?"

She cracked her knuckles again, something she'd rarely done since she was a bookie and some kid from another neighborhood had threatened to horn in on her territory. "What's the matter, Morrie? I still scare you?"

"Shut up, you bitch."

"Call me a bitch again and I'll make you eat your tongue." She gave him a sweet smile, with one dimple.

Simon said, "All right, that's enough. Listen up, Morrie. We want you to tell us who hired you. It could save your life."

Morrie started whistling "Old Man River."

Lily laughed. "Come on, Morrie, spare us. You got a brain? Use it. Herman Monk is dead, shot three times in the back."

"I don't know no Herman Monk. Sounds like a geek. Don't know him."

That could be true. Simon said, "Monk was a loose end. He's dead. You're a loose end, too, Morrie. Just think about your lawyer for a moment. Who is he? Who sent him? Who's paying his bill? Do you really think he's going to try to get *you* off?"

"I hired him. He's a real good friend, a drinking buddy. We watch the fights together down at Sam's Sports Bar, you know, over on Cliff Street."

Lily said, as she tapped her fingers on the Formica surface, split down the middle by bars, with Simon and Lily on one side, Morrie on the other, "He's setting you up, Morrie. You too stupid to use your brain? You know he told the sheriff that he took your case pro bono?"

"I want a cigarette."

"Don't be a moron. You want to die, hacking up your lungs? He said he took you on for free, out of the goodness of his heart. I want you to just think about all this. What did your lawyer promise you?"

"He said I was getting out of here, today."

"Yeah, we heard," Simon said, and it was true, according to Lieutenant Dobbs. The judge had called and was prepared to set bail. "You know what's going to happen then?"

"Yeah, I'm going to go get me a beer."

"That's possible," Lily said. "I hope you really

enjoy it, Morrie, because you're going to be dead by morning. These people really hate loose ends."

Morrie said, "Who did you say this Monk geek was?"

Lily said, "He was the curator of the museum where my grandmother's paintings were displayed. He was part of the group who had four of the paintings copied, the originals replaced with the fakes. When it all came out, when it was obvious that things were unraveling, he was shot in the back. That's why they wanted you to kill me. They were my paintings and here I am doing what they knew I'd do—stirring things up until I find out who stole my paintings. I wonder how long before they shoot you, Morrie."

"I'm leaving town, first thing."

"Good idea," Simon said. "But I see two big problems for you. The first is that you're still in jail. Your lawyer said he was going to get you out? Who's going to pay the bail, Morrie, and that's your second problem. Your pro bono lawyer? That's possible, what with all the money from the people who hired you in the first place. So, let's say you walk out of here, what are you going to do? Hide out in an alley and wait for them to kill you?"

Morrie believed him, Simon knew it in that

moment. Simon waited a beat, then said, "Turns out I can solve both problems for you."

"How?"

"Ms. Savich here will drop charges against you, we'll get you out of here without your lawyer knowing about it. To sweeten the deal, I'll give you five hundred bucks. That'll get you far away from these creeps, give you a new start. In return you give me the name of who hired you."

Morrie said, "Look, I'm going to sue her the minute I get out of here. Five hundred bucks? That's jack shit."

Simon's gut was good. He knew he was going to get Morrie. Just one more nudge. He turned on the recorder in his jacket pocket. "You know, Morrie, Lieutenant Dobbs and the DA don't really want me to cut any deal with you. I had to talk them into it. They want to take you to trial and throw your butt in jail for a long time. Since Lily hurt you pretty good, it's more than your word against hers. You'd be dead meat, Morrie."

It took only three more minutes of negotiation. Simon agreed to give Morrie Jones eight hundred dollars, Lily agreed to drop the charges, and Morrie agreed to give them a name.

"I want to see her sign papers and I want to see the money before I do anything."

Lieutenant Dobbs and the DA weren't pleased, but knew that Morrie was incidental compared to the person who'd hired him.

Lily, in the presence of Lieutenant Dobbs, an assistant DA, a detective, and two officers, signed that she was dropping the charges against one Morrie Jones, age twenty.

Once they were alone again, Morrie said, slouching back in his chair, "Now, big shot, give me the money before I say another word."

Simon rose, pulled his wallet out of his back pocket, and laid out the entire wad. There were eight one-hundred-dollar bills and a single twenty. "Glad you didn't wipe me out completely, Morrie. I appreciate it. That twenty will buy Lily and me a couple of tacos."

Morrie smirked as Simon started to slide the hundred-dollar bills through the space beneath the bars. "Tell me a story, Morrie."

"I don't exactly have a name. Hey, no, don't take the money back. I got just as good as a name. Look, she called me. It was this woman and she had this real thick accent, real Southern, you know? Smooth and real slow. She didn't give me her name, just Lily Frasier's name. She described her, told me where she was staying and to get it done fast.

"I went right over to the bank, picked up the money, then I went to work." He slid his eyes toward Lily. "It just didn't quite work out the way I wanted."

"That's because you're a wimp, Morrie."

Morrie half-rose out of his chair. The jail guard standing against the wall immediately straightened. Simon raised a hand. "How much did this woman pay you to kill Lily?"

"She gave me a thousand for a down payment. Then she was to have five thousand to me when it was done and on the news."

"This is not a good business, Simon." She stared at Morrie. "I was only worth six thousand dollars?"

Morrie actually smiled. "That's all. You know, I would have done it for less if I'd known you then."

Simon realized that Lily was enjoying herself. She was having a really fine pissing contest with this young thug. He pressed his knee against her leg.

But she had one more line. "What I did to you I did for nothing."

Simon just shook his head at her. "Morrie, which bank?"

"Give me the money first."

Simon slid the money all the way through. Morrie's hand slid over it, presto. He closed his young eyes for a moment, feeling the money like it was a lover's flesh. "Wells Fargo," he said, "the one just over on First Street and Pine. The money was there in my name."

"You didn't ask who had left the money waiting there for you?"

Morrie shook his head.

"Thanks, Morrie," Lily said as she rose. "Lieutenant Dobbs thinks you'll be out sometime this afternoon. He's agreed not to tell your lawyer. My advice to you—get the hell out of Dodge. This time you don't have to be afraid of me. The woman who hired you—chances are good she wants you dead, and she's capable of doing it herself."

"You know who she is?"

Lily said, "Oh yeah, we know. She'd eat you with her poached eggs for breakfast. Hey, what happened to the thousand bucks she gave you?"

Morrie's eyes slid away. "None of your damned business."

Lily laughed, shook her finger at him. "You pissed it away in a poker game, didn't you?"

"No, dammit. It was pool."

Clark Hoyt was waiting for them in Lieutenant Dobbs's office. His arms were folded over his chest. He looked very odd. "I got a call from Savich. He was calling from Saint John's, in Antigua, of all places, said to tell you that all hell will break loose in the media really soon now, but that he and Sherlock are okay. It seems

that Tammy Tuttle got ahold of Marilyn Warluski and they're gone. There was a big situation
there at the airport. Savich called it a fiasco."

"Antigua?" Simon said. "I guess he couldn't
tell us he was there."

Lily said, shaking her head, "Dillon will not
be a happy camper about this."

Hoyt himself wondered what had happened,
but he said only, "Savich didn't give me any details, said he'd call again this evening. I told him
where you guys are staying now. Okay, tell me
who hired Morrie."

"Yeah," Lieutenant Dobbs said as he came
into his own office to see the two civilians and
the Fed. "Who was it?"

"It was my mother-in-law," Lily said. "No
doubt at all that it was Charlotte. She didn't
give Morrie her name, but that accent of hers—
it has so much syrup in it, you could sweeten a
rock."

Lieutenant Dobbs shook his head. "So now
you know, but there's still no case. Both Hoyt
and I interviewed the Frasiers—all three of
them—separately. In all three cases, their lawyer,
Bradley Abbott, a real son of a bitch hardnose,
was present. The Frasiers refused to answer any
questions. Abbott read a statement to us. In the
statement, the Frasiers claim all of this is nonsense. They are sorry about Mr. Monk, but it

has nothing to do with them, and this is a waste of everyone's time. Oh yeah, then their lawyer told us that you were nuts, Lily, that you'd do anything to get back at them, for what reason they don't know, but no one should believe a single word you say. We need more evidence before we can bring them to the station and put them in an interview room again."

Hoyt said to Simon and Lily, "We'll have two agents on Morrie Jones. Lieutenant Dobbs hasn't got a problem with that, especially since he's short officers right now. We won't let the little twerp out of our sight."

"Good," said Lieutenant Dobbs. "All right, listen up. I've got a murder to solve. As for you, Lily, you're just an attempted murder, so I guess I can let you slide just a bit. I understand this thing is more complicated than a Greek knot, and that all of it ties together."

Simon said, "If it's okay with you, Lieutenant, I'd like to go to Wells Fargo to see if there's a record of who gave Morrie a thousand dollars for the hit on Lily. That'd be too easy, but it's worth a shot."

Lieutenant Dobbs said, "She paid that little dip just a thousand bucks to off Lily?"

"Oh, no," Lily said. "I'm worth lots more than that. There was another five thousand bucks when the job was done."

Simon said, "Okay, then, let's get cracking."

On the way out the door, Lily looked at Simon for a moment, at his too-long, very dark hair, and realized she hadn't really noticed before how it curled at his neck. "Those little curls—they're cute," she said and patted his nape.

Simon rolled his eyes.

Hoyt, who was walking behind them, laughed.

Since Hoyt was along, they got instant cooperation at Wells Fargo. One of the vice presidents, who seemed more numerous than tellers at the windows, hustled onto the computer and punched up the money transfer transactions for the very morning Morrie had attacked Lily on the city bus.

Mr. Trempani raised his head, looked at each of them in turn. "This is very strange. The money was wired in care of Mr. Morrie Jones by a company called Tri-Light Investments. Any of you ever heard of them?"

"Tri-Light," Lily said. "I don't think Tennyson ever mentioned that company."

"Who are they?" Hoyt asked.

"All we have is an account number in Zurich, Switzerland. It simply lists Tri-Light Investments and the Habib Bank AG at 59 Weinbergstrasse."

"Curiouser and curiouser," Simon said.

Hoyt said, "I'll call Interpol and get someone to check this out. But don't count on finding anything out. The Swiss have duct tape over their mouths." He paused for a moment. "You suspect someone, don't you, Simon? And not just the Frasiers. Who?"

"If the owner of this Tri-Light Investments is a Swede by the name of Olaf Jorgenson, then we're confirming lots of things," Simon said.

"Makes sense," Hoyt said. "He's the collector, isn't he? That's how it all ties into Ms. Savich's paintings. You guys think he's the one who commissioned them."

"It's possible," Simon said.

Lily punched Simon in the ribs. "It's more than possible, Clark. Call us on the cell phone as soon as you know, okay?"

Hoyt said, "You promised no hotdogging. That means you don't go see Charlotte Frasier without having at least me along."

Hemlock Bay, California

Lily pointed to the Bullock Pharmacy, and Simon pulled into an open parking spot in front of Spores Dry Cleaners next door. An old man was staring out at them from the large glass windows that held three hanging Persian carpets, presumably just cleaned.

Ten minutes later, Lily came out of the Bullock Pharmacy carrying a small paper bag. She eased into the passenger seat and drew a deep breath. "It's such a beautiful town," she said. "I always thought so. You can smell the ocean, feel that light sheen of salt on your skin. It's incredible."

"Okay, I agree, lovely town, lovely smell in the air. What happened?"

"I had a real epiphany going into that pharmacy." And then she told him what had happened. There'd been about ten people in the store, and all of them, after they saw her, were talking about her behind their hands. They stepped away if she came near them, didn't say anything if she said hello to them. Lily was frankly relieved when Mr. Bullock senior, at least eighty years old, nodded to her at the checkout line. Evidently he was the spokesperson. He looked at her straight in the eye before he rang up her aspirin and said, "Everyone is real sorry you tried to kill yourself again, Mrs. Frasier."

"I didn't, Mr. Bullock."

"We heard that you blamed it on Dr. Frasier and left him."

"Is that what everyone believes?"

"We've known the Frasiers a long time, ma'am. Lots longer than we've known you."

"Actually, Mr. Bullock, it's very far from the truth. Someone has tried to kill me three times now."

He just shook his head at her, waved the bottle of aspirin, and said, "You need something stronger than these, Mrs. Frasier. Something lots stronger. You'll never live to be as old as I am if you don't see to it now."

"Why don't you talk to Lieutenant Dobbs in Eureka?"

He just looked at her, saying nothing more. Lily didn't feel like standing there arguing with the old man to change his mind, with the dozen other people in the store likely listening, so she just paid and left, knowing those people were thinking she was one sick puppy, no doubt about it.

"That's it. Nothing much, really." She waved the bottle of aspirin. "Thanks, Simon." He handed her a bottle of diet Dr Pepper, and she took two of the tablets.

"Isn't it interesting that no one wanted to speak to me," she said, "except Mr. Bullock. They were all content just to hang back and listen."

"It's still a beautiful town. Tennyson, Mom,

and Dad have been busy," Simon said. "How about some lunch?"

After a light lunch at a diner that sat right on the main pier, Lily said, "I want to visit my daughter, Simon."

For a moment, he didn't understand. She saw it and said, even as tears stung her eyes, "The cemetery. After I leave, I know I won't be back for a while. I want to say good-bye."

He wasn't about to let her go by herself. It was too dangerous. When he told her that, she simply nodded. They stopped at a small florist shop at the end of Whipple Avenue, Molly Ann's Blooms.

"Hilda Gaddis owns Molly Ann's. She sent a beautiful bouquet of yellow roses to Beth's funeral."

"The daffodils are lovely."

"Yes. Beth loved daffodils." She said nothing more as they drove the seven minutes to the cemetery set near the Presbyterian Church. It was lovely, in a pocket nestled by hemlock and spruce trees, protected from the winds off the ocean.

He walked with her up a narrow pathway that forked to the right. There was a beautiful etched white marble stone, an angel carved on top, her arms spread wide. Beth's name was beneath, the date of her birth, the date of her death, and beneath, the words *She Gave Me Infinite Joy.*

Lily was crying, but made no sound. Simon watched her go down on her knees and arrange the daffodils against the headstone.

He wanted to comfort her but realized in those moments that she needed to be alone. He turned away and went back to the rental car. His cell phone rang.

It was Clark Hoyt, and he was excited.

TWENTY-ONE

Saint John's, Antigua

There was nothing more for Savich to do in Antigua. Timmy Tuttle, with two healthy arms, had Marilyn, and Savich didn't want to even think of what he was doing to her.

Or maybe two different people had her, one wild-eyed man with black hair and two arms, and a woman with one arm and madness and rage in her eyes.

Savich couldn't stand himself. He'd set up Marilyn, gotten an FBI agent killed, along with a local police officer, and left chaos in his wake. He knew he'd see Virginia Cosgrove's sightless eyes for a very long time, and that long red gash that had slit her throat open.

Jimmy Maitland had taken his arm, trying to calm him down. "Batten down the guilt, Savich. I approved everything you did. We faced something or someone that shouldn't have been there. It happened. You've got to prepare to move on."

Maitland shook his head, ran fingers through his gray hair, making it stand on end. "Jesus, I'm losing it. There's nothing more we can do here. We're going home. I'm leaving Vinny Arbus and his SWAT team in charge. They'll keep looking for Marilyn and coordinate with local law enforcement. This confusion, Savich, it will unravel in time. There's an explanation, there has to be."

Savich didn't let Sherlock out of his sight. He realized soon enough that she was different—more quiet, her attention not on any of them, and he'd look at her and know she was thinking about what had happened, her eyes focused, yet somehow far away.

There was so much cleanup, so many explanations to give, most omitting the inexplicable things because they didn't help anyone to know the sorts of things that could drive you mad. And most important, there was no sign of the man who'd taken Marilyn Warluski from the Saint John's airport.

When they got back to Washington, Savich left immediately for the gym and worked out until he was panting for breath, his body so exhausted it was ready to rebel.

When he walked in the front door, feeling so exhausted each step was a chore, his son was there to greet him, crawling for all he was worth right up to Savich's feet, grabbing onto his pants leg. Savich started to reach down to pick him up when he heard Sherlock say, "No, wait a second."

Sean yanked hard on his father's pants, got a good hold, braced himself, and managed to pull himself up. Then he grinned up at his father and lifted one leg, then the other.

All the miserable unanswerable questions, all the deadening sense of failure, fell away. Savich whooped, picked up his son, and tossed him into the air, again and again, until Sean was both yelling and laughing, one and then the other.

It was Savich who wrote Sean's accomplishment in his baby book that evening. "An almost giant step for kid-kind." Then "The leg lift, one at a time—he's getting ready to walk, amazing. His grandmother says I started walking early, too."

In bed that night, Sherlock nuzzled her head into Savich's neck, lightly laid her palm over his heart, and said, "Sean brings back focus, doesn't he?"

"Yes. I was ready to fall over from working out so hard when I walked in the house, and then he crawls over to me and pulls himself up. Then he lifts each leg, testing them out, nearly ready to take off. I didn't think I had any laughter left in me, but I guess I do."

"Don't feel guilty about it. You should have seen Gabriella. She was so tickled when I got home, so proud of both herself and Sean that she couldn't wait to show off what he could do. Those leg lifts, I haven't read about that in any baby books. Gabriella got some video of him doing that with me. I swear she didn't want to leave this afternoon. I expect her husband to call me and complain about what demanding employers we are."

Savich settled his hand on her hip, kneaded her for a moment, thinking she'd dropped weight, kissed her forehead, then turned on his back to stare up at the dark ceiling.

"Dillon?"

"Hmm?"

"I waited until Sean was in bed and we were lying here, all relaxed."

"Waited for what, sweetheart?"

She took a deep breath. "I've remembered some stuff that happened in that room at the airport."

Hemlock Bay

Hoyt said, "You'll never believe this, Simon!"

"Yeah, yeah, what, Clark?"

"Lieutenant Dobbs, he's got—"

Simon heard the slight shifting in sound, perhaps a small movement in the backseat of the car, but just as he knew something was different, he felt something very hard come down over his right temple. He slumped forward on the steering wheel, his forehead striking the horn.

It blared.

"Simon? Simon, where are you? What the hell happened?"

Lily heard the horn. Their rental car? But Simon was there, surely. Then she realized something was very wrong. She was on her feet in a second, racing down those beautifully manicured paths to the visitors' parking lot. She heard the man running behind her, just one man; she heard the deep crunching of gravel beneath his feet.

She ran faster, veering away from the parking lot, running back into the thick stand of hemlock and spruce trees. She was fast, always had been.

She heard the man shout, but not at her. He was shouting at his accomplice. What had happened to Simon? The horn was still blaring, but it was more distant now. And then she realized that he must have fallen on the horn. Was he dead? No, no, he couldn't be, he just couldn't.

She was through the trees, out the back, and there was the damned cliff, miles and miles of it, running north and south. She had been here before, and there wasn't any escape this way. What to do?

She ran along the edge of the cliff, searching for a way down, and found one, some yards ahead just before the cliff curved inward, probably from sliding and erosion over the years. There was a skinny, snaking trail, and she took it without hesitation. There was nothing ahead except empty land dotted with trees and gullies. They'd get her for sure, that or just shoot her down. Maybe there was something there on the beach. Anything was better than staying up here and being an easy target.

The path was steep, and she had to slow way down. Still she tripped a couple of times, and the last time, she had to grab a bush that grew beside the trail to halt her fall. It had thorns, and she felt them score her hands and fingers.

She vaguely heard birds calling overhead.

She knew the men had to be nearly at the top of the trail now. They'd come after her. What was down here except more beach? There had to be someplace to hide, some cover, a cave, anything.

Her breath was spurting out of her, broken, tight. A stitch ripped through her side. She ignored it. She had to be calm, keep herself in control.

She kept her eyes on the winding trail. Wouldn't it ever stop? She heard the men now, yelling from the top for her to come back up, they weren't going to hurt her.

She managed three more steps, then there was a shot, then an instant ricochet off a rock just one foot to her right, scattering chips in all directions. A chip hit her in the leg, but it didn't go through her jeans.

She hunkered down as much as she could, twisting to the left, then the right, going down until at last her feet hit the hard sand on the beach. She chanced a look back up to the top and saw one of the men start down after her. The other man was aiming his gun at her. It was a handgun, not accurate enough at this distance, she hoped.

It wasn't. He shot at her three more times, but none of the bullets seemed to strike close to her.

She stumbled over a gnarly piece of driftwood and went flying. She landed on her stomach, her hands in front of her face. She saw wet sand, driftwood, kelp, and even one frantic sand crab not six inches from her nose.

She lay there for just a moment, drawing in deep breaths, feeling the stitch in her side lessen. Then she was up again. She saw the man coming down the trail, but he wasn't being as careful as she'd been. He was a big guy, not in the best of shape. He was wearing those opaque wraparound sunglasses, so she couldn't really make out his features. He had thick, light brown hair and a gun in his right hand. She watched him stumble, wildly clutching at the air to regain his balance, but he didn't. He tumbled head over heels down the trail and landed hard at the bottom, not moving. His gun. His gun was her only chance. She'd seen it flying. She ran to his side in an instant. She picked up a big piece of driftwood, realized it was soggy and not heavy enough, and grabbed up a rock instead. She leaned over him and brought the rock down on his head as hard as she could. She slipped her hand inside his coat and pulled out his wallet. She shoved it into her pocket, then saw the gun some six feet back up the trail, just off to the side, lying on top of a pile of rocks.

The man on top was yelling, firing, but she ignored him. She got the gun, turned, and ran for all she was worth down the beach.

Washington, D.C.

Savich felt his heart pounding faster beneath his wife's palm. He shot up, turned on the bedside lamp, then faced her. "Tell me."

"I remember being scared for you when I saw you go into that conference room. Then I'm sure I saw Timmy Tuttle dragging Marilyn into that security room across the hall. I ran into the room, the three other agents behind me. The room was empty. At least that's what I thought at first.

"I saw this bright light, Dillon. It nearly blinded me, and I swear to you, for some reason I just couldn't move. The light was right in front of that big window, and I know I saw Timmy and Marilyn in the middle of that light.

"I could hear the other agents yelling at each other. I realized they weren't seeing what I was. Still I couldn't move. I was just nailed to the spot looking at that white light. Then Timmy Tuttle grabbed Marilyn tight around her neck, and . . ."

"And what?"

"Dillon, I'm not crazy, I swear."

He pulled her against him. "I know."

"They just disappeared. It was like they were right in front of me, then they were in front of the window, and the window was bathed in the white light. Then they receded through that white light until they were gone. Then everything just seemed to close down. That's all I remember."

Savich said, "That's just fine, Sherlock. Well done. It fits right into the rest of it. It seems logical to everyone that Tammy Tuttle used some sort of mass hypnosis. You know how David Copperfield walked through the Great Wall of China? How he got sawed in half with millions of people watching, most of them on TV?"

"Yes. You think Tammy has this skill?"

"It makes sense. There she or he was with Marilyn, and then she or he just wasn't there. I think the whole thing was this big performance that she worked out to show us that we are dealing with a master. You know what else I think? I think Tammy knew I was trying to trap her and using Marilyn as bait. She knew we'd be at the airport waiting for her. She was ready for us. I also think she really wants us to believe that everything we saw was supernatural, beyond our meager brains. But it's not. She's just very, very good. She wanted to scare us all to death, paralyze us. I do wonder, though, why she didn't try to kill me."

Sherlock pulled away, stroked her fingers

over his jaw, and said, "I think it's because she couldn't get close enough to you. I've given this a lot of thought, Dillon, and I think you're one of the few people Tammy's ever met whom she can't hypnotize or perform an illusion for when she's up close to you. And if she can't get close to you without your seeing exactly what she is, then she can't kill you."

"You mean if I had been close to her, I wouldn't have seen Timmy, I'd have really seen Tammy?"

"Yes, it sounds reasonable. If she can't get close enough to you without your seeing her exactly as she is, then she knows she's at a disadvantage. When you were in the barn in Maryland with her, how far away were you standing from her?"

"Maybe two dozen feet."

"And she was always just what she was? Tammy Tuttle?"

"Yes. She called the Ghouls, but she didn't change. When I shot her, I saw the bullet nearly rip her arm from her body. I saw her fall, heard her yells of pain. She remained exactly what she was and who she was."

Sherlock said, "Then at the airport, she just couldn't get close enough to you to kill you. And she realized, too, that she couldn't get too close or you'd see her as she really is and kill her. She's being really careful after what you did to her at the barn."

Savich said, "Jimmy Maitland called me at the gym, told me that Jane Bitt in Behavioral Sciences allowed that just maybe it is possible that Tammy is a strong telepath in addition to all her illusion skills. She won't swear to it, says she doesn't want to get mocked out, but we should consider it, given the incredible control Tammy was able to exert at the airport."

Sherlock said, "So maybe she's got both this talent and skill in creating illusions. I think you were right. Tammy knew that you were setting her up. She also knew that you would bring Marilyn. For whatever reason, she wanted Marilyn back. I'm just hoping that she didn't want her back to kill her. Maybe she really is fond of Marilyn. Maybe Marilyn feeds her ego, makes her feel powerful because she's so very malleable and suggestible. Tammy can make Marilyn see, make her believe anything she tells her to believe. Didn't you tell me that Marilyn firmly believes everything Tammy says?"

"Oh, yes, and it's genuine, Sherlock. Even under hypnosis, Marilyn was frightened of Tammy and she believed everything she said to Dr. Hicks and to me. She remembered it as fact, for heaven's sake, so she had to have believed it."

Savich threw back the covers and jumped to his feet. He grabbed a pair of jeans as an afterthought and pulled them on. "I'm going to do some research on this with MAX."

He walked back to the bed, grinned down at his wife, pulled her up tightly against him, and kissed her until she would have just as soon he waited until morning to visit MAX. But she knew that brain of his was working again, asking questions, wanting to know everything, and fast.

"I won't be gone too long."

She lay back down in bed, shut off the table lamp, pulled the covers to her chin, and smiled into the darkness when she heard Dillon speaking to MAX down the hall in his study. She heard him laugh.

TWENTY-TWO

Hemlock Bay, California

There weren't any caves, not even one in-
dentation in the rock where she could squeeze in
and wait them out. Just a beach that went on and
on, driftwood piled all over it, and slimy trails of
kelp, dangerous when you were running.

But she had a gun. It was small and ugly, but
she wasn't defenseless. From what she knew
about guns, which wasn't much, it was a close-
range gun, useless at a distance, but if you got
near enough, it could kill a person quite easily.

The temperature dropped as the sun went
behind gathering clouds, whirling rain clouds.
Any minute now rain would pour down.
Would that help her or not? She didn't know.

Had there been three men? One staying with
Simon and the other two after her? Maybe there
were just two men and Simon could get away

and call for help. They'd been idiots—telling their FBI protectors that since they were just going to the cemetery and they wanted to be private, they'd meet them back in Hemlock Bay.

She stopped, bending over, her hands on her thighs, so tired her breath was catching and she was wheezing with the effort to breathe. She flattened herself in the shadow of the cliff and looked back.

Then, suddenly, she heard one of the men cup his hands around his mouth and shout, "Lily Frasier! We have Simon Russo. Come out now or we will kill him. That is a promise. Then we will call our friends to come at you from the other end of the beach. We will trap you, and you won't like what will happen to you then."

The man's words brought her breath back, straightened her right up. The man's voice was also thick with an accent—stilted, unnatural. Swedish. Well, damn, it seemed that Olaf Jorgenson himself had come, or sent his friends. She ran again, until she rounded a slight promontory and looked up. She had found her way out. Another narrow trail snaked up the cliff, much like the one she'd taken down. Two miles back up the beach? Three miles? She didn't make a sound, just shot up that trail, using her hands on rocks and scrubs, anything to keep her steady, knowing they couldn't see her until they came around the promontory themselves.

They couldn't kill Simon. They'd left him alone in the car. If there was a third man watching him, well then, they couldn't contact him. Unless they had a cell phone. Everybody had a cell phone. Oh, God, please, no. It had to be a bluff, it just had to be.

She slipped once, saw pebbles and small rocks gushing out from the cliff and pounding their way back down to the beach. She held still, then started up again. She was up to the top of the cliff in no time and running. The men would realize soon enough where she'd gone.

Hurry, she had to hurry. She hurt, really bad, but she thought of Simon, of his hair curling at his neck, and she knew nothing could happen to him. She wouldn't let it. Too much loss in her life, she couldn't bear any more. She came into the back of the cemetery, climbed the wrought-iron fence, and ran down the path toward the visitors' parking lot.

The horn wasn't blaring anymore.

Nearly there, she was nearly there. She saw their rental car, but didn't see Simon. She got to the car. He was stretched out on the front seat, unconscious. Or dead.

She pulled the driver's side door open. "Simon! Wake up, dammit! Wake up!"

He moaned, struggled to a sitting position. He blinked, finally focusing on her face.

"They're after us, two men, both with guns. I got away from them but we don't have much time. Scoot over, we're getting out of here. I'm going to drive us right to jail and have Lieutenant Dobbs lock us in. It's the only safe place in the world. No lawyers allowed. Just Lieutenant Dobbs. He can bring our food. We'll get Dillon and Sherlock out here. They'll figure this all out, and we can get the hell out of here."

As she spoke, she managed to shove his feet off the seat and push him toward the passenger door. "It will be all right. You don't have to do anything, see, I can drive now. Just rest, Simon."

"No, Lily, no more driving. You're not going anywhere, not anymore."

Lily turned slowly at that syrupy voice and stared up at Charlotte Frasier, who was pointing a long-barreled gun at her. "You've given us too much trouble. If I hadn't decided to oversee this myself, you would have escaped yet again. I always believed three times was a charm, and so it is. Get out of the car, Lily. Now."

Lily wasn't surprised, not really. Not Elcott, but Charlotte. Then she almost smiled. Charlotte didn't know she had a gun, too. Would

Charlotte take the chance of killing them here, in the cemetery parking lot? She believed all the way to her gut that Charlotte was capable of anything. She was still free, and Mr. Monk had been dead for three days now.

Then she saw the men running toward them. She had to hurry, had to do something. She opened the door, lifting one arm, hiding the other hand slightly behind her.

"Where's Elcott?" she said, wanting to distract Charlotte, just for an instant. "And that marvelous son of yours? Who loves me so much he'd like nothing more than to bury me? Aren't they hanging back there, waiting for you to tell them what to do?"

"Don't you dare speak of my husband and my son like that—"

Lily was clear. She raised the gun and fired.

Washington, D.C.
FBI Headquarters

Ollie Hamish came running into Savich's office. "We got him! We got Anthony Carpelli, aka Wilbur Wright. He was right there in Kitty Hawk on the Outer Banks. He was kneeling in front of the monument at Kitty Hawk and we came up on him and he just folded down like a tent and gave it all up."

For an instant, Savich was so distracted he didn't know what Ollie was talking about. Then he remembered, the guru from Texas who'd had his followers murder the two deputies and the sheriff, the Sicilian Canadian who'd attended McGill University and had an advanced degree in cellular biology. Savich said slowly, "Sit down, Ollie. You said he was kneeling at the monument? As in worshiping?"

"Maybe so. All the agents were so relieved at how easily it went down, they were celebrating, drinking beers at eleven o'clock in the morning. We got him, Savich. He'll go back to Texas and fry, probably."

"Probably not," Savich said. "Remember that he isn't tied directly to those killings, just hearsay from a woman who was pissed off."

"Yes, Lureen. Evidently they're holding her as a material witness. They've also picked up two more of Wilbur's people who were in the cult. Everyone thinks his own people will finally nail his ass. At least we got him and he's not going to be killing anybody else.

"Hey, Savich, you should be really pleased. After all, it was you and MAX who predicted he'd probably go back to Kitty Hawk."

Savich realized he was so caught up with

Tammy Tuttle that he didn't feel much of anything about Wilbur Wright. And it was a victory, a very clean win. Everyone would be very pleased. He smiled at Ollie. "I am pleased. MAX discovered sixteen more killings throughout the Southwestern U.S. that sound like the work of Wilbur. So there's lots of other crimes to tie in to this one; local law enforcement be brought up to speed and get with the program. Dane Carver is heading that up. Now that you've got Wilbur Wright, you can get our doctors on him and see what makes him tick."

"I really don't want to know."

"Unfortunately a jury will demand to know. Meet with Dane and go over all the other cases, then head down to interview Wilbur."

"When we caught him, I looked at him, Savich. You know, I don't think I've ever seen such dead eyes, and I've seen lots of bad folk up close and personal; but Wilber, he was just flat-out scary. You wonder what exactly he's seeing with those dead eyes. It won't be long before they extradite him back to Texas with more than enough evidence to fry his butt."

"You can bet the lawyers will fight extradition."

"Yeah, they'd prefer a state where there's no death penalty, but if we get enough evidence, it won't matter."

"We done good, Ollie. Now you and Dane sew it up, okay?"

"You got it." Agent Ollie Hamish leaned forward in his chair, clasping his hands between his legs. "I've heard all sorts of things, Savich, about what happened in Antigua. How's that going?"

Savich told him all of it. "We've got people working on where she learned her illusion skills so we can get a better handle on what she's capable of. There are more people scouring the airport in Antigua trying to find out how she managed to get away, questioning everyone in the area, searching all boats, all private charters."

Ollie said, "She's still got only one arm and, physically, she's in bad shape, right?"

"I don't know how bad it still is. Her surgeon said if she has an infection, she could be dead within a week without antibiotics. But if she doesn't have an infection, she could make it through just fine. He said she responded superbly to the surgery. I asked the doctor if anyone had ever reported seeing someone other than Tammy Tuttle or seeing her where she shouldn't be."

"Did he even understand what you meant?"

"Yes," Savich said slowly, "he did. He said that an orderly told him he'd just seen Tammy up and walking to the bathroom the day after surgery. When he went to check her, she was lying strapped down to the bed. Nobody believed the orderly. Then she escaped and no one could figure that out, either. Anyway, Ollie, how are Maria and Josh? He just turned two, right?"

"Yeah. He's running all over the house, opening every drawer, banging every pot. He yells 'no' at least fifty times a day, and he's cuter than the new puppy we just got, who peed on the shirt I was going to wear this morning."

Savich laughed. It felt good. He nodded Ollie out, then turned back to MAX.

A call came in an hour later. Tammy Tuttle had been spotted in Bar Harbor, Maine, where agents had showed her photo all over town, along with Marilyn's, and left phone numbers. A local photo shop owner had called the Bar Harbor police department to say she'd left film and was going to come back.

"I've got to get close to her," Savich said to Sherlock. He kissed her nose and left the unit, nearly on a run, shouting over his shoulder, "I've got to see Tammy with one arm, and not something she wants me to see."

"Please, not too close," Sherlock called out, but she didn't think he heard her.

It took very little time for Savich and six other agents to board a Sabreliner at Andrews Air Force Base for a flight to Bar Harbor.

He spent the entire flight telling the agents everything he could think of. It was time, Savich decided, feeling a weight lift off his shoulders, to let everyone know exactly what they were dealing with.

A psychopathic killer who is an illusionist, possibly a telepath. He had never seen anything like it, and he hoped he never would again.

He'd just finished telling all the agents about the Ghouls, detailing what Marilyn had told him and what he himself had seen. If they didn't believe him, they were cool enough to keep it to themselves.

One agent, a friend of Virginia Cosgrove's, didn't doubt a single word. As they were debarking from the jet in Bar Harbor, she said, "Virginia told me some things Marilyn Warluski had told her. It was terrifying, Mr. Savich."

"Just Savich, Ms. Rodriguez. I'm very sorry about Agent Cosgrove."

"We all are, sir." Then she managed a grin. "Just Lois, Savich."

"You got it."

"The thing is, guys," he said to all of them, "if you see her or him again"—he waved the artist's drawing under all their noses—"don't play any games. Don't even think about trying to take her alive. Don't trust anything you see happen, fire without hesitation, and shoot to kill. Now, I'm going to the photo shop, make sure there's no confusion. Then we'll get together at the local police department and get everything set up."

He wondered if the Ghouls would be with her, with Tammy as their head acolyte, their priestess of death.

He was becoming melodramatic. All he really knew as he walked into the photo shop, Hamlet's Pics, on Wescott Avenue, was that he was glad to his soul that Sherlock wasn't here, that she was at home, safe with Sean.

He spoke to the photo shop employee, Teddi Tyler—spelled with an "i" he was told—to verify what he'd said to the local police. Teddi repeated that the woman whose photo Savich was showing him had indeed been in the shop, just yesterday, late afternoon. He'd called the police right away.

"What did she want?"

"She had some film she wanted developed."

Savich felt his heart pound, deep and slow, and it was all he could do to remain calm and smooth. They were so close now. "Did you develop the film, Mr. Tyler?"

"Yes, sir, Agent Savich. The police told me to go ahead and develop it and hold the photos for the FBI."

"When did she say she wanted to pick the photos up?"

"This afternoon, at two o'clock. I told her that would be just fine."

"Did she look like she was in good health, Mr. Tyler?"

"She was sort of pale, but looked good other than that. It was pretty cold yesterday so she was all bundled up in a thick coat, a big scarf around her neck and a wool ski cap, but I still recognized her, no problem."

"Did you make any comment to her about how she looked familiar?"

"Oh, no, Agent Savich. I was really cool."

Yeah, I bet, Savich thought, praying that he'd been cool enough not to alert Tammy that he was on to her. One thing—Teddi Tyler was still alive, and that meant Tammy hadn't felt threatened, he hoped. Everything he'd told Savich so far was exactly what he'd told the local cops.

"I want you to think carefully now, Mr. Tyler. When she handed you the film, which hand did she use?"

Teddi frowned, furrowing his forehead into three deep lines. "Her left hand," he said at last. "Yes, it was her left hand. She had her purse on a long strap hanging over her left shoulder. It was kind of clumsy."

"Did you ever see her right hand?"

Again Teddi went into a big frown. "I'm sorry, Agent Savich," he said finally, shaking his head, "I just don't remember. All I'm sure about is that she stayed all bundled up—again no surprise, since it was so cold."

"Thank you, Mr. Tyler. Now, a special agent will take your place behind the counter. Agent Briggs will be in soon and you can go over procedures with him." Savich raised his hand, seeing that Teddi Tyler wanted to argue. "There's no way you are going to face this woman again, Mr. Tyler. She's very dangerous, even to us. Now, show me those photos."

Savich took the photo envelope from Teddi and moved away from the counter to the glass front windows. The sun was shining brightly for a November day. It didn't look like it was forty degrees outside. He slowly opened the envelope and pulled out the glossy 4x6 photos. There were only six of them.

He looked at one after the other, and then looked again. He didn't understand. All of them were beach shots, undubtedly taken in the Caribbean. Two were taken in the early morning, two when the sun was high, and two at sunset. None of them was very well done—

well, that made sense since she had only one
arm—but what was the point? All beach shots,
no people in any of them. What was this about?

He held the photos up to Teddi. "Did she say
anything about the photos? What they were?
Anything at all?"

"Yeah, she said they were vacation photos
she wanted to show her roommate. Said her
roommate didn't believe her when she'd said
how beautiful it was down in the Caribbean.
She had to prove it."

If Tammy hadn't lied, then Marilyn was alive.
She wanted Marilyn to admire the beaches in
the Caribbean.

He told Teddi Tyler to take off as soon as
Agent Briggs arrived. As for Briggs, he was a
natural retailer, experienced in undercover jobs.
He was fast, a good judge of people's behavior.
Savich trusted him. Briggs knew how dangerous Tammy was, knew everything Savich
knew.

They had three hours to get it all set up.
There were three agents undercover near Mar-
ilyn's boyfriend's house just off Newport Drive.
He doubted they would see either Marilyn or
Tammy at the boyfriend's house. Of course not,
Savich thought, that would be too easy.

Savich left, drew the salty air deep into his
lungs, and called Simon Russo on his way to

the meet with the other agents. He hadn't spoken to Russo or Lily in nearly thirty hours. He knew they were all right; otherwise Hoyt would have yelled out. Still, he wanted to know what was happening. He was worried about Lily, just couldn't help it. He knew Simon would protect her with his life, knew Hoyt and the Eureka police were with them all the way. But still, she was his sister, and he loved her deeply. He didn't want anything to happen to her. When he thought of what she'd already endured, he felt rage in his gut.

The more he thought about it, the more Savich worried.

He pulled his leather jacket collar up around his ears and dialed. Simon's cell phone didn't answer. Savich wasn't about to second-guess himself and try to believe that the battery was dead. He immediately put in a call to Clark Hoyt.

TWENTY-THREE

Bar Harbor, Maine

Clark Hoyt answered his cell phone on the third ring. "Savich? Good thing you called. We can't find Simon or Lily. Our guys have been sticking close to them, but when Lily wanted to go to the cemetery, everyone decided they'd be safe there, and so we agreed to give them some privacy. Jesus, Savich, they went after them in the cemetery!

"When they didn't show up in an hour at Bender's Café in Hemlock Bay, my agents called me, then drove to the cemetery. We found Simon's rental car and one of the Frasier's cars in the parking lot. There weren't any other cars around. We know Lily visited her daughter's grave because the daffodils she'd bought were there."

Hoyt paused.

"What is it, Clark? What else did you find?"

"Some blood on the front seats, Savich, just a trace, but there was blood on the parking lot cement, a good bit more. We're testing it. We fucked up, Savich. Jesus, I'm sorry. We'll find them, I swear it to you."

Savich felt fear twisting in his belly, but when he spoke, his voice was controlled. "The fact that you found the Frasiers' car there as well as Simon's—were the Frasiers taken, too? Or were the Frasiers a part of it and just left their car there? If they plan to come back, then why would they leave their car next to Simon's— that's a sure giveaway that they were involved."

"That's what we think."

"At least you didn't find them dead. They've been taken. By whom?"

"We're trying to track down the Frasiers, but nothing yet. They must be with Simon and Lily. Lieutenant Dobbs and I went to the hospital to see Tennyson Frasier. He claimed he didn't know where his parents were. Seemed to me that he really didn't care one way or the other. When we told him that Lily was gone, I thought he'd go nuts. This Dr. Rossetti—you remember, the shrink who wanted to treat Lily when she was still in the hospital after the accident? The guy Lily didn't like? Well, he was there with Tennyson. He got all huffy, said

Tennyson was a fine man, a great doctor, and his wife was a bitch and didn't deserve him. He then gave Tennyson three happy pills while we were watching. I'll tell you, Savich, I think Tennyson really doesn't know anything about the disappearance."

Savich was hearing everything, but he wasn't thinking a whole lot in that instant. He was flat-out scared. He wanted to leave Bar Harbor and fly immediately out to California, but he couldn't. He simply couldn't leave. It was that simple and that final. He said, "I'm not sure what I think right at this moment, Clark. And I can't break free. I'm up to my eyeballs right now." He drew a deep breath. "Actually, we're about to confront a psychopathic killer right here in Bar Harbor, Maine, and I'm in charge."

"Look, Savich, there are a whole bunch of us on this. We'll find out who took them."

Yeah, yeah, Savich thought, then said, "If this Olaf Jorgenson is behind this, we're talking about a lot of resources, like a private Learjet here, with flight plans out of the country. It won't be hard to find them."

"We're already on that. I'll call you when we get something. Ah, good luck in Bar Harbor."

"Thank you. Keep me posted."

"Yes, I will. Look, Savich, I'm sorry. Dammit, I was supposed to keep them covered, keep them safe. I'll do everything I can with this. I'll call you every hour."

"No, Hoyt, call me only if it's an emergency for the next three hours. Otherwise, I'll get back to you when I can." Clark Hoyt didn't know what nuts was, Savich thought, as he punched off his cell phone. He had to call Sherlock, tell her what was going on. Thank God she was home and safe. He didn't want her to hear about Simon and Lily from Hoyt or Lieutenant Dobbs. He had two hours and forty minutes left to set up the operation. He walked over to Firefly Lane to the Bar Harbor Police Department. He knew he simply had to try to stop thinking about Lily and Simon now. He had to concentrate on killing Tammy Tuttle.

He wanted to press his fingers against the pulse point in her neck and not feel a thing.

• Lily heard moaning, then a series of gasping curses that seemed to go on forever. Those curses sounded strange, long and drawn out. Then she heard crying. Crying?

No, she wasn't crying. Nor was she cursing. She felt movement, but it wasn't tossing her around; it was just there, all around her, subtle, faintly pulsing.

Simon. Where was Simon?

She opened her eyes slowly, not really wanting to because her head already hurt and she feared it would crack open when she opened her eyes.

There was a woman moaning again. Crying, then more of those soft, slurred curses.

It was Charlotte. Lily remembered now. She'd shot Charlotte, but she was still alive. And hurting. Lily at least felt some satisfaction. If her head hadn't hurt quite so badly, she would have smiled. She hadn't saved herself or Simon, but she had managed to inflict some damage.

She moved her head a little bit. There was a brief whack of pain, but she could handle it. She saw that she was sprawled in a wide leather seat, some sort of belt strapping her in. It cut into her belly and didn't hurt much, just a little tug, and that was a relief.

She saw Simon was seated next to her. He was strapped in, too. She realized then that he was holding her hand on top of his leg. He was looking toward Charlotte.

"Simon."

He made no sudden movement, just slowly turned his head to look down at her. He smiled, actually smiled, and said, "Shit, I knew I should have left you at home."

"And miss all this excitement? No way. I'm so glad you're alive. Where are we?"

"We're about thirty thousand miles up, a private jet, I'd say. How are you doing, sweetie?"

"I don't feel much like a sweetie right now. We're in an airplane? So that's that funny feeling, like we're in some sort of moving cocoon. Oh, dear, I guess maybe we're on our way to Sweden?"

"I guess it's possible, but why did you say it like you already knew."

"When those guys were chasing me down the beach, they shouted to me. They're foreign, very stilted English, Swedish, I think. I thought then that Mr. Olaf Jorgenson had gotten tired of waiting to have things done for him."

"You're right about their being Swedish." He was silent for a moment, then said, "You said you were running down the beach to get away from them?"

She told him what had happened, finding the trail back up, finding him unconscious, and then about Charlotte.

"If Charlotte hadn't been there, we would have gotten away and I would have moved us to the Eureka jail, no visitors allowed."

He picked up her hand and held it. "That crying and cursing—it's Charlotte Frasier. The pilot, who also seems to be a medic, has been working on her. You shot her through her right arm. Pity, but she'll be all right. Before you came awake, she was screaming that you were an ingrate, after all she'd done for you. She said she was going to kill you herself." He didn't add that she'd punctuated everything she said with the foulest language he'd heard in a long time.

She was thoughtful for a long moment, then said, "Are you all right?"

"Yes, just a slight headache now. How's your head?"

"Hurts."

"Ah, they see we're awake. Here comes Mr. Alpo Viljo. No, I'm not making it up, his name is Alpo. Sounds Swedish to me. He's an enforcer, a bodyguard maybe. I've never run into a real Swedish badass before. From what I've heard, he's the one who smacked his pistol butt against your head."

Alpo Viljo was indeed one of the men who'd chased her on the beach near the cemetery. He was even bigger up close, but really out of shape, his belly hanging over his belt, unlike most of the Scandinavian people she'd met. At least he was blond and blue-eyed. Had to be some Viking blood in there somewhere.

He didn't say anything, just stood there, his arms crossed over his chest, staring down at her.

Lily said, "What's your partner's name?"

He started, as if he wasn't sure he understood her, then said in his stilted, perfectly understandable English, "His name is Nikki. He's a mean man. Do not do anything to piss him off."

"Where are we going, Mr. Viljo?"

"That is none of your business."

"Why is Mr. Olaf Jorgenson bringing us to Sweden?"

He just shook his head at her, grunted, turned, and walked back to the front of the cabin, where Charlotte Frasier was still muttering a curse every little while.

"You got that, Lily? No pissing off Nikki. As for Alpo, I think he likes you. You do look like a princess, and maybe Alpo's a romantic man. But don't count on it, okay?"

She had to grin, even though it hurt her head to move her mouth. She looked out the window at the mountains and canyons of white clouds. She said as she turned back to face him, "Simon, I really do like your hair. Even messed up, it's cool the way it curls at your neck. Long, but not too long. Sexy."

"Lily," he said, leaning closer, his voice very low, "you're not thinking straight at the moment. I want you to close your eyes and try to sleep."

"I think that's probably a very good idea. All right. Maybe I could have some aspirins first?"

Simon called out to Alpo Viljo, and soon Lily was downing a couple of aspirin and a very large glass of water. She gave him a silly grin as her eyes closed.

And in that exact moment, Simon knew it was all over for him. He'd met a woman to trust, a woman loyal to her bones. She sent his feelings right off the scale. His princess, all delicate and soft and pale as milk—well, not right now, since she was still damp from the rain, her clothes torn and splattered with mud, and that hair of hers, all limp and tangled around her head; it was his opinion that she looked superb.

What was a man to do?

He eased a small airplane pillow between her belly and the seat belt. He leaned back against the seat and closed his own eyes.

Lily awoke thinking of her brother, knowing he must be frantic. Surely Hoyt and Dillon knew they'd been taken. But did they have any idea where? And, for that matter, why had they been kept alive at all?

She looked over at Simon's seat. It was empty. He was gone. But where?

She heard a man's deep voice say in halting English right next to her ear, "You eat now."

Nikki eased himself down into Simon's seat. He was holding a tray on his lap. It was the man who'd shouted to her on the beach, the man Alpo had said was mean.

"Where's Simon?"

The big man just shook his head. "Not your worry. Eat now."

She said very slowly, very deliberately, "No, I won't do anything until I see Simon Russo."

Nikki cupped his big hand around the back of her neck and dragged her head back. He picked up a glass of something that looked like iced coffee without the ice and forced her to drink it. She struggled, choked, the liquid spilling down her chin and onto her clothes, soaking in, smelling like coffee and something else. Something like pills went down her throat. She felt dizzy even before Nikki let go of her neck. "Why did you do that?"

"We land soon. Officials here. We want you quiet. Too bad you did not eat. Too thin."

"Where's Simon, you son of a bitch?" But she knew the words didn't sound right coming out of her mouth. She wished she'd eaten, too. She heard her stomach growl even as she fell away into a very empty blankness.

TWENTY-FOUR

Bar Harbor, Maine

Special Agent Aaron Briggs, neck size roughly twenty-one inches, biceps to match, a gold tooth shining like a beacon in his habitual big smile, nodded from behind the counter at agents Lowell and Possner. Both agents were dressed casually in jeans, sweaters, and jackets, trying to appear like ordinary customers looking at frames and photo albums.

It was two o'clock, on the dot.

Savich was in the back. Aaron knew he had his SIG Sauer ready, knew he wanted Tammy Tuttle so bad he could taste it. Aaron wanted her, too. Dead was what Tammy Tuttle needed to be, for the sake of human beings everywhere, particularly young teenage boys. He'd listened to every word Dillon Savich had said on the flight up here. He knew agents who'd seen the wild-eyed guy in Antigua who'd slit Virginia Cosgrove's throat, agents who couldn't explain what they'd seen and heard. He felt a ripple of fear in his belly, but he told himself that soon she'd be dead, all that inexplicable stuff he'd heard she'd done down in the airport in Antigua would then be gone with her.

The bell over the shop door sounded as the door opened. In walked Tammy Tuttle, wrapped up in a thick, unbelted wool coat that hung loose on her. Aaron put out his big smile with its shining, gold tooth and watched her walk toward him. He could feel the utter focus of agents Possner and Lowell from where he stood, his SIG Sauer not six inches from his right hand, just beneath the counter.

She was pale, too pale, no makeup on her face, and there was something about her that jarred, something that wasn't quite right.

Aaron was the best retail undercover agent in the Bureau, bar none, with the reputation that he could sell a terrorist a used olive-green Chevy Chevette, and he turned on all his charm. He said, "Hi, may I help you, miss?"

Tammy was nearly leaning against the counter now. She wasn't very tall. She bent toward him and his eyes never left her face as she said, "Where's the other guy? You know, that little twerp who spells Teddi with an 'i'?"

"Yea, ain't that a hoot? Teddi with an 'i.' Well, Teddi said he had a bellyache—he's said that before—and called me to cover for him. Me, I think he drank too much last night at the Night Cave Tavern. You ever been there? Over on Snow Street?"

"No. Get my photos, now."

"Your name, miss?"

"Teresa Tanner."

"No problem," Aaron said and slowly turned to look in the built-in panels, sectioned off by letter of the alphabet. Under *T,* he found Teresa Tanner's envelope third in the slot, which was exactly where he'd placed it himself an hour before. He picked up the envelope with her name on it, was slowly turning back to her, knowing Savich was ready for him to drop to the floor so he'd have a clear shot at her, when suddenly he heard a hissing sound, loud, right in his ear, and he froze. Yes, a hiss, like a snake, right next to him, too close, too close, right next to his neck, and its fangs would sink deep into his skin and . . .

No, his imagination was going nuts on him, but there it was again. Aaron forgot to fall to the floor so Savich could have his shot. He grabbed his SIG Sauer from beneath the counter, brought it up fast, just like he knew Possner and Lowell were doing, and whipped around. The photo envelope was suddenly in her hand; he didn't know how she'd gotten it, but there it was, and then both Tammy Tuttle and the envelope were gone. Just gone.

He heard Savich yell, "Get out of the way, Aaron! Move!"

But he couldn't. It was like he was nailed to the spot. Savich was trying to shove him aside, but he resisted, he simply had to resist, not let him by. He saw a harsh, bright glow of fire in the corner of the shop, smelled burning plastic, harsh and foul, and heard Agent Possner scream. Oh God, the place was on fire, no, just a part of it, but it was mainly Agent Possner. She was on fire—her hair, her eyebrows, her jacket, and she was screaming, slapping at herself. Flames filled her hair, bright and hot and orange as a summer sun.

Agent Aaron Briggs shoved Savich aside and started running, yelling as he ran toward Possner.

Agent Lowell was turning to Possner, not understanding, and when he saw the flames, he tackled her. They fell to the floor of the shop, knocking over a big frame display, and he was slapping at her burning hair with his hands. Aaron jerked off his sweater as he ran toward them, knocking frame and album displays out of the way.

Savich was around the counter, running toward the door, his gun drawn. Aaron saw him but didn't understand. Didn't he care that Possner was on fire? He heard a gunshot, a high, single pop, then nothing. Suddenly the flames were out. Possner was sobbing, in the fetal position on the floor, Lowell's shirt wrapped around her head, and Aaron saw that Lowell was all right, no burns that Aaron could see. He had his cell phone out, calling for backup, calling for an ambulance. And Aaron realized that his fingers looked normal. He thought he'd seen them burned, just like he'd seen Possner burned.

● Savich was running, searching through the streets. There weren't that many folk around, no tourists at all, it being fall and much too chilly for beach walks in Bar Harbor. He held his SIG at his side and made a grid in his mind. He'd studied the street layout. Where would she go? Where had she come from?

Then he saw her long, dark blue wool coat, thick and heavy, flapping around a corner just half a block up Wescott. He nearly ran down an old man, apologized but didn't slow. He ran, holding his SIG Sauer against his side, hearing only his own breathing. He ran around the corner and stopped dead in his tracks. The alley was empty except for that thick wool coat. It lay in a collapsed pile against a brick wall at the back of the alley.

Where was she? He saw the narrow, wooden door, nearly invisible along the alley wall. When he got to it, he realized it was locked. He raised his SIG Sauer and fired into the lock. Two bullets dead on and the door shattered. He was inside, crouched low, his gun steady, sweeping the space. It was very dim, one of the naked bulbs overhead, burned out. He blinked to adjust his vision and knew he was in grave danger. If Tammy was hidden in here, she could easily see his silhouette against the streetlight behind him and could nail him.

He realized he was in a storeroom. There were barrels lining the walls, shelves filled with boxes and cans, paper goods. The floor was wooden and it creaked. The place was really old. It was dead quiet, not even any rats around. He swept over the room, hurrying because he didn't believe she'd stayed in here, no, she'd go through the door at the far end of the storeroom. It just wasn't in Tammy's nature to hide and wait.

He opened the door and stared into a bright, sunlit dining room filled with a late-lunch crowd. He saw a kitchen behind a tall counter on the far side of the dining room, smoke from the range rising into the vents, exits to the left leading to bathrooms, and a single front door that led out to the sidewalk. He stepped into the room. He smelled roast beef and garlic. And fresh bread.

Slowly the conversations thinned out, then stopped completely, everyone gaping at the man who was in a cop stance, swinging a gun slowly around the room, looking desperate, looking like he wanted to kill someone. A woman screamed. A man yelled, "Here, now!"

"What's going on here?"

This last was from a huge man with crew-cut white hair, a white apron stained with spaghetti sauce, coming around the kitchen counter to Savich's left, carrying a long, curved knife. The smell of onions wafted off the knife blade.

"Hey, fellow, is this a holdup?"

Savich slowly lowered his gun. He couldn't believe what he was seeing, just couldn't believe that he'd come through a dank storeroom into a café and scared a good twenty people nearly to death. Slowly, he reholstered his gun. He pulled out his FBI shield, walked to the man with the knife, stopped three feet away, and showed it to him. He said in a loud voice, "I'm sorry to frighten everyone. I'm looking for a woman." He raised his voice so every diner in the big room could hear. "She's mid-twenties, tall, light hair, very pale. She has only one arm. Did she come in here? Through the storeroom door, just like I did?"

There were no takers. Savich checked the bathrooms, then realized Tammy was long gone. She might have remained hidden in the storeroom, knowing he'd feel such urgency he'd burst into the café. He apologized to the owner and walked out the front door.

In that moment, standing on the Bar Harbor sidewalk, Savich could swear that he heard a laugh—a low, vicious laugh that made the hair on his arms stand up. There was no one there, naturally. He felt so impotent, so completely lost that he was hearing her in his mind.

Savich walked slowly back to Hamlet's Pics. When he got there, he stood a moment outside the shop, incredulous. There'd been mayhem when he'd burst out of there. But now there were no cop cars, no ambulance, no fire engines. Everything was quiet, nothing seemed to be out of the ordinary.

He walked into the photo shop. There were three agents standing on the far side of the shop just staring down, talking quietly among themselves.

Agent Possner wasn't burned. There was no sign that there had ever been a fire in Hamlet's Pics. Agents Briggs, Lowell, and Possner stared back at him.

Savich walked out. He sat down on a wooden bench on the sidewalk just outside the photo shop and put his head in his hands.

For the first time, he thought the FBI needed to assign someone else to catch this monster. He'd failed. Twice now, he'd failed.

He felt a hand on his shoulder and slowly raised his head to see Teddi Tyler standing over him. "I'm sorry, man. She must really be something to get past you guys."

"Yeah," Savich said, and he felt just a shade better. "She's something. We'll get her, Teddi. I just don't know how as of yet."

She was still somewhere in Bar Harbor with Marilyn, she had to be. He got slowly to his feet. He had to get a huge manhunt organized.

In that instant, he realized that even if they didn't find her, she had every intention of finding him. She would hunt him down, not the other way around. And the good Lord knew, he was much easier to find.

Gothenburg, Sweden

It was cold, so bloody cold Lily didn't think she could stand it. Strange thing was that she knew she wasn't really conscious, that she didn't really know what was happening or where she was, but her body just kept shuddering, convulsing with the cold. The cold was penetrating her bones, and she felt every shake, every shudder.

Then, suddenly, she felt Simon near her, no doubt it was him because she knew his scent. She already knew his damned scent, a good scent, as sexy as his hair curling at his neck. His arms were suddenly around her, and he hugged her hard against him, pulling her so close she was breathing against his neck, feeling his heart beat steady and strong against hers.

He was breathing deeply, and cursing. Really bad words that Savich had never said even when he was pissed off, which had been quite often when they were growing up. What a long time ago. Sometimes, like now, she thought as she shivered, being an adult really sucked. She pressed closer, feeling his warmth all the way to her belly. The convulsive jerks lessened, her brain began to function again.

She said against his collarbone, "Where are we, Simon? Why is it so cold? Did they leave us beside a fjord?"

His hands were going up and down her back, big hands that covered a lot of territory, and he rolled her under him so he could cover more of her.

"I guess we're in Sweden. It's sure too cold in this room for us to be in the Mediterranean near Ian's yacht. I just woke up a while ago. They drugged us. Do you remember?"

"Yes, Nikki forced something down my throat. I guess you were already under. How much time has passed?"

"A couple of hours. We're in a bedroom, and there isn't even a heater working. The door is locked, and the bed is stripped, so we have no blankets or sheets. I didn't realize you were so cold until just a minute ago. Are you warming up now?"

"Oh yes," she said, against his neck, "definitely better."

He was silent for a long time, listening to her breathe, feeling her relax as she grew warmer. He cleared his throat and said, "Lily, I know this is an awfully unusual place and perhaps even a somewhat strange time to mention this, but I have to be honest here. You didn't do well picking your first two husbands. I'm thinking that you need a sort of consultant who could help you develop a whole new set of criteria before you try a third husband."

She raised her head, saw his bristly chin in the dim light, and said only, "Maybe, but I'm still married to the second one."

"Not for much longer. Tennyson is soon to be only another very bad chapter in your history. Then he'll be a memory, and you'll be ready to begin work with your consultant."

"He's scary, Simon. He married me to get to my paintings. He fed me depressants. He probably tried to kill me by cutting the brake lines in the Explorer. He's a very bad chapter, maybe the biggest, baddest yet, and my history isn't all that long. It's not particularly good for the soul to have both Jack Crane and Tennyson Frasier in your life."

"You'll divorce Tennyson just like you did Jack Crane. Then we'll figure out these new criteria together."

"You want to be my marriage consultant?"

"Well, why not?"

"I don't even know your educational background or your experience in this area."

"We can discuss that later. Tell me about your first husband."

"All right. His name is Jack Crane. He was even worse than Tennyson. He knocked me around when I was pregnant with Beth. The first and last time. I called Dillon and he was there in a flash, and he beat Jack senseless. Loosened three of his perfect white teeth. Cracked two ribs. Two black eyes and a swollen jaw. Then Dillon taught me how to fight so if he ever came around again, I could take care of him myself."

"Did he ever come around after you divorced him so you could beat him up?"

"No, dammit, he didn't. I don't think he was scared of me. He was scared Dillon would get every FBI agent in Chicago on him and he'd be dead meat. You know, Simon, I don't think having a consultant to select new criteria would help. You can be sure that I thought long and hard about Tennyson, given that Jack was a wife beater."

"You didn't think long enough or hard enough. You have trouble with criteria, Lily, and that's why you need a consultant, to keep your head screwed on straight, to see things properly."

"Nope, it's more than that. I'm simply just rotten at picking men. Your counseling me wouldn't work, Simon. Besides that, I don't need you. I've decided that I'm never going to get married again. So I don't need to consult you or anyone else about it."

"A whole lot of men aren't anything like your

first or second husbands. Just look at Savich. Do you think Sherlock ever has any doubts about him?"

He felt her shrug. "Dillon is rare. There are no criteria that fit him. He's just wonderful, and that's all there is to it. He was born that way. Sherlock is the luckiest woman in the world. She knows it; she told me so."

She was quiet for a moment, and he could feel her relaxing, warming up, and it was driving him nuts. He couldn't believe what he was saying to her.

She said into his neck, "You know, I'm beginning to think that once I marry a man, he turns into Mr. Hyde. He sinks real low real fast. But I guess you'll tell me it's because of my lousy criteria, again."

"Are you saying that all guys would turn into a Mr. Hyde?"

"Could be, all except for Dillon. But you see my point here, Simon. Don't be obtuse. With both Jack and Tennyson, I didn't believe either of them was anything but what I believed them to be when I married them. I loved them, I believed they loved me, admired me, even admired my Remus cartoons. Both Jack and Tennyson would go on and on about how talented I was, how proud they were of me. And so I married them. I was happy, at least for maybe a month or two. About Jack—he did give me Beth, and because of that I will never regret marrying him." Her voice caught over her daughter's name. Just saying her name brought back horrible memories, painful memories she'd lived with for so very long. It had been so needless, so quick, and then her little girl was gone. She had to stop it, cut if off. It was in the past, it had to stay there. She pictured Beth in her mind, decked out in her Easter dress of the year before, and she'd been so cute. She'd just met Tennyson. She sighed. So much had happened and now poor Simon was caught up in all of it. And he suddenly wanted her?

She said, "You can't possibly want to consult with me on this, Simon. I think you could say we've got a situation here; we might die at any minute—no, don't try to reassure me, don't try it. You know it's very possible, and you're trying to take my mind off it, but talking about Jack and Tennyson isn't helping."

He just kept holding her and said finally, nodding against her hair, "I understand."

"Stop using that soothing voice on me. You know you're not thinking straight. You know what? I think God created me, decided He'd let me screw up twice, and then He'd keep me safe from further humiliations and mistakes."

"Lily, you may look like a princess—well,

usually—but what you just said, that was bull-shit. I intend to make use of some proper criteria. You'll choose really well next time."

"Just forget it, Simon. I'm the worst matri-monial bet on the planet. I'm warm now, so you can get off me."

He didn't really want to, but he rolled off and came up on his elbow beside her. "This bare mattress smells new. I can make out more of the room now. It's nice, Lily, very nice."

"We're at Olaf's house, somewhere in Sweden."

"Probably."

"Why did . . ."

She let the words die in her mouth when the bedroom door opened, sending in a thick slice of bright sunlight. Alpo walked in, Nikki be-hind him. "You are awake now?"

"Yes," Simon said, coming up to sit on the side of the bed. "Don't you guys believe in heat? Is Olaf trying to economize?"

"You are soft. Shut up."

Lily said, "Well, we don't have your body fat; maybe that's the difference."

Nikki shouldered Alpo out of the way and strode to where Simon was sitting. "You get up now. You, too," he said to Lily. "A woman does not speak like that. I am not fat; I am strong. Mr. Jorgenson is waiting for you."

"Ah," Lily said, "at last we get to meet the Grand Pooh-Bah."

"What is that?" Nikki asked as he stepped back so they could get up.

"The guy who controls everything, the one who believes he's the big cheese," Simon said.

Alpo looked thoughtful for a moment, then nodded. "We will go see the Grand Pooh-Bah now." He said to Lily, "He will like you. He may want to paint you before he kills you."

Not a happy thought.

TWENTY-FIVE

Bar Harbor, Maine

It had been nearly a whole day, and there was no sign of Tammy Tuttle or Marilyn Warluski. There'd been dozens of calls about possible sightings, all of which had to be investigated, but so far, nothing. It was the biggest manhunt in Maine's history, with more than two hundred law enforcement people involved. And always there in Savich's mind was Lily and where she was. Whether she was alive. He couldn't bear it and there was nothing he could do.

He was nearly ready to shoot himself when Jimmy Maitland called from Washington.

"Come home, Savich," he said. "You're needed here in Washington. We'll get word on Tammy sooner or later. There's nothing more you can do up there."

"She'll kill again, sir, you know it, I know it,

and that's when we'll get word. She's probably already killed Marilyn."

Jimmy Maitland was silent, a thick, depressed silence. Then he said, "Yes, you're right. I also know that for the moment there's nothing more we can do about it. As for you, Savich, you're too close now. Come home."

"Is that an order, sir?"

"Yes." He didn't add that he was calling from Savich's house in Georgetown, sitting in Savich's favorite chair, bouncing Sean on his knee, Sherlock not two feet away, holding out a whiskey, neat, in one hand and a graham cracker in the other. Jimmy hoped the cracker wasn't intended for him. He needed the whiskey.

Savich sighed. "All right. I'll be back in a few hours."

If Sean had decided to talk while his father was on the phone, Jimmy would have been busted, but the kid had been quiet, just grinning at him and rubbing his knuckles over his gums. Jimmy hung up the phone, handed Sean to Sherlock, and said as she gave him the whiskey, "This is a royal mess, but at least Savich will be home sometime this evening. He's really upset, Sherlock."

"I know, I know. We'll think of something.

We always do." She gave Sean the graham cracker.

Jimmy said, "Savich feels guilty, like he's the one who's failed, like the murders of all those people, including our own Virginia Cosgrove, are his fault."

"He always will. It's just the way he is."

Jimmy looked over at the baby, who was happily gumming the graham cracker. He said, "Sean reminds me of my second to oldest, Landry. He was a pistol, that one, gave me every gray hair I've got on my head. If you ever get tired of this little champ, just give me a call."

He downed his whiskey and stared for a moment at the marvelous Sarah Elliott painting hanging over the fireplace. "I've always wondered about the soldier in that painting, wondered what he was thinking at that moment when he was frozen for all time. I wonder if there was someone at home who would grieve if he died."

"Yes, it's excellent. Has Dillon kept you in the loop about Lily and Simon?"

"He told me earlier that Agent Hoyt found the flight plan for a private Learjet owned by the Waldemarsudde Corporation that took off from Arcata airport bound for Gothenburg, Sweden. The CEO is Ian Jorgenson, son of

Olaf Jorgenson, the collector we believe is involved in all this."

Sherlock nodded and said, "Did he also tell you that we think his son is a collector as well?"

"Yes," Jimmy said. "Interesting, isn't it, that Charlotte and Elcott Frasier were also taken? Or maybe they went willingly because the jig was almost up for them here. Tennyson is still in Hemlock Bay. There's not a shred of evidence yet to connect him to the attempts on Lily's life or Mr. Monk's murder, or any of the rest of it. Seems to me that Lily's husband is his parents' dupe."

"Maybe so," Sherlock said. "It doesn't matter. Lily's divorcing him. Oh yes, Dillon has already called two cop friends he has in Stockholm and Uppsala. We know that Jorgenson has a huge estate in Gothenburg called Slottsskogen, or Castle Wood. It's about halfway up the coast of Sweden on the western side. Dillon said that one of his friends, Petter Tuomo, has two brothers in the Gothenburg police. They're on it. We haven't heard anything back yet."

Jimmy said, "Good, things are moving. Does Savich have friends all over the world?"

"Just about, thank God." She sighed, kissed Sean, who was wriggling to get down, and shook her head. "Everywhere we look, there's something horrible ready to fall on our heads.

We're terrified about Lily and Simon. We're praying that Olaf Jorgenson hasn't killed them."

"I can't see why he'd bother to kidnap them if he wanted them dead, Sherlock. There's got to be more going on here than we know."

Gothenburg, Sweden

An hour later, bathed, warm, and in fresh clothes, Lily and Simon preceded Alpo and Nikki down a massive oak staircase that could accommodate six well-fed people at a time. They were led to the other side of an entrance hall that was a huge chessboard, black-and-white square slabs of marble, with three-foot-tall classic carved black-and-white marble chess pieces lined up along the walls.

They walked down a long hall, through big mahogany double doors into a room that was two stories high, every wall covered from floor to ceiling with books. There were a good half dozen library ladders. A fire burned in an exquisite white marble fireplace with an ornately carved mantel that was at least two feet wide and covered with exquisite Chinese figures. There was a large desk set at an angle in the corner. Behind the desk was a man not much older than fifty, tall, blond and blue-eyed, fit as his Viking ancestors. He was tanned, probably from days spent on the ski slopes. The man rose as Simon and Lily were brought in. He looked at them, his expression gentle and sympathetic. She drew herself up. That was nonsense, and she wouldn't underestimate him. The man nodded, and both Alpo and Nikki remained by the door.

"Welcome to Slottsskogen, Mr. Russo, Mrs. Frasier. Ah, that means Castle Wood. Our city's largest park was named after this estate many years ago. Won't you sit down?"

"What is the city?"

"Sit down. Good. I'm Ian Jorgenson. My father asked me to greet you. You both look better than you did when you arrived."

"I'm sure that's true," Lily said.

"Your English is fluent," Simon said.

"I attended Princeton University. My degree, as you might imagine, is in art history. And, of course, business."

Lily said, "Why are we here?"

"Ah, here is my father. Nikki, bring him very close so he can see Mrs. Frasier."

Lily tensed in her chair as Nikki pushed a wheelchair toward them. In the chair sat an impossibly old man, with just a few tufts of white hair sticking straight up. He looked frail, but when he raised his head, she saw brilliant blue eyes, and they were cold and sharp with intelligence. The brain in that head was not frail or fading.

"Closer," the old man said.

Nikki brought him to within inches of Lily. The old man reached out his hand and touched his fingertips to her face. Lily started to draw back, then stilled.

"I am Olaf Jorgenson, and you are Lily. I speak beautiful English because, like my son, I also attended Princeton University. Ah, you are wearing the white gown, just as I instructed. It is lovely, just as I hoped it would be. Perfect." He ran his fingers down her arm, over the soft white silk, to her wrist. "I want you to be painted in this white dress. I am pleased that those American buffoons failed to execute you and Mr. Russo."

"So are we," Lily said. "Why did they want to kill us so badly, Mr. Jorgenson?"

"Well, you see, it was my intention to let the Frasiers deal with you. I understand they bungled the job several times, for which I am now grateful. I hadn't realized what you looked like, Lily. When Ian showed me your picture, I ordered the Frasiers to stay away from you. I sent Alpo and Nikki to California to fetch you back to me. They were clumsy also, but it turned out not to matter because you, my dear, are here at last."

Lily said slowly, "I don't look like anyone special. I'm just myself." But she knew she must look like someone who mattered to him, and so she waited, holding her breath, keeping still as his fingers stroked her arm, up to her shoulder. She saw that his nails were dark and unhealthy-looking.

The old man said finally, "You look exactly like Sarah Jameson when I first met her in Paris a very long time ago, before the Great War, when the artistic community in Paris broke free and flourished. Ah yes, we enraged the staid French bourgeoisie with our endless and outrageous play, our limitless daring and debauchery. I remember the hours we spent with Gertrude Stein. Ah, what an intelligence that one had, her wit sharper than Nikki's favorite knife, and such noble and impossible ideas. And there was the clever and cruel Picasso—he painted her, worshiped her. And Matisse, so quiet until he drank absinthe, and then he would sing the most obscene songs imaginable as he painted. I remember all the French neighbors cursing through the walls when he sang.

"I saw Hemingway wagering against Braque and Sherwood—it was a spitting contest at a cuspidor some eight feet away. Your grandmother kept moving the cuspidor. Ah, such laughter and brilliance. It was the most flamboyant, the most vivid time in all of history, all the major talent of the world in that one place. It was like a zoo with only the most beautiful, the wildest and most dangerous specimens congregated together. They gave the world the greatest art ever known."

"I didn't know you were a writer or an artist," Simon said.

"I'm neither, unfortunately, but I did try to paint, studied countless hours with great masters and wasted many canvases. So many of my young friends wanted to paint or to write. We were in Paris to worship the great ones, to see if perhaps their vision, their immense talent, would rub off, just a bit. Some of those old friends did become great; others returned to their homes to make furniture or sell stamps in a post office. Ah, but Sarah Jameson, she was the greatest of them all. Stein corresponded with her until her death right after World War Two."

"How well did you know my grandmother, Mr. Jorgenson?"

Olaf Jorgenson's soft voice was filled with shadows and faded memories that still fisted around his heart, memories he could still see clearly. "Sarah was a bit older than I, but so beautiful, so exquisitely talented, so utterly without restraint, as hot and wild as a sirocco blowing up from the Libyan desert. She loved vodka and opium, both as pure as she could get. The first time I saw her, another young artist, her lover, was painting her nude body, covering it with phalluses, all of them ejaculating.

"She was everything I wanted, and I grew to love her very much. But she met a man, a damned American who was simply visiting Paris, a businessman, ridiculous in his pale gray flannels, but she wanted him more than me. She left me, went back to America with him."

"That was my grandfather, Emerson Elliott. She married him in the mid-1930s, in New York."

"Yes, she left me. And I never saw her again. I began collecting her paintings during the fifties. It wasn't well known for some time that she'd willed paintings to her grandchildren, such a private family matter. Yes, she willed eight beautiful paintings to each child. I knew I wanted them all for my collection. You are the first; it is unfortunate, but we managed to gain only four of the originals before the Frasiers became convinced that you were going to leave their son, despite the drugs they were feeding you. They knew you'd take the paintings with you, so they decided to kill you, particularly since your husband was your beneficiary after your daughter's death."

"But I didn't die."

"No, you did not, but not for their lack of trying."

"You're telling me that my husband was not part of this plot?"

"No, Tennyson Frasier was their pawn. His parents' great hopes for him were dashed, but he did manage to make you his wife. It's possible he even fell in love with you, at least enough to marry you, as his parents wished."

She'd been so certain that Tennyson had been part of the plot. She asked, "Why didn't you just offer me money?"

"I knew you would turn me down, as would your siblings. You were the most vulnerable, particularly after your divorce from Jack Crane, and so I selected you."

"That's crazy. You invent this convoluted plan just to bilk me out of my grandmother's paintings?"

"Sarah's paintings belong with me, for I am the only one who can really appreciate them, know them beyond their visual message and impact, because I knew her, you see, knew her to her soul. She would talk to me about her work, what each one meant to her, what she was thinking when she was painting each one. I fed her opium, and we talked for hours. I never tired of watching her paint, of listening to her voice. She was the only woman I ever wanted in my life, the only one." He paused for a moment, frowning, and she saw pain etched into the deep wrinkles in his face. From the loss of her grandmother or from illness?

He said, his voice once again brisk, "Yes, Lily, I selected you because you were the most vulnerable, the most easily manipulated. Most important, you were alone. When you moved to Hemlock Bay, I had Ian approach the Frasiers. Tell them, Ian."

"I played matchmaker," Ian Jorgenson said and laughed. "It was infinitely satisfying when it all came together. I bought the Frasiers—simple as that. You married Tennyson, just as we planned, and his parents told him to convince you to have your Sarah Elliott paintings moved from Chicago to the Eureka Art Museum. And there our greedy Mr. Monk quickly fell in with our plans."

Simon said to the old man, "You managed to have four of them forged before I got wind of it."

Those brilliant blue eyes swung to Simon, but he sensed that the old man couldn't see him all that clearly. "You meddled, Mr. Russo. You were the one who brought us down. You found

out through your sources, all that valuable information sold to them by an expatriate friend
of mine who betrayed me, and then it was sold
to you. But that is not your concern. If she had
not betrayed me, then I would have all your
paintings now, and you, Lily, would be dead. I
am not certain that would have been best."

"But now you'll never get the other four,"
Lily said. "They're out of your reach. You
won't be hanging onto those you do have very
long. Surely you know that."

"You think not, my dear?" The old man
laughed, then said, still wheezing, "Come, I
have something to show you."

Three long corridors and five minutes later,
Lily and Simon stood motionless in a climate-
controlled room, staring at fourteen-foot-high
walls that were covered with Sarah Elliott
paintings. The collection held at least a hundred
fifty paintings, maybe more.

Simon said as he stared at the paintings,
slowly taking in their magnificence, "You
couldn't have bought this many Sarah Elliott
paintings legally. You must have looted the museums of the world."

"When necessary. Not all that difficult, most
of them. Imagination and perseverance. It's
taken me years, but I am a patient man. Just
look at the results."

"And money," Simon said.

"Naturally," Ian Jorgenson said.

"But you can't see them," Lily said as she turned to look at Olaf Jorgenson. "You stole them because you have some sort of obsession with my grandmother, and you can't even see them!"

"I could see them all very well until about five years ago. Even now, though, I can see the graceful sweeps of her brush, shadows and sprays of color, the movement in the air itself. Her gift is unparalleled. I know each one as if I had painted it myself. I know how the subjects feel, the texture of the expressions on their faces. I can touch my fingers to a sky and feel the warmth of the sun and the wind caressing my hand. I know all of them. They are old friends. I live inside them; I am a part of them and they of me. I have been collecting them for some thirty years now. Since I want all of them before I die, it was time to turn to you, Lily. If I'd only known at the beginning that you were so like my Sarah, I wouldn't have allowed those fools to try to kill you. Because you are resourceful, you saved yourself. I am grateful for that."

Lily looked down at the old man sitting in his wheelchair, a beautiful hand-knitted blue blanket covering his legs. He looked like a harmless old gentleman, in his pale blue cashmere sweater over a white silk shirt with a darker blue tie. She didn't say anything. What was there to say, after all? It was crazy, all of it. And rather sad, she supposed, if one discounted the fact that he was perfectly willing to murder people who got in his way.

She looked at the walls filled with so many of her grandmother's paintings. All of them perfectly hung, grouped by the period in which they were painted. She had never seen such beauty in one room before in her life. It was her grandmother's work as she had never seen it.

She watched Simon walk slowly around the large room, studying each of the paintings, lightly touching his fingertips to some of them until he came to one that belonged to Lily. It was *The Swan Song,* Lily's own favorite. The old man lying in the bed, that beatific smile on his face, the young girl staring at him.

Olaf said, "That was the first one of yours I had copied, my dear. It was always my favorite. I knew it was at the Chicago Institute of Art, but I couldn't get to it. It was frustrating."

Simon said, "So it was the first one you stole from the Eureka Museum."

"Nothing so dramatic," Ian Jorgenson said, coming forward. He laid his hand lightly on his father's shoulder. "Mr. Monk, the curator, was quite willing to have the painting copied. He simply gave it to our artist, replacing it with a rather poor, quickly executed copy until the real copy was finished. Then they were simply switched. No one noticed, of course. You know, Mr. Russo, I had hopes for you, at least initially. You yourself own a Sarah Elliott painting. I had hoped to convince you to join me, perhaps even to sell me your painting in return for a generous price and my offer of a financially rewarding partnership in some of my business ventures."

Ian looked toward Simon and his eyes narrowed, but when he spoke, his voice was perfectly pleasant. "My father realized you wouldn't agree after Nikki and Alpo described your behavior on the long trip over here. You were in no way conciliatory, Mr. Russo. Actually, my father's desire to make use of you in his organization was the only reason we bothered to bring you to Sweden. My father wanted to test you."

"Give me a test," Simon said. "Let's just see what I would say."

"Actually, I was going to ask you to give me your Sarah Elliott painting, *The Last Rites;* it is one I greatly admire. In exchange, I would offer you your life and a chance to prove your value to me."

"I accept your offer, if, in return, you give Lily and me our freedom."

"It is just as I feared," Olaf said and sighed. He nodded to his son.

Ian looked at his hands, strong hands, and lightly buffed his fingernails on his cashmere sleeve. He said to Simon, "I look forward to killing you, Mr. Russo. I knew you could never be brought to our side, that you could never be trusted. You have interfered mightily."

Simon said, "You had your chance to get *The Last Rites*, Mr. Jorgenson. Freedom for Lily and me, but you turned it down. Let me promise you that you will never get that painting. When I die, it goes to the Metropolitan Museum of Art."

Olaf said, "I do detest making mistakes in a person's character. It is a pity, Mr. Russo."

Lily said to Ian, "Is it true that you have Rembrandt's *Night Watch* aboard your yacht?"

Ian Jorgenson raised a blond brow. "My, my, Mr. Russo has many tentacles, doesn't he? Yes, my dear, I had it gently removed from the Rijksmuseum some ten years ago. It was rather difficult, actually. It was a gift to my wife, who died later that year. She was so pleased to look at it in her last days."

The old man laughed, then coughed. Nikki

handed him a handkerchief, and he coughed into it. Lily thought she saw blood.

Ian said, "As my father said, the Chicago Institute of Art is a difficult place, more difficult than even I wished to deal with. In the past ten years they've added many security measures that make removal of art pieces very challenging. But most important, my only contact, a curator there, lost his job five years ago. It was a pity. I didn't know what to do until you moved to that ridiculous little town on the coast of California. This Hemlock Bay."

Olaf said, "My son and I spent many hours coming up with the right plan for you, Lily. Ian traveled to California, to Hemlock Bay. What a quaint and clever name. It was such a simple little town, generous and friendly to newcomers, such as you and your daughter, was it not? He liked the fresh salt air, the serenity of the endless stretches of beach and forest, the magnificent redwoods, and all those clever little roads and houses blended into the landscape. Who could imagine it would be so simple to find such perfect tools? The Frasiers—greedy, ambitious people—and here they had a son who would be perfect for you."

"Did they murder my daughter?"

TWENTY-SIX

"You think the Frasiers killed your daughter?" Ian Jorgenson repeated, his voice indifferent. He shrugged. "Not that I know of." Lily suddenly hated him.

Olaf said, "I know you felt sorrow over your daughter's death. But what does it matter to you now who is responsible?"

"Whoever struck her down deserves to die for it."

"Killing them won't bring back your little girl," Ian said, frowning at her. "We, in Sweden, actually in most of Europe, do not believe in putting people to death. It is barbaric."

What is wrong with this picture? Simon wondered, staring at Ian Jorgenson.

"No," Lily said, "it won't bring Beth back, but it would avenge her. No one who kills in cold blood should be allowed to continue breathing the same air I breathe."

"You are harsh," said Olaf Jorgenson.

"You are not harsh, sir? You, who order people murdered?"

Olaf Jorgenson laughed, a low, wheezy sound thick with phlegm, perhaps with blood.

"No, I always do only what is necessary, nothing more. Vengeance is for amateurs. Now, you do not have to wonder again if the Frasiers killed your daughter. They did not. They told me that they'd been concerned because your daughter, by ill chance, had seen some e-mails on Mr. Frasier's computer, communications that she shouldn't have seen. They, of course, assured the child that the messages were nonsense, nothing important, nothing to even think about."

So that was why Beth had been moody, withdrawn, that last week. Why hadn't her daughter come to her, told her, at least asked her about what she had seen? But she hadn't, and then she'd been killed.

Olaf Jorgenson continued, "I understand it was an accident, one of your American drunk drivers who was too afraid to stop and see what he'd done."

Lily felt tears clog her throat. She'd happily left Chicago and Jack Crane and moved to a charming coastal town. She couldn't believe what it had brought them.

Simon took her hand, squeezed her fingers. He knew she was feeling swamped with the memories of her loss and despair. She raised her head to look at Olaf Jorgenson and said, "What do you intend to do with us?"

"You, my dear, I will have painted by a very talented artist whom I've worked well with over the years. As for Mr. Russo here, as I said, I hold no hope now of bringing him into my fold. He is much too inflexible in his moral code. It is not worth the risk. Also, he seems taken with you, and I can't have that. Isn't that interesting? You've known each other for such a short time."

"He just wants to be my consultant," Lily said.

Simon smiled.

"He wants you in bed," Ian said. "Or maybe you're already lovers and that's why he's helping you."

"Don't be crude," Olaf said, frowning toward his son, then added, "Yes, I fear that Mr. Russo must take a nice, long boat ride with Alpo and Nikki here. We still have two lovely canals left from those built back in the early seventeenth century by our magnificent Gustav. Yes, Mr. Russo, you and my men here will visit one of the canals this very night. It's getting cold now, not many people will be about at midnight."

Simon said, "I can't say I find that an appealing way to spend the evening. What do you intend to do with the Frasiers?"

Olaf Jorgenson said to Lily, not to Simon, "At the moment they are my honored guests. They accompanied you here since they knew they could not remain in California. Your law enforcement, and so on. They expect to receive a lot of money from me. In addition, Mr. Frasier already has very nice bank accounts in Switzerland. They are prepared to spend the rest of their lives living very nicely in the south of France, I believe they said."

Lily said, "After you've painted me, then what will happen?"

He smiled then, showing her his very beautiful white teeth, likely false. "Yes, yes, I know I am an old man, but I do not have much longer to live. I want you with me until it is my time. I was hoping, perhaps, that you would see some advantage in marrying me."

"Oh, is that why I'm wearing white? To put me in the mood?"

"You want manners," Ian said. He was angry, she could see it as he stepped toward her only to stop when he felt his father's hand on his forearm. Ian shook off his father's hand and said, "She is disrespectful. She needs to see what an honor it would be to be your wife!"

Olaf only shook his head. He even smiled again as he said to Lily, "No, my dear, you are wearing white because that is a copy of the dress I last saw your grandmother wearing in Paris. It was the day she left with Emerson Elliott. The day I believed my world had collapsed."

"You are good at copies, aren't you?" Lily said. "I am not my grandmother, you foolish old man."

Ian struck her across the face. Simon didn't say a word, just hurled himself at Ian Jorgenson, slamming his fist into his jaw, then whirled back and kicked him in the kidney.

"Stop!" It was Nikki and he'd pulled a gun that was aimed at Simon.

Simon gave him a brief bow, straightened his shirt, and walked away.

Ian slowly raised himself to his feet, grimacing in pain. "I will go with Nikki and Alpo this evening. I will be the one to kill you."

"All this," Simon said, marveling as he turned to Olaf Jorgenson, "and you raised a coward, too."

Lily lightly placed her hand on Simon's arm. She was terrified.

She said to Olaf, "Even if I found you remotely acceptable in matrimonial terms, sir, I couldn't marry you. I'm married to Tennyson Frasier."

The old man was silent.

"I don't ever wish to marry again, at least until I've seriously reconsidered my criteria. I don't think there's any way in the world that you would ever fit them. I'm married anyway, so it doesn't matter, does it?"

Still the old man was silent, thoughtfully looking at her. Then he slowly nodded. He said, "I will be back shortly."

"What are you going to do, Father?"

"I do not believe in bigamy. It is immoral. I'm going to make Lily a widow. Nikki, take me to my library." As Nikki wheeled him out of the huge room, Lily and Simon saw him pull a small, thick black book from his sweater pocket. They watched him thumb through it as he disappeared from their view.

"He's completely mad," Lily whispered.

Washington, D.C.

Savich walked through the front door of his home, hugged his wife, kissed her, and said, "Where's Sean?"

"At your mom's house—babbling, gumming everything in sight, and happy. I left your mom a two-box supply of graham crackers."

Savich was too tired, too depressed to smile. He raised an eyebrow in question.

She said, without preamble, "Both the Bureau and I agree with your plan. Tammy wants you, Dillon. She's focused on you. There's no doubt in anyone's mind that she will come here. I took Sean to your mother's because we don't want him in harm's way.

"Right before you got home, Jimmy Maitland issued a statement to the media that you were no longer the lead investigator in the manhunt for Tammy Tuttle. Aaron Briggs has replaced you as the lead. He said you were urgently needed to gather vital evidence in the Wilbur Wright case, the cult leader responsible for the heinous murders of a sheriff and two deputies in Flowers, Texas. You're traveling to Texas on Friday to begin working with local law enforcement."

He hugged her close and said against her hair, "You and Mr. Maitland got it done really fast. So I'm to leave on Friday? Today is Tuesday."

"Yes. It gives Tammy plenty of time to get here."

"Yes, it does." Savich streaked his fingers through his hair, making it stand straight up. "Have you got Gabriella safely stashed away?"

"Actually, she's at your mom's house during the day. Both of them are safe. She said she doesn't want to miss a single step that Sean takes."

But Sean's parents were missing his first steps, Savich thought. He felt brittle with rage, bowed with his failure.

He said finally, knowing that she wouldn't like or accept it, "She's scary, Sherlock. I don't want her near you, either."

She nodded slowly as she stepped against him, pressing her face to his neck. "I know, Dillon, but I couldn't think of anything else. Jimmy Maitland told me you'd balk because of me and Sean, and I knew I couldn't allow that. Now we've gotten both Gabriella and Sean to safety. Don't even think you can send me away. We're in this together, we always have been, and we're going to get her. We have the advantage here because we control the scene. We can act and plan, we can be ready for her, not just wait to react to something she does."

He held her tightly. He wondered if she could smell his fear, there was such a huge well of it. Savich kissed her and hugged her until she squeaked. "We've got to be ready for her, Sherlock, and I've got some ideas about that. I've been thinking about this for a good while now."

"Like what?" she asked, pulling back, looking up at him.

"She has the power to create illusions, to make people see what she wants them to see. Whether it's some kind of magician's trick or a strange ability that's inside her sick brain, the end result is the same."

He let her go and began pacing. He looked at his grandmother's painting over the fireplace, then turned and said, "You believe that she can't fool me if I'm close enough to her. If we can get her here in the house, I'll be close enough."

He came back to her, smiled down at her while he ran his fingers through her curly hair.

"Kiss me, Dillon."

"Can I do more than just kiss you?"

"Oh yes."

"Good. Dinner can wait."

All the world can wait, Sherlock thought, as she held him to her. "After dinner, I want us to go to the gym. It'll relieve all the stress."

"You got it. But if you have much stress after I'm through with you, I'll have to reassess my program."

And he laughed, actually laughed.

Gothenburg, Sweden

Bloated clouds hung low, blotting out the moon
and stars. They would bring rain, perhaps even
snow, before the night was over.

Simon was sitting low in a small boat, his
hands tied behind him. Alpo was rowing and
Nikki was beside him, the gun pressed against
his side. In a boat trailing them were Ian Jorgenson and a small man Simon hadn't seen before rowing.

The canal was wide, the town of Gothenburg
on either side casting ghostly shadows in the
dark light. There was just the rippling of the
oars going through the water, smooth and
nearly soundless.

The canal twisted to the right, and the buildings became fewer. There were no people that
Simon could see.

He very nearly had the knot on his hands
pulled loose. Just a few more minutes and his
hands would be free, and a little more time after
that to get circulation back into his hands and
fingers.

If he had just a bit more time, he had a
chance. But the buildings were thinning out too
much. They could kill him at any time without
worry.

He worked the knot, rubbing his wrists raw,

but that didn't matter. His blood helped loosen the strands of hemp.

"Stop!"

It was Ian Jorgenson. His small boat pulled up beside theirs.

"Here. This is fine. Give me the gun, Nikki, I want to put a bullet through this bastard. Then you can put him in that bag and sink him to the bottom."

Simon could feel Nikki leaning toward Ian to give him the gun. It was his last chance. Simon jumped up, slammed against Alpo, and dove at the small man in the other boat. Both boats careened wildly, the men shouting and cursing. As Simon hit the water, he heard a splash behind him, then another.

God, there was nothing colder on earth than this damned water. What did he expect? He was in Sweden in November, for God's sake. He wondered how long he had before hypothermia set in and he died. He didn't fight it, just let himself sink, quickly, quietly, trying not to think of how cold he was, how numb his legs felt. He had to get free or he would die, from the frigid water or from a bullet, it didn't matter. He worked his hands until he hit the bottom of the canal, twisted away from where he thought the other men were. He swam as best he could with only his feet in the opposite direction, back down the canal, veering toward the side, back to where there was more shelter and a way to climb out of the water.

He was running out of breath and he was freezing. There wasn't much more time. There was no hope for it. He kicked upward until his head broke the surface. He saw Nikki and Ian both in the water, speaking, but softly, listening for him. Damn, his hands weren't free yet.

He heard a shout. They'd spotted him. He saw Alpo rowing frantically toward him. He didn't stop to get Ian or Nikki out of the water, just came straight toward Simon.

At last his hands slipped free from the frayed hemp. He felt his blood slimy on his wrists, mixing with the water. It should have stung like a bitch, but he didn't feel much of anything. His hands were numb.

He dove just as he saw Alpo raise a gun and fire. The frigid water splashed up in Simon's face, close. Too close. He dove at least ten feet down and swam with all his strength toward the side of the canal.

When he came up, his lungs on fire, the boat was nearly on him. The second boat was behind him and now all the men were in it, searching the black water for a sign of him.

Ian shouted, "There he is! Get him!"

Gunshots split the water around him.

Then he heard the sirens, at least three of them.

He went under again, deeper this time, and changed direction to swim toward the sound of those sirens. It was so cold his teeth hurt.

When he couldn't hold his breath for another second, simply couldn't bear the water any longer, he came up as slowly as he could, his head quietly breaking the surface.

He just couldn't believe what he was seeing. A half dozen police cars screeched to a stop on the edge of the canal, not ten feet from him. Guns were drawn, men were shouting in Swedish, flashing lights on Ian and his crew.

A man reached out his hand and pulled Simon out of the canal. "Mr. Russo, I believe?"

TWENTY-SEVEN

Lily walked beside Olaf's wheelchair back to the main entrance hall with its huge black-and-white marble chessboard, its three-foot-tall pieces lining opposite sides of the board, in correct position, ready to be moved.

He motioned for a manservant to leave his chair right in the middle of the chessboard, squarely on the white king five square. He looked at Lily, who stood beside the white king, then glanced down at the watch on his veined wrist and said, "You didn't eat much dinner, Lily."

"No," she said.

"He's dead by now. Accept it."

Lily looked down at the white queen. She wondered how heavy the chess piece was. Could she heft it up and hurl it at that evil old man? She looked toward the silent manservant, dressed all in white like a hospital orderly, and said, "Why don't you get an electric wheel-chair? It's ridiculous for him to push you every-where."

Olaf said again, his voice sharper now, not quite so gentle, "He's dead, Lily."

She looked at him now and said, "No, I don't believe he is, but you soon will be, won't you?"

"When you speak like that, I know you aren't at all like your grandmother, despite your look of her. Don't be disrespectful and mean-spirited, Lily. I don't like it. I'm quite willing to present you the Frasiers' heads on platters. What more can I offer you?"

"You can let Simon and me leave with my grandmother's paintings."

"Don't be a child. Listen to me, for this is im-portant. In a wife I require obedience. Ian, I'm sure, will help me teach you manners, teach you to curb your tongue."

"It's a new millennium, Olaf, and you're a very old man. Even if you died within the week, I would refuse to remain here."

He banged his fist on the wheelchair hard, making it lurch. "Dammit, you will do what you're told. Do you need to see your lover's body before you will let go of him? Before you accept that he really is dead?"

"He's not my lover. He just wants to be my consultant."

"Not your lover? I don't believe you. You spoke of him as if he were some sort of hero, able to overcome any obstacle. That is nonsense."

"Not in Simon's case." She wished that she really did believe him capable of just about anything, even if it was nonsense. But she was hoping frantically that Simon wasn't dead. He'd promised her, and he wouldn't break his word. When they'd taken him but two hours before, he'd lightly cupped her face in his hands and whispered, "I will be all right. Count on it, Lily."

And she'd licked her dry lips, felt fear for him moving deep and hard inside her, and whispered back, "I've been thinking about those new criteria, Simon. I admit I sure do need help when it comes to men."

He patted her cheek. "You got it."

She'd watched the three men take him out of that beautiful grand mansion, watched the door close behind them, heard the smooth wheels of Olaf Jorgenson's chair across the huge chessboard foyer.

Olaf brought her back, saying, "You will forget him. I will see to it."

She glanced at the two bodyguards, standing utterly silent. They'd both come with them from the dining room.

"Do you know I have an incredible brother? His name is Dillon Savich. He doesn't paint like our grandmother; he whittles. He creates beautiful pieces."

"A boy's hobby, not worth much of anything to anyone with sophistication and discrimination. And you spend your time drawing cartoons. What is the name? Remus?"

"Yes, I draw political cartoons. His name is No Wrinkles Remus. He's utterly immoral, like you, but I've never yet seen him want to murder someone." She paused for a moment, smiled at the motionless manservant. "I'm really quite good at cartooning. Isn't it interesting the way Grandmother's talent found new ways to come out in us, her grandchildren?"

"Sarah Elliott was unique. There will never be another like her."

"I agree. There will never be another cartoonist like me either. I'm unique, too. And what are you, Olaf? Other than an obsessed old man who has had too much money and power for far too long? Tell me, have you ever done anything worthwhile in your blighted life?"

His face turned red; his breathing became labored. The manservant looked frightened. The two bodyguards stood straighter and tensed, their eyes darting from Lily to their boss.

She just couldn't stop herself. Rage and impotence roiled inside her, and she hated this wretched monster. Yes, let him burst a vessel with his rage; let him stroke out. It was payback for all that he'd done to her, to Simon. "I know what you are—you're one of those artists manqué, one of those pathetically sad people who were just never good enough, who could only be hangers-on, always on the outside looking in. You weren't even good enough to be a pale imitation, were you? I'll bet my grandmother thought you were pitiful, yes, pathetic. I'll bet she told you what she thought of you, didn't she?"

"Shut up!" He began cursing her, but it was in Swedish and she couldn't understand. The bodyguards were even more on edge now, surprised at what the old man, their boss, was yelling, the spittle spewing out of his mouth.

Lily didn't shut up. She just talked over him, yelled louder than he was yelling, "What did she say to you that last day when she left with my grandfather? Because you went to her, didn't you? Begged her to marry you instead of Emerson, but she refused, didn't she? Did she laugh at you? Did she tell you that she would even take that woman-hating Picasso before you? That you had the talent of a slug and you

disgusted her, all your pretenses, your affecta-
tions? What did she say to you, Olaf?"

"Damn you, she said I was a spoiled little boy
who had too much money and would always be
a shallow, selfish man!" He was wheezing,
nearly incoherent, flinging himself from side to
side.

Lily stared at him. "You even remember the
exact words my grandmother said to you? That
was more than sixty-five years ago! My God,
you were pathetic then, and you're beyond that
now. You're frightening."

"Shut up!" Olaf seemed feverish now, his
frail, veined hands clutching the arms of the
wheelchair, his bent and twisted fingers showing white from the strain.

The manservant was leaning over him now,
speaking urgently in his ear. She could hear the
words, but he spoke in Swedish.

Olaf ignored him, shook him off. Lily said,
smiling, "Do you know that Sarah loved Emerson so much she was always painting him? That
there are six of his portraits in our mother's
private collection?"

"I knew," he screamed at her, "of course I
knew! You think I would ever want a portrait
of that philistine? That damned fool knew
nothing of what she was. He couldn't have un-

derstood or appreciated what she was! I could, but she left me. I begged her, on my knees in front of her, but it didn't matter—she left me!"

He was trembling so badly she thought he would fall from his wheelchair.

Suddenly, Olaf yelled something in Swedish to his manservant. The man grabbed the handles and began pushing the wheelchair across the huge chessboard.

"Hey, Olaf, why are you running away from me? Don't you like hearing what I have to say? I'll bet it's only the second time anyone's told you the truth. Don't you want to marry me anymore?"

She heard him yelling, but she couldn't make out the words; they were garbled, incoherent, some English, some Swedish. He sounded like a mad old man, beyond control. What was he going to do? Why had he left? She stood on the king one square, leaning against the beautifully carved heavy piece, shuddering with reaction, wondering what she'd driven him to with her contempt, her ridicule. She couldn't run because she didn't doubt the two bodyguards would stop her.

Where was the manservant taking him? What had he said to him? The two bodyguards were speaking low, so she couldn't really hear them.

They stared at her again, and she saw bewilderment in their eyes. She wouldn't get three steps before they were on her.

Lily's rage wilted away and was replaced with a god-awful fear. But she'd held her own. She thought of her grandmother and wondered how like her she was. They'd both faced down this man, and she was proud of what they'd done.

She stood there, her brain squirreling madly about, wondering what to do now. She didn't have time to think about it. She heard the smooth wheelchair wheels rolling across the marble floor and saw Olaf coming toward her. This time he was pushing himself, his gnarled, trembling hands on the cushioned wheel pads. His two bodyguards took a step forward. He shook his head, not even looking at them. He was staring at Lily, and there was memory in his eyes, memory of that other woman, painfully clear and vivid. She knew that what had happened that day had struck him to his very soul, maimed him, destroyed what he'd seen himself as being and becoming. And now he saw what he had become after that day so very long ago.

Lily saw madness in his eyes; it was beyond hatred, and it was aimed at her. At her and her grandmother, who was dead and beyond his vengeance. Everything that had driven him, the decades of obsession with her grandmother as the single perfect woman, all of it had exploded when Lily had pushed him to remember the events as they'd really happened, forced him to see the truth of that day Sarah Elliott told him she was leaving with another man.

He came up to within six feet of her and stopped pushing the wheels. She wondered if he could make out her outline. Or was she a vague shadow?

He spoke, his voice low and steady as he said, "I've decided I won't marry you. I have seen clearly now that you don't deserve my devotion or my admiration. You are nothing like Sarah, nothing at all." He lifted a small derringer from his lap and pointed it at her.

"The Frasiers are dead. They weren't worth anything to me alive. And now, you aren't either."

The bodyguards took a step forward, in unison.

He'd had the Frasiers killed?

Lily ran at the wheelchair, smashed into it as hard as she could and sent it over onto its side, scraping against the marble floor. Olaf was flung from the chair.

Lily didn't hesitate. She ran as fast as she

could, to fall flat behind the white king. She heard two rapid shots. The king's head shattered and fragments of marble flew everywhere.

She heard Olaf yell at the bodyguards, heard their loud running steps. She stayed flat on the floor. Several shards of marble had struck her, and she felt pricks of pain, felt the sticky flow of blood down her arm, rolling beneath her bra, staining the white dress.

She heard Olaf cursing, still helpless on the floor. He was screaming at his bodyguards to tell him if he'd killed her yet.

The bodyguards shouted something, but again it was in Swedish so she didn't understand. They didn't come after her, evidently because he wanted to have this pleasure all for himself, and they knew it.

She began moving on her elbows, behind the queen now, toward the great front door, behind the bishop. She looked out toward Olaf. One of his bodyguards was bending over him, handing him his own gun.

The bodyguard picked Olaf up and set him again in his wheelchair, then turned the chair toward her. And now Olaf aimed that gun right at her.

She rolled behind the knight. She wasn't any farther than ten feet from the front doors.

"I like this game," Olaf shouted and fired.

The bishop toppled, shattering as it fell, falling over her ankles. She felt a stab of pain, but she could still move her feet, thank God. She moved solidly behind the knight and stilled.

Olaf shouted again. Then he laughed. Another shot, obscenely loud in the silence, and she saw a huge chunk of marble floor, not three feet from her, spew in all directions. He fired again and again, sending the white king careening into the queen.

Lily was on her knees behind the rook now, close to the front door.

Another shot whistled past her ear, and she flattened herself. One of the bodyguards yelled and ran toward her. Why?

Then she heard more shots, at least six of them, but they weren't from Olaf or the bodyguard; they were coming through the front door. She heard yelling, men's voices, and pounding on the door until it crashed inward.

Olaf and the bodyguards were shooting toward the door.

Lily lurched to her feet, lifted a huge shard of the bishop's white miter, ran toward Olaf, and hurled it at his wheelchair.

It hit him. Olaf, his gun firing wildly, straight up now, went over backward. His bodyguards ran as policemen fired at them from the open front door.

More gunfire. So much shouting, so much damned noise, too much. Simon was there, just behind the third policeman. He was alive.

There was sudden silence. The gun storm was over. Lily ran to Simon, hurled herself against him. His arms tightened around her.

She raised her head and smiled up at him. "I'm glad you came when you did. It was pretty dicey there for a while."

She heard Olaf screaming, spewing profanity. Then he was quiet.

Simon said in her ear, "It's over, Lily, all over. Olaf isn't going anywhere. It's time to worry about yourself. You're bleeding a little. I want you to hold still; there's an ambulance coming."

"I'm all right. It's just cuts from the flying marble. You're wet, Simon," she said. "Why are you wet?"

"I was careless. Be still."

"No, tell me. How did you get away from them? What happened?"

He realized that she just couldn't let it go, and he slowed himself, keeping his voice calm and low. "I dove into the canal to get away, but I couldn't. Then there were all sorts of cops there to pull me out of the canal and take care of Alpo, Nikki, and Ian. Nobody was killed. They're all in the local lockup. It was your brother, Lily. He called a friend in Stockholm who happened to have two brothers living here in Gothenburg. The police were watching the mansion, saw Ian and the boys stuff me in the car, called backup, and followed."

"I want to meet those brothers," she said. For the first time, she felt like smiling, and so she did, a lovely smile that was filled with hope.

TWENTY-EIGHT

Washington, D.C.

Late Saturday night, it was colder in Washington than it had been in Stockholm. The temperature had plummeted early in the day and the skies had opened up and sprinkled a dusting of snow all over the East Coast. Lily was finally in bed, her shoulder and back no longer throbbing from the shards of marble that had struck her. "Nothing important here—all surface pain," the Swedish doctor had said, and she'd wanted to slug him. Now she would probably have more scars.

When she'd said this on a sigh to Simon, he'd said, as he'd eased some pillows around her on the roomy first-class seat, that he liked banged-up women. The scars showed character.

"No," Lily had said as she let him ease a thin

airplane blanket to her chin, "what it shows is that the woman has bad judgment."

He'd laughed as he'd kissed her. Then he'd smoothed the hair off her forehead and kissed her again, not laughing this time.

Then Simon had cupped her face in his palm and said very quietly, since the movie was over and everyone was trying to sleep in the dimly lit cabin, "I think we're going to make a fine team, Lily. You, me, and No Wrinkles Remus."

Lily snuggled down under the blankets. She hoped Simon was doing better than she was. Like her, he'd been ready to fall flat on his face from exhaustion. She hoped he was sleeping.

Actually, Simon was turning slowly over in the too-short cot, not wanting to roll himself accidentally off onto the floor. He had managed to get the blanket carefully wrapped around his feet, no easy thing, since his feet were off the cot and on the big side. He'd taken up temporary residence in Sean's room, just down the hall from Lily, since the baby was still with Mrs. Savich. A precaution, Dillon had said as he'd helped Dane Carver, a new special agent in his unit, carry in the narrow army cot that would be Simon's bed. He'd announced to both men that he didn't care if he had to fit himself into Sean's crib, if that's what it took to get to sleep.

He knew she was okay, just down the hall. Not near enough to him for the time being, but Simon had plans to change that. He could easily picture her in his brownstone, could picture how he'd redo one of those large upstairs bedrooms to make it her work room. Great light in that room, just exactly right for her.

Simon was smiling as he breathed in the scent of Sean. Nice scent, but he would have preferred to be in the guest room with Lily, in her bed. He'd always been a patient man, which, he supposed, was a good thing, since he'd only known Lily for a little more than two weeks.

As for Lily, she didn't know why she couldn't sleep. It was after midnight in Washington, morning in Sweden. But she and Simon had been in Sweden such a short time, her body had no clue what time of day it was. She was beyond exhaustion, yet she couldn't sleep.

She was still very worried about her brother. Tammy Tuttle hadn't shown up, hadn't come after Dillon, and both her brother and Sherlock were frustrated and on edge, at their wits' end.

On Friday afternoon, as announced, Dillon had taken a taxi to the airport and checked in for a flight to Texas. Then, at the last minute, he'd deplaned and slipped back into the house in Georgetown.

Now it was Saturday night, well beyond the deadline, and Lily knew there were still agents covering the house. Jimmy Maitland wasn't taking any chances, and the very sophisticated house alarm was set.

Lily hoped that Dillon and Sherlock were sleeping better than she was. She knew they missed Sean. When they'd all come up to bed, they'd automatically turned to go to Sean's room.

She rolled onto her side and sucked in her breath at a sudden jab of pain. She didn't want to take any more pain pills. She closed her eyes and saw that huge room again, its walls covered with her grandmother's paintings. So many to be returned to museums all over the world. Olaf Jorgenson and his son would not be able to stop it. Ian would be in jail for a very long time. Olaf was in the hospital, in very bad shape.

After a good deal of time, she was finally floating toward sleep, when her brain clicked on full alert and her eyes flew open. She'd heard something. Not Simon or Dillon or Sherlock moving around, something that wasn't right.

Maybe it was nothing at all, just a phantom whisper from her exhausted brain or only a puff of wind that had sent a branch sweeping against the bedroom window. Yes, the sound was outside, not in her bedroom. Maybe it was in Simon's bedroom, just down the hall. Had he awakened?

Lily continued to wait, gritty eyes staring around the dark room, listening.

She started to relax again when she heard a creak. Just a slight pressure on the oak floor could cause a creak, but it was there and it was close. In the air, no longer heard, but she still felt it. Lily waited, straining to hear, her heart pounding now.

The scattered carpets covering the oak floors would mask any creaks, make someone walking hard to hear.

Lily lurched upright, straining to see. Too late, she saw a shadow, moving fast, and something coming down at her. She felt a deadening pain like a sharp knife driving into her skull.

She fell back onto the pillow. Just before she passed out, she saw a face over her, a woman's face, and she knew whose face it was. The mouth whispered, "Hi, little sister."

● Sherlock couldn't sleep. Dillon's arm was heavy over her chest, and he was close and warm, his familiar scent in the air she breathed, but it didn't help. Her brain wouldn't turn off;

it just kept moving, going over and over what they knew about Tammy, what they imagined but didn't know.

When she couldn't stand it anymore, Sherlock eased away from Savich, got out of bed, and pulled on her old blue wool robe. She wore socks to keep her feet warm against the oak floor.

She had to check the house again, just had to, though she'd already checked it three times, and Dillon had checked probably another three. She had to be sure. It was early Sunday morning, it was snowing, and Sean was at his grandmother's, safe. When would she feel secure enough to bring him home? Ever? It had to end. Tammy had to do something; it had to end, sometime.

She hoped the four agents outside weren't freezing their butts off. At least she knew they had hot coffee; she'd taken them a huge thermos about ten o'clock.

She got to the end of the hall and paused for a moment, feeling the house warm around her, breathing in its comforting smells. It took a moment, but Sherlock realized that something was different.

It was quiet in a way she wasn't used to. Too quiet. She realized that the alarm was off, the

very low hum you could barely hear wasn't
there. Panic lurched up into her throat.

She turned to look down the beautifully
carved oak staircase. She saw dim light pooling
at the bottom from the glass arch above the
front door, snowflakes drifting lazily down. She
took one step, then another, when a hand hit
her square in the middle of the back. She
screamed, or at least she thought she did, as she
went head over heels down the stairs. Someone
passed by her as she lay there facedown on a
thick Persian carpet, the breath knocked out of
her, barely hanging on to consciousness. She'd
struck her head, struck everything on her body,
and she could hardly move.

She thought she heard a moan, and then the
figure was gone. The front door opened as she
stared at it, yes, she was sure it was open, now
fully open, because she felt a slice of cold air
reach her face, and she shivered.

The front door stayed open. Only an instant
passed before she realized what had happened.
Someone had shoved her down the stairs.
Someone had just gone out through the front
door.

She managed to stagger to her feet, fear
swamping her. Tammy Tuttle, it had to be her,
but how? How had she gotten past the agents

and into the house? Why hadn't Sherlock seen her?

She threw back her head and yelled, "Dillon! Oh God, Dillon, come quickly!"

Savich and Simon appeared at the top of the stairs at the same time, both wearing only boxer shorts. A light went on.

"Sherlock!"

Savich was beside her, holding her tightly against him, then gently pushing her down, afraid that he was hurting her.

Sherlock came back up, grabbed his arms. "No, no, Dillon, I'm okay. Tammy—she was here; she shoved me down the stairs. The alarm was off and I was just coming downstairs to check. I heard a woman's moan. It wasn't me. Where's Lily? Dear God, check Lily!"

Simon was back up the stairs, taking them two, three at a time. They heard him yell, "She's gone!"

Dillon grabbed his cell phone to call the agents outside.

Simon turned on all the lights as Dillon was speaking to the agents. The front door was open and there was no sign of Lily. Somehow, Tammy had taken her out without Sherlock seeing anything.

Savich stood on his front porch in his boxer shorts, straining to see through the snow falling like a thin, white curtain in front of him, into the darkness beyond.

● Jimmy Maitland said as he sipped his coffee, so blessedly hot that it nearly burned his tongue, "What do the folk in Behavioral Sciences have to say?"

Savich said, "Jane Bitt is guessing, she freely admits it, but as far as she knows, no one has ever before encountered anything like Tammy Tuttle. She may have some sort of genetic gift, be able to project what she wants you to see. What's amazing is the scope. She had everyone in that airport in Antigua believing she was a man, and this is what makes her so unique. Jane said that even given that, we shouldn't focus exclusively on it—there's just no percentage to it. She says there's no beating her that way. We should focus on a woman with one arm who's twenty-three years old. What would she do? If we can predict that, she's vulnerable."

"But we don't know what she'll do, where she'd take Lily," Sherlock said.

"She was supposed to come after *me* here, not Lily—to tear my fucking head off," Savich said slowly, staring at his hands, which were clasped tightly together around Sherlock's waist.

Jimmy Maitland blinked. He had never heard

Savich utter a profanity before, and then he realized he was quoting Tammy.

Simon was on his feet, pacing in front of the two of them. He was wearing only wrinkled black wool slacks, no shirt, even his feet were bare.

"Listen, Savich, you know she took Lily because she figured it was better revenge than just killing you. Now, think, dammit. Where would Tammy Tuttle take Lily?"

It was nearly four o'clock in the morning and snow was still falling lightly. No one said a word. Savich sat in his favorite chair, leaned his head back, and closed his eyes. He felt Sherlock leaning against him.

Then Sherlock said very softly, "I think I know where she might have taken Lily."

TWENTY-NINE

Lily was colder than when she'd been lying on that naked mattress in Gothenburg. Her wrists and ankles were bound together loosely, with some sort of tape. She was lying on her side in a dark room, and it smelled funny. It wasn't unpleasant, but she didn't recognize it.

She was all right. She felt a dull throb on the side of her head, but it wasn't bad, and her side hurt, but that wouldn't kill her. No, it was the insane woman who had brought her here who could kill her.

Did she hear someone laugh? She couldn't be sure.

She gritted her teeth and tried working at her wrists. There was a little bit of movement; the tape wasn't all that tight. She kept pulling and twisting, working the duct tape.

Where was she? Where had Tammy Tuttle

taken her? She knew Tammy was utterly mad and smart, since up to now she'd managed to evade Lily's brother. She'd taken Lily because she was Dillon's sister. She thought it was better revenge against Dillon than just killing him.

Lily knew she was right about that. Dillon was probably driving himself mad with guilt. She kept working the duct tape.

What was that smell that permeated the air? Then she knew. She was in some sort of barn. She smelled old hay, linseed oil, yes, that was it, at least it was some kind of oil, and the very faint odor of ancient dried manure.

A barn somewhere. She remembered Simon asking Dillon where they'd first caught up with the Tuttle brother and sister, and he'd said it was at a barn on Marilyn Warluski's property near the Plum River in Maryland.

Maybe that was where she was. At least Dillon and Sherlock knew about this place. Was this Marilyn Warluski here with her as well? Was she still alive?

Dull, gray light was coming through the filthy glass behind her. It was dawn. Soon it would be morning.

Lily kept working the duct tape. She didn't want to think about how in all the years she'd used duct tape it had never broken or slipped off. But it was looser than before, she knew it.

Lily needed to go to the bathroom. She was hungry. Her side and shoulder were thudding with pain. Just surface pain, that damned doctor had assured her. She wished now she had slugged him. Let him feel some surface pain for a while, the jerk.

There was more light, dull, flat light, and she could see now that she was in a small tack room. There was an ancient desk shoved against the opposite wall, two old chairs near it. A torn bridle with only one rein was dangling from a nail on the wooden-slatted wall.

It was cold. She couldn't stop shivering. Now that she could see around her, see the cracks in the wooden walls that gave directly to the outside, she was even colder. She was wearing only her nightgown. At least it was a long-sleeve flannel number that came to her neck and down to her ankles.

But it wasn't enough.

She turned her head when she heard the door slowly open.

She saw a woman standing in the dim light. "Hello, little sister. How are you doing with the duct tape? Loosen it up a bit yet?"

And Lily said, "I'm not your little sister."

"No, you're Dillon Savich's little sister and that's more than close enough. That's just dandy." Tammy walked into the small room, sniffed the air, frowned for just a moment, then pulled one of the rickety chairs away from the desk and sat down. She crossed her legs. She was wearing huge-heeled black boots.

"I'm very cold," Lily said.

"Yeah, I figured."

"I also have to go to the bathroom."

"Okay, I don't care if you're cold, but I wouldn't make you lie there on your side and pee on yourself. That would be gross. I'm going to unfasten your feet so you can walk. You can go out in the barn and pick your corner. Here, I'll put the duct tape around your wrists in front of you. I wouldn't want you to pee on yourself." Lily didn't have a chance to fight her. Her ankles were bound. She could do nothing, just wait for the duct tape to go around her wrists again. At least they were in front of her now, even for just a short time.

"Here's a couple of Kleenex."

Lily walked ahead of Tammy into the large barn. It was a mess—overflowing rotting hay, random pieces of rusted equipment, boards hanging loose, letting in snow and frigid air. She quickly saw the big, black-painted circle. It was starkly clean. That was where Tammy and her brother had forced the two boys to stay while Tammy called her Ghouls.

"How about the corner over there? Hurry up now, you and I have lots to do. I don't trust you not to be stupid but it won't matter if you are. Move, little sister."

Lily relieved herself, then turned to face Tammy, who'd been watching her.

"How did you get into the house? The alarm system is one of the best made."

Tammy just smiled at her. Lily saw her very clearly now in the shaft of strong morning light that speared through a wide slash in the wall. She was wearing black jeans over those black boots, and a long-sleeve black turtleneck sweater. One sleeve dangled where her arm should have been. She wasn't ugly or beautiful. She just looked normal, average even. She didn't look particularly scary, even with her moussed, spiked-up dark hair. Her eyes were very dark, darker than her hair, in sharp contrast to her face, which was very pale, probably made more pale with white powder, and her mouth was painted a deep plum color. She was thin, and her single hand was long and narrow, the fingernails capped with the same plum color that was on her mouth. Even thin, she gave the overwhelming impression that she was as strong as a bull.

"I'll just bet your brother and that little red-headed wife of his were chewing off their fingernails waiting for me. But I didn't come when they wanted me to. That announcement the FBI character made on TV, I didn't believe it, not for an instant. I knew it was a trap, and that was okay. I took my time, found out all about the alarm, how to disarm it. It wasn't hard. Sit down, little sister."

Lily sat on a bale of hay so old it cracked beneath her. "I don't think you could have done that alarm yourself, alone. It would require quite some expertise."

"You're right. People always underestimate me because they think I'm a hick." Tammy grinned down at her, then began pacing in front of her, every once in a while looking down at her empty sleeve, where her other hand should have been. Lily watched her and saw the look of panic, then bone-deep hatred, cross her face.

"What are you going to do with me?"

Tammy laughed. "Why, I'm going to put you in the circle and I'm going to call the Ghouls. They'll come and tear you apart, and that's what I'll deliver back to your brother—a body he'd rather not see." Tammy paused for a moment, then cocked her head to one side. "They're close now, I can hear them."

Lily listened. She could hear the faint rustling

of tree branches, probably from the constant fall of snow, the movement of the wind. But nothing else, not even early-morning birds, no animal sounds at all. "I don't hear anything."

"You will," said Tammy. "You will. We're going to walk over to that black circle. You're going to sit down in the middle of it. I won't even tie your hands behind you. Now, move it, little sister." Tammy pulled out a gun and aimed it at Lily.

"No, I'm not going anywhere," Lily said. "Will the Ghouls still want me if I'm not in the circle? What if you've already killed me with that gun of yours? Will they still want me then?"

"We'll just have to see, won't we?" Tammy raised the gun and aimed it at Lily's face.

● Simon wished he were on his motorcycle, weaving in and out of the heavy, early-morning traffic. Why didn't Savich have a bloody siren? Why were there so many people at this hour?

When there was finally a break in the traffic, Savich pressed his foot hard on the accelerator. Simon looked out the back window, saw six black FBI cars, one after the other, coming fast, keeping pace with them.

"Tell me, Sherlock," he said, his heart thudding fast, hard beats. "We'll be there soon. Tell me about Tammy."

● Slowly, Tammy lowered the gun. "You think you're pretty cute, don't you?"

Lily slowly shook her head, so relieved she was nearly sick. She'd been ready to feel a bullet go right through her heart, to just be gone, and that was it. Sudden and final and she was dead. But she was still here, still alive, with Tammy, who was still holding that ugly gun.

The circle—it appeared Tammy wanted her in that circle, still alive. "Where is Marilyn? She's your cousin, isn't she?"

"You want to know about my sweet little cousin? I'm not real happy with her right now. See, she told your brother everything about me. Then he used her for bait. That was ruthless of him. I like that in a guy. She was waiting for me right there in the open, in that airport, standing next to that stupid agent who was supposed to be guarding her. From me. What a joke that was. I cut the agent's throat, and everyone saw a crazy young man do it. Everyone believed it, but it was really me.

"You want to know why I hate your brother? It's not hard. He killed my brother, shot my arm off, just left it dangling by a few strips of muscle, and I saw it hanging there and I thought I was going to die. And they strapped me down to this bed because your brother told them I was bad trouble, and then they cut the rest of it right off in the hospital and I nearly died. All because of your damned brother."

Then Tammy let loose, screamed to the rafters, "One god-damned arm! Just look at me—my fucking sleeve is empty! I nearly died from the infection, damn him to hell. He shot my arm off! After I set the Ghouls on you, after they've gnawed you to a bloody mess, I'm going to get him, *get him,* GET HIM!"

Lily kept her mouth shut, tried to pull herself together enough to work on the duct tape. She wished she could raise her hands and use her teeth, but Tammy would notice that for sure. At least her hands were still bound in front of her; that might give her some chance.

Tammy drew a deep breath as she slowly lowered the gun. Her eyes focused again, on Lily. "You're like him—stubborn."

"How did you get past all the agents guarding the house?"

"Stupid buggers, all of them. It was easy. There's hardly any challenge anymore. I didn't let them see me."

Lily didn't want to believe anything that outrageous, but she said, "And they couldn't see me either?"

"Oh yes. Nothing to it. Just dragged you out, wearing that cute little nightgown—sorry I didn't get you a coat. But I figured after you realized what was going to happen to you, you'd want to feel the cold, better than being dead and not feeling anything at all. Now, little sister, move into the goddamned circle!"

"No."

Tammy raised the gun and fired. Lily cried out, unable to help herself. She threw herself to the right, off the bale of hay, felt the hot whoosh of the bullet not an inch from her cheek, and rolled and kept rolling, pulling and twisting at the tape on her wrists. Another bullet hit a pile of moldering hay and spewed it upward.

Then Tammy stopped shooting. She walked over to Lily and stood still, staring down at her, the gun pointed at her chest. Lily looked up, frozen, afraid to move, afraid even to breathe.

Lily said, finally, "You have a problem, don't you, Tammy? The Ghouls won't come if I'm not staked like a tethered goat in that black circle, right? So get used to it. I'm not going anywhere."

Tammy didn't say a thing to that, just turned and walked away, her strides in those heavy,

black boots long and solid. Lily watched her
disappear into the tack room and close the door
behind her, hard.

It was so silent that Lily could hear the barn
groan as the rising wind hit it. Then Lily heard
a scream, a woman's scream, Tammy's scream
and two gunshots, loud, sharp.

Dillon ran out of the tack room toward her,
his SIG Sauer in his hand, yelling, "Lily! Oh my
God, are you all right, sweetheart? Everything's
okay. I got into the tack room, shot her before
she saw me. Oh God, are you hit?"

She felt such relief she thought she'd choke
on it. She yelled, "Dillon, you came! I kept her
talking, knew I had to keep her talking. Oh
God, she's so scary. Then she started shooting at
me and I thought it was all over—"

Lily stopped cold. Dillon was nearly to her,
not more than six feet away, when suddenly
Lily didn't see her brother anymore. She saw
Tammy. She wasn't holding Dillon's SIG Sauer;
she was holding that same little ugly gun that
was hers. Her brain froze. Just simply froze. She
couldn't accept what she was seeing, what was
right in front of her, she just couldn't. Oh, God.

"Honey, are you okay?"

It was Tammy's voice, no longer Dillon's.

Then Lily realized it really was Tammy. She
thought she'd seen Dillon because she wanted

to so much, and Tammy wanted her to. And Tammy thought it was working.

Oh God, oh God.

Lily said, "I'm okay. I'm so glad you're here, Dillon, so glad."

Tammy dropped to her knees beside Lily and turned her onto her side. "Let me get that tape off you, sweetheart. There, let me just slip the knife under the tape. Good, you've already loosened it. You could have gotten yourself free and away, couldn't you?" Then Tammy Tuttle pulled Lily against her and hugged her, kissed her hair. Stroked her single hand down her back. Lily felt Tammy's slight breasts against hers.

Tammy had laid the gun on the ground, just a hand's length away from her, not more than six inches. "Just hold me, Dillon. Oh, God, I was so scared. I'm so glad you came so quickly."

She cried, sobbed her heart out, felt Tammy squeeze her and kiss her hair again. Lily's hand moved slowly toward the gun, slowly, until her fingers touched the butt.

Tammy swept up the gun, tucked it into her waistband, and said, "Let me help you up, honey. That's right. You're okay now. Sherlock is just outside with the other agents. Let's go see them."

Tammy was holding her tightly against her side, walking toward the barn doors. No, not really toward the doors. She was swerving to the left now, toward that big black circle.

Just as Tammy flung her onto her back and into the circle, Lily grabbed the gun from Tammy's waistband, raising it at her.

Tammy didn't seem to notice that Lily had her gun, that she was pointing it at her. She'd turned toward the barn doors, raised her head, and yelled, "Ghouls! No young bloods for you this time, but a soft, sweet morsel, a female. Bring your axes, bring your knives, and hack her apart! Come here, Ghouls!"

The barn doors blew inward. Lily saw whirling snow blowing in, and something else in that snow. A dust devil, that was it. That was what Dillon had seen as well, wasn't it?

The snow seemed to coalesce into two distinct formations, like tornadoes, whirling and dipping, coming toward her. But they were white, twisting this way and that, in constant motion, coming closer and closer. Lily felt frozen in place, just stared at those white cones coming closer, not more than a dozen feet away now, nearly to the black circle now. She had to move, had to.

Tammy saw that something was wrong. She

pulled a knife out of her boot leg, a long, vicious knife. She raised that knife and ran toward
Lily.

Lily didn't think, just raised the gun and
yelled, "No, Tammy, it's over. Yes, I see you.
The minute you got close, I saw you, not my
brother. The Ghouls won't help you."

Just as Tammy leaped at her, the knife raised,
the blade gleaming cold, Lily pulled the trigger.

Tammy yelled and kept coming. Lily pulled
the trigger again and again, and Tammy Tuttle
was kicked off her feet and hurled a good six
feet by the force of the bullets. She sprawled on
her back, gaping holes in her chest. Her one
arm was flung out, the empty sleeve flat on the
ground.

But Lily didn't trust her. She ran to her,
breathing hard and fast, nearly beyond herself,
and she aimed and fired the last bullet not a foot
from Tammy's body. Her body lurched up with
the bullet's impact. She fired again, but there
was only a click. The gun was empty, but
Tammy was still alive, her eyes on Lily's face,
and Lily couldn't stop. She pulled the trigger,
like an automaton, again and again, until, finally, only hollow clicks filled the silence.

Tammy lay on her back, covered with blood,
her one hand still clenched at her side. Even her
throat was ripped through by a bullet. Lily had

fired six shots into her. Lily dropped to her knees, put her fingertips to Tammy's bloody neck.

No pulse.

But her eyes were looking up at Lily, looking into her. Tammy was still there, still clinging to what she was. Her lips moved, but there was no sound. Slowly, ever so slowly, her eyes went blank. She was dead now, her eyes no longer wild and mad, no longer seeing anything at all.

There was utter silence.

Lily looked up, but the Ghouls were gone. They were gone with Tammy.

THIRTY

Washington, D.C.

FBI specialists from the evidence labs went over every inch of the barn at the Plum River in Maryland.

They found candy wrappers—more than three dozen—but no clothing, no bedding, no sign that Tammy Tuttle had been there for any time at all.

There was no sign of Marilyn Warluski.

"She's dead," Savich said, and Sherlock hated the deadening guilt in his voice.

"We can't be sure of anything when it comes to that family," Sherlock said matter-of-factly, but she'd moved closer and put her hand on his shoulder, lightly touching him.

Two Days Later

It was late afternoon, and the snow had stopped falling. Washington was covered with a blanket of pristine white, and a brilliant sun was overhead. People were out and about on this cold, crystalline Sunday even as the national media announced the shooting death of the fugitive killer Tammy Tuttle in a barn in Maryland.

Lily came into the living room, a cup of hot tea in her hand. "I called Agent Clark Hoyt in Eureka, on his home number since it's Sunday. I just couldn't help myself, couldn't wait. Bless him, he didn't seem to mind. He said that Hemlock Bay was rife with gossip over the deaths of Elcott and Charlotte. The mayor, the city council, and the local Methodist church are holding meetings to plan a big memorial service. No one, he said, really wants to delve too deeply into why they were killed, but it's possible that the floating rumors could even exceed the truth."

Lily paused for a moment, then added, "I also called Tennyson. He's very saddened by his parents' death. It's difficult for him to accept what they did, that they used him—used both of us—to gain their ends. He said he knows now that his parents were feeding me depressants all those months and that they had been the ones to arrange for my brakes to fail when I was driving to Ferndale."

"But how did they know what you would be doing?" Sherlock asked.

"Tennyson said he called them from Chicago, just happened to mention that he'd asked me to drive to Ferndale, and when. I feel very bad for him, but I wonder how he could have been so blind to what his own parents were."

"They fooled you as well," Savich said. "At least enough. No one wants to see evil; no one wants to admit it exists."

Lily said, "I've decided to fly to California for the memorial service. I'm going for Tennyson. He's been hurt terribly. I feel that I must show him my support now, show everyone that I believe he was innocent of everything that happened. He knows I'm not coming back to him, as his wife, and he accepts it." She sighed. "He said he was leaving Hemlock Bay, that he never wants to see the place again."

"I can't say I blame him," Simon said.

Savich said, "Please tell Tennyson for us that we are very sorry about what happened."

"I will." Lily raised her head, listened, and smiled. "Sean's awake from his nap."

Both Savich and Sherlock were up the stairs, side by side, their hands clasped.

Simon smiled at Lily, sipped his coffee. Savich had made it, so it was excellent. He sighed with pleasure.

"So, Lily, as your new consultant, I think it's very good for you to go back for his parents' memorial service. It will put closure on things. It will be over. Then you will begin to move forward. Now, I've been thinking hard about this."

"And what did you decide, Mr. Russo?"

"I think the first step is for you to move to New York. It's never wise for a client to be any distance at all from her consultant."

Lily walked across the living room, gently placed her teacup on an end table, and sat down on Simon's lap. She took his face between her hands and kissed him.

Simon sighed, set down his own cup, and pulled her close. "That's very nice, Lily."

"Yes, it is. Actually it's better than just nice." She kissed his neck, then settled herself against him. "I just wanted to tell you that you're the best, Simon. I can't believe it's all really over—that I'm even going to get all my paintings back. But you know what? I want to stay in Washington for a while. I want to settle down, let the past sort itself out, and when I'm ready for the future, I want it to be with a clean slate, no excess baggage dragging along with me. I want to launch *No Wrinkles Remus* again. I want to be my own boss for a while, Simon."

She thought for a moment that he'd argue with her, but he didn't. He rubbed his hands up and down her back and said, "Our time together hasn't had many normal moments, like this. I think the consultant will need frequent visits, lots of contact, and both of us can think about things looking forward, not back."

She kissed him again and pressed her forehead to his. "Deal," she said.

Simon settled back and wrapped his arms around her, her cheek pressed against his neck. He said, "I forgot to tell you. An art dealer friend e-mailed me, said Abe Turkle is in Las Vegas gambling, and winning. He said Abe looked and acted like some big lumberjack; no one would believe for an instant he's one of the top forgers in the world."

"I wish I could remember what happened to that painting he gave me at his cottage."

The doorbell rang.

Dillon and Sherlock were still upstairs playing with Sean. Lily pulled herself off Simon's lap and went to answer the door. When she opened it, a FedEx man stood there, holding out an envelope. "For Dillon Savich," he said. Lily signed the overnight receipt and brought the envelope back into the living room.

She called out to Dillon. Shortly, Savich, carrying Sean over his shoulder, Sherlock at his side, came downstairs.

Dillon patted his sister's cheek. "What you got, babe?"

"An overnight envelope for you, Dillon."

Savich handed Sean to Sherlock and took the envelope. He looked down at it, bemused, and said, "It's from the Beach Hotel in Aruba." He opened the envelope, pulled out a sheaf of color photos. Slowly, he looked at each of them.

"Come on, Dillon, what is it?"

He raised his head and said to Sherlock, "These are the photos that Tammy took in the Caribbean to show to Marilyn." There was a white sheet of paper behind the last photo, just a few lines written on it. He read aloud.

"Mr. Savich, Tammy was right, the beaches here are very beautiful. I'm glad she didn't kill you."

MARILYN WARLUSKI